THE
PITHDAI GATE

A Senserte Caper

By Eric Zawadzki and Matthew Schick

Other titles by
Eric Zawadzki and Matthew Schick:

Kingmaker
Lesson of the Fire

Available at
fourmoonspress.com

Subscribe to our mailing list
on the website to receive
updates and offers.

Dedication

*For Kim, my wife, who continually teaches me
to see the world from a different perspective.*

Matthew Schick

*To Beth, my geeky, filk rocker wife:
There is no part of my life that has not been improved
by your presence in it, and many essential parts
of who I am now would not be there without it.*

Eric Zawadzki

THE FLECTERRAN VALLEY*

The Flecterran Union consists of Tremora, Aaronma, Pithdai,
Sutola, Petersine, Stormhaven and Jacobston.

Aflighan is northwest.
Turuna is west.

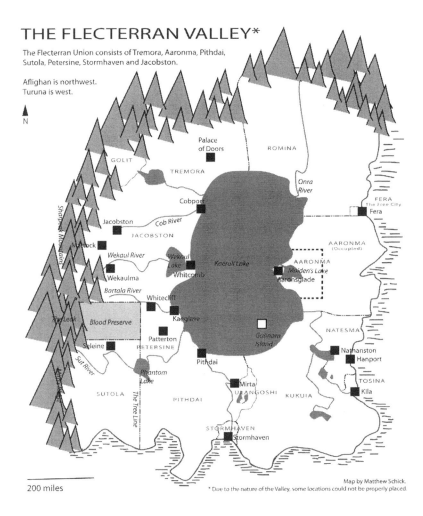

N

GOLIT

Palace
of Doors

TREMORA

ROMINA

Onra
River

Cobport

Sharpeak Mountains

Jacobston

Cob River

FERA
The Free City

Fera

JACOBSTON

Mutock

AARONMA
(Occupied)

Wekaul River

Wekaul
Lake

Kaerali Lake

AARONMA

Maiden's Lake

Wekaulma

Whitcomb

Aaronsglade

Bartala River

Whitecliff

The Leak

Blood Preserve

Kaeglave

Galinora
Island

NATESMA

Patterton

Seleine

PETERSINE

Sut River

Pithdai

Nathanston

Hanport

Phantom
Lake

Mirta

TOSINA

SUTOLA

The Tree Line

PITHDAI

URANGOSHI

KUKUIA

Kila

STORMHAVEN

Stormhaven

200 miles

Map by Matthew Schick.
* Due to the nature of the Valley, some locations could not be properly placed.

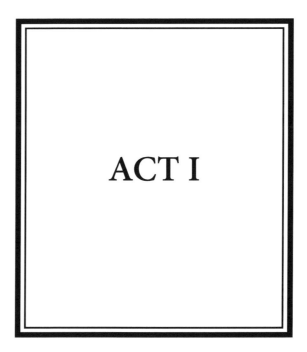

ACT I

Chapter 1

The crystal goblet captured the fading sunlight, its bright orange wine casting a scattered, amber shadow on a wooden table.

Reck held the glass up a little higher. He sat at a table near the western balcony of the mayoral estate in Mattock, a hamlet in the shadow of the Sharpeak Mountains. One ray of light reflected like a star off the edge of the glass.

"Wine made from mangoes I have had. Passion fruit is better, of course." The shadow danced as he brought the goblet to his lips and sipped it. "But both? And with orange? Like so much about life down in the Valley, it's almost painfully sweet. Can you blame us if we envy the ease and comfort you enjoy thousands of feet below us in your lands of endless summer?"

Reck was a Farlander, who were the tan-skinned, mellow-haired, round-eyed race of the three that inhabited the Flecterran Union. Short, fat, and gray-haired, he did not look dangerous. In Jacobston, the provincial capital twenty miles away and halfway down the Valley wall, Reck had the ear of the governor and a reputation as an honest and successful businessman who had risen to power in Mattock by means of careful investment and nearly prescient land purchases.

The amber shadow was much shorter when the goblet clinked against the table and Reck's small hand, with its half-bitten nails, released it.

"Ours is a dangerous livelihood in treacherous mountains plagued by unpleasant weather. We have one resource — gold — and we do nothing with it but try to purchase bits of your paradise. Yet you come to Mattock to steal our gold. Why?"

His pristine workman's boots scraped the floor as he leaned forward, clasping his hands on the table. The left sleeve of his red cotton shirt was buttoned, the right rolled back, exposing a long scar on his sweating forearm.

"Did you ever imagine, in your protected Petersine orchards, that life in the mountains could be so dirty and dangerous? You came to Mattock hoping to tame it. Did no one tell you that you can never conquer a mountain? You can only hope to survive it for a while." Reck bared his orange-stained teeth at his bound and gagged guest, pushed his hands on the table, and rose to his feet. He lifted the glass to his lips again. The sun had disappeared behind the mountains rising above Mattock like enormous white teeth — sharp and dense and threatening to tear all travelers to a shreds.

Nidela ad'Michelle of Petersine, a Wefal in her late middle years, sat silently, her lips unmoving under the rough wool gag. Her dress was torn halfway up her leg, and one shoulder sported a large bruise. Her dirty, disheveled golden hair had streaks of gray in it, and she had wrinkles near the long cut on her cheek. Her legs were crossed tightly, and her hands were tied behind her back.

Wefals were children of Farlanders and Wen. In other districts, they were the occasional consequence of Wen mingling with Farlanders. In Petersine, though, Wefals were the dominant race. They had the almond-shaped eyes and pointed ears of their Wen ancestors and the tan skin and unchanging eyes of their Farlander heritage.

Nidela's blue eyes never wavered from Reck's face.

"I used to sit on the balcony facing the Valley," Reck went on. "The evening light made glorious bursts of color among the greens of the trees. I would peer down at those shining lands and imagine I was a god looking down from the heavens at the wonders I had created. But lately, I find the mountains' majesty, their coldness, more comforting. They are cruel and demand respect. Do you understand what I am saying?"

The Farlander drained his wine, took the bottle and refilled his glass. He stayed a few steps away from Nidela, but spoke in a harsh whisper.

"If you had simply come here to set up a business, you wouldn't have had a problem with me. But no." He drank deeply, wiping his mouth with his bare forearm. His voice gained strength and anger. "You sent your man Gristo first. When I wouldn't accept his ridiculously low offer for my Mattock holdings, he insulted and then threatened me. He hired away all my workers at wages I could not match. He sent spies to infiltrate and sabotage my mining operations. And that was just the beginning — a little taste of what was yet to come. Cutting off my income clearly wasn't enough for him. I've endured constant theft — robbed, pickpocketed, burglarized, swindled at every turn — by strangers who vanish like puffs of breath on a cold day."

The glass was empty again. A cool breeze blew down from the mountains into the room. One of the two guards on the balcony moved to close the doors, but Reck waved to stop him. The Farlander sat down again, refilling his wine. He wiped his forehead with his sleeve.

"Then you arrived, claiming to be another of Gristo's hapless victims. You were looking for an honest partner, you said. I say, you were driving up the stakes." His knuckles were white on the goblet. "You exploited my desperate desire to regain any of the money Gristo had stolen. I mortgaged all my property on your advice — undoubtedly to another of your accomplices." The goblet rattled as he released it. He carefully wiped both hands on his shirt, then clasped them in front of him on the table again.

"You should have left then. You should have taken your ten percent interest and been content with that. You wanted more. You wanted the last of my gold. My strongbox — you know about that. You may have succeeded, too, if you had kept your Turu treasure hunter on your payroll for just a few more days, but now he works for me."

Reck showed his teeth again, spoke calmly and quietly. "And so you are here." He leaned toward her conspiratorially. "Gristo has my gold, but he knows I have you. I thought he would abandon you." He motioned to the two burly Farlanders standing guard at the paneled double wooden doors. The doors creaked open, revealing two more guards flanking a bound and gagged man.

Nidela's eyes never left Reck's face.

The Farlander on the left of the captive was Reg, Reck's most trusted lieutenant and enforcer. His body showed heavy muscles built by hard labor. His stern expression hinted that some of that labor had involved breaking things a lot more fragile than rocks.

The other escort was Tajek el'Nankek, an enormous Turu with a shaved head who was built like a wall of muscle. He dressed in simple breeches and mountain boots but wore no shirt, which made it easy to point out the individual muscles of arms and torso. Turu were distant cousins of Wen, but it was impossible to guess it by appearances except for the pointed ears and almond eyes. While Wen had skin as pale as mountain snow and straight hair the color of tropical flowers, Turu had skin as dark as basalt and kinked hair to match. Turu hailed from the desert nation of Turuna beyond the Sharpeak Mountains and were not a common sight in the Valley.

Their captive was a young Wefal with the smug look of some wealthy couple's younger son. He had coppery red hair tied back in a short ponytail, a curling mustache, and blue eyes. His lean body seemed to capture some small part of a Wen's graceful movement. When he had first come to Mattock, he had carried a rapier with an extravagant jeweled basket hilt and wore heavy gold rings and necklaces that made Reck look like a pauper by comparison. Gristo wore no weapon or jewelry now, unless you counted the manacles that bound his wrists together. Tajek held their prisoner's signature weapon in its slim sheath with one hand.

Reg and Tajek dragged Gristo across the room within sight of Nidela.

"I must admit, I am ever so grateful for this single act of loyalty," Reck told her with great satisfaction. "It will make this evening considerably more satisfying."

"I told you you'd regret not accepting my first offer, Reck." Gristo directed a stern stare on the Farlander like king waving for his headsman.

Reck managed a bemused smile, met Reg's eyes, and motioned with his chin. Reg buried a fist in Gristo's gut, doubling him over and leaving him wheezing on the floor.

Reck's smile broadened. "Did he bring it?"

"Yes, boss," Reg said. "I checked it, and it looks like all the gold is there."

"Bring it in. I want to make sure he's not swindling me yet again."

Reg motioned to the door guards, who nodded and moved into the hallway.

"Lead coins washed with gold, lead bars painted gold, nuggets of fools' gold — you've really made certain I've seen it all, haven't you?" Reck asked Gristo.

The Wefal opened his mouth to reply, but Reg kicked him in the ribs, turning the beginning of a laugh into a series of pained coughs.

"While I'm waiting for them to bring the strongbox up from the cart you stole from me, we're going to transact a little business." Reck smiled at Nidela. "First, you're going to tell me where you hid the rest of the gold you stole from me and restore the deeds of my land to me. After that, you're going to take a little trip to Jacobston." Then to the two balcony guards, "Remove her gag so we can talk."

Reck walked leisurely to stand over Gristo, who was still curled up on the ground with his manacled hands clutching his stomach.

"To Jacobston?" Nidela asked, voice quaking. "Are you going to have the bandits make us disappear like you made all those small-time Mattock prospectors disappear?"

"Ah, you fear me now that you're stranded in a snow-choked mountain pass." Reck didn't turn, but he smiled as Gristo looked up at him with wide eyes. "You might make it to Jacobston, or you might not. It depends on how difficult you make tonight's transactions."

The fear and pain suddenly left Gristo's face, and all the haughtiness returned. "There's your confession, Arrina."

Reck's brow furrowed. Somewhere behind him, glass shattered. He turned. Nidela had broken the ropes at her wrists and stood over one unconscious guard. Orange wine trickled down his neck. The other reached for his sword.

"Alive!" Reck shouted at the man. He rounded on Reg and Tajek. "Help get her under control!"

Tajek dropped Gristo's sword at the Wefal's feet and ran at Nidela, bellowing something in his native tongue. Reg glanced at the fallen weapon for the blink of an eye and grabbed Reck roughly, pushing him through the doorway into the hall.

"What are you ..." Reck began.

Then he saw Gristo on his feet with his hands unbound and his sword held at the ready. The Wefal gave him a mocking bow. Reck's eyes snapped from the sword to Tajek running into the melee on the balcony.

"The Turu's with them!" Reck shouted at the remaining balcony guard.

But it was too late. Even as the words left his mouth, Tajek ran past Nidela and punched the guard in the face, sending the Farlander backward over the railing. The man cried out as he plunged into the shrubbery below.

"Guards!" Reck shouted down the hall and was grateful for the thunder of running feet approaching.

Reg drew his own sword and stood between Reck and Gristo. "How did you slip the manacles?" Reg snarled as he crossed swords with the Wefal. He stepped into the room, leaving Reck alone in the doorway. "It couldn't be magic. I sweetened your lips myself."

To sweeten someone's lips meant to give them a taste of saat — a fruit whose incredibly sweet juice prevented the victim from using magic for several hours. Wefal, Wen, and Farlander were equally vulnerable to it.

Gristo smiled, parrying easily but giving ground. "Where do you think Tajek got them? Not all escape artists rely on magic, you may know."

Nidela grabbed the fallen guard's sword. She whipped it around in an experimental series of flourishes that belied her apparent age before nodding with satisfaction. Tajek ripped off one of the table legs, hefted it, and walked purposefully toward Reck.

Reg's eyes flicked to the two new opponents, and the moment's inattention cost his coat a button. He refocused on Gristo, gritting his teeth as he yielded the ground he had taken. "Boss, get out of here! I'll hold them."

Reck nodded and staggered into the hall. He met two of his guards coming up the stairs, their swords drawn. "Only two of you?"

The guards didn't slow down, but one of them spoke loudly as he passed. "We are betrayed. A few fight to defend your strongbox. All others have gone over to the enemy."

Reck turned. "Betrayed?" he shouted at their backs.

He saw the lead guard rush Tajek. The enormous Turu didn't even attempt to evade, and the blade hit him directly in the chest. The steel made a sound like metal grinding against stone before the blade broke off with a snap. Tajek, his bare chest entirely unharmed by the thrust, grinned and swung his table leg. The makeshift club caught his opponent across the chin and knocked him back through the doorway.

• • • •

Reck fled down the stairs. The main entryway showed signs of struggle. Several arrows stuck out of walls, floor, and furniture. The door hung open wide, its heavy iron locks broken to pieces like so much shattered glass. Reck took cover behind the doorframe and peered into the gathering twilight.

The cart Reg had brought back waited in the cobblestone square a few paces away. Reck could make out the shape of the strongbox under a canvas tarp in its bed. Two of his household guards lay unmoving on their stomachs behind the cart. Four others paired off against each other in the gap between mansion and strongbox, grunting and cursing as they parried and thrust with their rapiers.

Reck hesitated, but one of the guards glanced up from this mortal struggle just long enough to spot him.

"Sir, we're lost!" he shouted to Reck. "Take the cart and flee before the rest get here!"

As if to emphasize his point, the guard cried out as an arrow struck him in the back, near his left shoulder blade.

With a nervous glance in the direction from which the arrow had come, Reck ran to the cart and climbed into the seat. He wasn't used to this kind of excitement, and he wheezed as he snapped the reins to urge the two horses into a gallop.

As he fled his lost mining empire, arrows flicked over his shoulder, some sticking into the back of the cart. One came so close to his ear that Reck could hear it hiss. He didn't dare look back.

The cart nearly overturned as Reck turned it hard around the bend in the road that led to Jacobston. The rain of arrows stopped, and Reck heard no signs of pursuit. He slowed down only enough to prevent disaster.

• • • •

When Reck was safely out of sight of the mansion, the four guards who had been fighting over the cart put up their swords and untied the unseen cloth masks they wore. Instead of four Farlander guards, they were two Wen, one Farlander, and a Wefal.

All of them were young for their respective races. A Farlander who didn't know that Wen and Wefals aged more slowly would place them in their early twenties.

The Wen with the arrow in his back gave no indication that he had received a serious wound. He took off his coat, and the other Wen helped him remove the thick wooden disk hidden underneath that had stopped the arrow.

"Mathalla, remind Davur that he doesn't need to hit the target so hard when he shoots you," he said as he slipped the arrow the rest of the way through the coat and inspected the area below. "That one's going to leave a bruise."

"It's fine, Torminth." Mathalla gave him a rakish smile. "I've gotten worse from you."

The Wefal cleared his throat. "Can we stay focused, gentlemen? My sister may still be fighting for her life upstairs. Make safe her exit."

Torminth nodded, drawing his sword again. He ran the side of his hand down the blade just enough to moisten it with his blood, which turned into a line of fire along the sword's edge. The cut closed instantly to a deep red scar.

"Yes, Jonathan." Mathalla drew his sword, and the two Wen disappeared into the mansion.

Jonathan looked around the yard. "Any sign of Lastor, Michael?"

The Farlander shrugged and set to work tying up the two immobile guards on the ground. "He probably decided to help the brothers."

"I hope so," Jonathan muttered under his breath.

Three Wen with bows approached from behind the outbuilding — Davur, Ravud, and Vudar, from eldest brother to youngest.

"All clear?" Jonathan called to them.

"He's halfway to Jacobston, by now," Ravud called back with a laugh. The middle brother could see in the dark as easily as others saw in bright daylight.

"Good," Michael called back. "Help us get these guards inside before my spell on them wears off."

The trio put up their bows as they trotted over.

"Is Lastor with you?" Jonathan asked them.

"No," Davur said. "We thought he must be with you."

Jonathan and Michael exchanged a look.

"Maybe he decided to help with the guards inside," Michael suggested, but he didn't sound hopeful.

"Why do we even bring him for the blow-off?" Jonathan grumbled as they carried the unconscious guards into the mansion. "He never does what he's told. He always finds a way to make things more complicated. One day he's going to blow the swindle for us."

"Even worse than Stipator, right?" Michael asked.

Jonathan fell into a stony silence.

"I think you're too close to the mark," Ravud teased.

"Fewer jokes at Jonathan's expense and more keeping up your end of the unconscious Farlander," Vudar grumbled at his brother. "His feet are practically dragging, and we haven't even reached the stairs, yet."

"No sounds of battle," Michael noted. "That's probably a good sign."

Jonathan grunted. "Ravud, stand watch over our exit in case Reck or his thugs come back. I'll take your end of this one."

The Wen shrugged. "Someone should keep an eye out for Lastor, too. In case he's not with Arrina." He moved back to the doorway.

When they were halfway up the stairs, voices filtered down from the balcony room.

"Sister mine, what caused your treason?" Jonathan called up.

The voices stopped for a moment, and then Nidela responded. "Brother mine, was no good reason."

Jonathan let out a breath at hearing the agreed upon all-clear response. They hauled the unconscious guards into the room. The three guards already in the room sat with their backs against the far wall, their sheaths empty. Reck's lieutenant, Reg, sat in the only undamaged chair, his feet tied and his hands bound by the same manacles that had held Gristo, hands twisting in the bindings. His former Wefal prisoner sat next to him, encouraging the Farlander's efforts to figure out where the trick clasp was hidden.

Nidela looked at the unconscious guards as the four men hauled them over next to their companions.

"Unharmed, as promised," Michael assured her, "which is more than I can say for yours."

With one sweeping gesture he indicated the large lump on the back of the balcony guard's head, the black eye of the stairway guard Tajek had knocked down, and the bloody handkerchief the second stairway guard held to his right shoulder where a sword had pierced it.

Reg had several small, superficial cuts — missing coat buttons, slashes on his cheeks and across the backs of his hands, and a belt that would never hold up another pair of pants.

"Did you see what happened to the one who went over the balcony rail?" Nidela asked.

"Broken leg, we think," Davur said. "He was moving, just not very quickly. Poresa said she'll send Zori to tend to him."

"Sorry," Tajek said. "I may have caught him a bit too unawares."

"I'm sure he'll recover," Nidela said. She turned to Michael. "Wake them."

Michael made a small dismissive gesture. The two guards awoke with a cry of alarm but quickly realized they were unarmed and outnumbered.

"Who are you?" Reg demanded.

"I am Arrina ad'Anna, daughter of King Larus of Pithdai," she announced, and her body and facial features shifted even as she spoke.

The lines and stoop of age flattened. Her gray hair turned a blue-blond to match Jonathan's. When her flesh had stopped flowing like water around her skeleton, she was a tall young woman with long hair, a round-cheeked face, and smooth muscles.

The whole transformation took only a handful of breaths to complete, the result of years of practice effecting rapid changes. Some kinds of stage magicians could change clothes in the time it took to walk behind a tree. Arrina could do the same with her body, using Wefal internal magic to take on any guise she could clearly envision. A mirror helped get the details just right, but she could easily return to her favorite shapes without one.

"That Wefal there is my brother, Jonathan ad'Pithius. Twins, as you might have guessed."

Jonathan waved faintly but remained wary.

"Tajek el'Nankek you have already met, though his command of Flecterran languages is much better than he led you to believe."

The enormous Turu saluted. "My uncle sent me here to be a tunnel between Flecterra and Turuna. Too many rocks stand between us."

Reg's expression suggested there weren't enough rocks in the whole world.

"You haven't tried dislocating your shoulder yet," Gristo offered their captive. "It could help."

"Stipator, not your turn," Arrina admonished. "Sa'Michael ad'Aaron is our enchanter. He is the son of M'Elizabeth ad'Alice, one of Aaronsglade's most prominent Nosamae."

Michael tipped his head in acknowledgment.

"Davur, Vudar, and ... where's Ravud?"

"Keeping watch," Michael said.

Arrina looked at Jonathan with a raised eyebrow. She returned her attention to Reg and their other captives. "The three brothers ad'Marusak are the sons of Tafult, the high archon of Sutola."

The two brothers stood straight and unbowed in the Sutol tradition.

"Mathalla ad'Stontal is the eldest son of the vice primary of the Coastal Republic of Kukuia. Torminth ad'Revelan, his bodyguard and traveling companion."

Mathalla and Torminth put up their swords and bowed with both hands over their chests.

"Then there is the one you know as Gristo," Arrina said.

The Wefal stood up slowly and made a show of dusting off his pants while she spoke. He reached over and touched a point on the trick shackles, and before Reg could see they had loosened, he snapped them shut again.

"Cousin, nephew, or uncle to just about every well-bred family in Petersine," Arrina went on.

"And sometimes more than one of those at a time," Michael amended, and the Wefal gentleman only grinned.

"Famed among many as a battlemaster and by all as a prankster, this is Stipator ad'Bryan."

Stipator touched the first three fingers of his right hand to his lips in the Petersine gesture of greeting. "So sorry about your clothes, Reg. Unfortunate casualties of justice, much like yourselves." His smile grew ironic. "Also, it was funny."

"You can't all be the children of leaders of half the nations in the Flecterran Union!" Reg shouted over them. Michael and Stipator quieted, and Arrina looked at Reg expectantly. Their captive lifted his hands and dropped them into his lap again. "Some of them can't even be in a room together without coming to blows," he said hoarsely.

"The evidence states otherwise," Jonathan said.

"You didn't tell them about the others, Arrina," Tajek noted. "Maybe then he may have connected us to the stories."

"What stories?" Reg asked.

"Reck hired the bandits who have been attacking all the gold shipments coming out of Mattock," Arrina explained. "Between that and the sabotage and intimidation, he was able to take over so much of the land up here. The townsfolk asked us to get rid of the bandits. We decided to get rid of the bandit chief first, using the same kinds of tricks he used to drive his competitors off their land."

"The gold wasn't in the strongbox?" Reg asked.

Stipator smirked. "The gold was in the strongbox alright. But the strongbox isn't in the cart. Our team outside switched it for a box of lead right after you took me inside."

"Tomorrow, we take all the gold and land Reck stole and give it back to the people of Mattock," Arrina explained.

"Why not keep it for yourselves?"

"Not interested in money," Stipator said with a shrug.

"Then why go to the trouble?"

"Because we're the Senserte — the secret eyes of justice," Arrina told him. "It is our duty to punish those who let wealth and power corrupt them."

"Um, Arrina?" Jonathan said hesitantly. "I know you hate it when I interrupt your introductions, but have you seen Lastor?"

Arrina looked at her brother in slowly growing horror. "No. I thought he was with you."

· · · ·

Once the arrows stopped flying past and no pursuit seemed forthcoming, Reck let the horses slow to a trot. When night fell, though lit by Messegere and Chelestria — the yellow and blue moons — he ultimately slowed to a careful walk. High-speed travel along the mountain roads was dangerous enough by daylight. At night, it was downright suicidal.

Even at a walk, it could be dangerous to travel by night unless the traveler knew the road as intimately as Reck did. This applied both to the road and the highwaymen who patrolled it. *Nidela and her accomplices would never catch him before he reached Jacobston,* Reck gloated to himself.

Reck halted the cart near a finger of white stone that stood twelve miles from Jacobston. He climbed painfully out of the cart and walked cautiously to a tree on the far side of the road from the rock. He made a show of relieving himself on the tree before turning around to address the figures he knew would be waiting by the cart.

"Good evening, gentlemen."

The three stood with swords drawn, their faces concealed by shadow. Reck knew with certainty that archers waited out of sight.

"Mayor Reck," the lead figure said. "You choose a strange time to travel mountain roads."

"There is a bit of an emergency in Jacobston." Reck shrugged.

"It would have to be," the leader replied, and the man on his left snickered in a way that gave Reck pause.

"Some local rabble might be following me in hopes of slipping by with a shipment of gold," he explained as he approached his cart. "Don't let anyone else come down the road, tonight, but you can keep whatever they're carrying." He smiled, though the darkness spoiled the effect.

"Consider it a little bonus for adhering so faithfully to our arrangement."

"What's your cargo?" the leader asked casually.

Reck fought down the growing sensation that something was very wrong. "The usual — gifts for friends, some bribes to keep the governor's patrols from coming up here, a bit more to cover expenses."

If the gentle reminder that only Reck's bribes kept the bandits in business had an impact on the three, they gave him no sign.

"Kind of you to spend the last of your fortune protecting our livelihood, Reck."

The man on the leader's right muttered something and spat.

"We've heard the rumors from Mattock. Seems some competitor came up there and wiped you out." The leader put up his sword and clambered onto the back of the cart.

"Don't believe the lies of jealous men," Reck said, making a move to climb back onto the cart.

The bandit on the left barred his way with a sword.

"Oh, we didn't believe it," the leader continued, examining the arrows sticking out of the back of the cart. "At least not until you came down here after dark in a cart peppered with arrows carrying ..." He whipped the canvas off the strongbox. "... what would seem to be the last of your once-tremendous fortune in gold."

"I have no idea what you're talking about," Reck said, but the tremor in his voice betrayed him.

The leader jumped off the cart next to Reck and made a motion with his chin. Half a dozen more bandits came out of hiding and worked to remove the strongbox.

"It is your intention to sell the location of our hideout to the governor for the bounty. Then, once his patrols have gotten rid of us, you'll be able to take your time searching for whatever treasure we may have hidden in this area."

"Why would I do any such thing?" Reck demanded, but his eyes bulged as he watched the bandits carry off his precious strongbox.

The leader put a strong hand on Reck's fleshy shoulder to prevent him from chasing after his property. "We've seen the way you treated your business partners in Mattock. You'll recall that *we* were the way you treated them. Would you like to join your former friends, Reck? Oh how they'll grin when they see your face again."

"That's 'cause they're always grinning," the bandit in front of the cart giggled.

Reck tried to take a step back, but the bandit leader's hand held him fast. His eyes bored into the fat Farlander's.

"We're not as ungrateful as you are, Reck. After all, your last act as mayor of Mattock was to bring us a strongbox full of the last of your gold, so I'm willing to spare you a hot meal, a good night's rest, and what is left of your life." He gave a hearty, good-natured laugh. "I'll even throw in the cart and horses. You can sell them in Jacobston for enough to maybe start a new enterprise."

Reck tried to smile meekly, but his heart was pounding, and his knees felt like they wouldn't be able to hold him up much longer. He had no illusions now. He was pleading for his life. "That would be very kind of you."

The bandits led Reck into the pine forest where they lived, leaving the horses and cart tethered, for the moment, just out of sight of the road in a place where they hid captured carts and wagons until they could finish looting them. They didn't bother tying him up. They knew they didn't have to. He couldn't outrun them.

The bandits' hideout was an unimpressive collection of tents and cook fires. Reck ate and drank without appetite, not entirely sure they wouldn't slit his throat as soon as he fell asleep. *That might actually be a mercy,* he reflected gloomily.

The strongbox foiled all the bandits' efforts to force it open or pick its lock. Reck had no key, since that had been in Reg's possession. He maintained a quiet gratitude for that. He still wasn't convinced that Gristo hadn't somehow tricked Reg into taking a chest of gold-washed lead for one filled with gold coins, nuggets, and ingots. If the bandits discovered Reck had brought them nothing of value, they would probably slit his throat despite their protestations of gratitude.

When sleep came, it brought nightmares of abject poverty with it. Reck woke to crushing anxiety in an abandoned camp. The strongbox was gone. At least he was still alive, and if the bandits had been true to their word, he would still be able to get some money for his horses and cart.

Reck reached the spot where the cart had been, but nothing was there.

"No," Reck moaned, falling to his knees. Then he was weeping the tears of a terrified and broken man.

"Good," a pleased voice said. "I've been waiting for you to cry."

Reck looked up. A Wen boy of perhaps fourteen years sat on a tree branch ten feet up, swinging his legs in a way that should have sent him plunging earthward. He had bright orange hair and green eyes.

"Are you with her?" Reck shouted at him.

The boy cocked his head. "Does it really matter? All the terrible things you have been doing to others for the last year have now been visited upon you. Justice is served."

"You steal a man's fortune for yourselves and call that justice?" Reck snarled.

The Wen smiled. "Of course not. We Senserte don't work for money. We don't deal in half-measures either. Your wealth, including the cart and horses, will go to all the Mattock families you robbed."

"I didn't rob them!"

The boy shrugged. "You put them out of business through intimidation, sabotage, and hired violence. You robbed them as surely as we robbed you."

"What of the bandits? I may have forced my competition out of business, but they actually killed people for money."

The Wen sobered. "The strongbox is ensorcelled and therefore easily tracked. An enchantress is leading one of Jacobston's patrols to them. Your bandits' fates will be every bit as ... appropriate as yours."

"Why are you telling me this?"

The boy hopped to his feet on the branch. "You gloated over Arrina when you had her completely in your power. I'm here to balance the scales. Best of luck in your new life."

The boy stepped off the branch and vanished, leaving only an echo of his childlike laughter — which faded quickly — and Reck was alone.

Chapter 2

Arrina removed her mask and set it on the stand in front of her. Starting with the tips of her slightly pointed ears and moving to her temples, she massaged her nut-brown skin where the mask had touched it. Almond eyes stared back at her in the wagon's mirror as she ran long, slim fingers down her jawline and around her mouth, wiping off the glue like any other actor would wipe off her make-up.

Arrina took a steaming, lavender-scented towel from the plate below the mask. Dabbing at her face, she glanced at the mask again.

It was nothing more than a piece of colored silk the size of a human face, secured with a piece of string and vegetable glue. When she attached it to her face, however, Farlander magic transformed her features to those of Mad King Rupert — who thought he could give up the responsibility of his throne to his children without losing the title of king, thus leading to incessant greed and in-fighting until all his children predeceased him.

In a chest under the preparations table were velvet drawers that held all the masks of the traveling players Arrina's troupe traveled with. Michael, the troupe's lead enchanter, had made them, but they had originally been Jonathan's idea. Michael and Jonathan had designed most of the clever devices the traveling show used in its performances — tricks of the trade to which it owed much of its impressive reputation. The masks could make the wearer look like anyone — on the stage or off — a nondescript beggar, a well-known local official, even an arrogant Petersine businesswoman.

"Are you decent?" her brother, Jonathan, asked from the other side of the door.

"Yes. Come in."

The door opened, and her twin brother stepped inside. They looked nearly alike, though Jonathan's blue-blond hair was cut short. "The night sky's clear, and Messegere is waxing. If you have letters, Davur and his brothers will send them."

Arrina met his eyes in the mirror. She heaved a sigh of relief as she pulled open a drawer full of rolled up letters. They hadn't had a clear night in a month, which had kept them from sending or receiving letters by arrow.

Davur stood just outside the door. He was slightly taller than either of them and slim as a sapling except for the steel strong muscles in his arms and shoulders, which were visible through the form-fitting leather jacket he wore. His green eyes matched all those of his race, for all Wen eyes changed colors with the season — green in spring, blue in summer, brown in autumn, and grey in winter. "The leaves of the Valley are evergreen," went the Pith saying, "Only the eyes of the Wen change with the turning of the year." He carried a longbow slung across his chest and a quiver of bright-feathered arrows at his back. He held a basket filled with letters in one gloved hand.

Wen children possessed powerful magic but only kept one or two random magical talents when they reached adulthood. Sometimes when a Wen child made a wish, magic granted it — what Wen called a mirakla. In some cases, miraklas remained long after the child grew up, aged, and died. Most were small — a new kind of plant or animal, a strangely permanent localized weather pattern, or a bow that shot arrows of fire. It was said that Wen children had created squawkers and most of the other creatures of Flecterra.

Less commonly, a wish had a large and lasting effect, but this was so rare that most things attributed to major miraklas were more likely myth than truth. Some Wen claimed Farlanders and Wefal owed their magic, if not their very existences, to miraklas, for example, while others claimed the creation of the stars, the sun, and the four moons.

But even the most skeptical Farlander couldn't deny the existence of the Messegere moon shot.

Unlike every other heavenly body, the yellow moon traveled from west to east, going through all its phases in a little more than a day. Its month began when its new moon phase took place at noon, which happened once every thirty days. Any Wen could take advantage of the Messegere moon shot simply by affixing a letter to an arrow and firing it at the yellow moon as it waxed any clear afternoon or night. The messenger arrow would disappear to seek its recipient, arriving as the moon waned and the sky was clear.

"Do you think the clouds will stay away long enough for us to get some arrows back tonight?" Arrina asked as she handed him her own stack.

"Hard to say," Davur admitted. "The mountain weather is nothing like the Valley. It would be nice to get some news from home, but we worry less than our families, I think."

Arrina nodded. "I'll let you see to it."

"And I'll let you get dressed," Davur said. Jonathan nodded once in her direction and followed the Wen into the night.

Once they were gone, Arrina stripped the broad blue robe from her shoulders, taking with it much of the shoulder itself and revealing the straps that held the padded cloth and wood armor that had made her into the stout, aged king. A pair of twists and the armor unhinged on the side, and after a bit of contortion, she placed it on its stand. A hop and jump, with an oomph as she hit her head on the ceiling, and the thickened legs stood apart from her slimmer ones. These black carapaces joined the rest of the costume, hooked to the stand for transport.

Although she didn't need the masks or magic costumes to change her appearance, a Wefal's body paid a price for using magic that Wen and Farlanders did not. Wen magic never wavered. Farlander enchanters spoke of becoming fatigued from using too much magic, growing less able to keep casting more spells, but it was just a metaphor. Wefal magic was no different from physical exertion, and mystics using it needed to eat and drink more, slept longer, and experienced sore and cramped muscles. So Arrina saved her Wefal magic for the troupe's real business.

Arrina stripped off her soaked underclothes and wiped the sweat from her body with the lavender-scented towel. She was the very image of a beautiful Wefal woman — long blue-blond hair and a lean, toned physique with that little bit of softness to store extra energy for magic. She hadn't simply grown into the woman she saw in the mirror each day. An internal mystic chose the form of her body as surely as other people picked which clothes to wear and kept that shape for as long as she wished.

Wefal men with her abilities did it too, of course. Stipator certainly hadn't earned his incredible strength and speed through constant exercise. She strongly suspected that some of his other physical attributes were not natural gifts, either. Her upbringing prevented her from asking; it would be rude and hypocritical besides.

There was a timid knock on her wagon door. Arrina grabbed a sheet and put her ear near the door.

"Who is it?"

"It's me. Etha. I wanted to ask you a favor, but if this is a bad time …"

Screening her body with the door, Arrina opened it a crack. A short Farlander stood on the top step, blushing to the roots of her shoulder-length, brown hair. Etha ad'Lisa was a short, slightly plump woman with a complexion unusually dark even for a Farlander. She was a year older than Arrina, but had a high voice, round face, and girlish figure that made her perfect for playing child roles in the troupe's shows.

Arrina suspected Etha sometimes resented that. She had been mistaken for and treated as a child her whole life. Etha often alluded to receiving similar treatment from her family, since she was the youngest of more than a dozen grandchildren. She had made it clear from the start, though, that she would endure anything in the service of the Senserte — even if it meant playing nothing but children and minor roles. But Etha had gotten so used to being treated like a child that she sometimes assumed anyone offering her advice or a kind word was patronizing her.

"As good a time as any, Etha," Arrina said, waving her inside and closing the door behind them. "Come in and have a seat."

Arrina grabbed a robe from a nearby peg and pulled it on as Etha sat down, back straight and hands crushing her skirts. *She looks as wound up as one of Jonathan's clockwork contraptions,* Arrina thought.

"I'm ready for something more challenging," the Farlander blurted. She blushed, again. "I know I've only been traveling with you for a few months, but I've learned so much, and I think I can do more for the Senserte than you've let me do so far."

Arrina suppressed the urge to sigh. "I know you can, and I promise you will. It's not that I don't think you can handle more. It's just … the part chooses player. We'll try to find you a bigger role in the next job."

"I'd be much more useful if I could use magic."

Ah. So that's what this is about. "Michael has agreed to take you on as an apprentice."

"I know, but I think he'd rather spend his time enchanting new masks than teaching me. I haven't done anything except answer riddles and learn the history of the Nosamae." The words shot out of her like arrows from Davur's bow — fast and sharp.

"From what I've heard, that's how enchanters start teaching their apprentices."

The Farlander seemed to note Arrina's hesitation. "I know you can't force him to teach me faster, but can you at least talk to him about it when you see him?"

"Of course, Etha." Arrina gave her an encouraging smile she hoped didn't look as patronizing as it felt.

"Thanks, Arrina," Etha said, looking relieved. "I'll let you get changed."

Changed? Arrina thought, reaching for clean underclothes. *I forgot that's what I was trying to do.*

When she stepped out of her wagon a few minutes later, she wore a long-sleeved red and yellow dress and elegant sandals. Her hair was brushed and braided, and a white shawl covered her shoulders against the evening chill.

The troupe's wagons were neatly parked in two rows on the side of the road leading into Mattock. The clearing they had performed in was across the road and downhill a little. Sounds of a late party drifted up from it, and at a regular pace, a bowstring slapped a glove and an arrow disappeared toward the heavens. The cold mountain wind moved her shawl more than it affected the arrows.

Lights were on in two of the wagons: Michael's and Jonathan's. That was good; she wanted to talk with them anyway. Well, one of them.

She knocked on Michael's door. She heard the familiar creak as he stood from the corner of the small couch he had, and saw his legs' shadows moving as he approached the door. He always stopped to look at who was out there, no matter where they were.

The door opened, and he smiled broadly. "Arrina, a wonderful performance as always. Come in out of that wind."

"Are you talking about the play or the job with Reck?" she asked as she settled down on the couch, not half a step from his narrow bed.

Michael shelved two notebooks and carefully put away his ink and pen as he answered. "The play, of course." Without asking, he poured her a glass of passion fruit wine from a pitcher on the table. Another glass showed he had already finished his allotted one cup for the evening.

She took it, glancing at his bed again. She wondered if she could get him to sit there with her, but before she could suggest it, the familiar creak happened, and he settled down in his corner — not too close, a professional distance. A whiff of musky cologne spoiled the illusion of innocence.

Why is it always so complicated with Michael? She wondered, not for the first time, and turned her attention to him. Patience always worked.

He wore a white, long-sleeved shirt and brown, functional trousers. He had removed the large collection of rings he typically had on his fingers, but he still had four earrings in each ear.

Not that he would ever be seen without those, she thought, and smiled as he subconsciously touched one.

He smiled back.

"Jonathan asked me ..." he said even as she said, "Etha wanted to know ..."

Laughing, she waved him to go first. The wine helped warm her.

He shrugged. "Might as well get it out of the way. Jonathan wanted me to ask you to remind Lastor and Stipator to ..."

"To stick with the plan," she pronounced gravely, mimicking her brother's voice.

Michael chuckled. "Yes, those are his words exactly."

"He says it after every performance. He's known Stipator since he and I were fourteen." She shook her head in wonder. "Has our swashbuckling hero ever passed up an opportunity to improvise his way into the leading role?"

Michael chuckled again. "I know, and you know, but you know how your brother gets. It's his job to keep the players out of trouble."

"I'll tell him — again — when he gets back."

"And Lastor?"

"We have to find him first." She heaved a sigh. "Lastor is our wild card. We can't know when — or whether — he will show up, but we're always glad when he does. I don't know if I want him to always stick to the plan." She sighed again. "It's not much longer until he has to grow up."

"Wen magic ..." Michael trailed off. "What that must do to those kids. Sixteen, eighteen years old, living a life where nothing can even touch them, and then it's gone. They lose the wild freedom Farlanders and Wefals finally are finally getting."

"It's hard on them," she agreed. This was not the way Arrina had hoped the conversation would go. It reminded her of her younger half-brother Kaspar, heir to the Pithdai throne. He had lost his magic four years ago, and he still mourned it by obsessing over the magic of other races — within the Flecterran Valley and far beyond it. She sipped her wine pensively.

"You said Etha had asked you to talk to me about something?" Michael prompted.

She pushed away the dark thoughts gladly. "Yes. She wants us to give her more responsibility."

He raised one bushy red eyebrow at her. "She wants me to teach her magic more quickly, you mean."

"That's a big part of it," she confessed. "A third enchantress could be useful, but I know it takes a Farlander years to wield magic for the first time."

Michael retrieved the pitcher and his glass and poured them both one. Arrina was astonished, and it must have shown because he blushed.

Clearing his throat, he said, "How much do you know about the apprenticeship of enchantresses?"

"Etha thinks it's boring, and I know it's riddles, history, and poetry. Insufferably boring," she added, grinning. "Wielding magic comes much later."

He leaned toward her, expression so serious Arrina regretted being flippant. His voice was low, nearly a whisper, and she thought she heard thunder. "If I revealed a few closely guarded secrets to Etha, I could teach her the basics in a few weeks."

Arrina's eyes widened.

"Do you know why I won't?" He held up a finger for emphasis, and the room darkened a little. "With the enchantments that come easiest to me, I could fill you with such awe that you would prostrate yourself on the ground at my feet. I could spy on you invisibly and noiselessly in order to slit your throat before you even felt the knife." She felt more scared with each word he said, and the thunder seemed louder. "I could strip away Lastor's Wen magic and teach him the meaning of a life with consequences."

Arrina gulped her wine, dribbling some on her chin.

Michael sat back, the intensity gone, and he continued in a near whisper. Her fear slowly melted away. "But I would never do any of those things — not just because they would be wrong, though they would be, but because I can't make them last forever. Every enchantress's spell breaks eventually. You would remember that I had bowed you down with my magic, and what would you think of me then? Lastor may well discover I was behind his taste of mortality, and how do you think he would respond?"

"Badly," Arrina acknowledged, wiping her chin. "But do you really think Etha would ..."

"No, but I have an obligation to be absolutely certain before I give her the ability to do so." Michael lifted his finger again. "Don't think that means enchantresses do it out of pure altruism. We've learned from past mistakes. The Nosamae enchantresses overstepped their boundaries once, and it sparked a war between Wen and Farlanders. As it turns out, Wen children and Farlander enchantresses are very well-matched in magical combat."

"The Nosamae War," Arrina said, remembering the history. The Nosamae had eventually lost, but tens of thousands of Wen children died, much of the Valley burned, and Aaronsglade was razed to the ground. The once proud country of Aaronma was taken from the Nosamae, and now the Council ruled only over the rebuilt Aaronsglade. Eventually, enchantresses like Michael could practice openly and without fear of persecution, but even that was only a few generations old.

Michael shifted in his seat and gave her a wan smile. "I'm sorry. I didn't mean to bore you with history lessons."

"I don't find them boring. It sounds like it would make a good subject for a new play," she told him.

"Oh please don't." He chuckled, his mood lighter. "The Council of Aaronsglade has been trying to make everyone forget that unfortunate little chapter of history. If they find out I'm directing a play about it, my mother will tie me up and use me for fish bait."

Arrina took the two empty glasses and stood up. Business was done. It was time to move this forward. She put them on the table and purposefully leaned toward the door.

"Leaving so soon?" Michael said, on cue, in a tone Arrina knew meant he definitely hoped she wasn't.

She collapsed back onto the couch, a little closer to him. "Do you have any idea how cold it is out there? I'm at least staying here until I'm warm again!"

"Please let me get you a blanket," he said, standing up.

While he collected an extra blanket from a trunk, she inched a little farther toward his corner. The couch gave her away, creaking gently. He turned back, face softened. He seemed to have finally reached the same scene as her. He unfolded the blanket for her, and squeezed into the corner of the couch she had left him. His arm wrapped around her shoulder, and she curled into his warmth.

Arrina knew Michael wasn't exaggerating his abilities. Magic was a part of both of them — a source of power and strength that had helped the Senserte earn their reputation. But she also knew he would no more do anything to hurt her with his magic than she would hurt him with hers.

"I can understand a bit how Etha must feel," Michael said abruptly. "Her mother raised her pretty much on her own. That's something you, me, and her have in common."

This wasn't what Arrina wanted to talk about just now, but she saw no reason to change the subject right away. "Actually, we saw our father a lot when we were growing up. Even after Kaspar was born he visited us every three or four days. There's a secret tunnel between the palace and my mother's house."

"Not much of a secret if you're telling me about it."

Arrina jabbed him in the ribs playfully. "If I didn't think you were safe, I wouldn't be sharing a blanket with you."

"I suppose not," he admitted. "Etha grew up dreaming that she would one day find her pirate father and in some way make him accept her as his daughter. My father was murdered when I was too young to remember him. The enchanter who killed him escaped Aaronsglade and went into exile far from the Valley. I used to have elaborate fantasies about tracking him down and avenging my father."

"What changed?"

"When I was fifteen I found out the killer died when I was about five years old. He got involved on the losing side of some kind of local civil war. I'll never have a chance at revenge, just as I don't think Etha will ever meet her father."

"Mmm," Arrina murmured agreeably.

"Pirates tend not to live long lives," Michael elaborated.

"No." She wasn't sure what else to say.

They sat in silence for a few minutes.

"The rigged election skit sure brings back memories, doesn't it?" Michael asked. "Remember that job in the Republic? What was the name of that town?"

It took a moment for Arrina to retrieve it. "Lubalu."

"That's the one. Its conch stayed in power forty years using every trick he could come up with. He switched vote boxes, arrested people he thought would vote against him, and bribed ballot counters. He even had the lens responsible for certifying the election results in his pocket."

"We barely broke a sweat on that one. Stipator and Zori tried to liven it up by seeing how many times they could mispronounce 'Lubalu' without the conch's cronies realizing they weren't actually talking to their boss. Jonathan about had a fit when he found out about that. I don't remember who won."

"I had forgotten about the mispronunciation game. Anyway, I just remember how upset the conch was by the end of the blow-off."

"The people we punish usually are," Arrina said drily.

"Well yes, of course, but the whole town's population was, what, eight hundred?"

"Six."

"Right, six hundred. Being in charge of just six hundred people meant so much to him that he would take ridiculous measures to keep anyone from removing him from power. It wasn't like he had life and death power, either. He was the spokeperson for the village council of a town of six hundred. It just doesn't seem worth the fuss."

"Are you saying you're bored, Michael?" she asked teasingly. "Are your talents being wasted on small-time dictators and insignificant crime bosses?"

"Not at all. Places like Mattock and Lubalu are the ones who need us. Pithdai, Aaronsglade, and the rest have their own police forces. I mention it because it always amazes me how much people will do for so little. The world is so huge. Why squander your life trying to maintain your hold over some ceremonial post in a tiny village somewhere?"

"Have plans to conquer the world, do you?"

Michael barked a laugh. "Mira's deft hands, no! 'More power, more enemies,' my mother used to tell me."

"Less competition, I suppose. Not a lot of people lining up to be the conch of Lubalu. If he had tried something like that in a city large enough to matter he wouldn't have lasted forty years. Might not have lasted four."

"True enough."

"Not all of our targets have small ambitions, you know. Remember that potion-maker last fall?"

"The one who thought he could use the hair of his enemies to poison them?"

"That's the one. He probably still thinks he could have conquered Sutola if we hadn't stopped him."

"Arrina, he was out of his mind. I pitied him, to be honest."

"He murdered three people before we arrived, Michael. Was he really worthy of your pity?"

"Perhaps not, but I find it a bit difficult to hate someone whose mind has been warped by Wen magic, and I think he qualifies. Poresa felt the same way."

"Poresa has a soft heart. It's a marvel she still travels with us."

"I think she believes she moderates some of Stipator's zeal," Michael said.

"Heh. Jonathan has been trying to moderate Stipator since he and I were fourteen. I don't think anyone can make him less incorrigible."

They settled into an easy silence, simply enjoying each other's presence.

"Feeling warmer?" Michael asked suddenly.

She simply nodded, the top of her head rubbing against the inside of his shoulder.

"Mind sharing?"

She smiled up at him as she pulled the blanket out from under herself and slid it around his back. He glanced down at her a moment before looking away, slightly flushed. Arrina glanced at the front of her dress and noticed the bodice had slid down rather far. She sat up to adjust it and then leaned into Michael's arm again. He pulled his side of the blanket around so he could hug her close as they sat.

They stayed like that for a little while before Arrina felt his lips against the top of her head — just a single gentle peck.

"Mmm. Maybe we should come up to the mountains more often," she said softly, tilting her face up toward him.

He smiled and leaned toward her, lips slightly pursed.

Tchunk! A slender wooden shaft suddenly materialized between their faces, sinking through the back of the couch and into the wall behind it. Both of them jumped back away from the message arrow in surprise. After the initial shock passed, Arrina and Michael looked at each other and burst out laughing.

Weather permitting, a Messegere moon shot arrow always reached its target — even ones indoors and away from windows. It never hurt anyone, but it always managed to make an entrance that its recipient could not possibly miss.

"Midnight and all is well!" Arrina announced, still laughing. "And I have a guess about the current weather."

Michael plucked the rolled letter off the shaft and looked at the seal. "Is it for me or you?"

"It's from your father." He held out the letter to her. "He has interesting timing," Michael added with a small laugh.

Arrina's eyes scanned the page rapidly. She stood up, letting the blanket fall from her shoulders. "I need to talk to Jonathan."

"Your hands are shaking." He had a note of worry in his voice. "What's wrong?"

"It's Kaspar. He's been kidnapped."

Chapter 3

First-time visitors to Jonathan's wagon often described it as messy. This didn't do it justice. A room with unwashed dishes, empty bottles, and dirty laundry scattered everywhere was messy. A room pressed into service as storage for unused furniture, unwanted art, and incomplete sets of tableware was messy.

Jonathan's wagon wasn't messy. It was a wilderness, a trackless jungle no outsider had any business entering without extensive preparations or, even better, an expert guide.

Like a jungle, its flora of books, sketches, maps, and hastily scribbled notes sprang up wherever it could find purchase. Most held some potentially nourishing information, but some were poisonous. Useful reference books stood in teetering stacks with books filled with debunked myths or works of fiction disguised as truth. Blueprints abandoned as impractical or outright dangerous looked exactly the same to the untrained eye as useful ones. A page filled with complex calculations might have a single, trivial mathematical error that rendered it worthless, but there it sat near all the pages with no mistakes.

The fauna was even worse. Tools lounged on tables and chairs like predators awaiting a renewed appetite for the hunt. Mechanical devices ranging from tiny springwork masterpieces to large, counterweight-driven contraptions lurked under ever chair and behind every pile of dog-eared tomes. Nearly all of them were cannibal scavengers who lurked in the paper jungle, silently lusting for the flesh of their brethren even as they feared these rivals for gears and screws and mainsprings.

This jungle saw its share of death, too. Failed experiments and obsolete machines lay like corpses in all the unused corners of the wagon, slowly picked over for useful parts by other, more successful devices. This strange decomposition of contraptions happened slowly, and a casing or a winding key might lie in the wreckage for a month or more after the core idea had fled like the animating soul of living thing.

Some of these devices posed a serious hazard to the casual visitor who did not know to keep close track of his extremities. Not only was the rapid-fire crossbow wildly inaccurate, it sometimes threw a bolt up into the face of its operator. The perfectly innocent-looking lock on the table was meant to drive a (potentially poisoned) needle into the finger of any thief who tried to pick it, but at the moment it could shoot nearly a foot through the air without warning. The pulley of one experimental climbing harness sometimes popped a wheel, turning a smooth, easy climb into a sudden and potentially fatal descent.

When visiting this peculiar jungle, it was best not to touch the local wildlife. Even then, travel could be perilous. Sketches, maps, and wadded up notes covered everything, and no one could tell which rolling paper hills were simply piles and which concealed a lurking box of rusty nails or a herd of free range ball bearings. When Jonathan warned people to stay out of a particular section of the wagon because they might spring the concealed bear trap, only first-time visitors laughed. Everyone else stayed away from that spot.

Jonathan himself transformed into another creature when he was in the wagon — like a game warden raised in a city who has spent decades tending a particular tract of wilderness. Back home, he could discuss poetry and music, debate politics and theology, and enjoy all the other comforts of civilization a well-bred young man might indulge in. But in the wagon, he spoke only of tools, machines and mathematics, and any attempt to convince him to do otherwise was as futile as coaxing a kiss and a cuddle out of a lover while swimming in shark-infested waters.

No one knew this territory as well as Jonathan did. No one wanted to. No one needed to. If it could be found in his wagon, Jonathan could locate and retrieve it at a moment's notice. If it didn't exist he would set his jaw and disappear into the paper and brass wilderness for hours or even days at a time. When he returned to civilized company, he would have the requested prize in hand like the pelt of some rare and danger- ous animal. Jonathan never boasted or complained about these expedi- tions because, as he would be the first to admit, he lived for those hunts.

As he read the letter Arrina had brought into his wagon, Jonathan looked hopeful that he could solve it with something in his wagon. The expression wasn't quite rage, but something more akin to the determination of an athlete who enjoys overcoming the challenges of the competition even more than achieving victory.

Arrina sat cross-legged on a chair her brother had cleared for her benefit. She already had the letter memorized:

> *King Larus of Pithdai,*
>
> *As you can probably confirm by his handwriting in this letter, I have your heir in my custody. If you wish to see him, deliver all the paintings kept in Pithdai's throne room and art archive to Gulinora Island before the next time Chelestria is full. Late delivery will cost your son a finger each day. Attempt to apprehend or cheat me, and you will never see your son alive. Do not think I don't know which paintings you will not wish to deliver, and don't think I cannot tell an original from a forgery.*
>
> *Send only one ship. Do not send Wen children or Farlander adults. Instruct your representative to come to shore unarmed and prepared to follow my agents' instructions without question or hesitation. Anything less could result in the end of your family line.*
>
> *I sincerely hope you will arrange this transaction with a minimum of delay, difficulty, or spectacle.*
>
> *Sincerely,*
Prince Kaspar of Pithdai

And the second page:

> *Dear Arrina,*
>
> *Come to Pithdai at once. You and Jonathan will be my agents in the enclosed matter. This is a state secret. Share it with no one.*
>
> *Love,*
Father

Jonathan looked up from the letter and met her gaze. He dangled it in one hand as if threatening to feed it to all the other paper in his wagon. "This is a trap."

Arrina nodded. "It could be a forgery."

"We can't risk that."

"No," Arrina agreed. "We have to return to Pithdai more quickly than the wagons can get us there. Horses may not be fast enough, either."

"Father doesn't know where we are or how much his letter was delayed," Jonathan mused, and Arrina immediately saw the set of his jaw as he considered the problem. "We can't assume he'll send someone else if we don't get there soon enough."

"I don't want him to send someone else. He knew what he was doing sending us to do this. He knew we would come up with a plan and do something unexpected."

He raised an eyebrow at her, and his hands reflexively fidgeted with the hazardous lock. "Like tell all the Senserte that Pithdai's heir has been kidnapped?"

"For starters."

He paused, staring into the middle distance for a moment. "Do you have a plan for what to do when we get to Pithdai?"

"Not yet. Do you have a plan for how we're going to get there in, say, eight days?"

Jonathan's hand deftly evaded the needle as it shot out of the lock and disappeared into the paper underbrush on the floor. "The beginnings of one. Give me until the strike meeting tomorrow night."

"We're going to wait an entire day?"

He shook his head. "We won't make it on horseback. If my idea works, we can make the trip in maybe four days."

"Four hundred miles in four days?" Arrina asked incredulously.

"Less than one, if the winds favor us," he countered.

"Do you need any supplies from the other wagons?"

Jonathan surveyed the diverse wilderness around them. "Not tonight. Get some sleep. You have a show to put on in the morning. If I keep you up all night fetching canvas and candles, Michael will strangle me."

"He'd never get past the bear trap."

"That old thing? I dismantled it weeks ago and used the parts to make jaws for my wind-up panther." He carefully escorted her to the exit.

"Wind-up panther?" Arrina asked, glancing around the wagon to see if he was joking.

Jonathan grinned broadly, pressed the letter into her hands, and closed the door between them.

The mountain winds had picked up, and Arrina pulled the shawl tighter around her shoulders in a vain effort to shut out the chill. She briefly considered returning to Michael's wagon but dismissed it. She wasn't really in the mood for cuddling or conversation tonight, and going to him in her current state would only frustrate him.

He would be glad for a chance to soothe me.

But her feet carried her back to her wagon. She didn't really want to burden him with her troubles. Kaspar's letter would make trouble for the Senserte soon enough. She'd give Michael a night of rest without having to worry about how they would continue operating without Jonathan and her.

When her wagon came into sight, what Arrina saw brought her up short. Michael sat on the steps outside, underneath the hanging lantern.

Guilt instantly flooded her. "Sorry," she mumbled. "I should have at least stopped by to say good night."

Michael didn't leap up and grab her in a crushing embrace at the sound of her voice, but he didn't have the storm cloud look he could wear when deeply provoked. He simply looked up from the book he was reading, his face a mask of compassion.

"It's understandable. Are you leaving for Pithdai?"

The frankness of the question surprised her. Arrina suddenly realized how little time she had spent with her brother. Michael couldn't have been waiting for her here unless he had come here soon after she had left his wagon.

He knew I wouldn't be coming back tonight.

"Yes," Arrina said.

Michael closed his book and stood up. "Tonight or at first light?"

She shook her head. "The morning after the strike meeting. Jonathan has some plan to get us there faster, but it will take time."

He looked grim, jaw set. "Will you tell the others?"

She walked up the stairs to her door. "We're not about to sneak off in the night without letting the rest of the Senserte know."

"Can you talk about it?"

Arrina paused with her hand on the door latch. "Yes."

"But you don't want to." There was no accusation there, just simple recognition.

Arrina considered this for a long moment. "I don't," she said, "but I should."

"If you want to wait until tomorrow, I'll understand. After you left, though, I couldn't help but wonder how anyone could have kidnapped the heir of Pithdai."

Arrina turned. "You think it's a forgery?"

"Not necessarily. It just sounds like a pretty impressive crime. Any chance it happened while your brother was traveling on business for your father?"

"You realize we have a play to perform in the morning, don't you?"

Michael shrugged. "We just freed Mattock from the shackles Reck had them wearing. I think they'll forgive a few missed lines."

"Missed lines?" Arrina demanded, almost offended. "You know very well it wouldn't come to that!"

It wasn't until Michael quirked a small smile that she realized he was joking. "Your move, Arrina. Invite me in, come back to my wagon, or tell me to go away. I forgot to bring that blanket with me, and this wind is brutal."

Arrina pushed the door open and waved him inside. She threw herself into the comfortable chair at her dressing table, while he sat on the nearby stool.

"Is there a chance Kaspar was traveling?" he repeated.

Arrina shook her head. "I doubt it. Father rarely lets Kaspar leave the palace."

That had always been a point of contention between father and son. Kaspar often spoke of joining the Senserte or just plain traveling around the Flecterran Union, though Arrina knew he was secretly fascinated with the idea of traveling far beyond the Valley. Larus refused to consider anything like that.

The king of Pithdai was very old even for a Wen. It had been a near miracle that he had even been able to sire Kaspar — so much so that rumors persisted that the king had entrusted the deed to someone else. He was extremely protective of his heir for that reason.

"And I'm guessing he has guards around him at all times."

"The very best — the homeguard." Arrina frowned. She did not envy whoever had been on duty when Kaspar vanished. Father would not be lenient with them, assuming they survived the kidnapping.

"And visitors have their lips sweetened before they are allowed to enter the palace."

"That's fairly standard throughout the Union."

Michael ticked off points on his fingers. "So that means someone got into the palace without having their lips sweetened, overpowered Kaspar's homeguardsmen, and spirited away Pithdai's heir?"

Arrina's frown deepened. "And they apparently evaded capture. Magic."

"Or agents inside the palace," Michael amended. He crossed his legs at the ankles, stretching. "Probably both. We should assume whoever it was operates the same way the Senserte does."

"Not all the spies need to have left after Kaspar's abduction. Father would want to make it clear that he wasn't making any moves against the kidnappers."

"Kidnappers. It could not be done alone," he muttered, nodding. "More and more like the Senserte, then." He closed his eyes.

Arrina watched his bushy eyebrows twitch as he thought it out. The Senserte called him "the Director," and not just because he filled that role for their plays. He had a gift for finding the logical arguments their marks might take, for asking the questions that led to the insight to do things that would tip the scales in the Senserte's favor. And he could do it all from behind the scenes.

"But why do it at all?" Before she could answer, Michael shook his head. "Clearly it's a powerful lever against your father, but what's the specific motive? Destabilizing Pithdai? Exacting political or economic concessions?"

"The kidnappers are demanding most of the paintings in Pithdai's palace, or they'll kill Kaspar."

Michael's brow wrinkled in confusion. "I'm sure they're all priceless national treasures, but why kidnap the crown prince to get them?" He shook his head again. "Do you remember that clean-and-replace swindle we ran against those poison dealers who were using hollowed-out sculptures to hide their product? I mean, if they could make the prince disappear, a few paintings should be easier."

Now Arrina shook her head. "It wouldn't work even for the Senserte. When the king isn't holding court, at least a dozen homeguardsmen stand watch over the throne room. The paintings there are never taken off the walls, and only adult Wen with sweetened lips are allowed to clean them. It's the same with the palace art archive, except those paintings are never cleaned."

Michael blinked. "You assign twelve elite guards for empty rooms?

That's a new wrinkle. You Pith take your art very seriously."

Arrina managed a weak smile, fighting the growing worry gnawing at her belly. "Not without reason. Not all miraklas involve flora and fauna, and the miraklas of Pith children quite often take shape in canvas and paint."

"Nosamae Descending," he breathed. He closed his eyes again.

"That's the most famous, but certainly not the most dangerous."

His blue eyes snapped open. "Pithdai has paintings more dangerous than the one that ended the Nosamae War?"

"At least Nosamae Descending requires so many other, lesser miraklas that activating it is probably impossible." She shrugged. "In Pithdai, though, I know of six paintings that are doorways to other worlds. Empire of Brass allows travel both ways, because an army of brass soldiers walked out of it a few centuries back. We lost seven thousand soldiers turning back that invasion, and three thousand more were on the far side of the painting when the masons finished covering it with a brick wall. Pith scholars were pretty sure that a mere cloth cover prevented passage, but our generals didn't want to take any chances."

Michael's eyes bulged. "Mira's golden locks! Why didn't they just destroy the painting?"

"Miraklas are nearly indestructible."

"Nearly? It seems worth the effort to get rid of something like that."

Arrina sighed. *Farlanders will never understand Wen magic. They're used to magic that has rules.* She wasn't sure she'd ever understand it either, but she had spent her life around Wen.

"It's more complicated than that. It takes a mirakla to destroy a mirakla, and it usually has to be a mirakla intended to destroy that mirakla, and you're talking about something most very young children never even manifest. Most of those that do only produce very minor ones. Even the Wen have absolutely no idea what causes miraklas."

"So you can't eliminate the danger. You can only contain it."

"Exactly."

"But doesn't that mean delivering this ransom is completely impossible?"

"Yes, but I'm not sure the kidnappers know that."

"Or care."

"Or care," Arrrina agreed.

Michael closed his eyes again, leaning against the wall. Arrina felt her own eyes drooping, and was just wondering if Michael had fallen asleep when he sat up again, brushing his hands on pants.

"I have absolutely no idea what the kidnappers actually want," he said. "If they were merely incompetent, they couldn't have kidnapped Kaspar in the first place. If they want a specific painting, they could have just asked for it by name. If they wanted Kaspar dead, they could have killed him, rather than waiting until the ransom doesn't show up."

Arrina felt even more worried. Those were all of her conclusions, too. *If Michael can't figure out something new about this ...* She didn't let the thought finish, saying, "Smells like a conspiracy, doesn't it?"

"It smells like us, to be honest."

"Except without the justice. My father has enemies, but he has never done anything to anyone to justify something like this."

"Do you think that's why he's sending you — to find out who is behind this and render judgment?"

Father certainly knows what kind of work we do. Arrina hated the idea that he thought he could simply point the Senserte at his problems of state and expect them to do his dirty work. The Senserte never took direction. They chose their marks based on consensus agreement between their members.

Arrina knew she couldn't just turn her back on her half-brother, though. Kaspar could be childish and egotistical at times, but he was her blood. Besides, his death could set off a succession war for the throne of Pithdai. Larus had no siblings, but he had plenty of cousins.

"You're right," she said, her stubborn anger rising. "Except for one thing."

"What's that?"

"If they're powerful enough to kidnap Kaspar, they probably aren't the ones who will be waiting for us to deliver — or not deliver — the paintings. We're Senserte. We need to find out who is pulling the strings and punish them, not their accomplices — willing, unknowing, or otherwise."

Michael held up his hands. "Even if you weren't looking at me like you might stab me to death for disagreeing with you, I won't argue with you on that count."

Chapter 4

Nearly an hour after the final performance of Mad King Rupert, Arrina finally reached her wagon. The people of Mattock pressed gifts on her at every step — everything from carved wooden whistles to small casks of liquor they had distilled Mira-only-knew-where, to coins minted from gold that once belonged to Reck. She played the part of the grateful leading actor, even though her heart really wasn't in it. Jonathan hadn't come out of his wagon all day — not that it was unusual, but Chelestria would be full all too soon. If whatever contraption he was cooking up failed, Kaspar would suffer for it.

In the end, the only thing that allowed her to escape the press of bodies was Michael's thunderous announcement that the acrobats and jugglers would be performing their impossible feats of physical skill. Arrina barely had a chance to remove her King Rupert mask before there was a knock on her door.

She sighed and opened it. Jonathan stood outside looking and smelling like a hunter who had spent a week in the wilderness, not just a single day in a mere wagon. His blue-blond hair was tossed wild and greasy. Grime coated his hands and fingernails. His eyes were bloodshot, and he had buttoned his torn shirt wrong. But his eyes shone with victory.

"I told you I'd get it done in time for the strike meeting," he said with a slightly manic grin.

"You look like one whom Death would pity," she told him, quoting from the scene in Company of Fools after Wen children cover a Farlander scoundrel in honey and feathers. "Come inside. I'll pour you some wine, and you can tell me exactly what it is."

"It's not quite done. I need Michael's help for the last part, but I'm almost certain it will work. I'll show you after the strike meeting. But I'll take the wine." He dropped onto a bench mounted to the wall.

Arrina had not even reached into the cabinet for the wine before there was another knock at her wagon door. *Really? Can't a lady change clothes in peace?* "Who is it?"

"It's me," Michael answered. "Can I come in?"

"Yes."

"Stipator is back with Lastor," he said from the doorway. "Afternoon, Jonathan."

Arrina met Jonathan's eyes briefly before returning her attention to Michael. "Did they bring us any complications?"

"It doesn't look like they were followed by a mob." He shrugged. "Beyond that, I think you can guess the answer."

Arrina's heart fluttered. Stipator and Lastor could turn even the simplest job into an elaborate web of complications. Stipator loved a challenge and knew he could talk his way out of just about any problem his clever flourishes might get him into. Lastor still possessed the nearly literal invulnerability of all young Wen, able to rely on his magic to solve any problem his careless tongue could cause. She worried about them both nevertheless. "Send them in."

Michael nodded. "I'll see you both at the strike meeting."

He left, and Stipator sauntered through the door with a smug smile. He still wore his absurd, overly ornamented rapier, and it was really a wonder that their marks didn't pick him out at once based solely on the reputation of his sword.

Lastor trotted at his heels. Arrina recognized the Wen teenager's mischievous grin and nervous fidget. He couldn't wait to talk about what he had been doing the night the rest of the Senserte had been tricking Reck into fleeing the last of his once-immense fortune.

Jonathan slipped past them and closed the door. He said nothing as he sat on the small stool near the entrance, but his frown — not quite a scowl, but quite close — said everything on his mind. Arrina's brother did not always have the same appreciation for the pair's antics that she did.

"Did you accomplish what you set out to do?" she asked Lastor.

Stipator's brilliant topaz eyes twinkled at her, and he twitched his obscene curling mustache with perfectly manicured hands. He beamed down at the Wen like a proud father. "I think you could say that. Tell her how you left Reck in the woods with nothing but his clothes."

Arrina listened to Lastor's account in silence. Jonathan's frown deepened with every sentence. The Wen boy had told the bandits most of the Senserte's plan to stop Reck, which helped convince them to take the strongbox containing Kara's tracking ring back to their real hideout.

"They left the cart and horses like I asked, so when they all had gone, I drove them to a farm a few miles away and left a note," Lastor added. "And when Reck returned and his last hope had disappeared, he fell over and cried. That's when I taunted him. He needed to know why, Arrina."

Lastor looked at Arrina expectantly, a bright smile on his face. Jonathan was looking at her, too, practically demanding her disapproval. Stipator, clearly deciding Lastor's gambit was cause for celebration, opened one of Arrina's good bottles of wine while the Wen was retelling his exploits and started pouring it into four glass tumblers.

Arrina took a breath. "I'm sure both Kara and the governor's patrol will appreciate your cleverness. She wasn't convinced we'd be able to trick the bandits into taking the bait, but that's clearly no longer a problem. That means she can finish her business down there more quickly. Well done."

That was all true, and Lastor beamed to hear it.

Michael and Kara were both enchantresses, but they had specialties. Michael was adept at illusions and enchanted devices. Kara focused on gathering intelligence, whether that meant magical surveillance, asking around, or forging convincing documents to make her look like a legitimate official of some kind.

Jonathan looked neither convinced nor remotely pleased. Arrina spoke before he could berate Lastor.

"However, I'd like to offer some suggestions to keep in mind in the future."

"Yeah, yeah," Lastor said, accepting the glass from Stipator. "Stick to the plan." He winked at Jonathan.

"I wish you would follow my words instead of just hearing them," Jonathan muttered.

"Actually, you handled yourself well on the night of the blow-off," Arrina said. "I wanted to address the way you sabotaged his mining equipment."

"No one got hurt in any of the fires, just like you made me promise," the Wen protested defensively.

"I know, Lastor. It wasn't that. I just think it would have been better if you had let Reck's men see you do it."

"What?" Lastor and Jonathan asked at once with equal confusion, but Stipator nodded as he sipped the wine.

"Think about it from his perspective, Lastor. Reck knows someone was setting those fires, but not who. He has no proof that it's us. Gristo and Nidela always have alibis. But he can't appear to have no idea who is behind it, because that makes him look incompetent. So what do you think he does?"

Lastor considered this at length, one finger dipped in the wine until it began to steam. Arrina knew the question would intrigue him.

"He needs to punish someone," Arrina said when she was sure he was stumped. "So he blames someone unpopular who could have done it and punishes that person."

Horror replaced interest on Lastor's face, but Arrina couldn't tell whether he was moved by the prospect of the innocent suffering or by the idea that someone else was getting the credit for his handiwork. "But he was punishing the wrong people!"

Arrina nodded sagely and fixed him with a very serious expression. "That's because you let him do it. If people had seen a distinctive figure at the site of every fire — even one who disappeared right away and couldn't be found anywhere in Mattock — Reck's people wouldn't have accepted his claim that he was punishing a saboteur who had infiltrated their operations. They would know it was some mysterious vigilante. Does that make sense?"

"A little," Lastor said with a frown of concentration. "That would have been harder, though. They might have put out the fires in time."

"Do you think Stipator cuts off buttons and slices belts because he wants to show off his swordsmanship to people like Reg? Of course not. Every second a fight lasts gives his opponent more time to get lucky and kill him, but Stipator takes the most correct path, not the fastest or easiest." Arrina put a hand on his shoulder. "That's part of being a Senserte. We're not swindlers. Swindlers will steal from anyone they can trick, and if some bystanders get hurt or lose money along the way, well, that's their bad luck. But we are the Senserte — the eyes of justice. We're only interested in punishing the guilty, which means no one who is innocent should suffer because of one of our schemes, not even if it is at the hands of the ones we're here to punish."

"I know," Lastor said, clearly chastised. "I guess I just didn't think of the vigilante mask."

Arrina removed her hand and smiled at him. "Next time you will. I know you didn't mean for anyone to get hurt because of you. We all have to learn somehow, and sometimes experience is the best teacher we have out here on the road."

Lastor nodded. "I'll remember. I'm glad you're not mad about what I did to Reck."

"Not at all," Arrina assured him. "You should go get some dinner. Pine trees don't grow fruit like the trees in the Valley do. You must be hungry."

"I am a little, yeah." Lastor put down his nearly boiling glass of wine. "I'll see all of you at the strike meeting."

The young Wen ran out the door, which Jonathan closed behind him. Her brother still looked displeased.

"Why didn't you remind him to stick to the plan?" he demanded. His voice was low but filled with frustration.

Arrina carefully took Lastor's glass of wine and blew on it. "Lastor is a wild card," she said, repeating the old familiar argument. "We know we can't depend on him, so we're just thrilled when he shows up."

"You know," Stipator mused, staring at the tumbler in his hand as he turned it to catch the lantern light. "You could give him an important task so he stops feeling like you don't trust him. Who knows? He might surprise you."

Jonathan shook his head vigorously. "That would be even worse."

"Lastor is excellent at creating distractions," Arrina said. "Reck was so focused on the fires that he fell for swindles we didn't even expect to work. He's also good at disappearing when he needs to."

"That's just Wen magic," Jonathan noted. "Eventually it will go away."

"That's at least a year away, and probably two years from now," Arrina said. "Until then, it still gives him an advantage on these jobs. And he's learned a lot since he joined us a few months ago. He's just young, not foolish or stubborn — at least no more so than we were at his age."

Jonathan shrugged. "Two against one, how am I supposed to argue?" He took his tumbler of wine. "You're right about his ruse with the bandits. That will save Kara days, if not weeks. I still think Lastor was lucky Reck wasn't murdered on the spot, but as Slock says in The Prince of Stormhaven, 'The window's broken, the gold is stolen, but look, the man, his blood's still flowing. What crime was committed then?'" He stood up. "I should probably let you get changed and pick Michael's brain about

the, um ..." He trailed off, his secretive smile returning. "The surprise."

Jonathan took his glass and slipped out of Arrina's wagon, leaving her alone with Stipator.

"You were supposed to make him curious about this gold vein, not insult him and challenge him to a duel. " Irritation crept into her voice, but Stipator seemed not to notice it.

Like Arrina and Jonathan, Stipator was a Wefal. Unlike her, he had been born of Wefal parents in Petersine. Arrina's father was King Larus of Pithdai, the ancient seat of Wen civilization. Larus had taken Arrina's Farlander mother as his mistress during the lonely grief between the death of his first Wen wife and his marriage to his current queen.

Arrina and Jonathan had inherited their mother's charm and good looks. Wefals couldn't inherit titles in Pithdai, but Larus had given them both the best teachers his magnificent wealth could buy. Stipator, though thirty years old to Arrina and Jonathan's twenty-five, had become her favorite teacher.

Stipator shrugged. "It's not like he would have accepted, although that would have made this job a lot easier." He smirked. "Besides. It was funny. You should have seen the look on his face when I fed him the same lines he's been using on the smalltime prospectors he's been strongarming into selling their claims to him."

King Larus had chosen Stipator ad'Bryan because he was a Wefal from a good Petersine family who could help them master their magical abilities. Magic came to Wen as naturally as breathing, though they lost most of their incredible abilities as teenagers, retaining only one or two talents as adults. Farlanders and Wefals, though, needed to learn magic from someone else. Even then, the magics of Wen, Farlanders, and Wefals were completely different from each other.

Wen commanded the elements, shaping wind, fire, plants, and animals. Farlander enchanters were adept at illusions, charms, spying, and making magic devices. Wefal mystics had one of three types of magic, and they had as little choice in the matter as Wen adults did in their magic talents. Internal mystics like Stipator and Arrina could change and control their bodies. External mystics like Jonathan could manipulate nonliving objects as if with a thousand tiny, invisible fingers. Mental mystics like Poresa, another of their traveling companions, could read and control minds. The different kinds of Wefal mystics could also work together to create more complex effects, something almost unthinkable for Wen and Farlander magic-wielders.

Stipator's Wefal magic was hardly his only gift, however, and certainly not his greatest passion. He had the tongue and soul of some trickster god — seeking out and punishing the powerful, corrupt, and unrepentant. Arrina respected that in him — loved him for it, on the best of days. She wouldn't be here in Mattock if she didn't. But sometimes he got a bit carried away.

And if this next job is half as complicated and dangerous as Michael thinks it is, Stipator's audacity could get him killed. She didn't want that.

"It just wasn't part of the plan, Stipator," Arrina said with a sigh. "You were only supposed to lure him to the stream we seeded with gold and convince him to buy land you never even owned for ten times as much as it's worth — just the first of many cons to cheat him out of the money he cheated out of others."

"He didn't just cheat them, Arrina." His eyes filled with anger. "He arranged mining accidents. People died."

"We came here to rob him, Stipator, not execute him. Threatening violence only put Reck on his guard and convinced him to respond in kind. People like Reg and the guards were doing their jobs. The situation in Mattock was not of their making."

Stipator shot her the "I know what I'm doing" look he usually reserved for times when he knew she had a point.

She waited.

"Sorry, boss. I got a bit carried away."

Arrina laughed. "Now suddenly I'm 'boss' again? Your improvisations certainly made our little game more complicated, but some of the more colorful flourishes did work in our favor."

Stipator nodded, immediately picking up her train of thought. "He thought we were here for the gold, so he assumed we sought profit. But we never needed to steal his money — just convince him to give it away."

Arrina patted Stipator on the cheek fondly. "By the time we finished with him, I'm sure he did indeed wish he had taken your offer of five thousand."

Stipator shivered slightly and took her hand in both of his and kissed it. He fixed her with an exaggerated sultry look. "You really know how to get a guy all worked up, you know that, Arrina?"

She brushed her lips against his. "Just be a dear, and stay out of trouble long enough for me to get out of costume."

"Of course." Stipator stayed sitting with his glass of wine and toyed with his mustache, watching her intently. "This seems as good a place as any."

Arrina eyed him. "Watching me change clothes hardly counts as staying out of trouble." Her tone was serious, but they both knew she was teasing.

He shrugged. "Nothing I haven't seen before."

That was certainly true. Traveling performers, as a rule, weren't particularly easy to embarrass, and Stipator and Arrina had not exactly spent the first year of their travels together shooting each other awkward looks and blushing.

Nevertheless, she needed some time to herself.

She stood up and shooed him toward the door. "Get out. I need to get ready for the strike meeting. I'll see you there."

Stipator looked hurt but did as she said.

It's feigned, she knew. *He's still playing his little game of desire.*

"And don't forget to close the door behind you," she called after him, forcing a teasing note into her voice.

Once he was gone, Arrina stripped off the costume. As she pressed the lavender cloth to her face, the harsh reality of what she and Jonathan had to do pressed in on her. Someone wanted to kill her half-brother, which would break her father's heart and plunge her homeland into chaos. Arrina wasn't close to her stepmother, but nor did she wish her to suffer. Arrina, Jonathan, and the Senserte were the only ones standing between Pithdai and catastrophe, and she wasn't even sure if the others would go along with her plan. This wasn't about rescuing the poor and helpless from rich and powerful abusers. This was a more political job than any they had ever done before.

She allowed herself a few private tears, removed the cloth, and prepared to pitch the swindle to her peers.

Chapter 5

Messegere was well on its way to full before Arrina reached the mess tent, which had been cleared out for the strike meeting. Walking in, the cheerful conversation of her fellow Senserte filled the tent. She reached to pull the flap closed behind her, but a quick head count showed Kara was not there yet. She was probably still helping the Jacobston patrols with their search for the bandits.

"If they'd noticed you were walking on the puddles instead of step-ping in them, they would have known you weren't one of Reck's guards," Jonathan chided Mathalla playfully. The Wen among them often forgot that the talents that came naturally to them sometimes caused them to stick out among Farlanders and Wefals.

Jonathan had somehow found time to shave, wash, and change clothes since his brief visit to her wagon, Arrina noted.

Torminth leapt to Mathalla's defense. "Guards who would have no-ticed he was walking on less than an inch of water would have also no-ticed you forgot to take off your jewelry. Do you think they could afford gold rings on what Reck paid them?"

Stipator hooted a laugh at this as he struggled to remove the cork from a bottle of tropical fruit wine he had plundered from Reck's cellar.

Jonathan looked at Stipator, keeping his face straight with obvious effort. "One day someone is going to recognize you by that ridiculous basket hilted sword."

Stipator shrugged as he wiggled the cork with thumb and forefin-ger. "I've no interest in touching another man's sword." He nodded at Mathalla and Torminth where they sat together on a wicker chair made for two. "No offense, gentlemen."

"None taken," Mathalla assured him with a cheerful grin.

Stipator opened his mouth as if to say something more, but the cork abruptly gave way, and wine sloshed onto the front of his pants. The Wefal cursed softly.

Jonathan chuckled. "At least try to curb your enthusiasm in handling your own, Stipator."

Everyone burst into laughter at this, even Etha, who often seemed uncomfortable around such humor.

Stipator contained himself more quickly than the others, though his lips quirked up under his mustache. He leaned back slightly in his chair and spread his legs wide. "Are any of you ladies interested in a private little wine tasting?"

Etha shook her head, looking away awkwardly. The Wen men laughed, as did Jonathan. Poresa and Zori, as usual, played along automatically.

"Is it a sweet wine or a dry wine?" Poresa asked in mock innocence.

Poresa was a Wefal a couple of years Arrina's junior with grey eyes and strawberry blond hair braided down her back. Garble and Jabber — the parrot-billed monkeys known as squawkers — slept on her shoulders.

Zori leaned forward slightly and regarded Stipator's pants with a weighing look. "It looks like a wet wine," she pronounced gravely.

Zori ad'Korona was a Wen with bright blue hair. At forty years old, she was the oldest in the tent, but Wen longevity meant she looked no older than Stipator.

"They've been warned about you," Arrina added, strolling into the large tent. "And perhaps I should also warn you about them. I hear they run with a gang of swindlers."

Poresa opened her mouth to respond, but the sound of Arrina's voice woke Jabber, who clapped his hands together and squawked, "Arrina! Arri-na!"

This roused Garble, who took up a counter-cry, "Arr-ina! Arr-ina!"

Arrina crouched and held out her arms, and both the squawkers leapt from Poresa's shoulders to run onto Arrina's. They squawked her name in her ears for several seconds before she could convince them to settle for nuzzling her cheeks instead, the odd mixture of fur and feathers tickling her face.

Eventually, the two squawkers calmed down and returned to Poresa, nuzzling her ankles until she leaned down to let them climb back onto her shoulders.

"Is Kara coming?" Arrina asked.

"Any second," Poresa assured her. "Ah, there she is."

Kara ad'Molly jogged into the tent, pulling the cord to lower the flap and motioned for them to begin the strike meeting as she took a seat next to Jonathan. She had a nearly olive complexion, dark brown eyes, and black hair braided to halfway down her back. Her clothes were sturdy and practical — breeches, riding boots, and a wool coat over a plain blouse. The abundance of jewelry she wore gave the lie to her common appearance — gold necklaces, rings set with rubies and sapphires, and fine golden threads that wound through her hair.

"Good. We're all here," Michael said. He glanced at Stipator. "Shall we start?"

Stipator set down his glass of wine and stood on his chair. "Due to concerns about possible fraud in the previous election of the Senserte chair, the High Council has elected ... I mean, the High Council has decided by mutual consensus to adopt a new method of electing a chair of these proceedings. The High Council believes this will be less susceptible to manipulation. Lastor?"

Lastor pulled aside a sheet and picked up the small wooden box hidden underneath it. He held it up for all to see.

"Inside that box are slips of paper with each of your names on them — one name per slip and one slip per name. Whoever's name comes out of the box is the chair of this strike meeting. The selection is completely random — as random as the decision to let Poresa select the name of the ... I mean draw one of the slips out of the box at random. She'll even be blindfolded."

"Actually, we're fresh out of blindfolds," Lastor said, embarrassed.

"She will have her eyes closed as she ..."

Poresa snorted a laugh. "I know what you're thinking, Stipator. I'm not falling for that one again."

"She will respect the democratic process by turning her head so she can't see the name on the slip of paper until it is completely out of the box."

"Fine." Poresa walked over to Lastor, reached into the box, and pulled out a small piece of paper.

"And whom has fate elected as our chair?" Stipator asked dramatically.

"Arrina."

"Again?" Stipator sounded shocked. "Well, Arrina, it looks like fate has favored you once more."

Poresa slid a second, hidden slip of paper out from behind the first. "Fate must really approve of her election," she said with a mischievous smile. "This one has her name on it, too."

"Fraud?" Stipator demanded. "Who could possibly be behind this travesty? The High Council will surely investigate this rigorously!" He glanced nervously at Arrina. "Assuming our newly elected chair will fund our investigation?"

Vudar produced a golden dai, which he tossed to Arrina. She caught it sunburst-side up and handed it to Stipator, who accepted it solemnly.

"I assure you the criminals behind this will be brought to justice!" Stipator walked from person to person, making motions of searching them for weapons and contraband. He "confiscated" each of their purses as he went. At last, he came to Lastor, handed the young Wen the dai Arrina had given him, and winked. "That's for the election. You've done the right thing."

Lastor bowed slightly and ran out of the tent with the box.

Stipator returned to Arrina, looking crestfallen. "I'm sorry, lady chairwoman, but we were unable to bring the perpetrators to justice."

Mathalla and Torminth walked up behind Stipator and put one hand on each of his shoulders.

"Who are you?" Stipator demanded. "Can't you see we're trying to govern over here?"

"We are the Senserte," Mathalla told him in a grave voice. "The Eyes of Justice saw what you did. By the time you have received the full measure of your punishment from us you will wish you had never tasted money or power."

The little skit ended, and its players returned to their seats as Arrina took her place near the drying soup kettles at the edge of the tent.

"Lord Treasurer, what was the cost of this venture?" she asked.

"8,874 dai, 37 silver chel, and some small coins," Vudar announced nonchalantly. "Nearly a thousand dai more than we expected."

"Does anyone object to giving away the 125 and change to make it a nice round thousand dai over budget?"

In virtually any other setting, that question would have brought everyone to their feet in outrage. A family could live frugally for a year on a single golden dai. Most wealthy households would consider a hundred dai a year extravagant, and ten thousand exceeded the total annual budget of most small towns.

Among those gathered at the strike meeting, it earned small shrugs and an agreeable shaking of heads. The voting members had their allowances as the children of wealthy families, the sum of which totaled about 20,000 dai per year. The member nations of the Flecterran Union also provided a general budget that approached 100,000 dai from their military budgets to fund the activities of the Senserte.

This was the magic of taxation. Millions could unknowingly fund what thousands would never willingly pay for. One part charity, one part secret police, the Senserte had no shortage of money.

"Very well. Distribute the funds before we go, Lord Treasurer," Arrina said.

"Yes, Lady Chairwoman," Vudar said.

"Next order of business. Lord Director, have you tallied the votes?"

Michael nodded once and handed a rolled up piece of paper to Arrina. She broke the seal and read from it. "Tajek el'Nankek, please rise."

The enormous Turu set down his glass of wine and stood in front of her. He looked nervous, but that was only to be expected.

"The Senserte are an elite order that takes its members from every nation and race in the Flecterran Union — Wen, Wefal, and Farlander," Arrina said. "We rise above the politics of our homelands and our peoples, and we band together in common cause. We are the eyes of justice who see the corruption of the rich and powerful. We are the ears of justice who hear the cries of the weak and poor. And we are the hands of justice who humble the arrogant, ruin the miser, and utterly destroy those who threaten peaceful folk with violence. Our quarry is not the scapegoat, the cat's paw, or the accomplice. It is our sacred duty to seek the source of the corruption and eradicate it. Would you accept that duty if offered a place among the Senserte?"

Tajek simply nodded once.

"No one comes to the Senserte with a pure heart. We must overcome the same temptations to which our enemies have succumbed. No one of us is infallible or invulnerable. It is only by serving justice that the Senserte are pure. Only our dedication to establishing group consensus and living out democratic ideals makes the Senserte infallible. And only our perfect loyalty to and trust in each other ensures that the Senserte never fail. If offered a place among the Senserte, will you have as much faith in them as you do that the sun will rise in the morning? If offered a place among the Senserte, will you be a worthy vessel of their trust?"

"Yes and yes," Tajek said gravely.

"As you have no doubt guessed, your role in the demolition of Reck's ill-gotten empire was a test of your skills, resolve, and dedication to the principles of the Senserte. You injured one of Reck's guards unnecessarily in the final showdown. It was an accident, but the Senserte must be better than those we punish. Hurting those who stand between us and our quarry damages our reputation as heroes in the eyes of those we protect. Do you understand?"

"Yes."

"We sent you to convince Reck of the truth of Gristo's claim to have uncovered a major gold seam. This was a simple role, as befits a provisional member of the Senserte. You got a bit carried away with the outsider act. The simplest deceptions are usually the most effective."

Arrina saw Stipator mouth the words "am glad to peel oranges with you" from where he sat behind Tajek, and she had to suppress a smile of her own. The Turu was fluent in Wenri, the common tongue of the Flecterran Union, but he could pretend to barely understand the simplest words. As they intended, Tajek looked suitably chastised by this reminder.

"Finally, you are Turu. You will never blend in among the people of the Flecterran Union. Without a magical disguise, you will always be an outsider, and even with a disguise, your accent may yet betray your true origin. Furthermore, because you are Turu, you owe no loyalty to the people the Senserte protect. None of us know much about your homeland, so we cannot even guess at your true motivations. We have only what you have told us of an uncle who wishes you to be an envoy of the Nankek to the Wen. Never have the Senserte accepted a member who was not a citizen of a nation within the Flecterran Valley. If we offered you a place among the Senserte, it would be completely unprecedented. Can you understand why we might hesitate?"

"The Wen and Turu were once one nation," Tajek said severely. "We have more similarities than differences. My uncle has no designs on the Flecterran Union, and I wish nothing more than to win your trust and show that our differences are not so much."

Arrina made a show of looking at the Senserte sitting behind where Tajek stood. After a moment, she folded the paper and put it down, returning her attention to the big Turu in front of her.

"You got into your part, which isn't always a bad thing in our line of work. It ended up opening up many other opportunities, and you ended up playing one of the most important roles in the job."

That was an understatement. Convinced that Tajek's magic could find gold and that Gristo had no further use for the Turu, Reck had hired him to look for gold in the mountains. The pound of gold Reck paid Tajek each day allowed the Senserte to seed more rivers and mines, which Tajek then convinced their mark to buy for extravagant sums.

Stipator couldn't contain himself anymore. "Nothing ever goes exactly as planned," he said with a grin. "You did well, kid."

The Turu rumbled a laugh and looked over his shoulder. "Six years younger than me and will live half as long, and you call me kid?" He turned back. "But I am glad my mistakes were small. I will do better next time, Arrina."

She sat down abruptly in her chair and motioned Tajek to have a seat. The severity of ritual went out of her, and the other Senserte relaxed, as well. "Tajek, you can handle yourself in a fight, and metal can't hurt you because of your magical talent. That alone makes you intimidating. I think we've only seen the first of many ways your outsider act can work to our advantage."

"And the fact that I'm a Turu?"

"It's never happened before, but so what?" Arrina shrugged. "I still don't quite understand why you came to us when you could have approached one of the Wen nations and gotten the envoy treatment, but if you're willing to risk your life with us, you're welcome to be one of us."

Tajek beamed. "Thank you, Arrina. I will not disappoint."

She cocked an eyebrow. "Don't thank me. Thank all the Senserte. We put these things to a vote, as you have seen."

"I know."

"Are we going to discuss where we're going next?" Lastor asked, clearly bored with the ceremony. "Because there are rumors of Aflangi bandits riding down from the Winteeth Mountains to attack villages in Tremora."

"I'm more interested in the lake pirates who have been attacking boats on Kaeruli," Mathalla said.

"Only because you won't get your feet wet," Zori told him with a laugh.

Arrina sighed heavily, and this uncharacteristic response to the prospect of new jobs attracted the attention of all the Senserte but Stipator, who remained oblivious to the change in mood. Zori drew his attention to it.

"I need to make one announcement before we get into that," Arrina said, her voice carrying more because of her long time on the stage than because she wanted to be heard. "Jonathan and I received a letter from our father last night. Someone has taken our brother Kaspar hostage, and the king has asked us to take charge of delivering the ransom."

The Senserte met this announcement with murmurs and frowns.

"We're leaving first thing in the morning, and we'll be gone for at least a month or two," Arrina explained.

"Someone kidnaps the heir to Pithdai's throne, and you think we're just going to let it slide?" Stipator asked with an expression she knew all too well.

He smells a challenge in this. Now I'll never talk sense into him. She looked at Jonathan pleadingly.

Lastor took Stipator's lead, looking indignant at the very thought of anything that interested the Wefal battlemaster. "Yeah. We're the Senserte. We can't let anyone get away with kidnapping our family members!"

"This is outside of our mandate," Arrina reminded them. "The Senserte punish those among the rich who hurt the poor. My father isn't poor, so if he needs more help, he can always send more. This isn't Senserte business. This is personal business. It concerns only our family."

"Perhaps it is, as you say, a family matter," Michael said, tapping his lips with an index finger. "What demands are the kidnappers making of your father?"

Arrina resisted the urge to glare daggers at him. *Don't think I can't tell what you're doing.*

"The kidnapper is demanding all the paintings in the palace of Pithdai," she said, trying to sound like this wasn't at all unusual.

"What an odd request," Torminth said at once.

"I know Pith miraklas often take the form of paintings," Davur said. "Is there anything remarkable about these?"

Had Michael already told the others, or was Davur suspicious for some other reason? Arrina wanted to lie. She was extremely good at lying — a professional, even. Poresa would know though, and it was bad form for one of the Senserte to lie to the others about anything important.

Not that it never happens.

"Many are miraklas, yes."

"Dangerous?" Davur persisted.

"In a few cases, extremely dangerous."

"Are any dangerous enough to throw the entire Flecterran Union into chaos?" Michael asked innocently.

This time, Arrina really did glare daggers at him, though he pretended not to notice.

"Like Nosamae Descending?" Poresa asked.

Etha gasped. Kara shook her head. Davur and Vudar whistled softly in unison. Tajek looked confused.

"Nosamae Descending?" he asked.

"It's not really worth explaining," Kara answered. "It is a miraklan painting — one of two nearly identical ones with opposite effects. It is harmless unless you recreate the scene in the painting, which requires six specific lesser miraklas."

"What happens if you do, though?" Tajek asked.

"They change how well magic works within the Valley. Nosamae Descending broke the power of the enchantresses at the end of the Nosamae War," Poresa offered. "Nosamae Ascending was intended to make their rule over the Flecterran Valley permanent, either by making Farlander magic stronger or by greatly weakening Wen magic."

"Wouldn't that be bad?"

"Each of the six keys to them was entrusted to one of the other Flecterran nations to guard," Davur said. "The people of Sutola take that charge very seriously, as I'm sure do the other nations."

Mathalla elaborated on this. "Stormhaven and Kukuia received the wedding rings from the paintings, but neither believed the paintings should ever be activated, so they sent them away on ships and cast them into the ocean thousands of miles away."

"Without the six miraklas, the paintings are just curiosities," Kara said with a note of finality. "I'd be more concerned about the other miraklan paintings Pithdai has."

Arrina took a deep breath and told them about Empire of Brass.

Chapter 6

Torminth broke the long silence after Arrina's explanation. "These stakes make madness tossing dice," he murmured, quoting from Empress Korona III.

"The coins lie on the table, and we cannot quit the game," Poresa responded, reciting the next line of the play. Garble twitched awake at the sound of her voice. She scratched the top of his feathered head.

Davur pursed his lips. "Pithdai cannot possibly think to meet these demands. It would be like turning over Sutola's Forbidden Orchard to an invading army."

"And its Hidden Vineyard and Deep Reaches, as well," Vudar added.

Davur shot him a warning look.

Vudar spread his hands. "It's not like they don't at least suspect that those are real."

Davur sighed. "I didn't know about Empire of Brass, but I've heard enough about the other miraklan paintings of Pithdai to recognize that giving all of them to a kidnapper would not have a happy ending. It could strain relations between Sutola and Pithdai. It could even mean war, if someone uses those miraklas in a way that harms Sutol interests."

"Can't you just explain this to your father?" Lastor asked. "He's Sutola's ruler, right?"

Davur shook his head. "Sutola isn't a monarchy. It's an archonate. The High Archon can be overruled or even stripped of power by the Council of Leaves."

"My father may not have a choice," Arrina said. "The succession of the Pith monarchy is at stake."

"His personal legacy is at stake, not Pithdai's succession," Kara amended. "Yours is the oldest nation in the Valley. This is not the first time a monarch left no heir."

Davur shrugged. "Pithdai, Aaronma, Jacobston — something similar has happened to every nation."

Kara shook her head. "Given the choice between his heir's safety and the peace of the Union, the right course of action should be clear to King Larus. If he hands over all those miraklas, perhaps it is he the Senserte will be forced to bring to justice."

Arrina looked at the black-haired Farlander, her mouth open in shock. In his spot near the back of the gathering, Jonathan's face mirrored hers.

"That would definitely be outside our mandate, Kara," Zori said crisply. "This is not how the Senserte work."

"No one wants Nosamae Descending to fall into enemy hands, Kara, least of all the Nosamae," Michael observed. "King Larus has brought this to the Senserte..."

"To Jonathan and Arrina," Kara countered fiercely.

Michael brushed the objection to the side. "Who have brought it to the Senserte. Pithdai's king is no fool. He knows very well how delicate a political position he has been put into. He also knows he can rely on us to prevent any of these miraklan paintings from being used against the Union. Would you demand he risk a war of succession? Many thousands would die in that, as well, which would also be bad for the Flecterran Union."

"It is dangerous even to bring such things into play," Kara said, but with less anger in her demeanor.

Michael continued like a counselor making a shrewd case. "Pithdai and Aaronma have fought each other in some of the fiercest wars in the Valley's history. If there is one thing my people know about the Pith Wen it is that they cannot be trusted to hold up their side of the bargain." His lips twitched into a brief smile. "You mark me. Larus is looking for a way out of this deal. We are his best chance of turning the game around on these kidnappers."

Arrina waited a long moment for Kara or anyone else to respond. The other Senserte respected her, trusted her judgment as their de facto leader. On this matter, though, she didn't dare drown out any dissenting voices. Jonathan would always take his cues from her.

"This affects all the Senserte, and each of you should have a voice in it," Arrina said into the silence. "Michael, I think you've made your position clear. Is there anything else you'd like to add?"

He shook his head slightly.

"Davur?"

The eldest Marusak looked to his younger brothers. Ravud shrugged, but Vudar frowned. Davur motioned the youngest brother to speak.

"I dislike any compliance with these demands. I've read accounts of the War of Brass," Vudar said. "I'm not convinced it's safe to transport that painting even if we have no intention of going through with the exchange."

"How many miraklan paintings are involved?" Davur asked.

"Is there enough time to make replicas of the worst of them?" Vudar added by way of suggestion.

"Too many paintings and not enough time," Arrina admitted. "We don't know how familiar these kidnappers are with the paintings and whether they would detect a forgery."

"They might be in too much of a hurry to examine them closely," Davur suggested, "especially if they're afraid the homeguard could show up any moment and take away their prizes."

"Even someone who knows nothing of art can distinguish mirakla from forgery if they're an enchantress," Michael countered. "I'd know immediately unless I didn't bother to look. Besides, there might be agents in the palace, and they would be watching for that sort of gambit."

Davur looked thoughtful. "A couple paintings might not be missed. You might convince your father to hold back the ones that would imperil the entire Valley."

"Like Empire of Brass and Nosamae Descending?" Arrina asked.

"Nosamae Descending would be missed. It's too famous," Vudar pointed out. He shrugged. "It's harmless without the other six miraklas, so I say let them have it."

"It makes for a convenient sign of good faith," Davur agreed.

Arrina nodded. "I'll suggest it."

"Then you have our support," Davur told her.

"I can work up something to maintain the illusion that all the paintings are there," Kara offered, rubbing the ruby of her necklace. "It won't survive close scrutiny, but it should fool a hasty magical examination."

"I would appreciate that, Kara. Thank you," Arrina told her.

"I still oppose this whole thing," the black-haired enchantress reminded them. "I know Kaspar is your half-brother, but Pithdai can get another heir. But if the vote is against me, you know I'll support the

Senserte's mission."

Poresa put a companionable hand on Kara's shoulder. Garble scrambled on top of the Farlander's head and picked at her hair as if looking for insects.

"Poresa?" Arrina prompted.

"As a matter of principle, I'm with Kara. I don't like the Senserte being used as the tool of the strong to punish the weak, regardless of the crime. However, I'm pragmatic enough to recognize Ulangoshi is on Pithdai's eastern border. If your nation bleeds, so does mine."

"Is that a vote in support or opposition?" Michael asked.

Poresa pursed her lips. "Let's call it an abstention."

"Very well," Arrina said. "Etha?"

The short Farlander woman waved the question aside. "I haven't decided yet. Come back to me."

"Zori?"

The eldest of the Senserte sighed heavily. "This could get ugly, but I'm with you. We need to know whether our enemy is from within the Valley or outside of it, and I only trust the Senserte to find the true culprit."

"I'm in favor," Stipator said without prompting, twitching his mustache.

"Me too," Lastor piped up cheerfully.

"Tajek?" Arrina asked.

"By my count, you already have the votes you need to proceed."

Stipator clapped him on the shoulder. "That doesn't mean dissenting opinions don't matter to us. Sometimes it hones the plan. Sometimes it's just fun to be able to say you told us so when everything goes wrong."

Tajek raised an eyebrow. "From what I've heard, that is not a boast I wish to make. Turun miramani are much like Wen miraklas. Some can change the course of history, but it is best to be the ones guiding the simam instead of suffering it. I am in favor."

Arrina wasn't sure she followed that, but she nodded. "Etha?"

"Stormhaven also borders Pithdai. Like Poresa said, if you bleed, we bleed. I say yes."

"Jonathan?"

Her brother was still staring at Tajek, clearly as confused by his response as she was. "I am too close to this to vote. I recuse myself and abstain."

"As do I," Arrina said.

"Nine to one with three abstentions," Michael announced.

"Now that we've agreed on this mission, what's your plan for getting from Mattock to Pithdai to Gulinora Island in a matter of a few days?" Zori asked, folding her arms with a small smile. "Have Wefals and Farlanders learned to fly like Wen first-cyclers?"

"Jonathan?" Arrina prompted.

Her brother set down an empty tumbler on a nearby table and rummaged through a leather bag next to his chair. After a moment he produced what looked like a silk pouch with a loop of wire holding its mouth open. Another, smaller loop of wire holding a stub of a candle hung from the larger ring by four pieces of string.

"First off, I can't transport the entire traveling show to Pithdai, or even all the Senserte," Jonathan began, holding the wick of the candle to a nearby lantern. "That would take more cloth than we'll find within a hundred miles, and I'm not sure we could keep that much volume hot enough."

Jonathan held the pouch upside-down so the open mouth hung over the flame of the candle.

"Most of us will have to travel by road to Jacobston, barge to Cobport and then ship. That's a journey of 700 miles. So we won't be there when the advance group makes first contact with the kidnappers. They will be on their own until the troupe gets there."

The pouch slowly swelled as Jonathan spoke. The Senserte watched it with rapt attention.

"How many will be in the advance group?" Poresa asked.

"I had hoped to make a balloon for six, but it looks like we may have to be content with two."

Jonathan suddenly released the hanging pouch. Far from falling to the ground, it hovered in midair where he had let go of it. He pointed to spots on the pouch contraption as he spoke.

"The advance group will ride in the basket here. The basket would best be made from lightweight reeds, of course, but this isn't the climate for them."

"The stuff they use for baskets up here can't support the weight of two people, much less six," Michael elaborated. "The stronger materials are much heavier."

"Every pound counts, and I'd rather err on the side of caution than have the basket give out while you're hundreds of feet in the air or be forced to crash land because there isn't enough lift to sustain the weight of the passengers," Jonathan continued.

The tiny balloon drifted lazily in the air, rising higher by inches.

"The principles behind the balloon are sound," the Wefal assured them. "I'll oversee its construction to ensure it will do the job. We're going to need to sew together a huge bag out of as much lightweight cloth as we can find."

"We could make one out of tent canvas, but it won't be able to carry as much," Michael explained. "We'll be giving up a good part of the best clothes in our wardrobes, I'm afraid."

Zori clucked her tongue, but neither she nor anyone else objected.

"The design has some limits, though." Jonathan paused for a long moment, watching the balloon rise to the level of his head. "First, it's entirely at the mercy of the wind, as there is no way to steer it. Wind blows from the mountains to the Valley, so the balloon should go the right direction, but there's no way to predict its exact course. Second, there is no way to gain altitude once you lose it."

"We considered a couple ways of keeping a fire going in the basket, but none of them was practical, and all of them were dangerous," Michael added. "Yes, Kara, even a fire wand. The basket is just too flammable."

"Right. So we'll fill the balloon with as much hot air as we can before we untether it," Jonathan continued. "It will gradually lose altitude as you go, and I'm pretty sure that as you get into the warmer, wetter air of the Valley, you'll lose altitude even faster."

"Not dangerously so, though," Michael assured them.

The tiny balloon floated on a breeze coming from the tent entrance and flew over the heads of the gathered Senserte.

"Finally, descent," Jonathan continued. He licked his lips. "Given the elevation we're starting at, and if the wind cooperates, you should touch down gently more than half the distance you need to travel. If you need to descend sooner, you'll have to tear holes in the balloon to let the hot air out."

"That should be a last resort," Michael cautioned. "Once the balloon sinks, it can't rise again. Also, there's a chance that the pressure of the hot air through any hole will pull out the seams and, um, compromise the balloon's integrity. In short, you could crash instead of land."

"We'll do everything we can to make sure this is as safe a journey as possible," Jonathan said.

Etha gasped, and everyone looked her direction. The flame of the candle had flickered in the breeze and touched one of the strings, which ignited. The Senserte watched as the fire passed from string to pouch. In moments the bottom half of the balloon was alight, and a line of flame traced the seam to the top of the balloon.

Michael reached to try to put it out, but it was already too late. The whole contraption dropped to the ground like a hot coal, pouch still burning. Kara extinguished the tiny balloon fire with one foot.

An awkward silence fell over the director's tent.

"So," Jonathan said in a cheerful voice, "who wants to be in the advance group?"

ACT II

Chapter 7

The balloon floated over the mountains spread out farther and farther below them, buoyed by tiny bursts of fire from Lastor's fingers and driven forward on the wind he had called to their aid. Jonathan had been reluctant to let the young Wen go with Arrina and Stipator, but none of the other Senserte could guide the wind. Kaspar had that talent, but if he had been here, Arrina wouldn't have needed to fly by balloon. The weight of the third passenger was more than balanced by their ability to use magic to maintain altitude.

Arrina looked back at the mountains. She could just make out Jacobston drifting past far below them. The largest city in the region looked like an elegantly carved toy castle. Mattock had just passed out of sight, obscured by clouds.

"You should stand up, Stipator," she told the Wefal sitting at the bottom of the basket. "It's quite the view."

"That's fine," he mumbled.

She raised an eyebrow at him. "Don't tell me the big, brave battlemaster is afraid of heights."

"Heights don't bother me. I climb trees and rocks all the time, same as Lastor here. This is different."

"If you fall off a cliff, you're just as dead as if you fall out of a balloon," Lastor pointed out cheerfully. Another jet of fire shot from his fingertips and into the balloon.

Stipator shot him a betrayed look. "If I fall off a cliff or treetop, I might be able to catch something on the way down. Up here?" He shook his head. "Can we please talk about something else?"

Arrina leaned on the side of the basket. The cold wind tugged at her hair. "Like what?"

"I don't know. Maybe Lastor has some suggestions?"

"You and Jonathan don't talk about your half-brother much," Lastor noted. Spurt of fire. Gust of wind. "Is he as brave and noble as the Senserte?"

Stipator sighed. "It's as good a question as any, I guess. Do you want to talk first, or should I?"

Arrina frowned at the scenery below them but did not answer. They would be past Jacobston soon. They were making good time.

"I don't think anyone can answer that question yet," Stipator said, picking at the hilt of his rapier. "It's no secret he dislikes me, envies Arrina and Jonathan, and spends most of his time feeling sorry for himself."

"Stipator," Arrina warned, but she didn't move.

"It's true, Arrina. He's probably still mad that I couldn't convince your father to let him join the Senserte."

"Kaspar started to lose his Wen magic right before Stipator taught us how to use our Wefal magic. Every day, he watched us learn new powers while his own talents withered. He used to best us at everything without even thinking about it — archery, running, climbing, fencing, you name it. After Stipator came, though, the margin of victory got slimmer and slimmer until one day Jonathan surpassed him. Soon after that, I caught him, too. The harder he tried, the worse he lost."

"That must have been frustrating," Lastor said.

Arrina and Stipator shared a glance. She hoped Lastor would find the situation less frustrating than Kaspar had.

"Every Wen goes through it and gets over it," Stipator said, not sounding especially sympathetic. "Just like every Wefal has to get over the idea that most Wen and Farlanders will ever take him seriously."

"That's not true, Stipator," Arrina said absently.

"Isn't it? If the Wen took Wefals seriously, you would be your father's heir, not Kaspar."

That touched a nerve. She and Jonathan had grown up thinking Arrina would one day be the Queen of Pithdai. It had not been until they were twelve that their tutors had given them the bad news. *The laws of succession were written centuries ago. One day the Pith will update them, but they've not yet had a convincing reason.*

"Want another example? Look at the ransom note. Wen children and Farlander adults are potential sources of danger, even though most Farlanders never learn magic. Wefals, though? Pfft. What threat could we possibly pose?"

"Most Wefals don't learn magic, either," Arrina reminded him. "Being underestimated works to our advantage, too."

"True enough," he conceded. "It doesn't make it any less annoying."

"If we pull this off, I'm sure you'll convince these kidnappers not to underestimate Wefals in the future." Arrina watched the first green trees dot the grays and browns of the mountain landscape. "Father doesn't underestimate us. Otherwise he wouldn't have asked us to handle something this delicate. He knows what we can do, and he has some inkling of what the Senserte can do."

"Are you sure he doesn't just know you have a bunch of Wen and Farlanders willing to risk their lives for you?" Stipator asked.

Arrina shrugged. "Does it matter? I'm more than just my magic. That's something Kaspar didn't realize about himself until it was too late. Why do you think he took it so hard?"

"Presumably, he wouldn't have been kidnapped if he still had magic." Stipator folded his hands. "That can't be helping matters."

"Or maybe he'll find his own way out of this situation. He's naïve, not stupid."

"I somehow doubt it. Bright he may be, but capable of escaping from captors who found a way to kidnap him?"

"You and I do it all the time."

He barked a laugh. "Yes, but when you and I get captured, we do it with a plan. It's as deliberate as the homeguardsmen's patrols."

Arrina smiled and let the silence stretch on.

"Surely, you don't really think … I mean, why would Kaspar …"

"He wanted to join the Senserte, but Father wouldn't let him, remember?"

"Yes, but infiltrating … no. No!" Stipator shook his head vigorously. "It would be the stupidest thing he's ever done. He has no Kara or Poresa to scout. No Michael to equip him, and no Jonathan to extract him if it all goes wrong. Do you actually believe that?"

Arrina burst out laughing and turned to look at Stipator. "Of course not," she said as she bent over to tweak one end of his mustache. "I made you consider the possibility, though, didn't I?"

Stipator pulled away and smoothed it out again. "Is there a point to this absurd speculation?"

"Yes. Don't assume that someone who has been captured is just going to sit around and wait to be rescued."

Arrina turned back toward the mountains. The clouds were thicker now and had taken on a darker shade of gray. She frowned. A little tropical rain wouldn't hurt their balloon, but she didn't really want to end up soaked to the skin. Normally, she wouldn't mind. Rain in the Valley was warm and refreshing against the skin. But the wind carrying their balloon along was as cold as it had been in the mountains this morning.

She swallowed at that thought. Cold, wet clothes were unpleasant, but the falling rain would taste wonderful, just now. The air up here was so dry, and she missed the humidity of the Valley floor.

"How far do you think we've traveled?" Lastor asked as noon approached, and the shadow of the balloon blocked out the sun.

Arrina looked at the lands around them. The dark gray clouds obscured the mountains to the west completely, now. She frowned at them. It looked like a storm was brewing, and it was inching closer to them.

The Wekaul River meandered through the jungles of lower Jacobston to their north. A short distance to the east, jungle gave way to tropical rainforest. She couldn't see any large clearings, yet, which meant they hadn't crossed into the more populous region near the Petersine border. As she looked to the south, she spotted the most obvious landmark, and that cinched it.

"We're not halfway," she said at last.

"It's seven hundred miles to Pithdai from Jacobston, isn't it?" Lastor asked.

"Just about. They have to ride down to Jacobston, then catch a barge to Cobport. There's usually ships heading out from there, but finding one to get to Gulinora Island might take more time. By balloon …" She squinted at the landmarks again. "Maybe four hundred miles."

"Because the road follows the rivers and lakes?"

"Yes. Also, do you see that big red rectangle in the middle of the rainforest south of us?"

No one could mistake what she was describing. Amid the hundreds of shades of green all around them — jungles and tropical rainforests, mostly, but even small areas of farmland — nestled a rectangle of bright red. Its sides ran as straight as if they had been drawn on a map with a ruler.

Lastor nodded.

"That's the Blood Preserve."

"Why are all the leaves on the trees red?"

"Another of the miraklas in the art archives of Pithdai. There is a map of the Flecterran Valley with a big red rectangle drawn on it, labeled Blood Preserve."

Lastor barked a laugh. "And since it's red on the map, the mirakla actually made the rainforest here red?"

"Yes."

"That's not all," Stipator said, looking up at Lastor from the bottom of the basket. "You know how everyone sometimes dreams of terrible monsters hunting them?"

"Yes," Lastor answered slowly, clearly uncomfortable with the topic.

It was nearly impossible to frighten a Wen child because their magic protected them from almost everything. They still had nightmares, though, and they woke from them screaming and crying just as often as Farlander children did.

"Long ago, all the monsters in our nightmares roamed the Valley," Stipator explained gravely. "They used to eat entire villages — not because monsters need to eat but because that sort of thing inspired more nightmares. And every nightmare we have makes the monsters stronger."

Lastor looked a bit skeptical. "I've never seen any monsters."

"That's because of the Blood Preserve mirakla. One monster decided that eating a village wasn't horrible enough, so it got together with a bunch of its cousins, and they ate everyone in a city right where the Preserve is now. Only the children survived. The monsters thought that meant those kids would have more nightmares and so give rise to more monsters. But the Wen children were more angry than afraid, so they used the map to curse the monsters. Each time a monster comes to life, the map forces it to go to the Blood Preserve, and none of the monsters in the Blood Preserve can ever leave it. It was the end of the Age of Nightmares."

"Really?" Lastor asked, sounding more excited than afraid again.

"It's just one of Stipator's stories," Arrina assured him. "It has red leaves, which means some strange plants and animals probably live there. But it isn't a wilderness of monsters."

"Oh." Lastor sounded disappointed.

"Don't mind her. She's never gone into the Blood Preserve, so she has no idea what is in it."

"Are you saying you have?" Arrina countered.

"Mira's mercy, what kind of a madman do you take me for?" Stipator cried.

"What I'm hearing is that you haven't."

"Of course not. It's not so far from the border of Petersine that I haven't heard stories about people who have, though. Most never come back, and the ones who do aren't right in the head afterward. They wake up screaming every night and the things they remember about their dreams are so disturbing most people who hear about them have nightmares of their own for weeks afterward. The place is definitely cursed."

This only seemed to make Lastor more excited. "Can we take the balloon over it? It's a little bit out of our way, but it would be worth it if we could spot a monster!"

"I'm not sure that would be a good idea," Stipator said deliberately, though Arrina couldn't tell whether he was afraid of the Blood Preserve or simply didn't want his nightmare story ruined by the truth.

"Why not?"

Trying to keep a Wen child out of trouble by warning him of danger was as futile as driving off ants with an open pot of honey. Like all Wen, Lastor wouldn't really understand fear until his magic started to fade.

"As you say, it's out of our way," Arrina explained. "Besides, we probably wouldn't be able to see anything through the canopy."

"Oh." He sounded disappointed, but not so much that a leap out of the balloon seemed imminent. "Maybe another time?"

"Maybe," Arrina said vaguely. She looked at the clouds behind them. They were nearly black, now, and she could see flickers of lightning. She also couldn't help but notice the clouds looked vaguely like some kind of flying beast. She could make out a head, a long neck, leathery wings, and an impression of clawed forelegs.

You're imagining it, she told herself. *The Blood Preserve is at least fifty miles south of us, and Stipator was just telling nightmare stories. Probably getting me back for convincing him Kaspar is trying to act like a Senserte.*

"Lastor, is that storm catching up with us?"

"Yeah," Lastor said vaguely, shooting another spurt of fire into the heart of the balloon. "The mountain wind followed us farther than I expected. It's so cold and dry, and it just wants to pick a fight with the hot, wet air of the Valley. You know what happens when they meet. Kaboom!" Lastor clapped his hands together for emphasis.

Arrina blinked at him.

"It's not actually alive, though, right?" Stipator swallowed. "You're just, uh, personifying it."

"Of course it's not alive." Lastor laughed as though he had never heard a more ridiculous question.

Arrina and Stipator breathed a sigh of relief.

Lastor regained his composure. "It's an air elemental."

"A what?" Stipator asked. He shot a quizzical look at Arrina.

"They keep really young kids from getting lost in the sky," she explained. Then to Lastor, "But don't they only protect first-cyclers?"

"Mostly, yeah. Mine stopped bothering me when I was six and a half."

"Why would there be one here where there aren't any children?" Stipator asked.

Arrina blanched. "It's very difficult to kill a Wen that young, but not impossible, right? Is this what happens to an elemental if the child dies?"

"Sure." Lastor sounded nonchalant. "It goes mad and wanders around just sort of lashing out at everything that enters its territory — birds, mostly."

"Balloons?" Arrina asked.

Lastor frowned. After a moment, he said, "I guess so."

"Can you keep us ahead of it?" Stipator sounded on the verge of panic.

The young Wen's bright orange hair bobbed as he shook his head. "Balloons and Wefals aren't as light and fluffy as clouds."

A peal of thunder like a maniacal laugh rolled over them.

"We need to land until it passes," Stipator said in a tight voice.

"I know you're not standing and therefore don't realize this, but there is nowhere for us to land." Arrina gestured to the rainforest all around them.

Stipator sighed and stood up on wobbling legs just as the approaching cloud wall covered the sun like a cloak. With a pap, pap, pap, the first drops of rain fell on the canvas of the balloon above them. With far less dignity than Arrina was used to him possessing, Stipator gripped the edge of the basket and peeked out at the landscape far below them.

The wind picked up, tugging at their clothes and hair and driving surprisingly cold rain into the basket with them. Behind them, the wispy jaws, neck, wings, and claws pulled out of the bottom of the black tower of the storm cloud.

It looks like a fluffy, gray dragon, Arrina thought. *I can even make out the tail behind it.*

"Is that the elemental?" she asked.

Lastor nodded.

Streaks of lightning arced from the cloud to the elemental and to the tropical rainforest below.

"So we can't escape it. Can we drive it off, somehow?" Arrina had to shout to be heard over the wind and the rain now.

"Not without Michael or Kara!" he shouted back. "Elementals are mostly made of magic."

"You say elementals attack things that fly in their territory, right?" Stipator asked suddenly from the other side of the basket. "Can they hurt each other?"

"I don't know," said Lastor. "Why?"

"Because I think we're about to find out."

Arrina turned to where Stipator was pointing. A flickering heat mirage rose up from the leaves of the trees in the path of the balloon. She didn't notice at first, but as the mist thickened the air, she caught the impression of wings slowly unfolding to reveal something more within them.

Stipator shrank down into a crouch so he could just barely see over the side of the basket. "Any guess whether that's good news or bad?"

The rainforest mist formed a head whose jaws parted in a silent challenge, and the mountain cloud crackled with lightning and let loose an ear-splitting crash of thunder in answer.

Lastor's eyes widened. "This is even better than nightmare monsters." Arrina could hear tremendous awe in his voice. "I don't think they've ever seen a balloon before." He grinned.

The elementals moved with the slow deliberation of mountain cats stalking their prey. *They are like snakes,* Arrina thought, *pivoting for the quick strike.* The one below withdrew its head a little, and its eyes turned bright green. The one above crackled a little more urgently.

"Hold on to something!" she shouted, just as both elementals charged the balloon with the speed of raptors.

She struggled to wind one of the ropes around her right arm while clutching the rim of the basket desperately with her left. Stipator had already tied one end of an extra coil of rope around his ankles and the other end to the basket. Lastor didn't heed her at all. He perched on the rim of the basket with his hands empty and let out a steady torrent of wild laughter as rain ran down his face and the wind whipped his hair back and forth.

The mountain cloud reached the balloon first, its gray snout banging against the canvas like a dog pushing a very large ball with its nose. The basket rocked underneath them, though Lastor hardly seemed to notice. Then the elemental beat its wings, sending a shockwave of wind and rain that caused the balloon to dip like a cork on water.

Even as the mountain cloud sailed upward to make another pass, the rainforest mist struck the balloon a solid blow near its base. The basket, which had been rocking one way, abruptly rocked the other way instead, and Lastor's arms spun like a windmill to keep his balance. The mist's shimmering claws tore small holes in the balloon as it carried them up.

At that moment, the mountain cloud collided with the side of the balloon and sent it spinning southward. All the while, the storm clouds sent down sheets of cold water and blindingly bright flashes of lightning.

The rainforest mist's jaws closed on its rival's back right leg. The mountain cloud's thundering roar sent a bolt of lightning into the top of the balloon.

Stipator pointed at the smoking hole. "That can't be good."

They weren't losing altitude yet. In fact, the two elementals circled the balloon while snapping at each others' tails, and that seemed to be creating a powerful updraft. The balloon climbed higher and higher. The storm cloud above soon looked impossibly close. Stipator moaned as they approached it. Arrina looked far below them where a less threatening white cloud drifted quickly but harmlessly.

How far up are we?

For a flickering moment, Arrina thought she saw a castle on that cloud, and then the black cloud consumed them.

Chapter 8

The storm winds, rain, and hail buffeted the balloon even more relentlessly than the elementals, which spent more time fighting each other. The mountain cloud possessed more enthusiasm, but the tropical mist barely seemed to notice the chunks its enemy had carved out of its massive bulk. As the strokes of lightning and explosions of thunder around them grew less frequent, the mountain cloud lost its intensity as well.

Eventually, the mountain air elemental turned away from the balloon and flew away, presumably back to its territory, vanishing into the melting storm clouds. For reasons Arrina couldn't even begin to guess, the rainforest mist also lost interest in the balloon and sailed off into the gray.

The basket stopped rocking, and the afternoon sun peeked through the clouds above.

"I thought that would never end," Stipator said with a heavy sigh. He looked terrible. Arrina thought she had heard him vomiting during the worst of the turbulence, and a look at his mustache confirmed it. She grimaced.

Arrina had joined Stipator in the bottom of the basket, but she sat up now. "How badly damaged is the balloon, Lastor?"

The Wen had not left his perch on the edge of the basket even once, leaping from one end to the other to shout encouragement and insults at the dueling elementals. He jumped back into the basket, causing it to lurch. Stipator shot him a pleading look.

"We're losing altitude rapidly. On the bright side, it looks like we may get to see the nightmare monsters after all." He sounded legitimately cheered by the possibility.

Arrina scrambled to her feet and looked over the edge of the basket.

A sea of red leaves stretched out beneath them and for at least a hundred miles along their current course. At the rate they were dropping, she didn't like their odds of reaching the far side of the Blood Preserve before they hit the canopy. She glanced to the right, and the Preserve stretched out endlessly in that direction. She could just make out the edge to the left, a few miles from the horizon.

"Lastor, is there anything you can do to seal up some of those tears and get us more lift?" she asked, wincing as the words lashed out like a whip. *It's not his fault.*

The young Wen blinked at her. "Um, maybe?"

"Anything in the basket that will help is yours, but grab it now," Arrina told him. "Also, if you can get us more wind or turn us so we don't have to go as far to reach the edge of the Preserve, do that, too."

He nodded and grabbed some extra canvas and a sewing kit. "I'll do what I can."

Lastor leaped onto the basket edge and climbed up the side of the balloon.

"Stipator," Arrina said, turning her attention to the battlemaster, who looked even paler than he had during the storm. "I need you functional right now. I don't care how you do it."

He opened his mouth as if to object, then nodded instead. "What do you need me to do?"

"The basket is weighing us down. You're better with ropes than I am. I need you to secure us to the balloon with whatever gear we absolutely cannot part with, and then I'm cutting the basket free."

She hoped he wouldn't question her. There really wasn't any time. She wasn't even sure how high up they were — she just knew she was higher above the ground than she had ever been until today, but as the red leaves and black flowers of the canopy below turned their attention to the balloon, Arrina knew they were not nearly high enough.

Stipator set to work immediately. Arrina grabbed her backpack and emptied it into the basket. Extra food they wouldn't need once they were below the canopy. Water? They'd have to risk it. She kept one set of each of their warm weather clothes. They'd be sweltering in the jungles and rainforests if they stayed in their mountain wear. Compass. Letters identifying them and giving them access to credit.

The balloon lurched as the wind shifted suddenly, changing their course from south to east. She breathed a sigh of relief at that as she tucked two knives into sheaths at her belt and pulled the backpack over her shoulders. Green appeared just at the edge of the horizon.

"How far away is that?" she shouted in the sudden gale.

Stipator slipped a circle of rope around her and pulled it tight under her armpits. He had Lastor's bow and quiver of arrows slung onto his back over the safety line. His rapier and a machete hung at his hip on opposite sides. He held a dagger in his right hand and grabbed Arrina around the waist with the left in case one of their ropes didn't hold. Sweat ran down his face and arms as if he had been running for half an hour or more.

He's using magic to override his fear, and he's chosen to pay its price in exertion, she recognized immediately. Arrina wouldn't have chosen to tire her muscles like that right before what promised to be a physically demanding ordeal, but Stipator knew his limits. He glanced east.

"Maybe thirty miles."

"How fast are we going?" Her brow furrowed in worry. "And how quickly are we dropping?"

Lastor ducked out of the balloon, hanging like a squawker in front of them. "I can get us there in an hour. I think the elemental's coming back."

Arrina's head snapped back at the mountains, wreathed in gray clouds.

"It could just be rain," she said. Lastor gave her a confused look. They lurched again, and he ran back up inside the balloon, shouting something about loose skirts.

Stipator coughed. "The trees are getting very close very fast."

Arrina didn't even look. She just reached across and grabbed one of the four thick ropes connecting the basket to the balloon.

"Ready?" she asked, placing her knife against it.

He nodded and did the same.

"Do it," she said.

Both of them sawed at the ropes. Stipator's gave out a moment before hers did. The balloon rocked with the shift in weight. They attacked the other two ropes. The balloon lurched hard when Arrina's rope gave out, and Stipator's knife tumbled out of his grip and vanished into the red canopy that was rapidly approaching them below.

He cursed under his breath and struggled to get a grip on his machete, but it was on the wrong side. Overhead, there was a small tearing sound as the weight of the basket began pulling the canvas of the balloon apart. She noted with some worry that if it ripped too much, it would pull Stipator's line free, as well.

Arrina kicked one of her legs to spin them as much as she could and managed to hook the basket's last rope with the inside of her wrist. The extra tension tore the canvas above her even more. Twining a foot around the nearly cut rope, she sawed at it vigorously with the dagger.

"Hold on tight, Lastor!" she shouted.

The rope broke, and the upper end snapped up into her face, drawing a painful line against one cheek. The bottom half of the rope burned like a line of fire as it slipped along the inside of her calf.

The basket tumbled as it fell away. A few seconds later, it vanished into the canopy with a rustling crash.

The balloon lurched upward. No, not quite upward. They were still descending, but compared to how quickly they had been falling only a moment before, it felt like an ascent.

Arrina glanced at the eastern edge of the Blood Preserve and at the canopy rising toward them.

"This is going to be close," she murmured. She looked at Stipator. "Can you hold on for an hour?"

He nodded, teeth gritted and knuckles white as he gripped his rope.

Lastor suddenly appeared next to them, hanging by one hand from the tear in the canvas the rope had made. He shot a gout of fire into the balloon, and it stabilized a little more. The wind was stronger now. Arrina had hardly even noticed.

A long, bone-chilling howl arose from the rainforest where their basket had fallen. Snarls, chitters, and more howls answered it.

"Are those the nightmares?" Lastor asked. In her moment of inattention, he had somehow managed to hook his foot into the hole and was dangling upside-down inches above her head.

"I don't know, and I don't think I want to find out," Stipator said, staring up into the balloon.

"I do," Lastor said with a pout.

"If you leave the balloon, it will crash, and we'll both probably die," Arrina said.

She glanced down and saw several trees swaying as though something massive shook them in its enormous hands. *Please don't leave us, Lastor.* One could never be certain with a young Wen.

"Arrina is right. We need you to keep it as high in the air as possible and to get us past the boundary of the Blood Preserve before sunset," Stipator told him. "The worst of the monsters down there only hunt at night."

Arrina frowned at him, but the effect was probably lost on him at this range. "Are we safe up here?"

Stipator barked a laugh. "We're tied to a badly damaged balloon that's losing altitude above the Blood Preserve. Safe isn't the word I would choose, no." He frowned. "I don't know. Monsters that would scare a very young Wen are probably worth giving the benefit of the doubt."

"He's right," Lastor said thoughtfully. "Maybe they have really long tentacles or can shoot poisonous quills or can sing magic songs that will make us want to explore or..."

"Lastor, enough!" Arrina snapped. If she let her imagination ponder half the terrible powers magical monsters might possess, Stipator wouldn't be the only one who needed magic to keep a clear head. "We're really relying on you," she said more patiently. "This is your time to shine, Lastor. Stipator and I are literally dead weight right now."

"She's right," Stipator said, closing his eyes. "If you can get us past the Preserve, we'll be within the boundaries of Petersine, and I can get us to Pithdai from there. Just promise me no more balloons."

Arrina couldn't resist a laugh. "I promise."

She couldn't deny the balloon had been a brilliant solution to the problem she had given Jonathan. Granted, it had carried a bit of a risk, but so did any wild, unbroken beast if you jumped on its back.

The howls in the rainforest seemed to follow them wherever they went. She could almost imagine the creatures attached to the jaws down there, hoping the balloon suffered just one more little setback that would keep it from reaching safety.

The rope around Arrina had cut off her circulation. Both her arms had gone numb, and her chest would probably have bruises. That final rope had left a stinging cut on her check and a painful burn on her calf.

Arrina watched the red leaves below them — holding steady at just under two hundred feet. At this range, she could make out some of the Blood Preserve's fauna. Giant black butterflies and huge birds with beaks like swords flitted a few yards above the canopy. Monkeys with blood-red fur howled at the balloon from their perches in nests woven of human bones. Three fin-like crests occasionally rose up above the trees like those of circling sharks, but from the thunder these creatures left in their wake as they followed the balloon, Arrina had the impression these monsters were as tall as the huge trees of the rainforest.

Those three are probably just the only ones tall enough for us to see.

She pointed them out to Lastor, who soon overflowed with excited speculation.

"Stipator, we're not much higher than we'd be if we were canopy diving," she said, trying to calm him down.

"We're missing nice, comforting trees all around us, and the canopy is still too far below us."

"I don't know," Lastor said, standing horizontal from the edge of the balloon. "We might only be a hundred feet above the canopy now."

"How long, Lastor?" Stipator shouted back at him, sweating beading his face.

"It's hard to measure time..."

"Twenty minutes," Arrina guessed. More green than red stretched to the horizon.

The shark giants, as Arrina thought of them, still trailed them. The leaves teemed with hundreds of strange birds and clouds of swarming insects Arrina had no desire to examine more closely. All of them seemed to have claws, teeth, or beaks made for tearing into flesh. Once, the trio heard a snatch of strange music that filled them with terrific longing. None of them leapt to their deaths to pursue it, but they probably weren't close enough to feel the full power of the song. She could smell something like rotted flesh creeping up around them.

"How far? How fast?" Stipator whined.

Jonathan would have been able to calculate all this in his head. Kara could have scanned the area with magic and determined their position to within a hand's width. Arrina knew all the Senserte would not have fit in the balloon. They would of course reach the shores of Kaeruli as soon as they could.

She missed them anyway.

A few minutes later, Lastor shouted, and the balloon dropped sickeningly. Arrina saw a brilliant patch of blue through the top of the balloon, which was beginning to collapse in on itself. Lastor scampered up the inside like a spider pouncing on captured prey, leaping to capture Kara's second favorite maroon silk dress that had torn off at the sleeves and hung by the lace at its throat.

Stipator screamed, and Arrina felt something brush her foot. Her eyes shot down, and she caught a glimpse of a giant, toad-like creature with stubby wings falling away from them. Then something slammed into Stipator, crashing him into her, and sending her spinning.

She glimpsed the boundary of red and green before she was facing upward. Lastor filled the blue gap, reaching for the maroon dress. A winged toad leapt at them, tongue lashing out and missing her by inches. Flames shot down into the balloon. Stipator grabbed her hand and pulled her close. The balloon came to an abrupt stop in the air, and Lastor slid onto their rope, laughing. Stipator's sword flashed in his hand.

Arrina was facing down as they swung out over the boundary of the Blood Preserve, the balloon frozen in air just at its edge.

"Lastor, don't!" Stipator screamed in her ear, and then her stomach was in her mouth, the green canopy stopped moving below them for a split second, and she was falling.

Stipator pushed her away from him so they wouldn't get tangled up. "Canopy dive!" he screamed.

The balloon deflated, hanging like a cloud over the edge of the Blood Preserve as she flipped over and confronted the approaching canopy.

A thousand shades of green leaves stretched out around her from horizon to horizon like the waters of one of the Valley's vast lakes. Wind rippled across its surface, whipping into waves of green. Brightly colored flowers, monkeys, and birds speckled it all like sea foam composed of rainbows. Light-footed canopy cats born of Wen magic danced on the leaves, scampering away from the incoming balloon.

Even if Arrina had had more than one brief moment to count all the different kinds of plants and animals she could see from her vantage point a few dozen feet above the trees, she would not have been able to do it. Wen claimed that their children created new kinds of animals by the hundreds of thousands every year, and that was why the Flecterran Valley had so many varieties. Idle boasting, perhaps, but Arrina could believe millions of different creatures made their home in the rainforests and jungles of the Valley.

As she fell, the smells and sounds of the rainforest rose up to greet her. Sweet smells and sour smells. The smells of animal furs and feces, feathers and rotting, dead flesh. Hoots and chirps. Howls and screams. Roars and whimpers. Trills and whistles and more songs than a musician could compose in a lifetime — all held in a few brief moments of time and a few square miles of the rainforest's ceiling.

The Wen had long claimed the canopy was their native land. They reveled in its light and warmth and dramatic storms. They felt kinship with trees whose years numbered into the thousands. They claimed responsibility for all its brightly colored living things, its cornucopia of flowers and fruits — most nutritious, many magical, and some deadly poisonous. The Farlanders sometimes said it suited the Wen well because they loved nothing more than to look down on the other races, to soak up all the resources of the Valley and leave only their waste to those living in the darkness they allowed others.

Arrina plunged through the leaves of the canopy.

She braced for sudden impact and terrible pain. The leaves hid thick branches that covered the ground like great wooden ribs protecting the heart of the jungle. If she hit one at this speed, she would be lucky to get off with a broken ankle or dislocated shoulder. She had done only two canopy dives in her life, and most sane people would consider that two too many, Wefal magic or no.

The pain did not come. She had slipped between the branches of the canopy and into the dimness of the understory. The canopy sounds shifted as if she was underwater and listening to noises of the world above. New sounds rose up from beneath her, equally distant and muffled. The wild sweet smells of the leaves above mixed with the wet smells of decay from far below. Here was the world that connected earth to heaven. The browns below blended with the greens above.

The understory was also a world unto itself. Here, vertical lines dominated — from trunks of trees as wide as wagons to the narrower tips of younger trees straining toward the sun to slim, opportunistic climbing vines. Snakes and lizards and frogs dominated this layer, but birds, monkeys, and squawkers were not in short supply.

Different layer, different environment, same tremendous variety, Arrina mused.

She spied a sturdy-looking hanging vine. A twist in the air, an outstretched hand tingling as its blood flow returned. Her fingers closed around it. The rough surface scraped off several layers of skin, and her shoulder protested for one moment before she reinforced tendons with magic. She grabbed the vine with the other hand and squeezed. Her arms were so numb from the long time she had spent dangling by a rope that she had to use magic to manage even that.

Both hands left a trail of blood as they slid, slowed, and stopped at a small knot in the vine. Her vertical fall shifted into a diagonal swing at what was still a dangerously high velocity.

Her eyes were still adjusting to the dimmer light, but she picked out a tree and chose several clumps of vines that would serve her purpose. Suppressing the pain in her hands with another tiny flow of magic, she released the vine and grasped another, and then another.

At last, she was pointed directly at the trunk of a tree. She let the vine carry her the rest of the way, cushioning the impact with her feet. She bounced away and slid a few feet down the vine. She bounced against the trunk again and slowly rappelled down it using the vine. When she reached the end of the vine, she hung a mere thirty feet over a largely clear spot on the rainforest floor.

The air this close to the ground was still and heavy. It grew cooler and moister as she fell. It wasn't cold or even less than warm, but it lacked the sweltering tropical heat of the canopy. The smells of damp and decay and fecundity dominated. Day seemed like night down here, for the canopy blocked out almost all the light of the sun.

Arrina took a deep breath and let go of the vine. The croak of frogs and the buzz of insects filled her ears. The next sound she heard was a snap as her right leg shattered against a tree trunk concealed under the layer of fallen leaves and the bones of dead animals.

She held onto consciousness by the thinnest margin, sliding her magic into place to cut off the pain. Arrina lay there for a long minute, panting and taking stock of her injuries and her reserves.

The rope burns had been superficial, but she would have to do something about her hands if she intended to use either of them within the next week. Shin and calf bones? She wouldn't leave the rainforest alive if she didn't repair them and soon. They were too far away from a navigable river to simply splint them. Her acrobatics, pain control, and heightened reflexes had not come without cost, either — a pound of her flesh burned away by the effort, maybe two, and that was before any healing.

I'll need to gorge myself when we get to Pithdai to make up for today.

She could instead pay the price of magical healing in sleep, pain, or exhaustion, but that seemed ill-advised in this situation. Arrina focused her magic on healing the shattered bones in her leg and waited. This had been her most successful canopy dive, and she suspected Stipator was not far away, doing exactly what she was now. Internal mystics were known for self-reliance.

Lastor arrived maybe an hour later, riding the back of a giant, tree-climbing lizard with purple skin. He carried a huge, folded up leaf over one shoulder like a sack.

"Arrina?" He sounded worried.

"I'll be all right," she assured him. "Have you seen Stipator?"

"He'll be along after he rests. He took a canopy branch between the legs."

Arrina winced. Lastor misinterpreted it.

"Are you in pain?"

"No," she lied. Well, it wasn't a huge lie, but she couldn't continue to waste resources on suppressing pain when she had bones to mend.

Lastor brightened and clambered off the purple lizard, which scrabbled back up the trunk of the tree. "I brought you some food. I'm sure you'll need it."

He unfolded the leaf to reveal a small pile of fruit, none of which looked familiar.

"It's all safe," he assured her as he turned to go. "I'll have the rainforest weave you a hammock. I don't think we're going any farther tonight." He sounded apologetic, as if all of this was his fault.

"Lastor," she called.

"Yes?"

"Don't worry about the balloon. We would be just settling into Jacobston right now. Instead, we've traveled hundreds of miles on the winds you brought."

"You're always saying I need to think of consequences before they happen. I should have guessed the air elementals would attack the balloon. I also forgot how...fragile you can be." He sounded miserable.

She met his gaze in the half-light of the forest floor. "Stipator and I would have been dead many times today if not for you. You did everything you could think of to keep us safe, and we may be a bit battered, but you kept us alive. We could not have come this far without you. Thank you."

He brightened. "I guess you're right. You need me on this mission."

Arrina fought down a laugh but couldn't resist a smile. "I told you three times. We can't take you with us to Gulinora Island without endangering Kaspar."

"But they won't even know I'm there!"

"No, and that's final. This isn't our decision to make."

Lastor pouted. "Fine. I guess I'll go make camp now, since neither of you are going to do it."

The Wen vanished amid the shadows of the trees.

Arrina sighed and started devouring fruit. It wouldn't be enough. She would need to bring down some meat. She ran two fingers through the rotting vegetation next to her, upsetting the ants, beetles, and worms that lived there.

If all else fails, there are always plenty of grubs down here.

Chapter 9

Arrina woke up stiff in the woven vine hammock Lastor had created for her. Her lower leg still sported nasty bruises, but the bones had knitted together nicely overnight. Her mountain shirt had become makeshift bandages for her hands, which still stung from the day before. The minor rope burn on her leg barely even showed.

Her neck and wrists and ankles were a mass of mosquito bites, but that was a simple fact of sleeping in the rainforest. Any day she didn't wake up with a snake or a poisonous spider curled up under her clothes was a victory as far as Arrina was concerned. The durable, lightweight sleeveless top and legless pants were both reptile- and arachnid-free.

She checked the ground under the hammock before setting foot on the forest floor. Most of the things that crawled and slithered down here weren't dangers, especially to an internal mystic. Cusser ants, digger beetles, calf-bite lizards, spite wasps, and all the other stinging, biting, and parasitic floor-dwellers could ruin one's day or sap her already taxed resources.

Her backpack and traveling sandals had not been so fortunate. Arrina evicted several small lizards and a large, hairy spider that was not happy about taking its meal elsewhere. It waved its fangs at her in impotent rage, picked up the paralyzed wasp with its front legs, and ran away.

There was no sign of Lastor or Stipator.

She knew her former instructor could more than take care of himself, but he himself had been the one who gave her the stern lecture after she returned from her first attempt at canopy diving.

He took Jonathan and me into the rainforest to practice navigation as well as magic. I wandered off. Climbed the tallest tree I could find. Leapt like a Wen child...

Both her legs had been shattered like pottery. One arm was broken so badly that the bone had nearly impaled her on the jagged end when she landed face-first. A broken back and a shattered ribcage. Anyone but an internal mystic would have died within a few hours. It had cost her nearly twenty pounds of fat and muscle — a dangerous price to pay for a single incident, but spending a week sleeping on the forest floor would have been suicide. The layer teemed with scavengers that would have welcomed her still-warm flesh in their jaws.

She hadn't so much walked back to their camp as crawled.

Once Stipator had nursed her back to health, he told her exactly how stupid she had been to attempt something so dangerous before fully mastering her magic. She was an idiot for taking such a needless risk without knowing enough about the sport to maximize her chances of survival. Certainly an internal mystic could heal just about any wound, but even her magic couldn't reverse an immediately fatal injury.

And six months later, once I understood my magic better, he taught me how to canopy dive. I still burned more than eight pounds. He managed a flawless dive, but it cost him five. From what Lastor said last night, it sounds like he got hung up in the canopy where there are more predators than scavengers.

"Good morning," Lastor called down to her cheerfully from the branches of an understory tree.

Arrina sighed deeply. "How is Stipator?"

"Stipator is hungry." The familiar voice came from the far side of a nearby trunk.

The trees of the rainforest grew to incredible widths as well as heights. The ones around them were at least twenty feet across, with huge, ridge-like roots forming pyramids of wood that dug into the earth around them. They were the inspiration for the buttresses of Farlander cathedrals, she knew.

Arrina followed the sound of his voice even as Lastor jumped down from his vantage point to do the same. Stipator had cut a wide, bowl-like indentation into a section of log fully three feet thick. The hollow held a skinned monkey and a few plucked sweetbirds on a squirming mass of white floor grubs.

Stipator showed no signs of serious injury, but she could tell he had lost several pounds overnight. His belly was shrunken, and his shoulders and arms were less defined. Arrina's stomach growled in sympathy.

"Lastor, I would appreciate your assistance," Stipator said. He attempted to twitch his mustache, but his hand trembled, and the fingers missed their target.

"What do you need?" the Wen asked in a very serious voice.

"Fresh water and fire to boil it."

"And some fruit to accompany this meat," Arrina added.

Lastor nodded and walked up the trunk of a tree and into the canopy as easily as the Wefals walked on the ground.

"We were right to bring him, Stipator."

He nodded. "He's a good kid. You and Jonathan are a good influence on him. He really takes your lessons to heart. He'll make a good King of Tremora, one day."

Arrina grinned at him. "That's a hundred years off, surely."

Stipator shrugged.

"Exactly how badly did you manage to injure yourself? You look terrible."

Stipator looked a bit embarrassed. "I didn't make that dive under the best of conditions…"

"Lastor told me you took a branch between the legs."

"That's an understatement." Stipator winced in memory. "I was going so fast it snapped my pelvis like a twig, to say nothing of my, um, sensitive bits. Massive internal bleeding. The pain would have made me black out if not for magic, and the price of controlling it was not inconsequential. I then needed to stay awake and alert enough to keep predators and scavengers from eating me while I healed."

She looked at him appraisingly. "Ten, maybe twelve pounds?"

Internal mystics routinely used magic to monitor their current body weight down to the ounce. No one had a better idea of how much punishment their bodies could endure than an internal mystic.

"Fourteen." Seeing her worried look, he added, "That's not so very much for me. I outweigh you by a good thirty pounds on our best days. We'll stay out of trouble until we reach civilization."

A torrent of water fell on them both. Arrina squealed at the suddenness of it. She looked up and thought she could just make out the silhouette of a Wen in the canopy above withdrawing its hand from the giant urnleaf plant that had just been upended on their heads.

Arrina let down her blue-blond hair and wrung it out.

No doubt the only reason we can't hear him laughing is because the birds and monkeys and distance drown it out.

"We did ask him to bring us some water to boil," Stipator noted, indicating the indentation in the log between them, which was now brimming.

Lastor returned soon after with his leaf bag full of the canopy's bounty. They munched red- and blue-peeled bananas as he used Wen fire magic to bring the water to a boil without scorching the wood holding it.

When the white grubs began to float to the surface, Stipator and Arrina fished them out with carved wooden spoons and ate them while they waited for the larger animals to cook. Only Lastor refrained, saving his appetite for the birds. Unlike Wefals, Wen couldn't just eat all morning long, and he didn't want to fill up on grubs.

Arrina blew on a spoonful of grubs to cool them before putting them in her mouth. As she expected, they tasted fairly bland in the absence of any seasoning. She broke open a pomma — a red fruit with a tough outer shell like a coconut that hid hundreds of juicy blue seeds — and used them to add a bit of sweetness to the pasty blandness of the grubs.

Lastor snagged two sweetbirds while Stipator disjointed the monkey with his knife. Arrina held a slice of meat up for Lastor, who traded her a sweetbird breast for it.

Wen ate meat even less often than Farlanders, and Wefal mystics could regularly devour more than both put together in any given sitting. Internal mystics were especially prone to paying the price for their magic with their reserves of fat and muscle, especially given that they could replenish it nearly as quickly by using a small amount of magic to convert meat into Wefal flesh.

Once they had torn the monkey into pieces Stipator cracked open its skull and dug into the brain with his fingers. He offered Arrina the first bite of the spongy flesh, but she simply shook her head. She liked monkey brains well enough, but she knew they were one of Stipator's favorite foods. They had a rich, salty flavor and an exotic texture like the interior of floor grubs except without the interfering toughness of the skins.

Stipator had an almost beatific expression as he pressed each morsel against the roof of his mouth to feel it compress and then spread against his tongue. Arrina picked up the rest of her pomma, brushed off the excited ants that already swarmed over it, and continued picking out the blue seed berries. The meal wouldn't replace everything she had lost since yesterday, but it would fortify her for the rest of the journey to civilization.

They traveled east through the twilight darkness and rich moisture of the rainforest floor. Eventually they would reach one of the rivers cut across the Valley floor, and that meant a surer means of travel to Pithdai. They were only forced to drive off one panther on their first day of travel. It must have been desperately hungry to risk attacking three people.

Not desperate enough to press an attack in the face of Wen fire, though, Arrina thought.

The compass and Lastor's occasional trips into the canopy to check their position kept them on track. None of them were used to traveling overland on foot, so they made worse time than Arrina would have liked.

"We'll make up for it when we reach a river," Stipator assured her. "We'll have Lastor make us a canoe, and we'll find a sailboat at the first village along the way."

• • • •

Eventually, the rainforest gave way to neat rows of banana trees heavy with fruit. Cultivated land meant people nearby. It also meant an abundance of easily accessible food. Stipator relaxed noticeably.

"It's good to be home," he said, scratching at the clusters of bug bites on his arms.

"It's hard to believe we left Mattock yesterday morning," Arrina said, squinting in the sunlight.

"Yeah, it's just about midday and we're probably another day's walk to the lake."

"Do you know where we are in Petersine?" Lastor asked.

Stipator shook his head. "There are hundreds of fruit farmsteads along the border. The chances we'll run into anyone I'll recognize are..."

"Stipator ad'Bryan!" cried a woman with dark auburn hair as they passed between rows of orange trees.

Stipator barely missed a beat. "Calory, so nice to see you, cousin. These are my friends — Arrina and Lastor."

"Nice to meet you," Arrina said, resisting the urge to hide the pink banana she had been eating.

Guessing ages in Flecterra was often tricky business. Wefals lived twice as long as Farlanders, and Wen lived three times as long, but their bodies aged at the same pace for the first 18 to 20 years. A trio of

15-year-olds looked the same, but 60-year-olds certainly did not — a Farlander greybeard, a middle-aged Wefal, and a Wen in late early adulthood.

Calory was a Wefal half a generation older than Stipator. Short-lived Farlanders would have placed her age at 30, but she had more likely seen 45 years. She was of an age when she was as likely to be married with children as still happily unattached.

Much like ourselves, Arrina thought as Stipator chatted enthusiastically with his cousin about their relatives.

"Stipator, we shouldn't be leaving your friends standing among the oranges," Calory said suddenly, turning her attention to Arrina and Lastor. "Travelers, I extend to you the hospitality of my home, where I hope you will enjoy more satisfying fare than fresh bananas." She smiled at Arrina.

Arrina blushed slightly, but Calory simply laughed. The twinkle in her brown eyes bore a family resemblance to Stipator's. Arrina felt sure that if their hostess could grow a mustache, she would be twirling it right now.

"Please, follow me," Calory said as she turned and walked through row after row of fruit trees.

"How is my mother doing?" Stipator asked.

"She's raised the bounty on your head," Calory said breezily.

"Again? What is it up to?" He sounded unsurprised.

"Eight hundred dai."

Stipator whistled softly.

"Bounty?" Lastor asked.

"Oh yes," Calory told them gravely. "My cousin here is a renegade wanted for his crimes throughout Petersine."

"Only because they don't have what it takes to commit those crimes for themselves." Stipator smirked.

Calory ignored the interruption. "If I hadn't just offered him my hospitality, I would claim the reward for his capture in an instant. As it is, though, ah well. I'm not sure what I'd do with eight hundred dai anyway."

"Petersine succession is...complicated," Arrina told Lastor, who was looking more and more confused by the exchange.

"Oh, it's a joke, right?" Lastor said.

"Not exactly. In short, when Petersine was founded, Peter ad'Bryan, the first king, was overthrown by his centessor — his chief tax-gatherer."

"Terain ad'Marcus was extremely popular for doing the opposite of his job," Calory corrected her. "He was a tax-spreader."

"And he did not take the title of king, either," Arrina went on. "But the history lesson aside..."

"It happened again." Stipator twirled his mustache.

"This time, Patrick ad'Bryan the Glorious, a one-handed lute player from the outskirts, performed amazing feats of strength and dexterity and mental acumen."

"Acu what?" Lastor asked.

"What's important is that eleven years into Terain's reign, Patrick led half the country into Teraton, Terain's capital. It's called Patterton now. Terain, who was not a bad ruler, by the way, and did take care of our people for 100 green months, met with Patrick, and after a formal discussion..."

"Lost to history," Stipator interjected.

"Sure," Arrina said, shrugging. "Terain abdicated to Patrick."

"After that, it became traditional," Calory said. "Several centessors later, the whole folk hero thing became more of a show than a reality. And now, generally, it's a well-funded propaganda campaign by a handful of rich families."

"Please don't talk about my mother that way," Stipator said. Lastor laughed.

"Cousin Stipator here, though, he has become a true hero." Calory clapped a hand on his shoulder.

Lastor nodded. "He's Senserte."

"And he did a few things before he joined us too." Arrina smiled at Stipator, who twirled his mustache.

"But your mother is helping you."

"The bounty," Lastor said. "That seems like the brains in the monkey."

"It's perfect to keep the country aware that Stipator's still a real folk hero."

They were now standing just outside Calory's house.

Limestone, Arrina noted, recalling what she knew of Petersine's geography. *Either she's much wealthier than she looks, or we're close to Whitecliff.*

Whitecliff was a respectably large town near the Bartala River. They could buy a boat there. She resisted the urge to ask about it right away. It would be rude to accept hospitality and then leave right away.

Calory fed them a fried mixture of fruit, meat, and greens. She took note of Stipator's emaciated state, though, and tapped a cask of manioca — a beer made from cassava roots — and poured both Arrina and him large bowls of it. Manioca was one of the fastest ways to replenish lost weight, fatty cheeses being another, though it didn't appear Calory had any on hand. She allowed Lastor a small mug, but he wrinkled his nose after a single sip, so she took it for herself.

"So what story will you tell your neighbors this time?" Stipator asked as he finished his first bowl and refilled it from his cousin's cask.

Calory shrugged. "You could facechange, and I'll pretend I somehow didn't recognize your sword hilt until after you were gone."

"Are you actually a wanted criminal?" Lastor asked. "If so, why would anyone aid you?"

Calory and Stipator exchanged a look, no doubt silently arguing over who would be required to explain time-honored Petersine traditions to the foreigner.

"Is there a town nearby?" Arrina asked before they could reach a decision. "We need to buy a boat, and I'd rather get that out of the way today."

"Whitecliff is three miles east of here," Calory said with a victorious smile at Stipator. "We can stay at my house there. My cousin can explain the political realities of our country to your friend."

Stipator regarded his cousin with an unusually serious expression. "I'd love to put on a little show for your neighbors, Calory, but I'm afraid we really don't have the time. Our business is urgent."

Calory's brows rose at this. "My dear cousin, you have a reputation to maintain."

"I can facechange and slip away quietly."

Calory eyed the battlemaster's emaciated body. "Absolutely everyone around here recognizes your sword. " She smirked at him. "Don't think of it as a show. Think of it as me making sure you get on the road nice and early."

"Stipator isn't exaggerating, but he is also forgetting his manners as a guest," Arrina broke in. "As long as it doesn't delay us unnecessarily, I'm willing to put on a little show in exchange for your hospitality. What did you have in mind?"

Chapter 10

An hour before dawn, a heavy fist pounded on Calory's front door. "Open in the name of the centessor of Petersine!" The voice was gruff and without emotion.

Calory rolled out of her hammock and glided silently past the small mirror on the dresser to the window. Two men stood outside on her front porch.

The first was a middle-aged man with a slim rapier and a sheriff's badge in the shape of a four-pointed copper star. He wore a wide-brimmed hat. His features were shadowed in the dim light, but he did not stand like one on the alert to fight a dangerous criminal.

The second held a torch up high so it lit his bushy, blond beard. He wore ordinary clothes much like Calory's — a short-sleeved shirt, shorts, and traveling sandals. The only exception was a ridiculous hat with more brightly colored feathers sticking out of it than could be boasted by most tropical birds. He wore a belt of knives and a silver badge like the discs of four moons slightly overlapping in a rough square — the badge of a night hunter, the personal police of the centessor.

A double dozen of Whitecliff's peacekeepers gathered on the lawn behind them. They were clearly irregulars and deputies who had been roused out of their hammocks in the dead of night. Most carried spears or clubs, but three had neglected even to arm themselves. The flickering torchlight made them look more like a mob than a police force.

The night hunter pounded on the door again. "If you do not open to us, we will enter by force!"

Calory slipped on her traveling sandals and opened the door. The sheriff looked surprised to see her. He glanced at the night hunter and then back at her, and his posture grew suddenly wary.

"Are you Calory ad'Sina?" the night hunter asked.

Calory glared at him. "I should hope you check your addresses before you wake people up in the middle of the night, sir."

The sheriff doffed his hat awkwardly, revealing a nearly bald head with just a fringe of grey and auburn hair. "I'm sorry to wake you, Calory, but his papers appear to be in order."

"Answer my question," the night hunter growled.

Calory looked him up and down with disdain. "I should like to see these papers."

"And allow a wanted criminal to slip out while you peruse them?" The night hunter sneered. "I don't think so."

"Criminal?" Calory looked to the sheriff. "What is this about, Barkast?"

The sheriff crumpled the brim of his hat in his hands. "Hunter Tomsto heard a rumor that Stipator ad'Bryan was seen in Whitecliff yesterday. As you are Stipator's cousin, Tomsto believes the renegade may have sought your hospitality."

"You are Calory ad'Sina?" the night hunter persisted.

"You are Tomsto the night hunter?" Calory mocked. "Yes, I'm Calory. I'm one of Stipator's many cousins, and before you take that tone with me, I suggest you also remember who my aunt is."

"I am aware that you are the centessor's niece, miss," Tomsto assured her.

"Then you will understand that while I do not object to you searching my home for someone who isn't here, I will not have twenty-five people tracking mud into my house," Calory told them imperiously. "You and Sheriff Barkast may come inside, but the rest will have to wait outside. Do we understand each other?"

"And how do you intend to stop us?" Tomsto snarled.

"Look around. These are not your men. They're the sheriff's, which means they do as the sheriff says. The law applies to you and the night hunters as surely as it does to others. Given the choice between the demands of a so-called night hunter and the law of the land, I have faith that Sheriff Barkast will side with the law."

Barkast looked deeply unhappy about suddenly being made the center of attention.

The night hunter came to his rescue by throwing both arms into the air exasperatedly. "Very well. The house isn't that large. Two of us can search it as easily as twenty. Sheriff, have your men surround the house. I don't want him fleeing into the orchards the moment we're inside."

The sheriff, looking deeply embarrassed now, motioned to the peacekeepers, who fanned out. Calory stood aside and motioned for the night hunter to enter.

The sheriff followed them, picking at the guard of his rapier nervously. "Hunter Tomsto, I would like to offer my sincere apologies for doubting you. Until tonight, no one had ever seen Calory and one of the centessor's night hunters in the same place. I began to suspect..."

"That Stipator's cousin was hiring people to pose as night hunters?" he asked, casting an imperious expression at the sheriff. "I can't know for sure that she didn't, but I am glad I have put to rest your distrust, sheriff." Then to Calory, "Show us where guests stay when you have them."

Calory hesitated for just a moment before pointing through the dining room and into the spare bedroom beyond.

"That is an awful lot of dishes for one person to use in a single meal," Tomsto commented, indicating the pile of unwashed clay bowls on the dining table.

Calory opened her mouth to reply, but the night hunter motioned her to silence. He cocked his head. "Wait. Did either of you hear that?"

Calory shook her head, frowning deeply. Barkast continued toward the next room.

"I think I heard something upstairs," the night hunter whispered. "I'll go investigate. Behave yourself while your friendly sheriff checks out that room."

Out of the sheriff's sight, Calory glared daggers at the night hunter but followed Barkast. She picked up one of the bowls on the table and weighed it with one hand.

The hammock in the spare room was empty. Barkast whirled. Calory hid the bowl behind her back just in time.

"Sheriff! Behind you!" she shouted.

He turned, and Calory brought the bowl against the back of his head. The clay shattered noisily, and the sheriff collapsed onto the wooden floor. She ran into the dining room and snatched up another bowl.

"Why did you ..." she shouted, cutting off mid-sentence as she threw the bowl against one stone wall, where it shattered.

• • • •

Calory, disguised as the night hunter, ran back down the stairs. She took in the scene at a glance as she took off the belt of knives and badge.

Arrina, disguised as Calory, knelt beside Barkast among fragments of broken pottery, her hand pressed to the lump on his head. She stood up as her disguised hostess approached.

"Skull intact?" Calory asked in a whisper.

"Yes, but I'm afraid he'll have a nasty headache in the morning," Arrina said.

Arrina completed most of her transformation into the night hunter in the time it took her to say it. Green-blond hair replaced Calory's auburn. Breasts vanished, and a bushy beard grew out of a rough face. She took the belt of knives and badge from Calory and placed them over her clothes.

Calory's features shifted, too, although much more gradually. The beard fell out, and the green-blond hair slowly turned auburn. She handed Arrina the night hunter's outrageous hat. "Just keep them out until I finish changing."

"Looking for me?" Stipator's voice filtered down the stairs.

"That's your cue, Arrina," Calory noted, looking almost entirely like herself.

Arrina growled in her guise as night hunter but charged up the stairs. "Villain! You knocked out the other two, but you won't take me by surprise!"

Stipator stood in the second-story window and gave a little wave to the peacekeepers below before turning his attention to the approaching night hunter. "You're just calling me names because I stole all that money from the centessor's corrupt tax collector and gave it back to the ones he robbed."

"You stole his clothes, too!" the Arrina shouted back, improvising. "Not just the ones he was wearing — his whole wardrobe. Don't you think that's a bit excessive even for you, Stipator?"

Stipator gave a small shrug and posed in the window. "Excessive? Corruption is a serious problem, and I would have no tolerance for it if I were centessor!"

Arrina howled as he charged toward the window. Stipator jumped, and at that moment, a huge gust of wind swept past the house and extinguished all the torches. The peacekeepers shouted in surprise more than fear. By the time Arrina emerged from Calory's house in her night hunter disguise, Stipator had vanished.

• • • •

The manhunt lasted until well after dawn. Stipator and the night hunter leapt from rooftop to rooftop. Arrina, still playing the part of the night hunter, shouted threats and accusations. Stipator responded with taunts and grievances against the centessor. At last, he reached a building overlooking the river. Several small boats were tied to piers below.

Arrina cornered him there, and the hero and the night hunter confronted each other in full sight of the third-story windows of the taller nearby buildings. Arrina drew a pair of knives and attacked in a flurry of steel.

Stipator dodged the initial rush. The second time Arrina attacked, Stipator parried the knives with his bare hands by striking her in the wrists. With a pair of quick twists, the knives clattered to the roof and slid into the gutter.

She freed himself and drew two more knives but gave Stipator enough time to draw his rapier.

She lashed out without hesitation, a fearless defender of the current regime protecting the established order. Stipator parried both knives with impossibly swift strokes. He took a step sideways. The sword touched the hilt of one knife and deftly flicked it out of the night hunter's hand.

"I am not your enemy," Stipator told his opponent. "I know eight hundred dai is a lot of money, and you must really need it if you'd risk chasing me down."

Arrina drew another knife and held it in a reversed grip. She sprang forward, driving him back. The knife and swordplay continued in earnest, but Stipator never stopped talking.

"The drought has hurt a lot of families. Even I can't blame the centessor for that. I've been talking to some of the people in Jacobston, though, and there's a demand for manioca and tropical fruit wine up there. That won't make up for your losses, but it would bring much needed coin to Whitecliff's families."

Arrina rolled her eyes at that, and Stipator's sword point touched the bearded man's waist. A child squealed in delight from a nearby window and clapped her hands.

Stipator waved with his free hand and then disarmed his opponent in two swift motions. Arrina reached for more knives, but the knife belt snapped and slid onto the roof.

Stipator smirked and made a quick salute with his sword. "Think on my words, sir." He slid the rapier into its sheath. "Until then, farewell!"

Stipator sprang backward and over the side of the roof to the gasps of onlookers. He landed feet-first in a sailboat piloted by a lone Wen boy. The boy opened his mouth to object, but Stipator quickly pressed a small purse into his hand.

"Sail on! I'll go wherever the wind takes me, just as long as it takes me quickly."

Arrina roared in the night hunter's deep voice and made a running leap off the edge of the building. She pretended to misjudge the speed of the boat, and a large splash rose up from where she landed, dousing several workers on the nearby pier. Arrina came up sputtering and shouting at the fleeing boat from which Stipator was blowing kisses.

Arrina made a show of retrieving the night hunter's waterlogged hat and swam to shore. Laughter followed her, but she pretended to studiously ignore it. She pulled on the hat, which let out another torrent of water on her head. The bright feathers drooped low, but Arrina pretended not to notice, nor did she go back for the night hunter's belt. Instead, she marched in a huff southeast along the side of the river, shouting curses at anyone who came near her.

• • • •

The night hunter clothes dried after only a couple miles of walking. Except for the hat, which Arrina gave up on and threw into the undergrowth by the side of the river road. When she was a half-mile away from Whitecliff and well out of sight of anyone who might have seen the night hunter's showdown with Stipator, she picked her way past long-rooted trees to the edge of the river and waved to a familiar sailboat moored on the far side of the river.

The boat moved swiftly and seemingly heedless of the current. A Wefal man sitting near the bow tossed a canvas backpack to Arrina, whose hair had already turned blue-blond. A short trip behind a tree later, and the night hunter became Arrina again, now dressed in her own clothes.

"Was my performance satisfactory?" She let her whole posture project irritation as she climbed into the boat.

"Brilliant as usual," he told her, smiling as if he was oblivious to her frustration.

She didn't return it. "Good. I wasted a solid pound on that little farce."

"Relax, Arrina. " Stipator shrugged and indicated a small cask. "You'll have plenty of time to get it back before we reach Kaeruli Lake. My cousin supplied us well, and we won't need to leave the boat for the rest of this leg of the trip."

"Exactly what kind of swindle did I participate in back there?"

"Well, I have some powerful political rivals who are spending a lot of money to fake stories about their bravery. One of them even staged a hunt into the Blood Preserve and brought back what he claimed was one of the nightmares he killed with his bare hands. More likely just a bunch of animal parts cleverly sewn together."

"Why do you go to all the bother?"

"Well, it would be a shame to lose this election to some lazy cocoa merchant who won't even try to act like a folk hero until he has to storm the capital with a mob at his back."

"Can't you just spread stories that way, too? Why the theatrics?"

"Because I'm the real thing, Arrina. You know that. We're out there having adventures and rescuing the unfortunate from bad people in clever ways. The problem is none of these people are out there, so if I'm going to prove to them that I'm a folk hero, I have to find ways to convince them of it."

She shook her head and picked up an orange from their supplies.

"It doesn't make sense to you. Pithdai is a Wen monarchy. You've got your next king all picked out sometimes a century in advance. Petersine is a democracy."

"I know it's a tradition to elect a folk hero, but isn't this cheating even by your own rules? If one prince murders the heir to the throne, the Pith still don't crown him king."

"It's not the same thing. It's about visibility. People won't elect someone they've never heard of. And I am trying to change the tradition a little bit, at least. You heard my speech, right?"

Arrina threw a piece of orange peel at him, but her annoyance was fading. However absurd the Petersine succession traditions, it was really none of her business.

"Of course you did," he continued. "I agree we have to get past this obsession with rebellion and heroes and actually put people in charge who know what they're doing."

"Like you?"

Stipator looked hurt. "Not that it's your concern, but yes. I have all the advantages of education you and Jonathan do."

Arrina picked at the orange peel. "That wasn't really fair. Sorry."

Stipator brightened. "I was thinking that the night hunter of White-cliff might be swayed by my arguments and join me in my life as a folk hero..."

Arrina barked a laugh. "I am not going to play the part of your pet night hunter!"

They all laughed, and the sailboat continued down the river.

Chapter 11

They put in briefly in the small port city of Kaeglave. All of Kaeruli Lake stretched ahead of them. A Wen couple from Pithdai crewed Larus' Gift, the narrow, shallow draft 40-foot boat they were on. Martuerige and Jetty had received the boat as a gift when they retired from the service of the Pith royal family after half a century of service.

That was the official story anyway.

In truth they still served Pithdai. They primarily kept their eyes and ears open for news that would be of interest to the king — not exactly spies, but certainly more interested in the current events of other countries than most. Occasionally they transported the king's spies and Grey Diplomats into and out of foreign ports.

Nor were Martuerige and Jetty the only such agents Pithdai had in the Valley. Arrina's father had provided Jonathan and her with a list of them after the first time a mission had gone disastrously for the Senserte. "You have friends everywhere," Larus had assured them, "if only you know where to look for them."

Her father had been true to his word. Arrina had no illusions that he had given them a complete list of Pith agents, but she knew where to find help in most of the larger lake and river towns of the Flecterran Union. They brought the Senserte safely out of more than one crisis.

This was the biggest emergency yet, even if she couldn't tell them exactly what that emergency was. Telling the Senserte about Kaspar's abduction was one thing. Telling anyone else was out of the question.

"I wish the boat would go faster," Arrina said out loud, sucking at her cold tea.

"She's at hull speed," Jetty said, his tall Wen frame staring up at the taut sails. He frowned at her, a normal expression for the pale Wen. "And we're using the wind, if you know what I mean."

Arrina couldn't help staring out at the water in what might have been the direction of Gulinora Island.

Is Kaspar waiting for us there even now, or was that a lie? Arrina thought gloomily.

Stipator and Lastor entertained each other and mostly left her alone. Sometimes she was glad for the space. Most of the time she wished they would at least try to comfort her or distract her from her worries.

The trip across the corner of Kaeruli Lake took two days.

Having made their farewells to Martuerige and Jetty, the three Senserte hailed a public carriage and disappeared into Pithdai, heading for one of the larger marketplaces.

Where Aaronsglade and Jacobston were crowded and loud and smelly, with walls surrounding them that bespoke a warlike history, Pithdai was quite the opposite. It was a sprawling, manicured garden with open air markets, free-standing columns marking city blocks, and trees expertly planted and tended in a contemporary Wen tradition. Homes, some stone and brick structures on the ground but many the classic Wen treehouse, popped up wherever necessary, but never more than a handful in a block, leaving room for the many feral animals Pithdai was also home to.

The palace, a white and pink marbled set of buildings with three wings surrounded by dozens of gardens filled with every species native to the Flecterran Valley and many from around the world, was largely unprotected, less than a quarter-mile from the lake itself. The city had been sacked many times, by land and water, but it had regrown every time as well, and the people took pride in that.

The fruit stall they stopped in front of sold pomegranates, bananas, mangoes, star fruit, kiwis, and barrels of oranges, lemons, and limes. The owner, a sun-darkened Farlander with a broad hat, nodded at Arrina, Stipator and Lastor as they traded bronze lei for pieces of the fruit. Arrina peeled her orange and bit into it happily, feeling good to be home but slightly guilty she wasn't with her father.

We have to plan our approach. We have no clear idea what is happening inside the palace, and we can't afford to be dosed with saat or questioned by someone who might be working for these kidnappers. The balloon still saved us several days. We can make it to the rendezvous point.

Stipator and Lastor followed her lead without comment. This was her territory.

She led them to a part of the city filled with younger lemon and grapefruit trees. There were cobblestone roads here and more buildings than in most of the city. Here and there the trees had been cleared away entirely to make room for fields of maize, potatoes, and beans. The wind carried the sweet and sharp scents of a hundred kinds of peppers — green and red chilies, bell and fire peppers — as well as countless ground-cultivated spices like mint and sweet basil.

This was Spicetown, one of the wealthiest of the Farlander quarters of the city of Pithdai. Arrina hadn't planned on coming here. She expected to end up with some Wen cousin on her father's side, or perhaps one of the contacts Larus had set up to aid the Senserte.

But this was the right choice. Any one of Larus's relatives could be involved in Kaspar's abduction. Those of his relatives who weren't involved were every bit as likely to be watched. Arrina needed someone uninterested in the politics who would still help her no matter how odd the request might become.

The house was stucco, two stories tall, with a wrought iron gate at the front. Beyond the gate lay a large garden encircled by the building. The sweet smell of flowers wafted from it, but the view was obscured by carefully placed everlac bushes with bright purple blooms surrounded by veritable swarms of bees and hummingbirds.

Arrina tugged at the gate once, not surprised to find it locked. She automatically reached for her purse before remembering the ring of keys was still hanging on a hook in her wagon. At last, she reached for the nearby cord and pulled it.

A cheerful-sounding bell rang somewhere beyond the everlac bushes. Arrina waited for a few minutes and pulled the cord again.

"I'm coming," called a woman's voice from a narrow window above their heads.

Arrina took several deliberate steps away from the gate and looked up at the slit of a window. She caught a glimpse of a Farlander woman with gray hair struggling with something below and out of sight.

"Mom, it's me!" Arrina shouted up.

The Farlander finished the hidden labor and came to the window with a crank-loaded crossbow in both hands. The suspicion drained from her face in an instant.

"Arrina! I wasn't expecting you. I'll be right down." The head disappeared.

"Does she know about us?" Stipator asked, twisting his mustache. "I'd hate to be at the business end of that crossbow, and I'd appreciate any running start I can get."

Arrina laughed slightly and patted him on the arm. "Rest easy. You're not the first boy I've brought home, you know."

He eyed her. "That doesn't answer my question."

"Besides, she's a lousy shot."

"My ears are still good, though," the Farlander woman said as she slipped into the entryway between the everlac bushes and the gate.

Peggy ad'Anna had once been captivating, with long blond hair, delicate facial features, and an overall shape Arrina had all but imitated when designing her idealized body. Despite the family resemblance, Peggy was a Farlander. She had deeply tanned skin and round, brown eyes. She also lacked the pointed ears of Wen, Wefal, and Turu.

Arrina's mother was in her mid-50s now, which though young for a Wen or Wefal, was late middle age for a Farlander. Her hair was slate gray and pinned up into a tight bun as was the common Farlander fashion for widows and maids past their childbearing years. The corners of her eyes and mouth showed distinct lines.

For all that, the woman who had entranced the king of Pithdai had never left her. Even in her graying years, Peggy ad'Anna remained graceful and precise in every motion, moving as naturally as a butterfly flitting on the wind. Her brown eyes glinted with sharp intelligence and piercing wit.

Being mistress to a king and a mother to his Wefal children had hardened her, though. By Pith law, Arrina and Jonathan couldn't inherit land or titles at all, much less any of the ones their father possessed. This had not prevented criminals near and far from attempting to abduct and swindle them at every turn, and it had fallen to Peggy to protect her children from the predations of the greedy and ambitious. Her distrust of strangers and caution around visitors had preserved them from the worst, but her friends had keenly felt the loss of the fearless woman who had boldly flirted with the most powerful Wen in the Flecterrran Union.

It also might have something to do with the door in her basement that doesn't officially exist.

Larus provided for the twins' education, granting them access to the finest tutors in the palace from the age of six. Queen Aora ad'Mirana had insisted Peggy remain outside the palace, though. That act of jealousy rankled Arrina's mother. She had never had designs on the throne, and Pith law was clear on the subject. It was no sin to have loved a king and given him children. Her objections made no difference. Aora feared every potential rival for the king's attention, often without reason, and Peggy was the only woman who had so abundantly proven her ability to seduce Larus.

Peggy did not resent the king. She saw the necessity of keeping a queen happy. She recognized the importance of producing an heir. Larus's first wife had not succeeded in that, and he was old even by Wen standards.

Not so old that he doesn't enjoy midnight visits to his old mistress, though.

"You remember Stipator ad'Bryan, I think. Dad brought him to Pith-dai to be our battlemaster."

"My lady." Stipator touched the first three fingers of his right hand to his lips in the Petersine gesture of greeting.

The crossbow didn't rise, but nor did Peggy disarm it.

"This is Lastor ad'Remos, great-grandson of the king of Tremora."

The Wen gave her a little wave, but his eyes didn't leave the crossbow. It wasn't fear, Arrina knew. He was simply deciding on the most immediately entertaining way to respond to a crossbow bolt flying in his direction, if it went that way. Would a gust of wind simply turn it aside? Would it burst into flames that incinerated it before it reached him? Would he dodge it? Catch it? Turn it into a flower or fruit as it flew through the air?

"Mom, it's fine. They're friends."

Peggy lowered the crossbow and slipped the bolt out of its groove. She briefly disappeared back behind the everlacs, returning with a key and no crossbow.

"I have to be careful, honey. You know that," she explained as she unlocked the gate. "Come here and give your old mother a hug."

"Oh, Mom. You're not old," Arrina chided as she wrapped her arms around her mother.

Peggy laughed. "I'll be the judge of that, girl. Come in, all of you."

They obeyed, and Peggy locked the gate behind them.

The house was a kind of small fortress built to keep out burglars and beggars alike. The windows on the second story that looked out on the rest of the city were narrow slits barely wide enough to let in air and light but certainly wide enough for a crossbow bolt to exit. The windows on the first floor were even smaller, barely large enough for a hand to pass through. Cast iron spikes lined the edge and peak of the sharply sloped roof, every bit as functional as they were decorative. The walls wouldn't stand up to a mob with a battering ram, but they could certainly deter a less dedicated attacker.

The four of them passed through a gatehouse-like entryway. Arrina knew the arch above them was riddled with scores of inch-wide holes that hid a spring-driven contraption Jonathan had built for their mother. With the pull of a lever on the second floor, a forest of metal poles would descend into matching holes in the granite slabs below their feet, forming a three-dimensional portcullis held in place by a series of counterweights in the walls.

We all know which cloth my brother was cut from, Arrina reflected.

It was not the only hidden layer of security, Arrina knew. Each time Jonathan visited, he would add some new mechanism to their mother's house, though Arrina suspected none of them had ever been used. Certainly, even their mother's neighbors had no idea what clever spring-work devices protected Peggy's home from intrusion. Larus had an heir now, and his Wefal children seldom visited Pithdai anymore.

Not that anyone in the city would even consider abducting either of us after what happened to the last one who tried.

Arrina shook away that unpleasant thought as quickly as it occurred.

That little game had gotten out of hand. Arrina's parents had warned them constantly throughout their childhood about a hundred dangers only the Wefal children of the king of Pithdai need fear. Abduction was an oft-invoked bugaboo. Jonathan dutifully did as he was told, but Arrina always wanted to face those fears directly. This only got worse when she grew into her Wefal magic under Stipator's tutelage. Canopy diving was only the beginning, and it was only a matter of time before she challenged her fear of abduction.

Arrina had set out to make herself a tempting target to anyone who might sink to kidnapping the daughter of a king. She would wander the streets by night and sit in seedy public places, playing at being the rich, naïve girl. After several months, during a particularly bad economic time, someone finally took her up on her offer.

Her abductor was a Farlander fisherman who had lost his boat and both sons in a storm. The ransom he demanded of Larus for her safe return was a laughable 1,000 chel — not even 13 dai. The Farlander was rough-spoken and strong, but he treated Arrina well out of obvious terror of the king's reprisal. Unfortunately for him, he wasn't as clever as the kidnappers Arrina had been taught to fear. He came unarmed to the agreed-upon location fully expecting to receive his 1,000 chel in exchange for Arrina's safe return.

Instead, the homeguard captured him the instant she was out of danger. Arrina thought nothing of testifying against him at his trial. He was the evil kidnapper, after all. Somehow she had not realized that the crime she had lured him into committing was a capital offense. Moreover, Larus couldn't be seen to pardon a man who had confessed to kidnapping one of his children, as that would only embolden other would-be abductors.

Arrina had not wanted to know anything about the man's execution. Her father spared her the grisly details, but he made it clear that the Farlander had died while running through the rainforest by night, pursued by Wen hunters and their huge hound-cats.

From that, Arrina knew the death had not been swift or easy. Her kidnapper had died afraid, no doubt bleeding from dozens of small wounds deliberately calculated to cause pain and drive the condemned to keep running. Maybe he collapsed from exhaustion or fright. Maybe he injured a leg or foot badly enough that the hunters finished the job. Perhaps he stepped on a poisonous snake and died writhing as his lungs ceased to function. Possibly he attracted the attention of some other rainforest predator and died that way. A rainforest hunt could end a hundred different ways — none of them merciful, few of them swift.

The fisherman was only a poor man fallen on desperate times. Arrina had no legal right to call herself a princess, but she had all the wealth and other advantages of a king's daughter. She had harmed the man without cause, had tempted him with the explicit intention of bringing him to harm to satisfy her twisted, self-righteous sense of justice. She had killed him as surely as if she had broken free of his gentle restraints and strangled him in his sleep. Why? Out of a selfish desire to prove to herself that she wasn't afraid of abduction.

It was a painful lesson. She thought about it whenever the Senserte deliberated on whether one of the people under investigation deserved their particular kind of cold and absolute punishment. Arrina was not one to repeat her mistakes.

They passed into the garden beyond. Stipator stopped as soon as the everlacs no longer obscured his view. The garden was open to the sky and filled with thousands of different flowers. Lavender and rose, starlick and cheldrops, sunflowers, and orchids — the air was thick with the perfume. Peggy had arranged the flowers into complicated patterns of color, accenting the effect with fountains and landscaping.

The building that surrounded the garden looked nothing like it did from the outside. Balconies and large windows looked down at them. The walls were veritable mosaics of tiny flowerboxes and climbing flowering vines. Large, open doorways led into the house on all sides.

"Now, tell me," Peggy said once all of them were comfortably seated around the dining room table, "this is about Kaspar, isn't it?"

Arrina took a deep breath and started talking.

Chapter 12

The formal meeting room at Pithdai Palace was a Wen architectural ordeal, with pink marble pillars stretching from the sky to a tiled floor, and balconies supported by lacy buttresses from the walls bounding it. The craftsmen had grown and carved most of the still-living chairs from olka — the palace kept a gardener around to prune the chairs, which had always made Arrina laugh — but with the growth of the Flecterran Union and the age of the ruler here, new seats had been added. A fairly conspicuous one had purple cushions.

The room was empty save for three figures sitting in one of the balconies.

"This is where the Flecterran Union leaders meet?" Lastor asked in an excited whisper.

Stipator nodded. "When they're in Pithdai."

"Luckily, they will not be meeting this week, and no one else uses this room," Arrina explained. "Spies are less likely to watch it."

"But not certainly," Stipator reminded the young Wen, pointing up at the clouds progressing across the clear sky.

Lastor watched the clouds for half a minute before he said, "I don't think anyone's up there."

Stipator laughed and Arrina smiled.

A trio of serious-looking Wen dressed in the purple and pale blue livery of Pithdai entered the room, their hands resting lightly on the hilts of rapiers. They were members of the homeguard, which protected the king and his family.

"All clear," the tallest of them said. He was a tough-looking Wen with lime-colored hair.

King Larus Pithius hobbled into the room with the assistance of another homeguardsman. Two others brought up the rear and closed the door behind him. Arrina knew from long familiarity that two others would stand guard outside.

The Wen king looked up at the balcony. She raised a hand in greeting.

Her father was old even for a Wen. His hair was long, white and framed a face wrinkled and vein-marked. A patch covered one eye, from a duel when he was younger. The other was pale green, not the normal color of Wen eyes, a sign of his failing sight. He removed his teeth to sleep. But his hawkish nose and strong cheeks were mirrored in his younger son's face. Anyone who knew him when Kaspar was born would now say the younger was twin to the elder. Even at his advanced age Larus was not stooped and stumbling, and his ears and mind were as sharp as ever.

The king motioned his assisting homeguardsman to help him up the stairs to the balcony. The one with the lime-green hair seemed on the point of objecting but thought better of it. It took Larus several long minutes to reach the little circle of chairs Arrina, Lastor, and Stipator had set up. Her father eased into the fourth chair and put his braided wooden cane aside.

The homeguardsman with him reached into a pocket and removed a glass flask filled with a yellow liquid. He held it out to Arrina sternly, but Larus put his hand on the guard's wrist and shook his head.

"Arrina is my daughter, Absokol. I'll not have you sweetening her lips in her own home." Larus's voice was little more than a whisper, but it still had the edge of command to it. "Nor her guests. Leave us. We need to speak in private."

"But your majesty," the homegardsman objected, making a motion at Stipator's sword.

Larus's eye narrowed to a slit. "Obey me, or you'll join the last homeguardsmen to fail in their duties."

The guard's eyes fell. "Your majesty." He bobbed his head slightly and returned to the meeting room floor.

Larus turned his attention to Arrina. He smiled. "Give your father a kiss, dear."

She did so, her lip brushing his wrinkled cheek. "We came as fast as we could, Dad," she whispered in his ear.

Every other part of the king's body might be falling apart, but he still had his Wen talent, which was supernaturally sharp hearing. He leaned back in the chair, trying without much apparent success to get comfortable in it despite creaking bones.

"You need not whisper so softly," Larus said in his same rasping voice. "Architects designed the room to muffle sound from the balconies."

Arrina returned to her seat, but she continued to whisper. "It is only another precaution. Just like leaving your homeguardsmen down there." A motion of her head indicated the six Wen in the chamber below.

He nodded. "There are only three of you, and your Wen friend cannot come with you. Where are the others?"

"In transit. Bad weather kept me from receiving your arrow."

Larus frowned. "I feared that might happen."

Arrina made a helpless gesture. "We are here, and there is time. Do you still want us to deliver the art as planned?"

"Yes. It will take a few days to load it onto the Promenade." Larus's eye darted to one side and then returned to Arrina's gaze.

He still fears we might be overheard.

"Would you be amenable to our staying here in the palace?" Arrina asked, taking one of his hands and playing the part of the adoring daughter. "Whatever the circumstances of our arrival, I would like to visit some old friends."

"Of course. I've had your suite prepared in anticipation of your arrival. Stipator, you and Lastor can borrow Jonathan's, since he is not here to need it."

Suites whose entrances are merely a few paces away from each other.

"Dad, I would like to request a boon."

"Anything within my power, my daughter."

Her voice took on a deliberately sharp tone, one of carefully focused rage. "The homeguardsmen charged with protecting Kaspar failed in their duty. If you have not yet executed them, I would like some time alone with them. I want to see them suffer."

This seemed to momentarily throw him off balance. "I, uh, I'm afraid that's no longer possible, Arrina. The queen has already received that boon."

That's unfortunate, Arrina thought, but she threw her arms around his neck and made a small motion in Stipator's direction.

"Hey Lastor, do you see that purple chair down there?" Stipator said suddenly, and then he launched into a loud and lengthy explanation of who sat in which chairs when the Union's leaders met to discuss the country's problems.

"Softly, Dad. What of the archives?" Arrina breathed in her father's ear even as she used her magic to heighten her own hearing. Her heart was pounding in her chest at the thought of giving paintings as dangerous as Empire of Brass to a hostile force.

"Outer vault only."

That was a relief. The Pith kept the truly dangerous paintings in a hidden inner vault.

"Throne room?" she prompted.

"Can't risk it."

She barely nodded, and then they parted. Arrina had expected that answer. Anyone who had been to an official audience in Pithdai Palace would see the paintings on the wall. Someone bent on stealing Pith art certainly would know which ones were there. Not counting Nosamae Descending, three of the paintings there were miraklas.

Gates of Tremora was a painting of a carved wooden double door depicting the Wen of Tremora and Pithdai joining hands at the time they made the alliance against the Farlanders centuries ago. When the real gateway, the Pithdai Gate, in far away Tremora was opened, the doors in the painting would open too, and travelers could move back and forth between the painting and the doors as easily as stepping through them. The king of Tremora usually left those gates open as a sign of mutual trust, although neither sent envoys through the gates without permission.

Sun's First Rising showed a sunrise over the ocean east of Kukuia. The sun never moved, but the waves in the painting lapped against the sandy shoreline. Legend held that the painting had created the sun, so if anything ever destroyed it, the sun would cease to exist. As with all such mirakla stories, this might well be pure myth. Maybe the painting caused the sun to rise. Maybe it was nothing more than a pleasant view of the ocean.

The third mirakla was The Kind Lady, which had hung opposite the throne of Pithdai almost as long as there had been one. It was a portrait of a kindly looking Wen woman with lemon hair peppered with silver, smiling a bit enigmatically. Anyone who looked on that face would instantly recover from any ailment short of death or those brought on by age. Poison, injury, and illness were no match for The Kind Lady, and many Pith kings had survived assassination attempts as a result of her ministrations. Its theft would be a grave loss to Pithdai.

So her father intended to cooperate, at least partially, but he was also willing to take a risk. And he was arranging for her to investigate what she could about Kaspar's disappearance before facing whoever had abducted him.

"Would you like to know how those seven homeguardsmen died?" Larus asked.

Seven? Eight would have guarded Kaspar. Was that the one who betrayed him?

Something in Larus's expression warned her not to ask. She shook her head. "Perhaps we can settle into our rooms first, and you can tell me later." She knew they would discuss no such thing when spies might be listening.

"Of course. The midday meal is in an hour. Please join me."

The more she interacted with her parents in this situation, the more Arrina became convinced they could have kept their relationship a secret from all of Pithdai, if they had desired.

Father was never ashamed of my mother. He would have married her if the law had allowed and if he had already had an heir.

Peggy still had enough of the king's trust to prevent him from having the old entrance to his bedchamber from being walled up — or even from revealing it to the palace staff. The queen, of course, had her own chambers.

That had kept the three of them from being disarmed or having their lips sweetened to prevent them from using magic. Then it was just a matter of leaving him a token to meet them here — a purple banana taken from the fruit bowl and placed on the table to indicate a younger family member, and eight drops of wax on it to indicate the meeting place — and sneaking out of the king's chambers and into the meeting room. Arrina wasn't certain she would need to resort to disguises and other physical transformations, but even the tiny bit of enhanced hearing had served an important function.

The three of them settled in. Arrina's suite had duplicates of most of the tools and costumes in her wagon, with the exception of the ones Michael enchanted. Farlander magic kept for quite some time, but it faded away eventually. Besides, he hadn't developed spells like the masks until a few months after the Senserte had begun their travels. She added the pouch of wooden tokens Kara had enchanted to create the illusion that ordinary paintings were miraklas.

They ate the midday meal with her father, carefully maintaining an ambiance of small talk tempered only slightly by open worry about Kaspar's well-being.

He has lost faith in the loyalty of even the homeguard, Arrina realized.

After the midday meal came setat, the restful three — a period during the hottest hours of the day when almost everyone took a nap or, at the very least, sat around quietly and tried to stay as cool as they could. Late afternoon in Pithdai almost always brought rain to cool the air, but between the hours of noon and three, no one did much of anything.

Of course, Wen who still had their magic and Wefal internal mystics could ignore this rule. Arrina met Stipator and Lastor outside of Kaspar's suite. Larus had conveniently arranged for it to be left unlocked.

The trio crept into the suite warily. Arrina had prepared a few very good reasons to come to Kaspar's room that would make her interest purely filial. She was as much at home in the palace as her father was, and Stipator was hardly less welcome.

Arrina scanned the living room, which had been decorated in dark wood paneling. The decor was as tasteful as she remembered, but it lacked her half-brother's usual clutter, a trait he shared with Jonathan. His writing desk was completely bare. The bookshelves, once covered in layer after layer of books, had been carefully pruned to look neat and sensibly organized.

"He's done some growing up in our absence," Stipator mused.

Arrina frowned in concentration. She went over to the desk and pulled out one drawer. Paper and writing materials practically exploded out of the drawer, sending pens and sealing wax clattering to the marble floor. She picked up the scattered contents and stuffed them back into the drawer, barely getting it closed.

Stipator raised his coppery eyebrows at her.

"Is that your brother?" Lastor asked, pointing at a portrait hanging over the desk.

Kaspar as a Wen teenager stood in a brave attempt at a heroic pose, dressed rather awkwardly in the costume of a Marrishlander wizard. The boy wore heavy boots meant for wading through knee-deep water, a long-sleeved tunic of simple gray cloth, and a leather utility vest covered in pockets. A huge, bright green cloak with long sleeves hung over all of this, the heavy-looking hood pulled up so it buried most of Kaspar's pale Wen cheeks. The belt held at least six absurdly heavy knives, and the points of javelins stuck out of what looked like a giant quiver hanging from a leather strap on his back.

"Yes," Arrina said.

"It looks uncomfortable," Lastor noted.

No one with an ounce of sanity would wear a costume so unsuitable to the Valley's tropical climate. Arrina felt the stifling afternoon heat more strongly simply by looking at it. She didn't want to imagine how many hours Kaspar had worn that ludicrous outfit for the sake of the portrait. That the young Wen's face wasn't covered in rivers of sweat was pure artistic license.

It also doesn't capture the time he fainted from the heat while wearing it.

"That's new," Stipator said.

He walked over to what Arrina had originally assumed was an iron statue. In fact, it was some kind of suit of armor made of interlocking metal plates. Stipator rapped it with his knuckles. It barely made a sound except a low, slightly hollow clunk.

"This isn't a show piece," Stipator announced in clear surprise. He twitched his mustache. "It's a genuine suit of Aflangi plate mail custom-smithed to fit a Wen. It must have cost a small fortune, though I have no idea who he found to do work like this."

"It looks heavy," Lastor said softly. "I don't think I'd want to climb trees in that."

"Aflighan doesn't have many trees, and it's a lot colder there than it is in Flecterra." Stipator ran his hand along the front of the breastplate and up to the fluting at the shoulders and neck where it met matching shoulder and neck pieces. "I've seen diagrams in books, but I've never seen one up close. You see those metal pieces that stick up from the shoulders? I can't remember the word for them, but they're made to block a decapitating slash from a heavy longsword. And you see how it all locks into place over the chainmail weave underneath? That fluting deflects force away from the places that have to be thin enough to allow movement. Here, look at where the helmet locks slides into the gorget above the breastplate."

Stipator held up an imaginary sword to demonstrate. He swung in a broad horizontal stroke at the neck and mimicked getting his weapon stuck in the shoulder guard. He brought the imaginary sword down in a heavy overhead blow, but it deflected off the helmet and then harmlessly off the shoulder guard and to the ground. A heavy, two-handed swing at the torso, and the sword simply bounced off the thick plate.

"It doesn't cover everything," Lastor noted, becoming interested in the exercise. "A crossbow bolt could go through that spot between the, um, gorget and the bottom of the helmet. Bolt to the throat would slow anyone down. There's also that slit in the visor. An arrow could get in that way, too, and nothing would stop it."

"Yes," Stipator agreed. "Both those targets are tiny, though. An archer would need a perfect shot and a lot of luck."

Lastor shrugged. "I could do it. Give me a bow, and I'll show you."

Stipator opened his mouth to object, but no sound came out.

"The Aflangi don't have archers with Wen magic talents," Arrina said gently.

Lastor screwed up his face as he tried to contemplate this impossibility. Stipator chuckled and threw up his hands.

"Not very practical for someone in the Valley," the copper-haired Wefal admitted.

"Like the clothes in the painting?"

"Yes," Stipator told him. "Also, it would be incredibly heavy to wear. Aflangi train for years to carry around that much weight, and most of them can't stand up in it. They have to ride horses."

"Those poor horses," Lastor said in a soft voice, poking a thin finger through a gap in the plates in one armpit.

Stipator barked a laugh and opened his mouth to launch into what Arrina could only assume would be an explanation of different horse breeds.

"Later," she said. "Let's not forget ourselves."

"Where next, boss?" Stipator asked. "Bedroom, or do you not want to know your baby half-brother that intimately?"

Arrina thought of Kaspar's hasty effort to hide the clutter on his desk. "Let's spread out. Stipator, thank you so much for volunteering."

He gave a mocking bow with the salute of three fingers to his lips.

"Lastor, the bath. I'll check his dining room."

"What am I looking for?" Lastor asked.

"Things a Wen prince wouldn't keep in his bath," Arrina said.

He looked confused.

"I can't be more specific, Lastor. I don't know what we're dealing with." She shrugged. "It's either this or play lookout, but we don't have a lot of time."

The orange-haired Wen nodded solemnly and skipped away to obey.

Kaspur's private dining room had light, shutter-like doors that led out onto a balcony that overlooked Pithdai's citrus gardens. Even though the balcony was currently closed, Arrina could smell the sweet scents of the blooms and fruits of orange, lemon, lime, and mirafruit trees. In the dim light allowed by the shuttered windows, Arrina could make out six elegant chairs surrounded the beautiful wooden dining table. She opened a window to get a closer look. The two chairs nearest the door showed signs of daily use, but the other four clearly remained free of dust only because of the household staff. A sky blue vase decorated with the purple tree of Pithdai sat on the table. Arrina didn't recognize it at once, but that probably meant nothing.

She examined the cabinets where china plates, bowls, and kaf cups sat in a careful arrangement. One plate was missing from the set, and the antique silver was absent. Arrina checked the drawers and could find no sign of them.

She glanced at the table again and realized the silver candlesticks had also disappeared.

The housekeepers may have simply removed them to prevent temptation.

Arrina went out onto the balcony. A small wicker table and two matching chairs sat on the balcony.

Those weren't there when I was last in here, but that was nearly a year ago.

She examined the table and discovered the center was covered in drops and pools of wax that had melted into the tabletop.

Someone has been spending a lot of time out here, recently.

On a whim, Arrina examined the balcony railing and stared over the side three stories below. A vine-covered trellis linked ground to balcony. She idly considered whether she could have climbed up or down it, but dismissed it. It would never hold her weight. Her foot would go right through the...

Then she saw it. Halfway down. Not gap in the vines or even anything enormous, but there was a small hole in the trellis. As if someone climbed down with a rope and swung too much, putting the tip of one foot through the flimsy wood before continuing.

It would have been interesting to hear what Kaspar's homeguardsmen had to say about the night of his disappearance. She sighed. *If only*

Aora had waited until I got here so I could have asked them some questions.

"Arrina," Lastor called from inside.

"Did you find anything?"

"I found this in the tub. I collected as much as I could." He held out a tangled handful of long, black hair. "Stipator says you should come see what he found, though."

That isn't Wen or Wefal hair. Almost certainly a Farlander's. Who besides Kaspar has been bathing in his suite?

"Let's see what Stipator found."

Kaspar's bedroom showed the same hasty tidiness as his writing desk. The bed was carefully made, of course, the floors polished and the furniture dusted, but that was because of the household staff. Stipator had since delved into anything that didn't fall into their purview — dresser drawers, closets, trunks. Clothes lay scattered on the floor all around the room.

The mustached Wefal sat on a heavy wooden trunk, smirking as he fiddled with a twist of coppery hair with one hand while holding the other out of sight.

"Well?" Arrina prompted.

"First off, a lot of his clothes are missing, so I'm thinking he packed up and left. As to motive..." With a flourish, Stipator held up some pale green cloth. It took Arrina a fraction of a second to recognize them as women's undergarments — a large bustier — made of woven silk.

She fought to smother a grin, failed, and burst out laughing. "That took him long enough."

"I know, right?" Stipator agreed. "I was beginning to fear for the future of the kingdom." He tossed the undergarments onto the bed and made a show of wiping his hands on his pants.

"And no one found them during the search?"

Stipator shrugged. "They were stuffed into a pantleg at the bottom of the drawer. The people searching the suite must not have unfolded every piece of clothing the way I did. I remember all the best hiding places for romantic keepsakes from when I was a young lover, so I had an advantage."

Arrina shook her head. "This is beginning to tell a story."

"Boy falls in love with some girl or another. Mom and Dad don't approve."

"Or the law just won't let him marry her because she's a Farlander."

His eyebrows rose. "Right. In any case, Kaspar runs off with her."

"Just like dear old Dad, although my grandparents didn't live long enough to see that. Instead, he had large political factions angry at him. It only got worse when Jonathan and I were born."

"I imagine so, muddying up the succession like that." Stipator said it with a bitterness she knew he didn't feel and would probably never comprehend.

Arrina had grown up with the arguments that prevented Wefals from inheriting family titles in most Wen and Farlander countries. Wefal blood was stubborn. It took at least eight generations for a family to become Wen or Farlander again. In the meantime, you could have a short-lived king of Pithdai or a councilmember of Aaronsglade who could never learn the arts of enchantment.

"Not so much that," she explained patiently, "but Wen don't sire or bear children accidentally, so some of them thought he did it just to spite his detractors."

The first part of that statement was not an exaggeration or reflection of what was socially acceptable. Unlike Farlanders, Wen men could choose whether or not the sex act had potency, and Wen women could activate and deactivate their fertility cycles. Wen claimed it as another mirakla like the creation of the moons and Farlanders, but they probably didn't believe that, either. More likely, it was a physiological mechanism to protect against overpopulation. With life spans three times the length of Farlanders and near-zero infant and child mortality, exceedingly fecund Wen would soon multiply beyond the ability of their environment to support the population.

In addition, parents whose children still had their magic couldn't have more children unless their magic-wielding children actively desired younger siblings. This, at least, seemed to have more to do with childish magic than the bodies of Wen adults, but it served as a similar limit on procreation. Unless their child wanted more children in the household, even Wen couples who wanted larger families had to wait fifteen or sixteen years between children. This usually worked out to a lower lifetime reproduction rate in Wen than in Farlanders. A Wen with three children within five years of each other was almost unthinkable. Davur and his brothers were each only six years apart, which Wen considered as rare as triplets among Farlanders.

Wefals lived twice as long as Farlanders and could multiply just as quickly, so they could outstrip both their parent races in sheer birth rates. Many did, intentionally or not, which was why Petersine had become a force to be reckoned with in just two hundred years. It also made them more convenient sources of fear. If the Wefals were allowed to multiply at their current rate, the argument went, they would soon outnumber the Farlanders and Wen. The stubborn Wefal blood only made this fear stronger, convincing both sides that eventually everyone in Flecterra would be Wefal, and the Wen and Farlanders would cease to be.

"Oh," Stipator said at last. Petersine Wefals didn't like to be reminded of the reality of Wen and Farlander attitudes toward the hybrid race. He changed the subject with a heavy hand. "So you think she's a Farlander?"

Arrina shrugged and opened the door to leave. "The black hair Lastor found would seem to say so."

"Unless he had more than one lover," Stipator suggested, wagging his eyebrows suggestively.

"Or that," she conceded.

Lastor, who had been quietly examining the undergarments only moments before, stood up with empty hands and trotted after her.

Stipator got up off the trunk to join them. "Lastor, it is in bad taste to steal another man's romantic keepsakes."

The Wen looked at him with an innocent expression.

"Whoever she is, she gave her underthings to Kaspar, not you," Arrina said.

Stipator held out a hand, and Lastor grudgingly gave him the pale green clothing. Stipator returned them to the back of the drawer where he had no doubt found them.

"How did he sneak away from eight homeguardsmen without raising an alarm?" Stipator asked as they passed a small table with a bowl filled with colored sand that moved and shifted on its own — a minor mirakla no doubt created by a Turu child.

Arrina shrugged. "I'm still working on that. It could have been a mirakla or an enchantment."

"Or even an internal mystic accomplice?"

"That's less likely than a mental mystic, but yes."

"So we've narrowed it down to not an external mystic," Stipator said cheerfully.

"We know he ran away from home."

"Actually, we only suspect it," Stipator reminded her. "All we know is he has women's undergarments in his dresser, and even those could have been planted there after his disappearance."

"That's true, but I think the lady friend is real, and I'd say she visited him not long before his disappearance. I've seen the way you tidy up your wagon when you're expecting a woman to visit you, Stipator. The desk drawers remind me of that. There is also a romantic little table and chairs out on the balcony with evidence of long hours spent staring into each others' eyes by candlelight to support the lady friend scenario."

Lastor and Stipator both laughed at that.

Arrina smirked slightly. "At this point, I don't think we know enough to guess at how he left Pithdai without raising an alarm, and it might not even matter. We're still Senserte, so what we most need to know is whether Kaspar was abducted by his lover or by someone else. And are the kidnappers acting alone, or are they working for someone else? If so, who?"

At that moment, the sky opened up and showered the city with heavy rain, bringing some relief from the stifling heat. The rest of the palace would be waking up soon. The trio left Kaspar's rooms behind.

Chapter 13

They set sail aboard the Promenade at dawn, with Chelestria opposite the rising sun, waxing nearly full.

"We have three days," Arrina had told Captain Autil at dinner the previous evening. He had delayed departure because the evening storm had been heavier than most.

Autil nodded. "Promenade will get us there in two days. We'll raise the sails before dawn tomorrow, and arrive around noon the next day."

After a day sailing, with another stop during a ferocious storm — the lightning over the water was as amazing as it was frightening — she finally believed him. She stood at the rail near the bow, out of the Wen sailors' ways, and scanned the horizon for the first sign of the uninhabited, rocky outcrop that was Gulinora Island. Stipator sparred with the rail not too far away from her, darting in to etch his name lightly with his rapier, one stroke at a time. He was clearly very bored.

"I wish Jonathan and everyone else were here," she said.

"He would be a better sparring partner," Stipator answered, poking the rail with a flourish to make the "a".

Arrina turned around and leaned back against the rail. "They may not know if we reached Pithdai."

"Or that we nearly crashed into the Blood Preserve."

Arrina grimaced. They had recovered fully, and a little bit more at Stipator's urging, from that near disaster.

"We would be far more prepared for this meeting if they were here and knew what we knew."

He grunted, concentrating on creating an "o". Arrina saw that this was the third time he was finishing his name, and wondered how much Autil would forgive them for damaging his ship.

Her half-brother's disappearance was less of a mystery, but the motivation was not clear yet. According to her father, Kaspar's homeguardsmen had no memory of that night. As far as they could recall, the prince had been with them all night, but when it came time to change shifts, he had been missing. Frantic searches had not turned up any sign of him in the palace, and discreet search parties failed to locate him anywhere in the city. His escape had been swift, which spoke of careful planning, not impulse.

The accounts of the palace servants and those of Kaspar's homeguardsmen not on duty at the time supported the lady friend scenario. Over the last few months, Kaspar had become entangled with a Farlander woman from Aaronsglade named Sora ad'Serra and her Aflangi friend, Herald. Aora believed "Herald" was the title the man held in Aflighan, and not his real name. It probably didn't matter, but seeing his wife step out of her grief long enough to contribute had made Larus happier.

Sora was not an official representative of the Council of Aaronsglade. She at least claimed to represent the Aaronsglade Arts Council, though that had been yet another thing the rainy weather prevented Arrina from confirming or discrediting. Sora's reason for being in Pithdai seemed to have been to convince Aaronsglade's envoy to Pithdai, Ma'Carol ad'Melissa, of the wisdom of increasing funding to Aaronsglade's art schools and museums.

As if reading her thoughts, Stipator sheathed his sword and said, "That Sora woman's reasons for being in Pithdai were an excuse. She was there for something else."

Arrina nodded, lost in her thoughts. It was as good as saying she was there for a swindle. Arrina trusted his instincts, but the question remained whether Sora was acting on her own or whether Carol — and by extension, the Council of Aaronsglade — was in on the game. An arts advocate with enough money to employ a fairly large entourage was on a completely different scale from a conspiracy that touched the Council of Aaronsglade. That the envoy was Ma'Carol and not simply Carol meant she was not only an enchantress, but a member of the Nosamae.

It would make no difference if Sora was a Nosama or a rogue enchantress. With only a few exceptions, visitors to Pithdai's palace had their lips sweetened with saat to prevent them from using magic. Diplomats and their entourages were not exempt. Simply avoiding the initial dose of saat was no escape. Saat spiked the drinks at every state meal involving foreign dignitaries. Even the king shared in this leveling of ground, though the sharp hearing that was his Wen talent was hardly as potentially dangerous as the magic of Wen archers or Farlander enchantresses.

"Michael could do it," Arrina said out loud, just as Stipator pointed over her shoulder. She turned. Gulinora Island's rocky point had topped the horizon. They were, perhaps, an hour out now. She brushed her hair back.

"The Senserte do it all the time with the masks. The kidnapper or Sora or someone else could have hidden an enchanted item and snuck it into the palace."

"Ah, that." He twitched his mustache.

Arrina gripped the rail with both hands. "Even with tasa petals, an object enchanted by Farlander magic looks no different than one that isn't, right?"

Tasa petals came from the same trees as saat. They were the flowers that became the fruit. A few drops of sickeningly sweet saat juice would prevent anyone — Farlander, Wen, Wefal, or otherwise — from using magic for several hours. Tasa petals had a different link to magic. Anyone chewing the bitter leaves for a few minutes could see the magic enchantresses wielded. From her conversations with Michael, Arrina knew Farlanders saw this magic differently than other races did when under the effects of tasa petals. Wen saw white light around enchantresses who were actively using magic. Wefals saw Farlander magic in shades of gray, which had surprised Michael in a way she guessed meant that enchantresses could see colors.

"Tasa watchers have their limits," Stipator agreed.

"The guards don't search Kaspar when he comes home, but they would check any gifts he brought back." She chewed her lip.

"It's an impressive crime, kidnapping a crown prince from Pithdai Palace," he argued. "Maybe we could learn a couple new tricks from it that the Senserte can find a use for."

Arrina said nothing.

Stipator let out a sigh. "Fine. You're right. The goals of whoever the kidnappers are working for are of greater consequence to us. Still, knowing what they can do and how will make it easier for us to bring them to justice."

She really couldn't disagree with him on that point so she nodded once and changed the subject. "Do you think Lastor is still angry that we wouldn't let him come with us?"

"He'll be fine."

"He didn't even say goodbye to us when we left the palace."

"He'll forget all about it in a few days. If I know Lastor, he's looking for some villainy in Pithdai that he can punish." Stipator grinned wolfishly.

"I suppose you're right." Arrina left the rail. "I'm going to my cabin to get ready."

Stipator made agreeable noises and moved to do the same.

The changes Wefal internal mystics made to their bodies did not go away with the first taste of saat. Certainly they couldn't transform further or heal new injuries until the saat wore off, but muscles already magically enlarged didn't wither, nor did false faces melt away.

Enemies of the Senserte had captured Arrina before — had bound and gagged her and sweetened her lips — but she had never been at anyone's mercy. Arrina had no intention of being a victim today, either.

• • • •

"I have fifteen sailors trained with bow and sword," Autil protested for the fourth time as his men lowered Arrina to the sea in one of the ship's rowboats. "I can send half a dozen, no, eight!"

Arrina shook her head, exasperated. "Not yet, captain. There is too much we do not know, and they've ordered me to come alone and unarmed."

"And I'll be there." Stipator waved down to her from the rail. His neck had grown gills like a fish, and his hands had become webbed. Arrina knew his feet were flippers, and his skin would shift colors to blend in with his surroundings, which was why he was naked. It was important now, though, that anyone watching would see him on the ship. "I'll be nearby, and I'll be armed."

The boat touched the water, and Arrina looked up at the captain and crew again.

"This is an exchange of goods for a hostage," she said. "If you are attacked, don't negotiate or stand and fight. Return to Pithdai with all haste. Stipator and I can take care of ourselves."

"As you say, my lady," Autil said, and she wondered if he would listen.

The sun was high in the sky, and seagulls wheeled overhead. She watched the ship get farther from her as she rowed to the island. Its most prominent feature was its sharp stone peak, like a sundial. Some trees had taken root at the edges of the sand before the rock began, but Arrina doubted there were even any animals on it.

On the shore, a huge man with pale skin, blond hair and a thick, braided beard waited. Arrina focused on rowing, resisting the urge to look over her should to keep him in sight. Just knowing this stranger, decidedly un-Flecterran, was there made her skin crawl. She heard him splashing through the water just as the boat's hull scraped the shell-covered edge of the island.

She jumped out to pull the boat in, and he grabbed it with one hand three times the size of hers and hauled it effortlessly up to the beach. She caught the blue eyes and freckles of an Aflangi who was getting too much sun. She could not miss the deadly, beautifully crafted halfmoon axe on his belt.

"I am glad you could come." His voice was deep and powerful.

"Who are you?"

"You may call me Herald."

"That is not your real name."

Herald smiled. "Have you brought the paintings?"

"Yes. What interest does an Aflangi have in Wen paintings?"

"My interests are the Godhead's interests."

"What interest does the ruler of Aflighan have, then?"

"I will not answer that question. Who can speak for the Godhead?"

Arrina wasn't sure how to answer that question. Her knowledge of Aflighan was limited. The Godhead was its ruler, she knew, and Aflighan often went to war with its neighbors, though they had not conquered any lands south of the Winteeth Mountains at the northern edge of the Valley.

Everything else was probably legend. The Godhead was a thousand years old. He commanded armies of the dead. He could ensure the loyalty of anyone whose blood he had tasted, which was why his soldiers harvested a few drops of blood from every Aflangi child when they were born. Aflangi magic was not like any Flecterran race's magic, but all those powers seemed strange even from what little she knew of Aflangi magic.

Herald smiled at her the way Reck had when he thought he had the best of her.

"I will bring you to your brother soon. Then you will see that I am willing to make this exchange in good faith. If you brought all the paintings I demanded, I may forgive you for disobeying my instructions. Prince Kaspar is too old to regrow lost fingers."

Arrina's heart thudded in her chest, but she remained impassive. "All the paintings are on the ship. Once Kaspar is safely in my custody, I will arrange for you to receive them."

The Aflangi removed a glass flask from a pouch at his belt and held it out to her. The golden liquid inside could only be saat. She took it.

"You know what this is and why it is needed. Drink."

Arrina obeyed. A drop or a dram of the sweet liquid had the same effect. *It will not make me weaker or more vulnerable, just less adaptable.* She took a small mouthful and handed it back to Herald.

"Now your battlemaster."

Arrina didn't react. She was too good a swindler to be caught off-guard so easily. He could be bluffing, after all.

"You might have guessed I am not alone, either. I would not want there to be any fatal misunderstandings between us." The smile melted from his face, replaced with an iron stare. "Obey quickly, or we take fingers. Who knows? Perhaps I will give one to the Godhead as a gift, and then your brother will serve Aflighan as all soon will."

Arrina cursed inwardly, mind racing.

"Can I at least change into something more comfortable?" Stipator said as he appeared behind Herald, his signature rapier pointed directly at the Aflangi's back. The gills and flipper feet were gone, and the camouflage was fading rapidly.

Herald's face reddened, but his lips curled in a forced smile as he turned toward Stipator. "Dress."

Stipator walked over to Arrina's boat and pulled on his shirt, shorts, sandals, and belt. He slid the rapier into its sheath without comment and returned to Herald and Arrina.

"Your sword," Herald prompted.

Stipator looked nonplussed. "A battlemaster goes unarmed nowhere. Be content with saat and whatever advantage of numbers you have."

"The prince..."

"Is not the only one who cannot regrow his fingers," Stipator said darkly, rolling his shoulders back.

Arrina shot him a hard look.

"Stipator," she warned, but he shook his head in denial. "He can return to the ship, if you'd like," she told Herald.

Stipator reflected the same hard look back to her. This was no time for a disagreement.

Herald laughed. "Your sword does not frighten me. Drink the saat and follow. Let us finish this exchange before sunset."

"Before the saat wears off, you mean," she said.

Herald shrugged.

Arrina noted that Stipator had finished off the vial in one gulp.

I should have done that. Of course, Herald might not have been so accommodating if I had swallowed all his saat with an ally standing nearby.

They followed the Aflangi giant away from the beach. The trees were pandanas, interspersed with lake oats nearly as tall as Arrina. Behind the thin vegetation, the beach stopped, and the rocks began, a field of them leading all the way to the peak, with very little green between them. Arrina could see a white tent set up a hundred yards away across the rocks, and a young Farlander woman with light brown hair and a middle-aged Wen man dressed in the purple and blue of the homeguard.

Is that Tasticon or just someone who stole his uniform? She glanced over her shoulder. Between the slight rise of the dune and the lake oats, she could no longer see the Promenade. She looked down to catch her footing. Three hand-sized, rock-colored lizards looked up from within her small shadow.

"Sorry," she murmured to them as she gave them their sun back.

They stepped onto the larger, flat rock the tent was set up on. A Wen with bright pink hair stood up from behind the white canvas and casually aimed a bow at Stipator, who froze in place.

"Canolos!" Arrina cried, recognizing Kaspar's oldest friend, the son of the archon of Seleine, one of the oldest tree towns in Sutola.

His eyes did not even flick toward her.

"I told you I was not afraid of your sword," Herald told Stipator, laughing.

Strain showed around the battlemaster's eyes, and Arrina remembered Canolos's talent. If the Wen took aim with a bow, his target was arrested and could not move until Canolos loosed the arrow or lowered the bow.

A motion made Arrina turn her head slowly. The Wen in the

homeguardsman uniform had taken aim at her. Every muscle of his body seemed to strain. She froze as surely as if he had Canolos's talent, but shifted her attention to the Farlander woman.

She was young, probably younger than Arrina, and wore sturdy, well-worn clothing designed for outdoor travel. Her eyes were deep brown, and her hair was in one thick braid. Everything about her screamed practical.

"Well?" Herald asked her.

The Farlander simply nodded.

"You may bring out Kaspar."

No one moved. Arrina saw Canolos's eyes flick to the tent flap, and she saw it twitch, then move aside, as someone held it open for a middle-aged Farlander woman to step out. She stood up in the beating sun, but Arrina ignored her.

"Kaspar!" she cried as her brother stepped from the tent. Joy filled her as he smiled, then wavered as she noticed the smile was for the woman whom he had helped out. He handed her a wide-brimmed hat, which she put atop her lustrous black hair with a matching smile for Kaspar.

"Are you all right?" Arrina said levelly, looking for any sign of bruises or scars.

"I'm fine." He sounded completely unperturbed. "Did you bring them what they want?"

Arrina regarded the woman, whose smug smile was beginning to grate on her nerves. She must be Sora ad'Serra, the representative for the arts council. Slightly above middle-aged, Arrina thought. The lines on her face were carefully powdered, but they were there. She was slightly taller than Arrina, but larger all around. Her blouse was low-cut and transluscent, her leather shorts too tight. She wore a silver ring with four rounded stones set in a square — one each of green, blue, yellow, and black. She was not so much pretty as handsome, and Arrina wondered what she had told Kaspar to get him here.

"We have the paintings," she said.

Kaspar offered his hand to the woman, who took it and stepped forward.

"Please understand I am only interested in Pithdai's art," Sora said.

"Good. You have the art. You don't need to hold Kaspar hostage," Stipator said breezily.

It could still be Herald who wanted the art for Aflighan. Arrina didn't want to jump to any conclusions. The big Aflangi stood impassively between her and Stipator.

"Ah, but it isn't in my possession yet," Sora said. "Kaspar has told me about you…whatever you're called."

"Senserte," Arrina's half-brother supplied. He shrugged at her. "Of course Father would send you an arrow."

Arrina gestured dismissively, but felt bile rise inside her. Being known as professional swindlers would make their next steps harder. But knowing her opponents knew, that was an advantage by itself.

"Yes," Sora said, clicking open a paper fan and waving it briskly at her face. "From the stories he has told us, I would not be surprised if you have dared forgeries."

"We only received your letter a few days ago," Arrina said, wiping a drop of sweat from her brow. "There hasn't been time, even if we had wanted to. The king instructed us to cooperate fully with you as long as you return Kaspar to us."

"So he can send his homeguard to hound me to my death the way he did the man who abducted you for a ransom?"

Pray that you are so lucky, Arrina thought fiercely. *If I find out you're behind all this, you'll face much worse than Larus's wrath.*

Instead, she said, "Check the art first, if you want. We're not interested in double-crossing you. I want my brother back, and that's all."

The woman seemed to consider this. Her eyes went to Stipator's sword with its elaborate basket hilt. When she met Arrina's gaze again, her face was a picture of accusation.

"You are kidnappers," Arrina snapped. "My cooperation you have, but not my trust."

"Ma'Sora," Canolos said from where he pointed his bow at Stipator. Sweat dripped from Stipator's face, making his mustache sag. "Let it go."

She smiled at him. "Very well. Corina, are you ready?"

"Yes, Ma'Sora," the younger Farlander said.

Ma'Sora? Is she really a Nosamae, or is that just part of her cover story? Arrina wondered.

"The three of us will go to the ship," Sora said. "The rest of you, make sure they don't leave the clearing until we're ready to depart. We'll signal you when we've confirmed the paintings are genuine."

"You're taking our ship?" Stipator objected loudly.

"Yes." Sora snapped, then smiled sweetly at Arrina. "This is your last chance to let me know if they are forgeries or if you somehow forgot to include important masterpieces. I don't want to harm you any more than necessary, but if I don't find out until I get back to your ship, I'll have to send your father a clear message that my demands are not to be ignored."

Arrina made a calculation. If Sora was Kaspar's lover, she might know about the deep archives, too. "All the paintings in the throne room and the main archives are on the ship, including the miraklas. We left out the deep archives frankly because many of them are just too dangerous, as Kaspar can tell you."

Sora frowned in clear irritation but looked to Canolos for confirmation.

He nodded. "The one we want is in the throne room."

One? Arrina thought. *But which one?*

Sora looked relieved, but Stipator seemed to tense even more than he already was.

"Very well," the Farlander said with a small, strange chuckle. "It only seems fair that you should hold back a little, since you're not leaving this island with Kaspar."

"But you said," Arrina began.

"Of course I said," Sora interrupted. "But you are liars, and we are liars, and I enjoy your brother's company far too much to send him home so soon."

Arrina fumed. *As soon as the other Senserte catch up to us, we will track you down like a wild animal and give you an end worthy of your crimes.*

"You knew this would happen," Sora said. Her fan clicked shut.

"Yes, we did," was all Arrina would give her.

The Farlander smiled at her. "No threats of bloody vengeance? No dire predictions of the horrible end I will meet?"

"We didn't have any planned," Stipator told her with a smirk, "but I can improvise a few if it will make you feel better."

Sora turned her attention to him. "Stipator ad'Bryan. You're quite the folk hero in your native land, aren't you?"

"And elsewhere. I'd bow, but your archer seems to have me dead to rights, so forgive me for remaining upright."

"Would anyone recognize you without that sword of yours?"

"Despite my state of undress earlier, I'm not that prone to exhibition. It won't satisfy you the way it can when I'm attached to it, and it won't actually keep me from using it with someone else, since I just grow them back."

Sora held out her hand in Stipator's direction, her smile sour now.

"I'm sorry, honey, but pointing at it just doesn't do anything for me. If you want me to show you…"

The sword suddenly slid out of its sheath, flying through the air into Sora's hand. She didn't grab it quickly enough, though, and it clanged to the rocks. Kaspar hurried to retrieve it for her.

"I'd like to see you regrow this," Sora told him, pointing the sword in his direction vaguely. "Corina, let's go. Canolos, Herald, be certain they don't follow, but let them live. They've been more cooperative than I expected, and Arrina is family, after all."

After a few heartbeats, Corina and Sora took on the appearance of Stipator and Arrina. The two of them plus Kaspar left the clearing, heading back in the direction of the Promenade.

"Autil will not accept those women are us," Stipator said sullenly. "Corina doesn't look a thing like me. Her hips are all wrong."

"They have your sword," Arrina said. She thought he tried to shrug. She glanced at Herald. "Will she trick the crew or resort to enchanting our people?"

The big man smiled and adjusted his pose.

"Your arm must be killing you," Arrina tried with Canolos. "If you put the bow down, we won't move. Do you mind if we just sit down?"

"My arm is fine," Canolos replied. "You will remain standing, and you will wait."

"I hope they don't hurt Autil and his men," she muttered under her breath, then settled to silence. She considered what would be the fastest way back to Pithdai. It would still be at least four hours before either of them could use magic, assuming they were not dosed with saat again.

Her shadow grew almost six inches before a thunderclap rose from behind her. Herald looked up at the sky in the direction of the ship. "That's the signal."

The big Aflangi hefted his axe and walked up behind Arrina. She wondered if Sora really intended to let them live. The neck of her enhanced body could probably endure one stroke from the axe, but even the tallest tree in the rainforest could be felled with enough chopping.

The metal butt of the axe hit the back of her head, and she crumpled to the ground, feigning unconsciousness.

We'll lie here for a few minutes before chasing them down. Once the saat wears off, we'll steal their identities and get onto the ship, she thought.

It was one of the back-up plans they had discussed. Saat made it harder, but they could invent a reason for the delay.

There was a meaty thunk above her. Then another. Stipator swore once under his breath.

Canolos's talent is keeping him upright until he falls unconscious.

"This one has a thick skull," Herald noted.

"We'll take care of him," Canolos said. "Watch Arrina, Herald. She could be faking it. Tasticon, shoot his knees."

There was a long pause.

"Tasticon, obey!" Herald barked.

Stipator gasped as arrow after arrow sank into his legs. Arrina wanted to leap to his defense, but she could feel Herald looming over her, his axe poised to chop her down if she moved.

"Tell me, battlemaster," Canolos said casually. "Do you still think you can stand up, or is it safe for me to let you fall, now?"

"One more arrow to the back of the right leg should just about do it," Stipator growled, defiant.

"We don't want to kill either of you," Canolos said. "Arrina is probably only playing dead, and those little arrow wounds will be nothing but painful memories in a couple days. If either of you try to follow us, though, we will shoot you. You'll lose a lot more blood and maybe even lose consciousness. It would be a terrible loss for the Flecterran Union if you died before the saat wears off."

"What are you planning to do with the art?" Stipator asked.

"You can stop it with the folk hero act. No one out here will sing of your bravery, and it isn't as though any of us is going to tell you what you want to know so you can thwart us."

"We should get moving. He's just trying to buy time," Herald said. "Tasticon, you're rear guard. If you see them following us, shoot them."

They left, clattering over the rocks to the beach. After a few minutes, Stipator collapsed to the ground next to Arrina, his breathing ragged as he probed six different arrow shafts in his knees and thighs with his fingers. His blood dried quickly on the rocks.

Arrina slipped off both their belts and made tourniquets to stop the bleeding. The saat would wear off in just a few hours and Stipator's magic would do the rest provided he didn't lose consciousness before then.

"At least one enchantress, two Wen and an Aflangi," she told Stipator, whose eyes were half-shut against the pain. She wiped the sweat from his face and dragged him into the tent. "And they know at least a little bit about Wefal internal mystics and Senserte tactics."

"But," he whispered.

"Shhh," she said, pressing a finger to his lips. "I know what you're thinking. But are they operating on their own, or are they working for someone else?"

That question came to her even as it made her want to scream in rage. She had never wanted revenge so badly, but she was a Senserte. If Sora and her entourage had kidnapped Kaspar and stolen Pithdai's art on their own, they would face the appropriate justice. If they were working for someone else, Arrina had an obligation to punish the ones behind it all, first and foremost.

She wished she could believe she didn't have a personal interest in righting this wrong. It was easier to feel justified when she didn't know the people she was protecting.

ACT III

Chapter 14

Arrina wasted no time tallying up their possessions. Aside from the clothes on their backs and the tent Sora and her mad crew had left, they had nothing. The island had more possessions. In terms of rocks, they were as wealthy as the Godhead. In terms of water, they were wretched.

"It will rain later," Stipator rasped, head in her lap.

She couldn't let him sleep to heal until the saat wore off, so she rocked him and talked to him in the baking shade of the tent. Outside, it felt hotter. Gulinora was not on any trade route because the wind tended to ignore it.

"I'll rig something with the tent to catch water," she replied, but did not move. Nor did he object. She would also see if she could capture a lizard or two for them to eat. They would have to go to the beach before morning, and hope Jonathan and the Senserte were not running too late.

"So which of the miraklas from the throne room do you think they are actually after?" she said, tweaking his mustache. "Not that it matters, since they will no doubt find ways to abuse or make a profit off all of them, but I think it's pretty obvious. Sun's First Rising and Gates of Tremora seem unlikely, but The Kind Lady is a lot more immediately useful than Nosamae Descending."

His tongue moistened his lips. "I might believe that if they hadn't taken my sword."

"What does your sword have to do with it?"

"The basket hilt of that rapier has been in my family for two centuries. We've replaced the blade eighteen times, but what the rest of you mock is not as ordinary as you may think."

She could almost see the fat burning off his cheeks as he forced himself to sit up.

"Be careful," she warned him. "There're only lizards to eat, and I don't

144

know if I can catch them."

"I'll be fine," he said. "We just have to make it to the rain." He coughed and smoothed his mustache. "After the Nosamae War, each country took one of the miraklas needed to activate Nosamae Ascending and Nosamae Descending. Petersine didn't even exist at the time, but Wefals did. My ancestor, Bryan Premier — often called the founder of Petersine — received one of the six keys."

Arrina tried to remember Nosamae Descending. Someone was holding a sword with a basket hilt. "Theo's Sword. Mira's painted nails, how could we have never seen that before? What are its properties?"

Stipator barked an embarrassed laugh. "I should have thought that was as clear as one of Jonathan's plans. How many swordsmen do you know who can clip buttons and cut belts in the middle of a fight?"

She smiled at him. "Just one."

"Exactly. That was never me. It was the sword." He gave her a wry smile.

"Does this mean you've secretly been a terrible swordsman this whole time?"

Annoyance flickered across his face. "No, no, no. I'm still at least as good as Mathalla is. And far better than Jonathan. But you should spar with Etha sometime. It's like fighting bees."

Arrina frowned. As far as she knew, Etha had never touched a sword. "And now Sora or whoever she works for has it."

"Yes." He fanned himself. "Is it really cooler in here than out there?"

She nodded. "If Theo's Sword is such a priceless treasure whose theft could have horrible consequences, why were you just wearing it around Flecterra?" She didn't mean to sound angry, but she couldn't keep it completely out of her voice — not with Stipator. Instead, she stood up and looked for a rock sharp enough to cut rope.

"Think about it. You have a sword that makes whoever has it pretty much impossible to beat in a fight that just so happens to also be one of the six keys to a pair of miraklas that could make or break Wen or Farlander power forever. What is the safest place for it? In a museum or some palace archive? No matter how many clever protections surround it, someone always knows where it is. Kukuia and Stormhaven reached the same conclusion, which is why they hid their keys where no one would even think to look for them, even if they had the ability to identify them, which Kaftheans don't."

"Right, but anyone could have those keys now." Rock in hand, she grabbed one of the long ends of the tent ropes near a support and started cutting. "No one has stolen the keys from Sutola, Tremora, or Romina, and they're not right in front of everyone's face."

The edge in Stipator's voice could have cut the rope for her. "But someone just managed to force Pithdai to give away Nosamae Descending and half the other treasures in its archive because they knew exactly what they were, where to find them, and who had the power to deliver them."

Arrina said nothing. *Did we walk that blindly into this situation? Could Sora or her benefactor know Stipator would be here, on Gulinora, today?* It was too much coincidence.

"No one is stupid enough to steal Jacob's Bow or the Orb and Diadem of Elvenkind unless they are pretty confident of locating all the keys and one of the paintings," Stipator continued. "Agents of the custodian nation would hunt you for the rest of your short, desperate, unpleasant life. Kukuia and Stormhaven cleverly made it a complete waste of time to even attempt those thefts. That was the only thing keeping the other miraklas out of play."

"So you're saying Petersine decided the safest place for Theo's Sword was at the hip of one of their favorite sons?" Arrina asked.

"Exactly. In other countries, that might create an irresistible temptation. Wen and Farlanders both have something to gain or lose if one of the paintings is activated. But a Wefal has no direct stake in the game. In fact, we benefit from a balance between the other two races. If one wiped out or conquered the other, well, they'd be coming after us next. All that quiet fear and hatred they have toward us would stop being so subtle. Petersine knows the history before we Wefals had our own homeland — when we were the bastard race."

The word Wefal was only about three hundred years old, but Wefals had been around almost as long as Wen and Farlanders both lived in the Flecterran Valley. Before Wefals were Wefals, they had many names in Wen and Farlander dialects, most of them derogatory when translated. Half-Wen, Half-Farls and Halves were the kindest, and even they tended to treat Wefals as nothing more than "half us, half them" rather than something separate, which they clearly were. Some Wen and Farlanders still spat them out when they wanted to provoke a Wefal.

Peter Premier rejected all the names Farlanders and Wen gave him.

Wefal was a nonsense word, a kind of portmanteau of Wen and Farlander, but it was created by a Wefal. Wefals spread it among themselves. They took pride in it. By the time Bryan Premier founded Petersine, Wefals were Wefals even among the Farlanders and Wen.

Arrina looped the rope through the two holes she had cut in the roof of the tent, and pulled until it made a shallow curve in the canvas. She tied the other end of the rope to a rock. The walls of the tent leaned in a little more now, but water would funnel down the rope and they could drink it. The sky through the holes was brilliant blue and cloudless.

"I have left out one rather important detail," Stipator continued. "Originally, Petersine did keep Theo's Sword in the vault of a museum in the capital. About a hundred years ago, one of Bryan's descendants who thought like I do snuck into the museum with a replica of Theo's Sword and stole the real thing. So the museum curators think they still have Theo's Sword under lock and key. I'm not the only person in the family who knows about that, but some people in other branches of the family tree might not believe me if I told them I wasn't the one who stole it."

"Really? Do we need to keep you out of Petersine until you get it back?"

Stipator grinned. "Nah. I just made up that last part. Well, that very last part. The museum curators know Theo's Sword has been missing for a hundred years, but they've kept that a secret even from the rest of the country."

Arrina tightened the rope a little, then sat down to smile at Stipator, who smiled back. In the brighter tent, he was looking even thinner.

"Could Sora know about that?" she asked.

"She recognized it, I'm sure of it. I saw the way she appraised it at a glance. Whether she's a fraud in other ways, she knows her history."

"I was thinking that. If we have a rogue Nosama on our hands, getting Kaspar, your sword, and the paintings back could get tricky."

"Tricky?" Stipator smirked. "Nothing the Director can't walk us past, and you and Jonathan can't plan us past, and the rest of us can't act us past." He winced as he raised his hands and waved them around. "Swindle magic."

"Is that like Wen magic, or Farlander magic?" She laughed.

"No one does it better than the Senserte."

She shrugged, gazing up through the hole in the canvas, watching for signs of wind, clouds, or rain. The sky remained blue. The sun continued baking. She sighed. Tomorrow was the earliest Jonathan and the Senserte could arrive, and they would have to be on the beach for it.

A hand touched her foot, and she smiled over her shoulder at Stipator. He waggled his eyebrows at her suggestively. She pushed his hand away.

"What? There's nothing better to do."

"What of the other girl, what was her name?"

"I don't think I'm what she looks for in her men," he said with a smirk.

"You know what I mean. She's far too young to be a Nosama, but she could be an enchantress."

He rolled back, letting out a big sigh of his own. "Sora could make it look like the other one is an enchantress."

"Corina," Arrina remembered. She shook her head. "And Tasticon?"

"He's obviously under enchantment. A strong one."

She nodded. Tasticon had resisted. She heard Herald's order for him to obey again. But he had been able to do nothing about it.

"Herald has a lot to gain by problems here in the Valley," Stipator said. "I'd love to spar with him."

"He's their wild card," Arrina commented. A thread of a cloud had drifted into view. A breeze flicked the edge of the canvas. "We don't know much about his magic or his personal motives."

"Do you think they're not organized like the Senserte?"

She shook her head. "They are organized like a barrel of fruit. The Senserte are organized like...like Jonathan's wagon."

Stipator grinned broadly. "He knows where everything in it is, and anyone who doesn't is in trouble."

She frowned. "I'm leaping to conclusions. I'm scared for Kaspar. They might be like the Senserte, if whoever is behind it, if the group is big enough. Who we saw is not."

"It seems like a good conclusion to jump to. If we track down Kaspar's kidnappers and it turns out they're just really dimwitted art thieves, hey, I'm sure we'll be laughing at this in a year's time." Stipator closed his eyes and eased himself down. "We'll rescue Kaspar," he said. He looked incredibly weak.

"One more, Stippy," she pleaded. "Canolos." Another cloud slid across the sky.

The battlemaster didn't open his eyes. "He seemed downright apologetic about having Tasticon shoot my knees full of arrows, and he didn't lose his temper and shoot me one last time when I basically told him to, so he's all right in my book."

"He might hesitate to associate himself with murderers. He's the firstborn son of the archon of Seleine, but that isn't a hereditary position. Sutola wouldn't hesitate to punish him if he broke their laws."

"Seleine? That's where Jacob's Bow is."

"Another key."

"I'm so tired," he said, and panic rose in her. If Stipator was admitting to being weak, then he was on the verge of dying.

She moved his arm to one side and laid down next to him, cradling his wounded body against her own.

"Do you think the saat has worn off yet?" she said quietly, but his breathing had already eased in a deep sleep. *We'll have to chance it.* She brushed his hair to one side, smoothed his mustache. "Rest, my battle-master," she said. "We've still got a long way to go."

• • • •

The storm, when it came just before sunset, was short and hard. The water disappeared through the rocks almost before it could be caught. Arrina soaked all their clothes and squeezed some of the water into her mouth. She gauged they might each get another cup before their clothes dried. It would have to be enough.

Stipator slept deeply, but not comfortably. Arrina had not slept. Her mind was full: Sora, Corina, Canolos, Herald, and Tasticon. And Kaspar.

The way he had looked at Sora had surprised her. Her emotions surprised her, too. Had she found out about his first crush in different circumstances, no matter her age, she would have chided him and felt proud. Here, when this woman had spirited away her brother in a way that had led to the deaths of seven homeguardsmen, taken together with the clearly enchanted Tasticon next to them both, she could not help but feel enraged and a bit nauseated.

Kaspar is fine, she thought. *That's what we got out of this. And who all these people are. And we know now they want Nosamae Descending.*

That thought was another furious insect buzzing in her head that she could not swat away. No one had used Nosamae Descending since the end of the Nosamae War, but everyone knew Nosamae Ascending was the one that allowed the enchantresses to do what they had done. Why would Sora want Nosamae Descending?

Kara's voice echoed in her head. *It is dangerous to bring such things into play.* She had said it to warn the Senserte that Arrina's own father could be the person who had arranged for his own paintings to be stolen. Or his wife, Aora, who had a frigid love for her stepchildren.

Arrina forced herself to consider the thought. *If father or Aora hired Sora and her crew to activate Nosamae Descending, what does that mean?*

"It means a legacy for Kaspar. It means Kaspar is father's agent."

"What?" Stipator muttered from his sleep. His eyes flickered open.

Arrina said the next thing in her mind. "It means Kaspar's not enchanted."

Stipator sat up slowly, wincing as the muscles in his legs stretched. "Mira's discarded panties, Arrina, did you put these stones under me on purpose?" He blinked and scratched his face. "Did it rain?"

"Feeling better?" Arrina dragged herself back into the moment. "Have some water." She threw his shirt at him.

He gratefully started squeezing it over his mouth.

"How long was I out?"

"Not long enough, but we have to make it to the beach."

"What were you saying about Kaspar?"

She closed her eyes. "I was considering if my father had hired Sora and Herald to steal the paintings and activate Nosamae Descending to create a legacy for Kaspar. That would make Kaspar my father's agent in this, and therefore..."

"Kaspar's not enchanted, I heard that part. It's foolish and wrong."

"Yes, probably." She was convinced. "I cannot leap to any more conclusions. That is how we got to where we are now. From now on, we stick to the plan."

Stipator sighed and lay back down. "In another day or two. I don't think I can walk yet."

"Now," she ordered, starting to take down the tent. "You can walk fine. We have to get to the beach. Jonathan and company should be here tomorrow."

"If they're on time."

"Now, Stipator," she ordered. "You can sleep on the beach. It's much softer."

He propped himself up on one elbow slowly, and she could count the ribs on his usually well-muscled chest. "Promise?" he said, grinning like himself.

"Promise. Come on." She held out her hand to help him up.

Chapter 15

Jonathan and the Senserte were only a day late.

It rained again, which was a blessing, because the almost certainly tasty and nutritious lizards refused to hold still long enough for Arrina to capture a single one. Stipator slept the sleep of the mortally injured, and though he was no longer losing weight, he hardly had energy to lift his arm in greeting as Davur and Vudar hauled the rowboat up on the beach to gather them.

Arrina herself was sun-burnt, wiped out, and beyond exhausted. A whole day to contemplate Sora, Kaspar, and what all of it, or any of it, meant had left her imagining the world was trying to destroy her specifically.

The ad'Marusak brothers gave them water and fish before helping them to the boat, and when they finally boarded the Starfall, Arrina could hug her brother fiercely.

"I'm so glad to see you're safe," he breathed into her hair.

"Stipator, you idiot!" Zori said not far away as she examined the reduced Wefal on the deck. "What have you been doing to yourself?"

Stipator waved a hand dismissively, though he was clearly too weak to stand. "Oh, you know. Turning myself into an invisible fishman. Making my skin into armor. Getting shot full of arrows. The usual."

Zori harrumphed. "Vudar, get me some of that manioca. Lord Shot Full of Arrows here probably couldn't digest soft cheese."

"I was just telling Arrina that the first thing I was going to do when we got to safety was get blind drunk for a few days," Stipator said in a raspy voice that undermined his attempt at levity.

"Yes. You're quite the prophet," Vudar told him, handing the bowl of thick white liquid to Zori, who tipped it into Stipator's mouth.

Jonathan looked worriedly at Stipator.

"He'll be fine," Arrina told her brother. "He'll need a couple weeks without any action."

"Give me three days, and I'll be ready for a canopy dive," Stipator boasted.

"Less talking, more swallowing," Zori growled.

"What about you?" Jonathan said. "You've lost some weight."

Arrina briefly wished they lived in a colder climate where she could hide her scrawny thighs and calves. Some place where she could wear suits of metal or boots and cloaks that covered her whole body.

"Is the course set for Pithdai?" she asked.

"Yes," Jonathan said. "And don't change the subject."

She flashed a brave smile that would do Stipator justice. "I'll be ready by then. Feed me as much fatty meat and manioca as you can, and I'll spend the rest of the time asleep." She could put on a good ten pounds in a couple days by doing that, assuming the food supply held up.

Jonathan nodded. "Kara?"

"On it," the enchantress called back, ducking into the small hold.

"I take it the exchange did not happen as planned?" he prompted.

Arrina told them the story between mouthfuls of fish and swallows of manioca.

"Is Lastor with you?" she asked.

His face whole face twitched into a brief grimace. "No. He was in the balloon, so you'll forgive me for assuming he was with you."

"The ransom note said no Wen children. We told Lastor to stay behind in Pithdai."

"It's clear he didn't obey, as usual."

Arrina shrugged. "We suspected as much when he didn't show up to see us off."

"Do you have any idea where he might have gone?"

Arrina chewed on a piece of fish for a long, thoughtful moment. "Tremora."

"You think he finally got tired of being sidelined and so quit the Senserte and went home?" Jonathan asked incredulously.

Behind him, Davur, Vudar, and Zori burst into near-hysterical laughter. Jonathan granted them a smile to show he wasn't serious.

"He knows about the Pithdai Gate and Gates of Tremora. He knows he can step through them in Tremora and step out of the painting of them that Sora stole."

"No matter where the kidnappers go, he can find them just by going wherever they took the painting," Jonathan said, following her train of thought.

"Exactly," Arrina said, digging an eye out of her fish and popping it in her mouth. "Now you're starting to think like he does."

He continued. "He sends us an arrow to let us know where they are so that we can track them easily."

"And you've lost him again," Arrina said with a sigh, patting her brother on the arm.

Jonathan stared at her in open confusion.

"Anyone?" Arrina prompted.

"He tries to apprehend them himself," Zori answered without looking up from her patient.

Jonathan gaped. "But they have...and they want to steal...and the door is..."

"An enchantress, the Orb of Elvenkind, and in the same museum," Arrina supplied. "It's a terrible idea, but Lastor doesn't know what he's about to step into or what Sora really wants."

"You keep talking about them like Sora is in charge. It is possible that the Aflangi, Herald, is behind all this," Kara said from where she sat on the edge of the hold.

Arrina shrugged. "Based on what we know, any of them could be leading the group, or they might all be working for someone else. For all we know, this is a Nosamae plot."

Kara stiffened, clearly not catching the note of humor in Arrina's voice. "It isn't."

"Don't take it seriously," Jonathan told her. "She's just saying we don't know enough to punish the truly guilty. We're just swatting worker ants at this point. We need to locate the queen of the nest of rampart ants."

"Exactly," Arrina said. "We can't just chase these people around the Valley. We need to infiltrate them or turn one of them traitor against the leader. We have to find out whether they intend to activate Nosamae Descending or use the threat of it to force some other action out of the Flecterran Union. We need to know which keys they've stolen and which one they plan to steal next."

"And stop them?" Kara asked.

Arrina glanced briefly at Stipator, deeply asleep on the deck of the boat. "More than that. We are Senserte. We don't prevent crimes. We punish those who commit them and punish them absolutely." She hoped she sounded more righteous than angry.

"You mean for us to let them think they've succeeded," Zori said.

She nodded. "We need to send a clear message to anyone who might try to activate either of these paintings. The Senserte know who you are, and they will let you collect all the evidence against yourself they need to prove your guilt. And then they will punish you — mercilessly and without hesitation. No one in the world will pity you or think that you didn't deserve it."

"What's the plan?" Davur asked, sounding excited.

"We'll discuss the details in Pithdai," Arrina said. "I think we need to split up into three groups — one for Tremora, one for Romina, and one for Aaronsglade."

"Why Aaronsglade?" Zori asked.

"We don't know where Corina and Sora are from, though I'm guessing Aaronsglade. We need to find out more about them and determine if they're connected to something bigger."

"What about Sutola?" Davur asked.

"They already have what they need from Pithdai, and there is nothing for them in Aflighan. But we know Canolos is from Seleine, and we know that's where Jacob's Bow is kept. He can get them access to it, after which he has probably outlived his usefulness."

Kara's raven locks bobbed as she nodded. "They'll use him to get the Bow, and then they'll abandon him."

"Why not Kaspar?" Davur asked.

"Activating either painting requires a Farlander woman and a Wen man to recreate the marriage scene in it," Jonathan explained. "Sora probably finds it easier to control Kaspar than Canolos."

"Assuming someone else isn't behind these thefts, of course," Arrina added. "At the very least, Kaspar makes a better hostage. Father can't exactly admit publicly that he gave away Nosamae Descending to a known enemy of the Flecterran Union."

"If she thinks the Senserte are loyal to Pithdai, she is badly mistaken," Vudar growled.

Sutola and Pithdai had fought their fair share of border wars over the last several centuries. The countries hadn't had more than a few property disputes within Arrina's lifetime, but her father had sent soldiers to the border a few times during his long rule.

"There is one possibility you haven't mentioned yet," Kara said into the quiet that followed. "What if this was all Kaspar's plan? Are you prepared to take this as far as it must go even if it means destroying your father's heir?"

The other Senserte stared at her in shock for simply suggesting the possibility. Arrina waited, watching them. Kara had already shown her distrust of this decision once, and Arrina had circled these thoughts more than she should have while on the island.

"The more I learn about this situation, the more I think we should not have gotten involved in this." Kara spread her hands. "We have actually done more to help these kidnappers and thieves than we have to thwart them. If we had done nothing, they may never have assembled the keys. Theo's Sword would still be safely surrounded by more than a dozen of us. Probably Sora's group would have made a critical error during one of their heists, and justice would take its normal, boring course. As it stands, if someone not Senserte investigated what we have done and what we are about to do, they might well conclude that we are behind these thefts."

"She's right," Jonathan said, his jaw set. "This has a political dimension."

"We knew that when we chose to pursue it," Davur reminded them. "But we took a vote. We reached a consensus. You two told us the Senserte shouldn't get involved, but we ignored your advice and committed ourselves to your cause anyway."

"You can still..." Jonathan began.

"Absolutely not," Zori said in a voice like a whip as she pushed a lock of Stipator's coppery hair out of his sleeping face. "This painting is a threat to the entire Valley, not just the Union. I'm not going to trust some museum guards that haven't had a theft in a century to stop these people. They have enough magic and foresight to shut down Arrina and Stipator with just five of them. When was the last time you two came back empty-handed from a first contact?"

"Never," Vudar said. "They might not have the goals of the Senserte, but they make plans the way we do. We're the only ones who are a match for them."

"Stop it, all of you," Jonathan said more forcefully than usual. "Kara has the floor. Kara?"

"You haven't answered my question. Will you take this as far as you must, punish whoever is guilty even if the trail leads to your own house?"

Everyone watched Arrina and Jonathan expectantly.

"Yes," Jonathan said, looking miserable.

"Arrina?" Kara prompted.

Arrina steeled her will. *Of course this is not true. I am Senserte. I am the justice that punishes the ones who abuse their wealth and power.*

"Wherever the trail leads," she said firmly.

Kara nodded. "Then I will follow you both wherever you may lead and even at the risk that I will be accused, attacked, or killed for my association with you. Rest now, Arrina. I'm sorry for making your ordeal more trying than it has already been."

"She's right," Zori said. "You and Stipator need rest and food. We'll let you know when we reach Pithdai."

Arrina nodded and willed herself into a dreamless sleep.

Chapter 16

After some deliberation, the Senserte agreed to follow Arrina's plan to divide into three groups.

At the docks in Pithdai, Arrina hugged her brother again.

"It's not as though we've never been apart before," he said.

She smiled, patting his cheek. "Be careful, and stick to the plan," she said.

Jonathan, Stipator, Poresa, Kara, and Etha were taking the Pithdai-flagged ship Bronze Leviathan to Aaronsglade, a three-day sail northeast across Kaeruli Lake. Their job was to find out more about Sora ad'Serra and her accomplices to determine whether they were operating independently or working for someone else.

It was probably the most delicate of the three jobs, but Arrina had confidence she was sending the very best Senserte for the task.

He held her tight for another moment before letting go. "You know that if something unexpected happens, it will be Stipator's fault."

Michael came up behind them and made to shake Jonathan's hand. The Wefal dragged the Farlander into a close embrace.

"You'd think you two had never been apart," Arrina said, patting their arms.

Michael coughed into his hand. "Don't lose that letter to my mother, but don't use it unless you absolutely have to. It might get you out of a tough spot, but it could also land you an even worse one."

Aaronsglade was the largest city in the Flecterran Union, a beautiful, tall city of white stone and orange-tiled roofs, engulfing the isthmus it sat on with towering walls. It formed a wall between Kaeruli Lake and Maiden's Lake connected to the mainland by two large bridges over the canals connecting the two lakes.

The Senserte had been there, but they never stayed long and seldom performed. The work they did was far easier outside of the big cities, and it was generally more welcome in towns without a dedicated police force. The Watchers of Aaronsglade were all Nosamae — elite female enchantresses who made up the ruling class of Aaronma. No other city maintained such a close watch on its citizens and visitors.

"And stick to the plan," Michael added.

They all chuckled. "You too," Jonathan said, and boarded the Bronze Leviathan. Etha and Kara waved from the rail, and Arrina waved back.

Etha wanted us to give her bigger roles, and this certainly qualifies, Arrina thought.

The Nosamae of Aaronsglade hadn't exactly outlawed magic, but they enforced strict regulations on its use. Using magic required registration with the Nosamae. Moreover, each specific way the practitioner intended to use magic required a separate license and fee. A Wen who sent a message by Messegere moon shot without authorization faced fines even if she had a license to use her Wen talent. The Nosamae arrested those they caught with undeclared miraklas or enchanted objects and confiscated their contraband.

The cost of registering all the magic the troupe used in their performances would have been prohibitive even for the Senserte. Each mask would require a separate license. The ad'Marusak brothers would need to declare every one of the many minor miraklas they kept in their wagon. Lastor would probably be arrested after spending less than an hour in the city.

Arrina and Michael waited until the Bronze Leviathan had cast off before walking over to the pier where Marteurige and Jetty made their much smaller sailboat ready. Zori watched the ad'Marusak brothers load their belongings on board.

"Jetty has a very fast boat," Arrina said. "He's an old family friend, so be nice to him."

"Jetty says we can be at the mouth of the Onra River by the time that, how did he call it, wallowing behemoth the Bronze Leviathan even gets out of port," Zori said, glancing up at the morning sun. "I can handle the transportation arrangements from there."

"Romin miraklas?" Arrina guessed.

Zori grinned wickedly. "Something like that. Let's just say I raided the boys' dressers to make sure they had at least one spare pair of pants for when they wet themselves or worse."

Davur stopped near them and shook his head, a basket of bananas on one shoulder. "It isn't a secret to all of us, you know."

Zori wagged a finger at him. "Then don't you go blabbing to your brothers and ruining the surprise. None of you warned me about that bubbleberry wine of yours, either. I'm entitled to a bit of revenge."

Arrina didn't ask. She knew the ad'Marusak brothers kept a large supply of miraklan liquors in their wagon — a specialty of Sutola the way miraklan paintings were a specialty of Pithdai.

Arrina hugged her. "Be careful."

"Oh, sweetie, I was being careful for years before you could talk." Zori smiled. "Worry about yourselves. We'll send you arrows when we have news."

"Thank you."

Jetty raised the colors of Romina on his boat. He had turned out to have registrations for the ship for every Wen nation and Petersine. Michael and Arrina waved from the dock as their friends departed.

Romina's history had shaped its people into suspicious warriors. In ancient times, they had broken the invasions of the Gien Empire. During the Nosamae War, they had suffered bitter defeat at the hands of the Farlanders, and the grudge they bore their neighbor race still ran deep. They also treated Wefals as abominations of nature and left Wefal children on the rainforest to be devoured by scavengers. It was unsafe for non-Wen to travel there.

Although it laid claim to the Diadem of Elvenkind after the Nosamae fell, it never joined the Flecterran Union. Its last king had tried to convince the governing council to allow him to request Romina's admittance to the Flecterran Union, but they had refused him. The king had then disbanded the council and applied to the Union unilaterally.

But the king had misjudged the support he had from the army, and Commander General Rokia ad'Puisia had led the First Battalion against the palace in Meorna to a dreamlike success. No one was harmed, no blood was shed, and the king died peacefully in his sleep — or so the stories went. Arrina believed those tales no more than she believed Rokia had buried the Diadem of Elvenkind with the last Romin king.

That was ten years ago, and Romina thrived under Rokia, who promised that one day, when a fully mature formal democratic structure, judiciary included, was formed, she would step down. Until then, she would remain high commander. She was much loved among her people, though, and in the few foreign negotiations, even the council of Aaronsglade pressed to have her stay in power.

"It's a bit of a sad day," Michael said as they walked to their ship, Swift Wind, at the far end of the pier.

Arrina nodded. Stipator and she had recovered quickly, but all that time was spent planning, and she'd had hardly any time to be with her family. The Senserte had neither gone to the palace nor her mother's house, on the assumption that Sora might be having those places watched.

The docks bustled without thought to who walked on them. Pithdai was the largest port on the southern shore of Kaeruli. Several giant, three-masted ships bearing the colors of Aaronma and Jacobston dominated the wharves. A dozen two-masted ships of every province, including a Stormhaven vessel, filled the smaller piers, with a dozen more waiting on the lake to unload their cargoes. Arrina saw the pier master nod at them and make a note as she and Michael dodged a cart loaded with crates of nuts from Tremora.

"We're the next to depart," Michael said. "We had better hurry."

Swift Wind was a two-masted, triangle-sailed Tremor luxury cruiser, a larger version of Jetty's sloop and equally as fast. All it did was ferry passengers from Pithdai to Reqest, the port for Tremora on Kaeruli Lake. Arrina, Michael, Tajek, Mathalla, and Torminth had bought passage under false names.

The captain welcomed them aboard, and a mate showed them to their adjoining cabins. Two hours later, they had passed out of harbor, and the ship leaned precariously as the sailors sought to catch every breath of wind.

They passed the next three days exchanging stories of all the terrifying creatures that supposedly lurked in the deep waters of Kaeruli Lake. Tajek found these tales fascinating, but then he seemed to consider water of the depth they were sailing on frightening enough even without the monsters.

The Turu told them tales of miraklas in Turuna, which they instead called miramani. He spoke of giant monsters made of ice that defended his home-town. He explained about simam, the poison wind, and of Urgaruna, the lost crystal city that no one could ever find twice. He disagreed with Wen tales of the birth of the sun, moons, and stars. He spoke of golems made of stone and sand and earth, born to bring Turu children home the way air elementals brought Wen children back to their parents each night.

Prompted by this, Arrina told them about their encounter with the air elementals over the Blood Preserve, and of the strange creatures they had barely evaded there. Then the conversation came around full circle to the dangers of Kaeruli Lake. Mathalla told them about the ghost pirates.

The Shy Maiden was a miraklan pirate ship that could appear and disappear anywhere on Kaeruli Lake at the whim of its crew. Despite the name of the legend, the ghost pirates were not spirits of dead Wen. Much like Tajek's talent that made his skin impossible to cut or pierce, Wen children who would otherwise suffer a deadly blow simply vanished, reappearing hours or days later when the danger had passed. Rare Wen adults kept it as their talent. Tasticon, Kaspar's enchanted homeguardsman, had it.

Based on the accounts and legends of the ghost pirates, The Shy Maiden had a similar property and could bring its entire crew and cargo along when it vanished.

How must our stories sound to visitors from other lands? Arrina wondered. But she recalled a book she had read from Kafthey, full of conspiracy, mystery, romance, insurrection, and murder that was as outrageous as what she knew of the Blood Preserve.

They expected a direct confrontation with Kaspar's kidnappers, and so Arrina had taken most of the best fighters among the Senserte: Mathalla, Torminth, and Tajek. Michael spent the trip preparing for a battle against one or possibly even two enchantresses, including a rogue Nosama. He hardly spoke ten words to the other Senserte, even Arrina, and most of the things he said were apologies for not having time to enjoy their company. By the time they reached Reqest, though, Michael had a trunk of enchanted items for all of them.

They rented horses from the livery stable and rode to the edge of Reqest before Michael had handed anything out. They had a hard, three-day ride to the Palace of Doors, the capital of Tremora, but the road was good.

"Let's hope King Pirian ad'Remos will indulge us," Torminth said.

"He's Lastor's great-grandfather. Of course he will," Mathalla answered.

"There's a big difference between letting kidnappers come into the

Palace of Doors and letting them leave it with the Orb of Elvenkind."

Kara is right, Arrina thought as the first drops of rain fell. *If anyone investigated the Senserte without trusting us, we'd be found guilty of some horrible crime based on the circumstantial evidence alone.*

All that meant was they had to continue being worthy of the Flecterran Union's trust.

And that means following the trail wherever it goes. As soon as we're seen to play favorites, our credibility will vanish like morning mist.

Chapter 17

Like Pithdai, the capital of Tremora was spread out over many square miles, and it all revolved around a central structure. But the Palace of Doors was far more than a governmental building and home to the king. It was important enough, at the very least, to have leant its name to the entire city.

The king of Tremora's daughter, Mariah, who was Lastor's great-aunt, met Arrina and her companions when they were still two hours from the Palace of Doors. She was middle-aged for a Wen, which meant she was three times Arrina's age, and had a twinkle in her eye reminiscent of her nephew. Her pale green hair was pulled back in a tight bun, but wisps of it danced around her head.

Pirian sent his daughter to welcome us rather than having us arrested as soon as we set foot in Tremora. That's an encouraging sign, Arrina thought.

"May the grace of Mira bless you," Mariah said, hands folded as she bowed. "Welcome to the Palace of Doors. Allow me to take you into my home for the night. A meal and beds have been prepared for you, and refreshing springs are available."

Arrina returned the gesture. "And bless you, in Mira's name. We bring a gift for the people of Tremora." Mathalla stepped forward holding a gilded arrow. "May your hunt always be successful."

The middle-aged Wen brushed her wisps aside and took the arrow. "Has your father received an arrow from mine in the last few days?"

Mariah nodded even as she turned her horse back the way she had come. "We have. If the Pith seek the aid of the Tremor, we will of course accommodate you. We will speak more of this in private."

Arrina and her companions followed.

The road between Reqest and the Palace of Doors was broad enough that a broad ribbon of sunlight broke through the canopy to light it. Six wagons could drive abreast with room to spare, and three did even as they rode to the capital, carrying food and goods to the king's doors. But they were already in the city; like Pithdai, it spread all around them. Few people walked the road, but dozens of Wen could be seen in the canopy.

"Shanubu!" Tajek's amazed whisper cut through the silence.

Ahead, the jungle opened up more and the Palace of Doors rose, the mother of all the trees around it. From the outside, it appeared to be a tree with a trunk thirty paces across, its branches arching high over the jungle's canopy and studded with white flowers. Petals the size of Tajek's hands fluttered to the ground around them. The branches buzzed with Tremor children — the city's crèche, where the youngest Wen children lived until they reached the end of their first cycle.

Adults were not allowed among the branches, Arrina heard Mariah recite to her friends.

"Our children like to play tricks. I remember a game where my friend fired an exploding arrow at me to see how far I would fly before my air elemental caught me." Arrina could hear Lastor's excitement in Mariah's voice. "But something like that would seriously injure you or me."

"It's unbelievable," Tajek said. "I should tell my kluntra about this."

Mariah nodded. "I am surprised all Wen do not seclude their children like this. They are, after all, a final line of defense against danger."

Below its lowest branches, and starting as high as the tops of the wild forest around it, hundreds of beautiful carved doors covered the enormous tree, wrought from the wood itself, and ending well above their heads. Rectangular doors, round doors, square or triangular doors, double doors — there seemed no rhyme or reason to their design.

"Are the doors all like the Gates of Tremora painting?" Tajek asked.

"Very good." Mariah's eyes wandered up and down the big Turu appreciatively. "But not quite correct."

Many of the doors hung sensibly on the trunk, but dozens opened sideways or upside-down or at odd angles. A few were open.

"They will all lead us to the same destination, and none can be opened from outside the tree." Mariah smiled warmly at Tajek as they dismounted. "But, strange as this may be, our Palace of Doors has even better secrets."

Arrina had been here. Once inside, and past the narrow, interior defenses, what seemed like a tree was no longer a tree — it was a palace, a sprawling, labyrinthine structure riddled with doors, many of which did not connect to adjoining rooms. Some rooms were carved of living wood, others of packed earth or solid stone. Some said that every room of the palace existed in a different tree or underground chamber somewhere in Tremora or beyond. Others said the palace existed outside of the world, in the place the wizards of Marrishland called the Tempest and the enchantresses called the Void. In truth, not even the Tremor could say for sure.

Certain doors within the palace opened out to the trunk, where rope bridges and ladders allowed travel to the rainforest floor or to the rest of Tremora's home trees. Others, like the Pithdai Gate, led to faraway places. The mirakla of Tremora's Palace of Doors had no doubt seemed incredible and wonderful to the young Wen who had wished it into being, but it was impractical and sometimes annoying to navigate even for its residents. Some doors only worked one way, forcing those who walked through the wrong door to endure tiresome, circuitous detours. And if you accidentally left the palace through one of the trunk doors, you had to start back at the entryway.

Mariah led them to a broad wooden stairway that spiraled around one of the nearby trees. They climbed up and up until they reached a rope bridge leading to one of the lowest open doors.

"Father lives here for two reasons." By this point, Mariah had a hand on Tajek's well-muscled arm, and Arrina thought he was blushing. "First, it's a huge, beautiful place that is genuinely impressive to visitors. Secondly, it's impregnable."

"Of course, the tree is a mirakla." Tajek grinned as they stepped into the entryway of the Palace of Doors.

"You have to live here to understand. Have you heard of 'besieging the Palace of Doors'?"

He shook his head.

"It's an idiom for impossible tasks and useless effort," Mariah told him. "There is, in fact, only one means of entering the Palace of Doors that circumvents its defenses. Until recently it was entrusted to the care of Tremora's closest ally."

Here come the questions, Arrina thought.

Mariah looked over her shoulder at Arrina as she led them through doors seemingly at random. "The tale of how it fell into the hands of our enemies was not included in Larus' letter to my father."

"It's a long story," Arrina said.

"We Wen have long lives."

"Prince Kaspar was kidnapped."

"So your father explained in his letter."

Arrina breathed a small sigh of relief. Weather often delayed arrows sent using the Messegere moon shot. "And the Pithdai Gate is now closed?"

Mariah shook her head. "Not anymore. Lastor slipped through it before the arrow arrived. King Pirian hopes his great-grandson will eventually come back through the gate, but until then he refuses to bar it."

"Has no one attempted a rescue?" Arrina asked with a bit more steel in her voice than she intended. *Lastor is resourceful, but he is no match for an enchantress, much less a Nosama.*

She made a helpless gesture. "The kidnappers covered the painting with a cloth before anyone realized Lastor was missing. That blocks passage from the other side. They left a hole that is too small for a spear or arrow but large enough for them to peep out at us."

They entered the second floor balcony at the end of a long marble hall known as the Alliance Gallery. Bronze statues of famous kings and heroes stood on both sides of the gallery — the Pith to their left and the Tremor to their right. Two levels of wraparound balconies overlooked the lower level. The Pithdai Gate stood open on the ground floor at the opposite side of the hall, but the brown rectangle of a tarp filled it.

Arrina counted three dozen Tremor soldiers standing watch over the gate. Thirty stood on balconies or behind statues, bows held at the ready with arrows already nocked and ready to draw at the smallest sign of a threat. The remaining half dozen waited to either side of the Pithdai Gate with spears. All wore the red-and-blue checkered livery of King Pirian's door wardens — the Tremor equivalent of the homeguard.

"The door wardens are simply a deterrent. The Palace of Doors is still an unnavigable labyrinth to anyone who doesn't know it the way we do," Mariah explained. "However, I think you had better tell me the entire story."

Arrina lowered her head. "I would prefer to tell the king. We will need his approval to carry out our plan to restore Tremora's security and hopefully Lastor, as well."

"You already have a plan?"

Arrina looked to Michael, who nodded.

"The beginnings of one. We'll need to talk to the king before we can finalize it."

Mariah smiled slowly without showing her teeth. "My dear, I am the king's daughter and have his full confidence. If you win my approval for your plan, you have won his."

Arrina provided a detailed account of events but held back a few facts. However close their alliance with Pithdai, the Tremor did not need to know Kaspar might be in league with his abductors. She also revealed nothing about the whereabouts of the other Senserte. Arrina could see no way that Mariah or Tremora could be behind the theft of Nosamae Descending, but it was best not to take chances.

When Arrina explained their intention to let the kidnappers steal the Orb of Elvenkind, Mariah frowned deeply. "When I am told that someone means to steal a treasure from my home, my first impulse is to be more vigilant, not to leave the front door unlocked to make the thief's job easier."

Michael swept his gaze across the room once and gave a small sniff, not quite a snort of laughter, as though deciding exactly how he quickly could neutralize all the soldiers in the Alliance Gallery.

Or how quickly Sora or any other enchantress could accomplish the same.

"Does something amuse you, sir?" Mariah asked.

"These arrangements of yours endanger your nephew far beyond any protection they afford the Orb or any other object in the Palace of Doors," Michael said in his no-nonsense way.

Mariah blinked at him but said nothing.

He didn't raise his voice. "How long has Lastor been on the wrong side of the gates? Three days? Six? His abductors' patience surely has limits. Do you think an enchantress will sit idle in impotent rage while you stand your pathetic watch over this gate?"

Mariah flushed, but she looked more ashamed than angry.

For now. Don't push the Tremor too hard, Michael.

"The more time an enchantress has to prepare the more formidable she becomes." He abruptly laughed — a harsh, dismissive sound. "But an enchantress with a hostage? He has long since told her everything she needs to know to steal the Orb of Elvenkind. When next you see Lastor he will be entirely in her thrall, and you can only hope that it is merely an enchantment that binds him. Enchantments can be countered. Enchantments eventually end. But if she is a tenth as powerful as the Senserte fear the nephew who returns to the Palace of Doors will be a shattered remnant of his former self. He may behave normally — up until the point where he betrays Tremora and steals the Orb of Elvenkind for his dark mistress, of course — but the Lastor you knew will be gone forever."

Mariah looked torn between frightened and furious.

Arrina gently touched her arm. "Lastor is our friend, and we're as worried for him as you are."

Michael sighed, and the edge went out of his voice. "I fear for him because I have some knowledge of how much damage a renegade enchantress can do to mind and soul. This is not the first time I have been called upon to bring another enchantress to justice."

"Would it not be easier to set a trap and kill them when they come through the gates?" Mariah asked.

Yes, that would be easier, but it is not the Senserte way, Arrina thought, although she wasn't sure whether the Tremor would accept that. *No harm in trying.*

Arrina shook her head. "We are Senserte."

Michael spoke over her. "That would be ill-advised and could prove fatal to your nephew." He looked grim. "I'm forbidden from saying much on the subject, but oftentimes an enchantress's victims do not outlive her. I can neutralize a suicide spell but only while the enchantress still lives. Otherwise…" He trailed off.

Arrina had to fight the urge to stare at him in open-mouthed horror. He hadn't warned the Senserte of any such danger to Lastor.

Mariah pursed her lips. "How can we help?"

"Tell me more about the properties of the gates. Will magic pass through them? Arrows? Sound? Don't tell me no one has ever experimented with them."

Mariah hesitated for a moment longer, but when she gave in the words came out in a rush, like a well-practiced lecture. "Only light and living things can easily pass through the Pithdai Gate. To them it is an open door. Noises and scents do not cross from one side to the other. Inanimate matter, including miraklas, will not penetrate unless worn or carried by a human. The gate is as solid as a wall to these. As to magic, those on one side of the gate cannot be affected by the magic of those on the other."

Michael nodded. "Is it the same for the other gates in Tremora?"

She frowned. "I don't see how that is relevant."

Michael hooked a thumb over his shoulder in the direction of the door they had come through. "I need to know whether an enchantress will be able to detect soldiers on the other side of the door of this gallery. We're reasonably sure the kidnappers are only interested in the Orb of Elvenkind, but if they have a mind to assassinate the king or create other mischief it would be wise to prevent them from doing so."

"The doors in the Alliance Gallery function the same way as the Pithdai Gate," Mariah said stiffly. "If indeed this renegade enchantress is breaking Lastor as you claim she is I suggest you make your preparations quickly."

Michael nodded. "Clear your soldiers out of the room and we'll take care of the rest."

Arrina removed the rolled up letter from her pocket and handed it to Mariah. "Send this by arrow tonight. It offers an exchange — Lastor for the Orb."

"I thought your plan was to let them steal the Orb," Mariah objected.

"Yes, but we'd rather they do it at a time of our choosing," Michael explained.

Mariah didn't look convinced. "What if she refuses?"

Michael gave a mysterious smile. "I have a suspicion she won't be able to resist this opportunity. Mathalla, could you hand me the, um, special arrow?"

The Wen removed an arrow from his quiver and untied the piece of string that was all that distinguished it from the others. Michael took it and handed it to Mariah, who frowned at it.

Arrina tried to sound reassuring. "We will bring Lastor back to Tremora safely. He is Senserte, after all, as well as our friend."

Mariah turned away without comment and began issuing orders.

Chapter 18

When the last of the door wardens had left the room, Arrina turned to Michael. "Why didn't you say anything to us about any suicide spell?"

He shrugged. "However closely the Tremor and Pith are allied, do you think they would let kidnappers steal the orb and live to boast about it if they could exact bloody justice?"

"A lie."

"More of a bluff on the behalf of our opponents. Our reputations can be every bit as convincing as the magic we command." He smiled enigmaticly. "If such an enchantment existed, the knowledge of it was lost after the Nosamae War."

"I might have been able to convince her."

"And if you hadn't, this mission would end the instant Lastor was safe and we might never find out if the kidnappers were working for someone else."

Arrina didn't have a response to that.

Michael sighed and opened the small cedar trunk they had brought with them. "Not that enchantresses don't make for powerful enemies even aside from our mundane misdirections."

He removed several talismans that looked like simple wooden coins on short cords, each painted differently. Unlike miraklas, Farlander magic devices could take virtually any form, and they seldom looked remarkable. Something about Wen and Turu magic seemed to make miraklan devices beautiful to behold.

"Make sure you wear these medallions against your skin," Michael explained, handing one to Tajek. "They should feel cool as long as they're working, but they'll turn icy if an enchantress is using hostile magic on you. If that happens, it means the talisman is protecting you from all magic, including your own. Get away from the enchantress' magic, and the talisman will warm up, and you can use your own."

The big Turu put the talisman around his neck reverently. Arrina took the wooden talisman offered to her and put it around her neck. The wooden chip indeed felt pleasantly cool between her breasts.

"Another important thing to remember," Michael continued as if this was a classroom for elemental hunters. "The talismans aren't limitless. If the wood goes from icy cold to unpleasantly hot, it means the talisman's magic is almost exhausted. You have maybe a minute, maybe a few seconds. It depends on what is draining it. I've made plenty of extras, so keep spares on hand, but away from contact with your skin."

He handed a talisman to Mathalla, who handed it to Torminth. Frowning, Michael handed Mathalla another one. "If that happens, stop whatever you're doing, and get another talisman in contact with your body immediately. It doesn't have to be around your neck to work. That's just a convenient, out-of-the-way place."

He glanced at Arrina, then looked down. "If the talisman stops being cold, cool, or hot, it is no longer enchanted. That will happen if she hits you with so much magic that it uses up everything your talisman has. She might realize you have protection and decide to counter it. If one of your spares is still cool or cold, you might be okay, but if she counters the one you're wearing, she might counter all the ones you're carrying. I'll conceal a few extra talismans in places near the Pithdai Gate in case that happens."

There's a reason we call him the Director, Arrina thought, smiling. The Senserte largely looked to her for direction when it came to making and executing plans, but Michael's knowledge of the arts of enchantment made all of them except perhaps Kara look small and ignorant by comparison.

"If your talisman runs out, you are vulnerable," he warned. "I'll be countering any enchantments Sora throws your way, especially ones that might break your defenses, but if it turns out Corina is an enchantress, I might get stretched a little thin. This is important. Until you have a new talisman protecting you, don't believe your eyes, your ears, or even your skin. Anything could be an illusion."

Arrina spoke into the silence that followed. "Remember that we're here to lose the battle but take a prisoner. Tasticon is our best option. If they send Kaspar or Lastor against us, try to keep them from going back through the gate — especially Lastor."

"Lastor and Tasticon can both vanish if their lives are in danger. Should we take the opportunity if we have it?" Mathalla asked.

Arrina looked to Michael, who shook his head.

"She might dose them with saat, which means their magic won't protect them."

Mathalla and Torminth seemed not to like this answer, and Arrina couldn't blame them. Capturing an armed homeguardsman was no one's idea of a sane course of action.

"Michael should be able to counter any enchantments on them, as well, right?" Arrina asked.

"Yes," Michael agreed, but he hesitated on the end of the word. "Unless there are two enchantresses."

Torminth suddenly burst out laughing. "Michael, my old friend, you are getting as bad as Jonathan, but with Stipator's theatrics. We understand. This could be dangerous. You've given us the best tools you can, but you'll never be able to control the weather. That's nothing new to any of us."

Michael seemed unamused. His dark blue eyes were hard and unblinking as he spoke. "Wen are fond of telling Farlanders that we cannot comprehend Wen magic, especially miraklas. I won't deny the truth in that." He held up a finger. "However, it is equally true that Wen do not comprehend Farlander magic, especially the mastery of it required of a Nosama. If we face one enchantress, I am more than a match for her. Even two is not beyond my ability. But if either is truly a rogue Nosama, all of us are in deadly danger, and all I can do is minimize it. If we face a Nosama and a lesser enchantress or two Nosamae, we might go through this entire mission only to wake up at the end and discover we have been imprisoned for days or weeks — if we wake up from the illusion at all."

"You're scared," Tajek said solemnly.

"Terrified, and you should be, too. Pay attention to your talismans. Cool, cold, hot, and nothing. Nothing is the worst sign you can have. Arrina?"

"The door wardens provided us with a kind of map of the portals in this part of the Palace of Doors. The museum gallery where they keep the Orb of Elvenkind has one entrance in the ceiling that permits travel both directions and one hidden exit on the ground floor, so the kidnappers can only reach it by a single route that the Tremor will leave unguarded. I'll wait for them there and lead them through the secret exit."

"That sounds dangerous," Tajek noted with a frown.

"I don't intend to stand and fight them. The exit leads down a corridor with several other doors. It will spread them out so that Michael can subdue Tasticon, Lastor, or Kaspar. We'll let any of the others go."

"What about the rest of us?" Mathalla asked.

"Tajek, I want you on the ground floor of the main gallery in case something goes wrong. The door opposite the Pithdai Gate leads back to the secret exit. Michael, can you work up something to hide him from sight?"

He considered for a moment. "It will be a small screen and not something that moves with him. Otherwise it would interfere with the talisman."

"That should suffice."

"Then yes, I can."

"Good."

"How will I know if matters have gone wrong, and what am I to do about it?" Tajek asked.

"If the kidnappers don't simply take their prize and run, we need to convince them to retreat. We can't allow any more of us to be captured."

"Or killed," Torminth said with a grin.

"Or killed. If it looks like we just can't win, Mariah has soldiers waiting behind the other doors of the Alliance Gallery. Hopefully the appearance of a few score door wardens will frighten off the kidnappers."

"Unless it turns out to be an invading army instead of a small group of thieves," Mathalla said.

"Or a Nosama," Michael said, his mouth a thin line.

"At which point I doubt we can convince the Tremor not to use deadly force," Torminth said.

"Don't bring them into this unless you must," Arrina cautioned. "The Senserte have done this sort of thing many times. Outsiders don't always share our reluctance to spill our targets' blood, so we try not to involve them unless we've no other choice."

"I understand."

"Mathalla and Torminth, you'll be waiting in doorways just past the secret exit. When the kidnappers run past you, come out and attempt to capture Torminth or Kaspar."

"And Lastor?"

"Leave him to me," Michael said. "I assume I'll also be nearby in the corridor — close enough to observe the enchantress but far enough away not to attract immediate notice?"

Arrina nodded.

"What happens if they don't take the bait?" Mathalla asked.

"If?" Torminth laughed. "How about when?"

Arrina sighed. "If that happens, split up and regroup at the Alliance Gallery. You all know your routes back here, right?"

A few murmurs and nodding heads.

"Our objectives are the same. Capture Lastor, Tasticon, or Kaspar. Let the other kidnappers escape with the orb but make a show of fighting hard to prevent that."

"And don't die or get yourself captured," Tajek said.

Torminth turned to Mathalla. "I like this one. He catches on quickly."

Chapter 19

A trapdoor opened in the ceiling of a museum gallery, permitting a single shaft of filtered sunlight to fall on the pedestal below. The chamber's darkness seemed strange because the gallery had numerous window slits in the walls clearly intended to provide light. Yet only stars shone through them.

A rope descended into the darkness, coiling slightly at the base of the pedestal upon which rested a golden orb the size of a large orange. A figure blocked the trapdoor briefly as it climbed down confidently. Within moments, sunlight illuminated the climber.

Corina was dressed in climbing leathers — thin gloves, soft boots that crisscrossed up her calves to just below the knees, and protective straps for her forearms and knees. A utility belt held several tools for foiling locks and five three-inch-long copper rods marked with painted numerals, as well as a slim stiletto. Her braid was pinned up to her head like a crown, a few strands tickling her nose.

She touched soundlessly onto the wooden floor and scanned the darkness beyond her shaft of sunlight, seeing nothing. She could see nothing beyond the pedestal. Corina picked up the golden orb and hefted it. It was lighter than it looked. She examined the details of its surface, knowing there would be a map of the world as the Wen knew it carved into the artifact.

The Orb of Elvenkind was smooth and blank — an obvious fake.

In the darkness, Corina heard a soft slapping, like a hand repeatedly coming into contact with a smooth, solid object. She removed one of the copper rods from her belt, checked the painted number, and held it above her head. Bright light illuminated the whole chamber, as if it had suddenly been bathed in sunlight.

An all-too-familiar Wefal woman with long blue-blond hair and a rapier at her side stood between two brass suits of armor. She casually tossed a heavy-looking gold orb covered in jewels and etched borders up and down, each catch producing a meaty slapping sound.

"Looking for something, Corina?" Arrina grinned ferally.

The enchantress returned the rod to her utility belt, though the light remained, and made a small motion with her hand in Arrina's direction. Arrina's amulet went icy cold.

"Who do you work for?" Arrina asked her calmly.

Slap. Toss. Slap. Toss. Slap.

Fear flickered across Corina's face. "I mustn't," she whispered. Then she shouted. "Canolos!"

Another shadow fell across the trapdoor, and Arrina froze in mid-throw. The orb rolled over her wrist and fell heavily to the stone tiles below. Corina gave her a weak smile as she retrieved the Orb of Elvenkind.

"Trust me. You want no part in what your boss is going to get out of this," Arrina said. She couldn't move her arms or legs, but the magic didn't immobilize her mouth.

"Corina, let's go!" Canolos shouted. "She won't be alone."

"I'm not doing this for our boss," Corina said softly as she stuffed the orb into a pouch at her belt and took hold of the rope. "I'm doing this for him." She tilted her head up toward the trapdoor.

"For Canolos?" Arrina hissed back.

Corina didn't answer as she climbed. Canolos had to relax his aim to let the Farlander through, and when the moment came, Arrina grabbed the rope and climbed it as quickly as her magic would allow. She got two-thirds of the way up before Canolos cut it. Arrina had expected this, as well, though she made a good show of falling clumsily and knocking herself unconscious.

The trapdoor slammed shut. Arrina leapt to her feet. A tug on the arm of the brass armor on the right, and a door opened. She stepped through it.

"Regroup! Regroup!" she shouted as she ran down the corridor, waving her arms wildly.

Torminth and Mathalla stepped through a pair of doors behind her. Mathalla looked as though he had just won a bet.

"You heard her, gentlemen," Michael called from around a bend in the corridor.

In moments all four of them had stepped through different doors, racing along separate routes back to the Alliance Gallery.

• • • •

Arrina burst into the main gallery. The Pithdai Gate hung wide open on the other side, affording a view of what looked to be the deck of a ship. Sora and Herald stood just in front of the gate. They looked surprised to see Arrina. Sora quickly raised a hand, and Arrina's talisman turned to ice against her chest.

"Surrender!" Arrina shouted, drawing her rapier.

"You are in no position for demands," Sora called back with a sneer. "Look upon the power of the Nosamae and humble yourself!"

The gems of Sora's silver ring flashed green, yellow, and blue, and Arrina's talisman went cold again.

Her ring must be a wand. Enchantresses didn't need wands, Arrina knew, but they sometimes used them to save their strength, storing spells in them for later. Unlike the talismans or the masks, only enchantresses could use them. *But wands don't glow when they're used.*

"You came better-prepared this time, but it will do you no good," Sora said, twisting her ring.

The balcony door above Arrina banged open, and she could just make out the rasp of Michael's soft-soled shoes on the marble floor above. He didn't speak. He didn't need to. Sora's intent expression revealed the contest of wills taking place between enchantresses.

Herald noticed it, too. He removed his halfmoon axe from its loop at his belt and moved forward. He looked at Arrina's rapier, and a smile slowly spread across his face as he approached her.

"Such tiny weapons you little people have," he said. "They are like the ones our children play with when they can hardly walk."

"In my country, the children play with mountains and order the flow of rivers," Tajek said as he stepped from behind the pillar where he been hidden, directly between Arrina and Herald. He had at least bothered to wear a shirt, but his hands were empty. "Any child can play with swords and axes. It takes a man to fight without them."

More doors opened. Torminth strolled out on the ground floor to Arrina's right, his finger sliding along the blade of his sword, igniting in the warm air. Mathalla appeared one floor above him, breathing heavily.

"Where are Kaspar and Lastor, Sora?" Michael demanded, his voice barely betraying the strain of his duel with her. "This was to be an exchange — your prisoners for the Orb of Elvenkind."

Sora's mouth hung open, face a mask of concentration. Sweat rolled down one cheek.

"By coming through the gate you consented to the terms of the offer we sent you by arrow," Michael continued.

Corina and Canolos emerged from a balcony door opposite Mathalla. Sora's eyes flicked in that direction.

"Pitiful fools!" she shouted defiantly, the ring flashing again. "Your puny magic is no match for the power of a Nosama!"

Torminth's eyes went wide. He rushed forward to threaten Sora, his sword and skin an inferno of yellow flames. His sword stopped moments before striking her, ringing as it was parried by an invisible enemy — Tasticon, concealed by the other aspect of his Wen talent.

"Catch!" called Corina, throwing the Orb of Elvenkind over the edge of the balcony above Sora.

All the eyes in the room followed the orb as it fell. Sora smiled as she reached up with both hands to catch it.

A shadow fell across her as Mathalla sprinted into the empty space between the two balconies. He reached out and snatched the orb out of the air as he ran.

"Stop him!" Sora snarled at her companions on the balcony.

Mathalla turned toward Michael's balcony and brought back his arm just as Canolos fumbled an arrow onto the string of his bow. Canolos took aim, but Mathalla had already tossed the golden sphere away.

It was a clumsy throw, well short of Michael and to the right. The orb clanged off King Pithius Premier's bronze head and rolled between Arrina and Tajek.

Arrina took three quick steps and scooped up the orb. Herald roared and raced toward her, his axe moving in a blurring arc. Tajek stepped directly in the weapon's path, and sparks flew off the Turu's side where the blade hit.

"Go, Arrina," Tajek said as his fist flew into the Aflangi's jaw, throwing him back across the floor to Sora's feet.

Herald was laughing as he stood up, seemingly unfazed. Behind him, Torminth swung wildly at the air with his flaming sword, trying to find his invisible opponent.

We need to bring Mathalla back into the fight. I can't do all the acro-

batics myself, Arrina thought.

She ran toward one of the statues, intending to vault off it to reach the balcony. Her talisman suddenly went cold again. Corina had one of her copper rods in one hand, looking down at her. With a snarl, Arrina threw the orb at Canolos, instead, hoping to make him flinch. He didn't, but Corina ducked with a yelp. Arrina's amulet faded back to cool.

Mathalla abruptly regained control of his limbs, and Corina turned her rod back toward Michael.

He probably disrupted Canolos's talent.

Arrina scanned the gallery to determine where she could be most useful. She had really hoped Sora would bring Kaspar or Lastor, but perhaps the offer of an exchange had only convinced the enchantress to leave them out of this.

Herald swung his axe at Tajek over and over — torso, arms, neck. The Turu returned the attacks blow for blow — head, knees, stomach. The axe made sparks but did not move Tajek. Herald seemed to hardly feel blows that should have had him whimpering on the floor, though he sported a bruise over his left eye and a bleeding lip and nose.

It looks like Tajek has Herald under control.

Beyond the battling giants, Torminth held Tasticon at bay with the fire surrounding him. Sora pursed her lips and focused briefly on Torminth. Her spell failed, clearly neutralized by the talisman, but Torminth's fire flickered out. In that moment, Tasticon's rapier pierced deeply into Torminth's shoulder, and the wounded Wen bellowed in pain.

Arrina reached for her sword and took a step, but Sora's satisfaction was short-lived. Mathalla's fist connected with her cheek, sending her to the floor with a grunt. She crawled toward the gate while Torminth and Mathalla circled the spot Tasticon had been a moment before.

The balcony it is, then, Arrina thought as she tore her eyes away from the battle on the ground.

Magic surged through her legs as she used a statue of King Noriks ad'Pithius as a step and leaped to the balcony. Canolos and Michael had crossed swords. The Wen's bow lay on the floor, its string sliced neatly. His quiver had tipped over, and arrows littered half the balcony.

Canolos made a clumsy lunge, and Michael parried it awkwardly. Canolos staggered forward, and Michael nearly lost his balance as he stepped out of the way. Both men were poor fencers, but an expert opponent was sometimes less dangerous than an incompetent one.

Arrina drew her sword, and Canolos froze in place, eyes slightly closed.

But an enchantress doesn't need to be an expert swordsman to ensure victory.

As if reading her mind, Michael looked at Arrina and smiled to let her know he had everything under control. Then Canolos's eyes opened, and the embarrassing duel continued.

Beyond the pair, the Orb of Elvenkind had rolled along the balcony toward Michael's original position, and Corina was crawling after it on all fours. Arrina kicked one of the arrows as she walked. It rattled as it rolled past the young enchantress.

Corina looked over her shoulder and saw Arrina coming toward her with sword drawn. Her eyes went wide as she rolled onto her back. She scrambled back as she yanked another of the copper rods out of her utility belt.

Arrina's talisman went cold and then cool. Corina discarded that rod and pulled out another. The talisman went cold, but Arrina only continued her slow, menacing approach. Another rod and another. The Orb lay forgotten on the floor.

At the edge of her vision, Arrina saw Torminth clutch at his throat, his eyes bulging. She feared the worse, but there was no blood. He staggered over to one of the statues and removed one of the hidden extra talismans, relief flooding his features. Sora's look of triumph turned to irritation.

"Get it, and let's go!" the elder enchantress shouted.

On the floor between them, Corina continued to empty her supply of copper rods at Arrina, and then she simply focused her will at the approaching Wefal.

Lastor's head appeared from behind the railing on the second floor opposite of Arrina. His smile was beyond manic, even insane. In spite of that, she was glad to see him on this side of the gate.

"Michael!" she called, pointing.

He nodded, and Canolos lowered his sword.

The sound of tortured steel dragged Arrina's attention to the ground floor. Herald's axe had shattered against Tajek's magically protected chest. The Aflangi had torn the arm off one of the bronze statues. As Arrina watched, Herald hit the Turu with it, the metal ringing in the air as if he were futilely sawing at a slab of granite with a bread knife.

Tajek's grin suddenly melted as he touched the talisman under his chest, and he backpedalled away from Herald as quickly as he could. Near the door, Sora smiled at him.

"Arrina, behind you!" Michael shouted.

He needn't have bothered. She heard the sound of cloth rustling violently as it fell toward her from the balcony above, could feel the wind that rushed up to meet the descending figure. Arms wrapped around Arrina from behind. Her first impulse was to throw the attacker off the balcony with enhanced strength.

"Work with me, sis," the assailant hissed in her ear, and that distracted her just long enough for him to throw her off the balcony.

Kaspar's face looked down at her as she fell. Arrina clutched for her magic to brace her body for the landing, only to realize her talisman was still freezing cold. Michael's gasp was practically a shriek. She tried to right herself, but there was no time.

The air below Arrina rushed up to meet her, cushioning her fall mere inches before she landed. She looked up at Kaspar with questions in her eyes, but he had already turned away from the balcony. Her amulet felt like it was on fire.

She reached a hand into a pocket for a spare but found it neither warm nor cold. One of the enchantress's spells must have removed its magic.

I need to avoid attention for a moment.

The nearest spare talisman was under a loose floor tile just beyond where Herald and Tajek still fought. Herald had finally discovered Tajek's invulnerability only extended to metal and was in the process of pummeling the Turu with bare fists that struck with impossible strength. Tajek's left arm hung limp, and blood dripped from a split lip. The Aflangi's body had taken substantial punishment, too. He was limping, and one eye had swollen shut.

Arrina grabbed her rapier where it had fallen a few feet away and got to her feet. Staying clear of the melee, she took a few uneasy steps toward the hidden talisman.

Canolos gave a cry. Michael must have released control of the enchantment when Arrina had fallen. The Wen jumped from the balcony railing, landing in front of her with a slight dip of the shoulders, his sword held at the ready.

"I will not let you harm her," he hissed, launching into a series of swift attacks.

Arrina gave ground, watching his movements even as she tried to puzzle out what he was talking about. He was limping noticeably. The fall had been an imperfect one, and he had twisted his ankle landing. As she tried to circle with him, Canolos cut her off, clearly trying to prevent her from moving past him.

Does he know my talisman is at the end of its power?

Then Arrina realized Canolos was the only thing left standing between her and Sora, who was again engaged in a silent battle of wills with Michael on the balcony. The Wefal fenced with the young Wen carefully but not aggressively, afraid that she would hurt him badly before he played his part in Sora's plan.

Or at all. He's obviously loyal, smitten, or both. He's not the motive force of this group.

Tasticon had become invisible again. Having both taken painful injuries at the point of homeguardsman's sword, Mathalla and Torminth had grown desperate. They formed a wall of whirling steel, shielding themselves with rapiers even though they couldn't see their attacker.

On the second floor balcony, Corina gave a cry of triumph. A moment later, she and Kaspar jumped down to the ground floor. Lastor did not follow them. Arrina caught a glimpse of a golden sphere cupped in Corina's hands before she and Kaspar ran past Sora and through the Pithdai Gate, appearing on the deck of the ship beyond.

"Canolos, Herald," Sora called urgently as she drew out a reed tube.

The young Wen feinted clumsily and toppled a nearby statue into the space between him and Arrina. He hobbled quickly through the gate after Corina and Kaspar.

In one quick movement, Sora put the tube to her lips, pointed it in Michael's direction, and blew. A small dart flicked toward the balcony, and Michael gave an alarmed cry.

Herald punched Tajek one last time, flinging the Turu backward. Then he turned and retreated after his companions.

"Tasticon, rear guard," Sora said, and then she stepped through the gate, as well.

"Michael!" Lastor shouted overhead. The enchantress had apparently dispelled whatever enchantment had held him.

What have you done to him, woman? Arrina thought fiercely, but rather than racing over to Michael, she charged toward the gate.

She saw nothing between it and her, but Mathalla and Torminth hadn't suffered further injuries, so she could guess that the enchanted homeguardsman would intercept.

The perspective of the Pithdai Gate tilted abruptly, now pointing directly at the ship's deck. The boards whipped down the wall like some miraklan waterfall.

Arrina's fingers clutched the cord around her neck as she ran, pulling the talisman out of her shirt. It burned without in her hand. She toughened her skin as much as she could.

The perspective flipped again, and the gate looked up at a clear sky. Seagulls wheeled overhead.

The tip of Tasticon's sword should have plunged into her shoulder, but it glanced off the carapace she had grown under her shirt. Arrina feinted with her sword. The talisman cord snapped in her hand, and she hurled it in the homeguardsman's face.

Tasticon flickered into visibility. Behind him, Gates of Tremora plunged into water and started to sink. The surface above it was a wall of sunlight flickering and flashing.

Tajek hit the side of the homeguardsman's head with a large fist, knocking him sideways and prone. Arrina had not even noticed him come up behind her.

The painting sank slowly — a precious mirakla that symbolized the peaceful union of two of the most ancient Wen nations. On the balcony behind her, Lastor shouted Michael's name again.

Arrina put up her sword, called on her magic, and dove through the Pithdai Gate.

Chapter 20

The shock of the cold water was not nearly as bad as the sudden disorientation. She dove sideways through a door and down toward the bottom of a lake. Suffocating liquid and a burning in her eyes Arrina had fully expected, after all. Almost immediately, though, arms flailing, she oriented herself in the water and pushed toward the surface.

Arrina's magic was already working, already growing gills on her neck and a protective coating over her eyes. She glanced all around, looking for the ship. Sora's group had changed ships — a fast-moving racing yacht instead of the sturdier hull that was the Promenade. Arrina couldn't see its name, but it did not look nearly large enough to carry all the paintings they had demanded as ransom.

They must have sold or hidden the others.

As her eyes adjusted to the brighter light, Arrina noticed figures standing on the stern. One of them pointed at her, and she remembered she no longer had the protection of Michael's talisman. She took a deep, unnecessary breath and dove, kicking webbed feet.

The water was murky. She couldn't see the painting. For a panicked moment, she wondered if it was sinking faster than she could swim. Assuming the thieves hadn't left Kaeruli Lake, the bottom could be very, very far beneath the surface.

Some Wen legends claimed there were parts of Kaeruli that were bottomless, and the terrible thing about Wen legends was many of them turned out to be true. She thought about the creatures in the Blood Preserve, which reminded her of the ghost pirates of The Shy Maiden. And that made her think about sea monsters.

Arrina kicked her webbed feet harder and tried to push that thought out of her mind.

There could be currents down here that would push a large, flat object farther than they would a smaller, humanoid one.

She remembered a game she and Jonathan had played with coins and a glass aquarium. The trick was to drop lei and chel into the water and try to get them to land on the little ceramic castle at the bottom. It looked easy, but the coins flipped and slipped sideways as they sank. In the end, they had lost interest. After an afternoon of the game, only one coin had reached its destination.

Jonathan's magic would make it easy now. Arrina wished not for the first time that her brother could have been with them. *They'll need him in Aaronsglade even more.*

A glimmer below her and several yards to one side caught Arrina's eye. She squinted at it as she kicked closer. She could see hints of daylight, like a well-lit room in the afternoon — the way the gallery was illuminated.

The light vanished again as the painting flipped over in the unseen currents. Arrina maintained her course, hoping it would eventually turn back toward her. Her body politely warned her that the pressure was more intense than she had designed it to endure. She reinforced it, shedding another half-pound of body weight to pay the price of her magic, and swam on.

There it was again. She kicked vigorously, shedding a few ounces more weight to add to her speed. It flipped again, but this time she could see a beam of light shining out from it. It couldn't be more than thirty feet below her, though it seemed to be tumbling almost as quickly as she was swimming.

Flip. Its light shone in her eyes, momentarily dazzling them. Flip, and she still saw after-images for several seconds. Arrina thought she saw its light fall on the lake bed. Flip. She closed her eyes against the light and swam on.

I must be close to shore. I can't be more than a couple hundred feet down.

Flip. She opened her eyes, and this time the light shone into endless depths below the painting's face.

I must have imagined it, she thought, but doubt crept in.

She swam down a few more feet. Her hand brushed some falling object. Flip. Arrina caught it halfway through its longwise turn and stopped her descent. The sunlight shone out from the painting like some miraklan lamp. The painting was too large for her to grab both sides from this angle, so she contented herself with clutching one end desperately with both hands. She turned herself upright and began her ascent.

The painting's light flickered out into the water beyond, where Arrina could make out the shapes of fish as numerous and varied as one would expect of a place so near Wen habitation. They came in as many shapes, sizes, and colors as the wildlife of the rainforest. Most were perfectly ordinary collections of a few fins and a wide mouth. Others glowed slightly or seemed to flicker in and out of existence. Arrina saw a pair of snakes with scales of bright red, orange, and yellow slithering through the water as if it were land.

Mira's endless variety, Arrina thought as she slowly made her way upward. She hadn't thought through her next step with the painting. She couldn't very well tread water forever, and if she went through the painting and back into Tremora, it would sink again. *Once I get it to the surface, I can make a plan.*

A few fish swam through the painting. No doubt they were flopping around on the floor of the Alliance Gallery. It was a strange sort of fishing net, for sure, but some of the fish were probably safe to eat, and fried fish sounded very good right now. The day's action had taxed her reserves.

The light fell across a surface not far below her. It had the colors of stones and algae, but Arrina knew with absolute certainty that the bottom of the lake had not decided to follow her to the surface. Even worse, it was moving sideways with a patient, almost lazy, undulation. Then it narrowed to a long, slim tail of brown and green, below which was nothing but murky water.

A moment later, the current of the thing's passage rocked Arrina, nearly ripping the painting out of her grip. Its light tilted ever so slightly, and Arrina saw the bottom edge of an enormous bottom-rear flipper. It was moving farther away, but it was also ascending.

If her body had still been adapted for it, Arrina would have gulped. Instead, she started to swim more frantically, her blood feeling suddenly cold in her veins. The pressure on her chest and ears lightened somewhat, and the water grew less murky.

Arrina knew she needed to slow her ascent to prevent diver's sickness. Magic could keep her from dying of it, but she had expended too much energy already. She hovered about halfway to the surface, taking advantage of the pause to get a better grip on the painting. A few motions of her arms and legs, and she managed to turn it so her fingers could clasp both ends. The back of the painting blocked her face. Arrina frowned and used her feet and knees to slow it as she let the painting slip through her fingers until she could see again.

The diffuse sunlight beam illuminated an eye twice the size of Arrina's head. Its pupil contracted, and an enormous, lizardlike head at the end of a sinewy neck turned toward her. She got the impression of huge, many-toothed jaws that reminded her of stories of the sharks who lived in the ocean. The maw didn't look quite large enough to swallow her whole, but there was no mistaking her role in the predator-prey relationship.

With heart pounding in her aching ears, Arrina resumed her ascent. The sea monster swam toward her inexorably but didn't appear to ascend quickly enough, whether because the sunlight from the painting was blinding it or because it had a cat's instincts for playing with its food. Either way, Arrina was more than a little relieved when its jaws snapped closed fully a yard below her feet.

Illuminated as it was by the light from the painting she held in her arms, Arrina got a long, close-up look at the creature. It had a lizard's head as big as she was. Its eyes stuck out of the sides of its head on short, fleshy stalks. The underside of its skull was an enormous jaw like that of a shark, complete with row upon row of daggerlike teeth. Its long neck was not quite as wide as she was, but it stretched out fully ten feet, where it attached to a wide, flat torso with scales in the pattern of the lake floor. This trunk continued for twice the length of the neck before tapering off into a long tail with a ruffled dorsal fin ending in a tail fin at least six feet high.

It passed underneath Arrina at the same slow pace, and this time the wake of its inexorable passage sucked her down and sent her spinning like a slow top. She fought the current for several long seconds before stabilizing enough to resume her upward path.

She couldn't see the lake monster. The light of the painting illuminated only schools of smaller fish.

It could be right behind me.

Arrina bit back panic and pirouetted in a slow curve, the beam of light scanning the water around her like the beacon of a lighthouse.

Nothing.

She tilted the painting at an angle and circled, slowing her ascent but shining the painting at the water below her.

Enormous jaws loomed up out of the darkness from below, reaching for her. Arrina's eyes went wide, but she twisted clear, feeling the scales of its neck rub rough and sharp against her arm.

She thought briefly about drawing her knife and stabbing it or even, more desperately, of grabbing it around the neck where it couldn't bite her. She dismissed both options instantly. Her grip on the painting was tenuous enough. If she let go with either hand, it would slip away into the depths once more, and she wasn't sure it was safe to attempt a second dive.

The top of the creature's torso slammed into her, sending Arrina spinning along its length until she was too dizzy to tell up from down. Then the monster's wake sucked her sideways.

The painting slipped from her hands, and she barely caught it with her knees before it tumbled beyond her reach. She struggled for several long seconds to regain her grip on the painting. This time she kept the face of the painting carefully pointed toward the departing sea monster.

I can't afford another surprise like that one.

Her heart was pounding, and she felt slightly light-headed, which she feared meant she was using up air faster than her gills could collect it from the water around her.

The sea monster rolled over on its back, exposing a broad white belly and showing off one set of huge forward flippers and two sets of stabilizing pectoral fins. It arched its neck and body, turning into a vertical, downward dive.

Maybe it lost interest, Arrina thought as she kicked slowly upward. She could use magic to slow her heart rate, but she knew that might be an exchange of one route to unconsciousness for another. *Better to stop exerting myself so much and recover before there is any more excitement.*

She continued sweeping the painting's light in horizontal and diagonal arcs as she ascended. Its beam was less distinct by virtue of the waters being less dark.

I must be near the surface, she thought with no small amount of relief.

Then she remembered that the surface was still somewhere on Kaeruli Lake, probably far from land. She couldn't very well hop back through Gates of Tremora, or the purpose of coming here in the first place would be lost.

One crisis at a time, she told herself.

She glanced upward and realized she could make out the silvery white surface of the lake as it undulated only a few yards above her. She surged upward, feeling as if some unseen current was pushing up from the bottom of the lake.

One is, she realized almost too late.

Arrina glanced down in horror even as she tried futilely to swim clear of the massive jaws rising up from the depths directly below her. She tucked her knees up behind the painting, which was the only thing that kept her from losing both feet as jaws like a massive steel trap closed over canvas and frame.

Any other painting would have splintered and torn instantly, but Gates of Tremora was a mirakla, so ordinary rules did not apply. Nor could the sea monster gulp it down whole, since it was wider than its neck even at its shorter dimension.

Arrina took what advantage she could of the monster's confusion at biting something its jaws couldn't swallow, crush, or maim. She clutched the top half of the painting desperately, keeping its seven-foot length between her and the creature's teeth. The sea monster made an attempt to fit more of the painting into its mouth, failed, and tried again with the same result.

It pulled the painting with the attached Wefal down to the depth of its huge torso, but Arrina remained elusive.

Mira's golden sandals, I hope it doesn't decide to dive.

But when the sea monster resumed swimming only a few seconds later, it stayed at the same depth, perhaps twenty feet below the surface, while it worked out the problem of the morsel on the other end of the unbiteable painting. Arrina suspected it couldn't stop swimming for very long.

It might also be too dim-witted to realize that no matter how long it swims, I'm not going to come any closer to its jaws.

The creature's mouth opened slightly, and for a moment Arrina held out hope that it was going to let go of the painting. But it still had it wedged between the sides of its mouth.

I feel like a piece of fresh meat hanging on a long stick in front of a starving panther.

Then she felt something thick and rubbery brush her ankle from behind the painting.

A tongue?

Arrina rolled onto the front side of the painting, balancing on the edge of the frame to keep from falling back into Tremora. She peeked over the back edge of the painting and saw a many-suckered appendage sliding along its surface.

A tentacle.

That gave Arrina pause, but she didn't have much time to respond to it, for the tentacle slipped around to the front of the painting, seeking her. Arrina pushed against the current at her back, her legs kicking out of the creature's reach.

The painting isn't going anywhere while that thing's jaws are around it, Arrina thought, letting go with the hand nearest the tentacle and drawing her knife with it.

She crouched against the top of the frame, knife held at the ready. The tentacle snaked forward, and she slashed at it. The tentacle withdrew just as quickly, dark red blood dribbling out in a tiny cloud where she had cut it. The monster's eye stalks waved in irritation.

Without warning, it started to descend.

No! Not now.

Its mouth tentacles probed the canvas as the monster dove. The shimmering underside of the surface faded from Arrina's sight. The light from the painting shone in the creature's mouth and illuminated its eye stalks. The tentacle passed through the surface of the painting.

Arrina tried to slash at it again, but she was barely still holding onto the frame, and the blade fell well short.

All at once, a large cloud of blood exploded out of the surface of the painting. The tentacle withdrew into the monster's mouth, but only a ragged stump remained of it.

One of the others must have cut it off. They've probably been watching this the whole time, but even Lastor's magic isn't ideal for an underwater fight.

The painting lurched as the sea monster flung it clear of its jaws. It snapped once at Arrina's leg, and she only barely managed to interpose the painting between her and its jaws. As it swam past her, Arrina stuffed the knife back in her belt, gripped the painting tightly in both hands, and braced for the wake.

The creature's tail swatted her to the side in the monster's eagerness to leave, and that actually pushed Arrina clear of the strongest of current. Now she had a plan. Arrina kicked into a steady ascent. As the sunlit surface came into view, she felt the water groan around her as if the lake itself were in pain.

You were probably more curious than hungry, but if you hadn't been so stubborn, you'd still have your mouth tentacle, and I'd be breathing fresh air by now.

At long last, Arrina's head broke the surface. She desperately wanted to take a deep lungful of the surface air, but she wasn't convinced the sea serpent was gone for good. Instead, she lifted Gates of Tremora as far above the surface of the water as she could. It was only about halfway, but that was enough.

Mathalla leapt out onto the surface of the water, his arms and chest bouncing off the waves as though some invisible skin covered its surface. As the Wen got to his feet, Lastor jumped out of the painting as well, skidding along the surface like it was covered with a layer of soft mud on a rainy day. Mathalla took the painting out of Arrina's hands.

"Where to next?" he asked her.

Arrina tread water at his feet and glanced around them. Sora's yacht was probably a mile away. They could chase after her, but that was beside the point just now.

Dangerous, too. I don't have my talisman, Lastor never had one, and if Mathalla's activated, he wouldn't be able to walk on water like this.

"Head away from Sora's group and find the nearest land or ship you can," Arrina told him. "We'll use the Pithdai Gate to meet you there."

Mathalla nodded.

Arrina felt another groan in the depths below, vibrating her abdomen. *It's coming back!*

She reached for the edge of the painting, and Mathalla accommodated her, though he couldn't actually lift her out of the water.

"Watch out for that lake monster. I think it's angry at you for cutting off its tentacle."

"That wasn't me," Mathalla said.

"It's coming back?" Lastor cried cheerfully, clapping his hands together. "Then I'm going to ride it!"

Arrina didn't bother commenting. Instead she dragged herself through the painting and onto the slick pile of fish and blood on the other side of Gates of Tremora.

Chapter 21

"Where's Michael?" she demanded the instant she stood up, gills and flippers gone.

The Senserte stood together, still breathing heavily.

"I'm here, Arrina," Michael's voice called down from the balcony where he had fallen only a short time earlier. He sounded groggy but not exactly at the point of death. "Sleep toxin, I think."

Arrina let out a heavy sigh of relief. She wanted to run up to him, throw her arms around his neck, and cover his face with kisses, but she contented herself with collapsing into an exhausted heap on the floor, heedless of the many-colored fish flopping on the tiles all around her.

"What of you?" Tajek asked, laying one enormous, black-skinned hand on her shoulder.

"I'll sleep well tonight and eat even better," she said. "Did we accomplish what we set out to do?"

Torminth pointed at where Tasticon lay on the floor, seemingly asleep. The large lump on the back of his head told her the homeguardsmen hadn't been rendered unconscious by one of Michael's enchantments. "Throwing the talisman at him was a stroke of brilliance. You countered his unseen presence talent and broke the enchantment on him at the same time."

"Only because the enchantresses didn't cast any other spells on me afterward," she confessed. It had been a reckless, impulsive action. "Sweeten his lips. We need to ask him some questions when he wakes up. Maybe he only served them under enchantment, or maybe he had some other reason for going with Kaspar instead of leading the other homeguardsmen to the prince before he could leave the palace." She hated even suggesting that one of the homeguard might be less than absolutely loyal.

Torminth nodded and moved to do just that.

"Where is Mariah?" Arrina asked as she realized Lastor's great aunt and her soldiers were not in the gallery.

"Still waiting in the wings," Torminth said as though answering an innocent question, but the look on his face told her he understood her completely.

"Michael. Analysis?" Arrina prompted.

"I have good and bad news," Michael said from above, his voice still thick with drowsiness. He peeked between gaps in the balcony railing, propped up on one arm. "Both Sora and Corina are enchantresses."

"We also have two enchantresses," Tajek noted.

Michael's head bobbed slightly, but when his forehead touched the marble rail, it took him an obvious effort of will to raise it up again. "That's the bad news. I can assure you however, that neither is a Nosama."

"That must be a relief to you," Arrina said.

Look at us — too weak even to sit up and still playing our respective roles from the floor, she thought, smirking slightly.

"Of course. I was willing, of course ... wherever the trail leads, you understand."

Tajek sat down on the toppled statue with his shirt rolled up and pressed to his mouth. He clutched his side, which showed dark bruises even against his black skin. "You worried that we might need to punish your Nosamae."

"I was worried we would have to punish *a* Nosama," Michael clarified. "That would have been a daunting task, I assure you. I hold quite a high rank for an enchanter, but even the least of the Nosamae could reduce me to begging for bananas in the streets of Stormhaven. If we set out to punish *the* Nosamae, well, quite frankly I don't think we could do it no matter how clever we got."

"We'd need Nosamae Descending," Arrina supplied.

"Yes," Michael agreed. "Over the course of our fight, I performed some analysis of both their tactics. They might have hidden strengths or deliberately played to their weaknesses just to lull us into a false confidence, but I don't think so."

Always careful to strew caveats and disclaimers ahead of any statements you make about other enchantresses, lest you claim more knowledge than you have, Arrina thought with a wry smile.

"We understand you're speculating," Torminth assured him from where he had finished pouring a small amount of saat into the unconscious homeguardsman's mouth.

"The younger one, Corina, appears to be a generalist. Some of the magic she used is uncommon outside of Marrishland, and though she clearly uses wands, they lack the, um, nuance of the devices I create for you. Our Sora is an almost pure charmer. Of that I have very little doubt. Were it not for the talismans, she may have added all of us to her little gang of art thieves."

"That would explain how she convinced the crew of The Promenade to take her somewhere other than Pithdai," Arrina agreed.

"Generalist? Charmer? What do these words mean?" Tajek asked. "Are they like the talents of Wen and Turu?"

Michael pulled himself up, gaining whatever measure of a lecturer's dignity he could while sitting on the balcony floor and talking through the openings in its railing. "All enchantresses must learn the basics of all Farlander magic." He trailed off, looking up into Tajek's earnest face. "Do you really care?"

"Absolutely," Tajek said, while Torminth and Mariah shook their heads. Arrina held up a hand to conceal her smile.

"Think of it as learning a craftsman's trade," Michael said, then stopped. He raised a finger, then dropped it. "Look, there's a lot of techniques and spells, and no one can be a master of all of them. So people choose. I'm an artificer; I specialize in enchanting objects so they have magical properties. Kara's a diviner. She mastered all the ways to collect information."

"It overlaps," Arrina interjected. "Kara enchants objects, too, and Michael knows some ways to collect information."

"But my skills with artificing are broader, and Kara doesn't have to enchant to collect information."

"So that's diviner and artificer. What are charmers and generalists?" Tajek asked.

"Generalists don't have a specialty. Some of them make a conscious choice to learn a little bit of everything, but most simply never received a formal education after graduating as enchantresses." He tugged at an earlobe. "Charmers are far more dangerous. They can force people to do their bidding."

"That's what the Nosamae War was about," Arrina said.

"Yes. It's not forbidden, though, but nearly all enchantresses frown upon it. Wen and Farlanders alike remember how enchantresses abused the specialty in the wars."

"That would be your begging for bananas comment," Tajek noted. "How can it be that your Nosamae have not forbidden such arts?"

"Some think they should, but most charmers don't bow down the innocent. They're quite often used as jailors or police. A single charmer can instantly stop a brawl or halt a thief's escape without so much as a bruise given or received. Such enchantresses can force out the truth in a court of law without resorting to threats, which greatly simplifies matters. Executions are extremely rare because a charmer can prevent criminals from repeating their crimes." Michael said it all as if this was the most normal thing in the world.

Not that Pithdai can criticize Aaronsglade's law enforcement, Arrina thought, remembering the horrible fate of that poor fisherman who had abducted her. That reminded her of the task Stipator, Jonathan, and the others had in Aaronsglade. *If the Nosamae catch them in the act, will I recognize what returns to me from Aaronsglade, or will a charmer steal away Stipator's ability to lie?*

"He's coming to," Torminth announced, and all attention turned to the homeguardsman.

Tasticon tested his bonds once, his mouth moving as he realized his lips had been sweetened. Arrina dragged herself toward him.

"Tasticon, do you know who I am?" she asked.

His eyes were neither haunted nor in the least bit concerned. He spoke as if he had been asked this a hundred times. "Stop testing me. I've already told you I won't betray him."

"Sora's enchantment has been broken," Arrina assured him. "Prince Kaspar has been kidnapped, and we need to rescue him."

Tasticon snorted a laugh. "Why don't you save your doubts for Herald, Sora? You can't still believe he's helping you out of friendship. Or Canolos. Do you think him incapable of jealousy?"

Arrina frowned and glanced up at Michael, who was watching the interview with a frown of his own. Tasticon abruptly slumped into a doze.

"Didn't the talisman break the enchantment?" she asked.

Michael looked extremely disgusted. "This isn't magic. It's a charmer trick. Sora knows some of the darkest secrets of her craft."

"This enchantress can control a man's actions without magic?" Tajek demanded, aghast. "And you say charmers should not be banned?"

Michael's face was a storm, his voice cold. "I assure you that a charmer who would do this without due cause will not go unpunished."

Arrina had never seen him like this. It was a little like how he had spoken of enchantment in the wagon in Mattock, the near-bravado with which he had explained why he did not teach magic to Etha more quickly. But this was not an act.

I think I would rather be hunted to death than suffer whatever sentence Michael would pass right now.

She was used to the ruthlessness with which Stipator and Lastor dispensed punishment. She herself seldom showed mercy once the Senserte had determined guilt and passed sentence. But this was a strange attitude to see in Michael.

"Can you undo what Sora has done?" Arrina asked quietly.

Michael shook his head, the storm still on his brow. "He believes all of this may be an illusion intended to trick him into revealing his motives. She has probably staged many opportunities for him to betray her, and he has learned to reject them. Whether or not he was loyal to Sora at the start, he will remain unfailingly loyal to her as long as he believes this is just another test. It is far easier to do than to undo. Even with a charmer, he may never recover."

"Poresa could do it."

He considered this for a long moment. "Possibly. It would mean slicing out weeks of his memories, though, including many of the ones we actually need intact."

Arrina pursed her lips. As far as she knew, he was right. Poresa didn't like talking about that element of her magic, though. She bent her mental powers to telepathic links and detecting lies, but Arrina knew the mental mystic had occasionally needed to remove memories. As with charmers among Farlanders, it appeared such things were frowned upon by mental mystics.

Torminth and Tajek looked slightly uncomfortable at the topic of discussion, and Arrina thought she knew why. For them, magic was a child's defense against danger, and by the time they were old enough to abuse their magic like Sora or Poresa could, they had already lost it.

"I will continue questioning him," Arrina announced. "Can you make me look and sound like Sora?"

Michael shook his head. "I got a good look at her face, but she didn't say much. You're probably better off playing the tempting illusion."

Arrina nodded. A moment later, Tasticon woke and regarded her with unimpressed eyes.

"I see you still haven't bored of this illusion," he said.

"You said I shouldn't trust Herald. Why?" Arrina asked, trying her best to be haughty.

Tasticon's lips twitched into a smile. "Now you take interest. You may have noticed he is an Aflangi — an official envoy of the Godhead, no less. Aflighan has long had its eye on its neighbors to the south. He would welcome another civil war, especially one that breaks the power of Farlanders or Wen to wield magic. All those Wen provinces on the northern border of the Valley ..."

"You think Aflighan means to invade?"

"I think Aflighan will invade if you carry out your plan."

"What plan?" Arrina asked.

She had hoped that might convince him she wasn't Sora, but the homeguardsman only shook his head with a knowing smile. "Temptations within temptations."

It seems pretty obvious that it involves one of the two paintings from the Nosamae War.

"And Canolos?"

"He certainly knows the truth about you and Prince Kaspar by now. Canolos must suspect that his friend is now his rival for your affection. Your protestations of using the prince as a shield against King Larus sound flatter by the day."

Mira's shapely calves, what has Kaspar gotten himself involved with?

"What of Corina?"

"She's really the least of your concerns," Tasticon said with only a small tremor in his voice.

A lie. Arrina said nothing, though.

"I'd be more concerned about keeping Prince Kaspar on your side. His continued good health is the only thing keeping King Larus from sending the entire Pith nation after you. You heard what happened to the last royal kidnapper, didn't you? Sixteen hours he ran. Thirty-six hours more before they let him die." Tasticon quirked a haughty smile. "That was for an illegitimate daughter. If my prince decides you are no longer worthy company, your execution will take far, far longer."

Arrina resisted the urge to wince. *An exaggeration,* she told herself. *He's probably trying to protect Kaspar even now.* That made sense. Sora no doubt still needed Canolos to steal Jacob's Bow, but Kaspar was no longer essential.

"What can you tell me about Arrina and her companions?"

"They are well-meaning children playing at being heroes. Clever and stubborn, certainly, but no match for a Nosama."

Arrina made a surreptitious gesture in Michael's direction, and Tasticon slumped.

Torminth spoke first. "Homeguard don't receive a lot of training in espionage, do they?"

Arrina choked out a laugh and threw a dead fish at him. The Wen ducked it easily.

"Interesting that he even bothered to lie," Michael mused.

"A misdirection," Arrina suggested. "Notice how little time he spent on Corina?"

"It sounded like he's trying to sow discord between Sora and her companions," Torminth noted. "You're right, though. He didn't plant any doubts about her."

"Does your father have Farlander spies working for Pithdai?" Tajek asked.

"Possibly, but I doubt any are enchantresses," Arrina told him. "Michael, is it possible we're not the first ones investigating this?"

"I can't be certain, but I find it unlikely in this case. Corina is too young for a Nosama, and the Nosamae would not send anything less than one of their own. Besides, the Nosamae are not Senserte. If they knew Sora intended to restart the Nosamae War, they'd arrest her and all her associates immediately."

"Even if one of her associates is the heir to the throne of Pithdai?" Arrina pressed him.

Michael hesitated. "A fair point, but that still doesn't make Corina a Nosama."

"Why is Tasticon protecting her?" Arrina asked.

"You missed it!" Lastor shouted at them cheerfully from the Pithdai Gate. "I was riding the sea serpent and waving at you, but nobody was watching, and then it went back into the
lake."

The gate opened into the interior of some structure made of cut limestone blocks. Mathalla stepped through a few moments into Lastor's rant.

"Where was it?" Michael asked the big Wen.

"Phantom Lake. I put it in the lighthouse at the mouth of the Sut River."

Heads nodded. Phantom Lake was situated in a space between Petersine, Pithdai, and Sutola, a few dozen miles southeast of the Blood Preserve. The Sut River came down the mountains and passed through Seleine on its way into Phantom Lake.

"As we expected, they're going to Seleine for Jacob's Bow," Arrina said.

Jacob's Bow had belonged to a famous Farlander hero — the only Farlander ever to win an archery contest against Wen bowmen. The legends disagreed on how he had done it or whether his bow had been a mirakla before the contest or long afterward. How it had ended up in a town in Sutola instead of somewhere in the country named for Jacob also remained the subject of legends.

"What next?" Mathalla asked.

"If we follow them too closely, we risk catching up before the others are in position," Torminth noted.

"If we let her get too far ahead, she'll have time to obscure her trail," Michael said.

"We need proof," Lastor broke in. Everyone looked at him in some surprise, but he ventured forward. "We're Senserte, right? We only punish the person in charge. We have to make sure Sora isn't someone's dupe."

No one spoke for a long minute.

He's right. Until the moment someone — Farlander or Wen — attempts to activate one of the two paintings, we can't know with certainty who is really behind this.

"We'll give them two days' head start." *More than that fisherman had, but is that less cruel or more?* "We need to recover from our injuries anyway."

Lastor nodded. "I was gonna say you look pretty terrible, Arrina."

She grinned at him. "How good of you to notice."

It's true, though. I'm not even fully recovered from the canopy dive.

The young Wen grinned. He struck a formal pose he clearly had not yet mastered. "Welcome to Tremora. Allow me to take you into my home for the night. I will prepare a meal and beds for you. There is a clean river a couple rooms away, if you would like to bathe yourself." He eyed Arrina with an impish smile. "Although it looks like some of you have already had one bath today."

"Thank you, brother," Arrina responded with easy formality. "We will accept your hospitality."

Lastor beamed.

"We ought to tell your family that you're safe," Arrina said. "Your aunt was worried about you."

Mariah did not look worried, but considering how carefully she examined Lastor for any sign of injury, she clearly had been. That the exchange had succeeded seemed to please her somewhat, although she remained cool toward the Senserte until they showed her they had reclaimed Gates of Tremora. This unexpected windfall occasioned a relieved sigh from her and the Tremor door wardens.

Their heir is safe, and the inviolability of the Palace of Doors has been re-established, Arrina thought.

The Tremor closed the Pithdai Gate against any surprises. Lastor begged his great aunt to let him serve the duties as host, and Mariah acceded to this request almost gratefully.

Clearly a busy woman.

Once the Senserte were alone again Torminth spoke up. "We should exchange arrows with the others, weather permitting. The gate could be helpful in that."

"Two skies make for two chances at clear skies," Mathalla agreed.

Still not likely during the rainy season, but any news would be welcome.

Michael joined them just outside of the gallery. He was walking a little unsteadily, but so were most of them.

"Aren't any of you going to ask me what I found out about Sora and the others while I was with them?" Lastor asked cheerfully as he led them through seemingly random doors and into impossible rooms.

"We had assumed you were under Sora's spell," Tajek said.

Lastor shook his head. "I was pretending."

Arrina looked to Michael for confirmation.

"There was an enchantment on him."

"It was a disguise," Lastor persisted.

"It's not impossible," Michael admitted. "It's possible to create an illusion of a charm, but it's seldom useful."

"It was fake, I tell you!" Lastor snapped, petulant now. "Are you going to argue with me or let me tell you what I found out?"

No one spoke for a long moment, so Lastor began talking.

Chapter 22

Lastor stepped through the Pithdai Gate from the Palace of Doors and into the murky, damp hull of a ship. The smell of moldy wood and rotting fish assailed him, and the deck bobbed and rocked under his feet.

His momentary blindness woke his magic, and a pair of hanging lanterns suddenly flared to life. They had no oil in their reservoirs, but that made no difference. Had there been no lamps at all, the lamplight would have found him.

The hold was piled high with dozens of paintings, in far different order and location than when he had first jumped through the Pithdai Gate. Most were still covered in their waterproof tarps, but the motion of the ship had uncovered a few. The covering of Gates of Tremora lay on the floor a yard away, deliberately pulled aside.

He listened. His Wen hearing devoured all the sounds of the ship around him. He heard the crew calling to each other, passing orders and information. Most of the sailors sounded Pith, but a few others were sprinkled in. Except … Lastor held still and really listened. The voices were wrong. They lacked emotion. They didn't curse or joke as ordinary folk did while they worked. He sifted through them all, seeking something useful.

Two men spoke near the bow. One had a deep, gruff voice with a strange accent. The second Lastor recognized as the clear, proud voice of Canolos, Kaspar's friend.

"I don't think it's an act, Herald." Canolos sounded exasperated. "She can't keep her hands off him. She's barely even looked at me since we left Pithdai."

"Enchantress or not, she's still a woman. She knows she needs you more than him. Who cares who she beds, as long as she marries you?" Herald sounded irritated, tired of the argument.

"Maybe I should find a new farl bride!" Canolos hissed sharply.

"You fool. You need her far more than she needs you. Defy her, and you'll envy the homeguardsman."

"I already do. He at least gets to watch." A small snort of laughter. "Perhaps they let him join in, sometimes."

Herald clearly had no patience for this. "Keep your eyes on the goal. Once you've activated the painting, all Wen will regain their childhood magic, and you can do what you like to the farls. Subjugate them. Butcher them. Breed with them ..."

"Never that," Canolos interrupted, sounding disgusted by the prospect. "I'll not sire any mules."

• • • •

"Did Canolos really say that?" Arrina demanded.

"Not exactly, but he may as well have," Lastor said evasively.

"But that's not what he said," Michael prompted. "Are you stretching any other details?"

Lastor blushed and let out a long-suffering sigh. "You're ruining my story." When no one leapt to his defense, though, he spoke hurriedly. "Canolos and Herald really are plotting to use Sora to activate Nosamae Descending. They're afraid of her, too."

"Was this Sora's plan or one of theirs?" Michael asked.

Lastor looked to Arrina. "Do I have to answer questions now, or can I tell the rest of my story?"

Arrina waved him on.

• • • •

Another pair of voices reached Lastor's ears — Kaspar's and a woman's.

"Rowing is harder than I thought," Kaspar said. "My back and shoulders are sore, and look at these blisters on my hands."

"I tried to warn you," the woman chided. "You'll have a few days shipside to recover. I'll try not to wear you out too much along the way."

"I'm looking forward to seeing Aaronsglade," Kaspar said, seeming to ignore the hot sultriness of his companion. "How high up is the third tier of the city?"

"You'll see soon enough," she said. If the rebuff bothered her, she didn't let it slip into her voice. "We won't stay long, though. We must go to Seleine."

"Seleine? I thought …"

"I hadn't explained the next step to you yet," she said. "But you will hear it now. Tasticon, move. Let Kaspar sit next to me."

There was a pause as the players in the room rearranged themselves.

"That's much better," she said. "Here. Let me rub out those knots while we talk."

"Seleine?" Kaspar prompted.

"Oh, yes dear. One of the museum's pieces is there, too. We'll drop anchor two days east of the city."

"That wouldn't happen to be Jacob's Bow, would it?" Kaspar asked.

"We'll make an art specialist out of you yet!" the woman cooed.

"Sora, darling, you know the connection between it and both Nosamae Ascending and Nosamae Descending." A note of betrayal tinged his voice. "People might accuse us of trying to activate one of them."

"Jacob's Bow belonged to the Farlanders long before the Wen stole it, you know."

"Sutola's champion won it fairly in an archery contest."

"No matter how it made its way to Sutola, it belongs to the Farlanders."

"Will you pretend to kidnap Canolos to convince his mother to give it to you, or do you mean to steal it?" Lastor frowned at the heat Kaspar used.

"Neither, my love," she said placatingly. "Canolos has promised to convince the leaders of Seleine to give it to me."

Kaspar seemed soothed. "It's an irreplaceable national treasure. Why would they do that?"

"My dear, you know I love you, don't you?"

"Of course, darling."

"Then please don't take it the wrong way when I tell you Canolos thinks I intend to marry him."

"What?!?" Kaspar sounded both shocked and wounded.

"Now, now. You knew when we met that you weren't my first."

"It's not that. It's just …"

"Just what?"

"Nothing."

"You say that, but these knots in your shoulders don't agree that it's nothing. Does it make you jealous to know I was your friend's lover?"

"Was?"

"I've fallen out of love with him, though he's clearly still mad for me. All that time in bed with him was becoming wearisome. He's such an impulsive man, prone to tantrums. I knew that if I told him my feelings had changed, he would renege on our agreement. I kept up my little charade for the sake of the museum, but then I met you, and I knew you would be my last as surely as I would be your first."

"What did you tell him instead?"

Sora gave a small, cool laugh. "I told him I was seducing you to get Gates of Tremora, of course! And now that we have it, I've convinced him that I'm keeping you around to keep your father from sending his homeguard after me. Canolos practically grew up in Pithdai, so he fears King Larus even more than most of Pithdai's enemies do."

"Your object is to activate Nosamae Ascending, isn't it, Sora? You know I won't be party to that. When my brother and sister catch up with you …"

"The Senserte aren't coming. They're all dead."

"What? How?"

"Herald oversaw the execution of Stipator and Arrina. Poison for the others. I have my agents."

"You monster!" Kaspar cried.

Sora merely purred in response. "Oh I do so love it when you call me nasty things, my prince. Do sit down while I change into something more suitable to the occasion. I don't want you to hurt yourself when my wicked enchantment finishes bringing you to heel."

"What about Lastor?" Kaspar demanded through gritted teeth.

"Still at large, I'm afraid, but my servants will catch him eventually."

There was a sound like the cracking of a whip and then grunts of pain.

• • • •

"Lastor!" Arrina shouted with a laugh. They sat at a dining table in a glass dome underneath the crèche; Mariah insisted it was impervious to the Tremor children frolicking above with jets of flame.

The young Wen winked. "I just wanted to make sure you were paying attention." He nibbled on an ear of corn. Arrina snatched another half-chicken from the tray.

"We are," Michael assured him. "Which portion of that was actually true?"

"You guys are no fun at all sometimes," Lastor declared with a pout. "Sora was at least pretending to be in love with Kaspar and plotting to trick Canolos. It doesn't sound like Kaspar knows Sora is trying to activate a painting, but it sure seemed obvious to me, so unless he's stupid he should figure it out soon, right?"

"And the lie about killing the Senserte?" Torminth prompted, sticking a forkful of roasted poultry from his plate into Mathalla's mouth.

"I think I like yours better," Mathalla murmured after swallowing. "Trade?"

"I made that up, too," Lastor confessed. "Oh, and I don't think Sora charmed Kaspar at all — not that I could tell, at least."

"Anything else?" Arrina asked.

"They really did have sex," Lastor told them cheerfully.

"Did it involve a whip?" Mathalla asked innocently as he and Torminth swapped plates.

The young Wen sighed heavily. "No. I made that up, too."

"Well thank Mira for small mercies," Arrina said with a laugh. "Tell us the rest of your story."

• • • •

Lastor quit listening.

He stood in silence in the ship's hold, staring at the paintings. He knew he could merely grab them all and send them back to Tremora, but that would put Arrina's brother in danger. No, he couldn't leave the ship without bringing Kaspar back with him, but he needed a plan. He waited in silence, listening for Kaspar and Sora to resume their conversation. The key to unraveling the enchantress's scheme must be there.

A hand covered his mouth an instant before he felt a dagger blade at his throat.

"Don't struggle, and you won't be harmed," whispered an unfamiliar woman's voice in his ear. "Who are you?"

The hand moved away just enough to let him speak. Lastor knew he could escape whenever he wanted, so he decided there was no risk in telling her the truth.

"Lastor ad'Remos."

"You're with the Senserte. You came through the Pithdai Gate, didn't you?"

"Yes."

The blade left his throat.

"Why would you do such a thing?" She sounded urgent.

"I'm here to rescue Kaspar."

"You should go right back through that painting and close the gates on the other side. Sora thinks we can sneak into Tremora through the front gate and find the Orb of Elvenkind by just asking directions, but the Palace of Doors is completely impregnable."

He slowly turned to face her. "Don't you work for Sora?"

"Yes, which means I really shouldn't help you." She slid the dagger back into its sheath between her breasts and heaved a sigh. "I'm Corina ad'Michelle of the Aaronsglade Art Council, Acquisitions Department. Your Senserte friends probably don't believe that's who I actually work for, but if they listen a little while longer without interrupting, they'll realize that's exactly how our conversation went. You won't find out the truth until later, so neither will they."

"I think your boss plans to activate Nosamae Ascending. We have to stop her."

"We can't. She's a Nosama, which means she's much too powerful even for both of us to fight."

Lastor puffed out his chest. "You might be surprised what I can do."

"I could have incapacitated you before you even knew I was there, and I'm not a tenth the enchantress Sora is. Besides, if we attack her, all the Nosamae will come after us, and we definitely can't fight all of them."

"The council is behind this plot?"

"I don't know." Corina sighed heavily. "She lies to everyone about everything. She offered to take me on as her assistant, even though I barely graduated as an enchantress. She told me it will put me on the quick path to becoming a Nosama like her, but she doesn't seem interested in teaching me anything. I know enchantresses often treat apprentices a little like servants, and I really do want to be a Nosama, but some of it is a bit, well, demeaning."

"So she has Kaspar under her spell?"

"Not the way you think." Her eyelids dropped demurely. "He's actually in love with her, the poor boy. He's afraid of what his father will do to her if he escapes."

"Which means I can't really rescue him, because he won't want to go."

"Exactly."

"Does he know she told King Larus that she had kidnapped him?"

"The ransom note was his idea. He also told Sora everything he knows about the Senserte — their identities, abilities, and methods."

"Why?"

"He doesn't want any of them to get hurt."

"What does he think will happen if Sora activates Nosamae Ascending?"

She shrugged. "He doesn't believe me when I tell him that's what she's doing. She's convinced him that she's stealing back art that belongs to the Farlanders for her museum."

"Her museum?"

"She's the head curator at the Nosamae War Memorial Museum."

"Is she, or is that another one of her lies?"

"At the least, she can walk in and out whenever she wants. I've seen that with my own eyes. I helped her set more wards on the exhibits. She seemed worried about thieves."

• • • •

Arrina stood up. "Lastor. Is that another half-truth?"

The younger Wen tilted his head in confusion. "Which part? She didn't actually talk about how the Senserte were going to interrupt my story. I thought that was pretty obvious."

"The museum," Arrina said emphatically. "Does Sora run it?"

"Well, yes. Why would I lie about something like that?"

Mathalla and Torminth were already on their feet and racing toward the exit, bows and quivers in hand.

"What's wrong?" Lastor asked, sounding as worried as he looked confused.

Arrina pressed her hands to her temples. "Jonathan and many of the other Senserte might be in terrible danger. We thought the Aaronsglade Arts Council was something Sora made up, like our disguises."

"Oh," Lastor said.

Michael rubbed Arrina's back gently. His voice was soothing. "Kara and Jonathan won't go in blind. You know that."

He's probably right. Kara's research will turn up Sora's name, and Jonathan will call off the whole thing.

Stipator was a part of that group, too, though.

He might smell a challenge in it and venture in without enough back-

up. He's probably regained a lot of the weight he lost in our first encounter, but he's not at full strength, and he doesn't have Theo's Sword anymore.

Then there was Etha.

Every bit as eager to prove herself to the rest of the Senserte as Lastor but with none of his Wen invulnerability.

That left Poresa.

She respects Jonathan but pretty obviously fancies Stipator at least a little bit. If it came right down to it, which one would she follow?

That assumed she would take a side at all. Poresa tended to get frustrated in situations where other people were arguing instead of working together.

She can literally see both sides in any argument, and that can paralyze her when she needs to be decisive.

"Do you want to hear the rest?" Lastor asked timidly.

Michael stood behind Arrina's chair and massaged her shoulders. "Please continue."

• • • •

"Why should I trust you? You work for her."

"She pays me well for my skills, but that doesn't mean I want a Nosamae Empire."

"Why not? It would make your magic more powerful, too."

"During the Nosamae War, it was just Wen versus Farlander, but now we have the Wefals to consider. With the power of Nosamae Ascending, we can easily beat the Wen, but the Wefals, too?" Corina shook her head. "Ulangoshi has an army of Wefal mystics, and Petersine has no shortage of them."

"You're afraid of the Wefals?" Lastor asked. This seemed like a strange worry to have.

"They could turn the tide against us. Internals make even more convincing disguises than enchantresses, making them perfect spies and assassins. The telekinetic powers of external mystics are formidable. And mentals?" Corina shuddered.

"I guess they might be able to make you forget how to use magic, since it's something you have to learn to do."

"Yes. And all that is assuming she succeeds. If she fails, such an obvious plot by an enchantress to bring us back to the Noasmae War would be much worse for all enchantresses. The Wen still don't trust us, and even the Farlanders remember the abuses of the old Nosamae. I don't want to spend the rest of my life in hiding."

"Why keep working for her? Are you afraid she'll succeed and then track you down to wreak horrible revenge on you for betraying her?"

"A little. But mostly it's ..." Corina trailed off, a blush creeping into her cheeks. "Kaspar."

"Kaspar?"

"I used to be adventurous like he is. I fell in with people I naïvely thought I could trust who got me in trouble. The things I did, the enemies I made. I can never go home." She trailed off again, and when she spoke again it was in a rush. "But none of that matters to him. He says everyone deserves another chance. No one is beyond redemption. And if I've turned away from who I used to be he sees no reason why he should dwell on it."

Lastor's brow wrinkled as he tried to puzzle this out. "And Sora?"

"Yes." She managed a wry smile. "He says he can make her a better person if he loves her enough. She treats him better than she used to, and I'm not ungrateful for that even if it means I can't have him like that."

"Oh. You mean you fancy him."

She nodded slowly.

"My friends and I will have to rescue you both, then."

"But she's ..."

"No match for us," Lastor interrupted, striking a heroic pose. "But we need to find out more about her first."

Corina pursed her lips and considered this offer for a long moment. "I have an idea. If it works, you'll be able to spy on Sora safely, and it might even help convince Kaspar that Sora isn't going to become the person he wants her to be."

"I like plans that involve me," Lastor said with a grin. "What is it?"

Corina smiled mysteriously. "It will take me a day or two to work out the details. It's not exactly something I learned in training. Can you come back through the gates the day after tomorrow?"

"Can't I hide out here?"

She shook her head. "Too dangerous. You've already been here too long, and they'll miss me if I don't come back up soon."

"Fine, then," Lastor agreed with a small pout. "Day after tomorrow."

• • • •

210

Lastor suddenly broke off his story to take a drink from his juice glass.

Michael was looking at him intently. "What happened next?"

Lastor smiled sheepishly. "The next part was kind of weird and boring at the same time. When I came back, Corina cast a spell on me. She had a complicated explanation for how it worked, but it didn't make any sense to me."

"What did it do?" Michael asked.

"It charmed me without charming me. You know how enchantresses can make someone do whatever they want?"

Michael didn't dignify that with a response.

"Um, well, usually the person being charmed can't help themselves. They just obey without question. This was different. It was more like a little voice in my ear telling me to obey, pretend to fall asleep, beg for mercy, or whatever, but it didn't make me do it. Corina said as long as I listened to that voice, Sora wouldn't know I wasn't actually charmed."

Michael seemed to consider this. He smiled in clear appreciation. "That's an interesting solution to an unusual problem. I'm not sure I buy her 'barely graduated' story. That was a clever bit of composition in not a lot of time, especially for a generalist."

"Are you sure the Nosamae aren't already investigating Sora?" Arrina asked.

Michael shook his head. "She's still too young to be a Nosama. If she turns out not to be the one behind these thefts, though, I'd like a word with her about her educational prospects."

Arrina eyed him. "That almost sounded dirty."

Michael blushed. "No. Nothing like that. I just mean I'd like to assess her abilities."

Lastor burst out laughing. "What kind of abilities would those be?"

"Would it be a private interview?" Arrina asked, joining in on the teasing.

Michael sat down in his chair with a short harrumph, crossing his arms in silent protest. "Please continue, Lastor."

• • • •

"What have you brought me, Corina?" asked a woman's voice that was at once cloying and irritated.

Sora had black hair heavily mixed with gray, as well as blue eyes rheumy with the partial blindness of old age. Wrinkles creased her face like a whithered and dried out fruit — crow's feet as broad as river deltas, smile lines that dwarfed the mouth they flanked, and a forehead so craggy that it made the topography of mountains look like the head of a drum. Her hands were like skeletal claws upon which spotted, shriveled skin had been hapharzardly hung, complete with yellowed fingernails that resembled those of a toothless and blind dog.

She dressed scantily in tight black leather shorts and a matching too-small halter, neither of which could quite conceal the sagging of her wrinkled breasts or enormity of her butt. Her clothes certainly emphasized the varicose veins in her legs and the hairy moles that blemished leathery arms. She wore enormous, heavy-looking silver earrings that had long since pulled open holes in the lobes big enough to stick her finger through. The black, rawhide whip completed her costume perfectly.

• • • •

"Are you going to let me continue?"

Mathalla clapped Torminth's shoulder as they fell against each other laughing. Arrina swiped some bread along the bottom of her manioca bowl and suppressed her own grin.

"We already saw her," Michael said. "Can you finish with no more exaggerations?"

Lastor nodded with a broad grin. "Sure."

• • • •

"I captured him in the hold with the art," Corina said. "He came through the Pithdai Gate."

"That's Lastor," Kaspar said. "He's one of the Senserte."

The prince of Pithdai wore comfortable clothes of superior quality — no doubt brought with him when he ran away with Sora. Loose-fitting shorts, an embroidered blue tunic he hadn't bothered to lace, and sandals with straps studded with small gems. His thin silver crown looked like vines braided together with leaves, and the rapier at his side had an all-too-familiar basket hilt.

Lastor wanted to ask him what he was doing with Stipator's sword, but Corina's spell warned him against it.

"They still defy me?" Sora demanded, flushing in rage.

Kaspar shrugged. "Of course. That's what they do."

"Perhaps I should send your father the finger I promised," Sora growled, but she took Kaspar's hand in hers and patted it. "Not yours, my love. One of the crew will certainly have fingers like yours we can use."

Again, Lastor wanted to object, but the spell stopped him. He raged silently.

"I don't think that's necessary," Kaspar told her with a lover's smile.

"Have you questioned him yet?" Sora asked.

Corina shook her head. "Not in detail."

"But you at least have him charmed."

"Of course, Ma'Sora." Corina assured her deferentially.

"Let me look. You're not exactly a charmer," Sora said quickly, like a mother fussing over her not-very-bright daughter's schoolwork.

Sora scrutinized Lastor carefully, no doubt with magic. Standing behind her, Corina was as tense as the springs in one of Jonathan's mechanical contraptions. At the end, though, the aging enchantress nodded.

"This is more complicated than it needs to be, but I guess that's only to be expected from a neophyte like you."

"I wanted to make him obey you as he does me, Ma'Sora," Corina said, her voice quaking.

"Kneel," Sora commanded.

Lastor obeyed without question. He kissed the woman's warty feet for good measure. Sora took a large step back, and Lastor crawled toward her on hands and knees, lips puckered to continue. Fortunately, Corina's spell seemed to make it easier for him to suppress his laughter when Sora took another step back, this time taking cover behind Kaspar.

"Stay," Corina said.

Lastor obeyed, sitting back on his haunches and holding both hands against his chest like the paws of a dog. He panted slightly but resisted the urge to bark.

This spell really has no sense of humor, Lastor mused in a pout that never reached his face.

A smile crept across Sora's face, and she came out of hiding. "We'll make a Nosama out of you yet, Corina. Tell me, is he housebroken?"

The spell warned Lastor that lifting a leg at that moment would not be taken well, so he refrained, though it took an effort of will.

Corina opened her mouth to reply, but Sora had already lost interest in her.

"Tell me, Lastor. Are your friends coming through the gates, next?" Sora asked.

"No, Ma'Sora," Lastor said in a faraway voice, as if he were not aware of the sounds he was making. "They don't even know I'm here."

"How well do you know the Palace of Doors?"

"I grew up in it, Ma'Sora. I know every door."

"Do you know where we can find the Orb of Elvenkind?"

Lastor saw Kaspar's brows knit in consternation, on the point of objection.

"Yes, Ma'Sora," Lastor droned. "I can lead you to it."

Sora's smile broadened. "And so you shall, but first I want to know everything you can tell me about the Pithdai Gate, the place where the Orb is kept, and all the ways to move between them."

Lastor began speaking. When it was done, Sora had Corina cover up the painting of the Gates to prevent anyone from coming through and confined Lastor to the hold for the remainder of their voyage.

Corina came down a few times a day to bring him food and drink and to renew her enchantment. They dropped anchor outside of a Farlander town Lastor didn't recognize to transport Pithdai's miraklan paintings to a racing yacht. At first, Lastor assumed it was Sora's, but it soon became clear that she had never set foot on it before.

"She had to get rid of the Wen crew," Corina had explained to him in furtive whispers while the other members of Sora's group were otherwise occupied. "She couldn't keep them charmed forever."

When they reached Aaronsglade the next day Sora left Corina on the yacht and forbade Lastor from leaving the hold while the rest of them unloaded most of the paintings. Once they set sail several boring days later, Lastor's wind magic became the yacht's main source of propulsion. Canolos knew how to sail, but he seemed content to put forth the minimum necessary effort. Lastor gathered they were on the east side of Lake Kaeruli, travelling west and south as swiftly as the ship could navigate the waters. He noticed Herald had not come with them from Aaronsglade.

By the time the yacht left Kaeruli and entered Phantom Lake, Sora declared that it was time to put their plan into action. Instead of the ruses and manipulations the group had used to acquire other works of art, this would be a straightforward, smash-and-grab burglary.

Corina and Lastor had agreed beforehand that if there was any resistance in the palace, that would be his cue to allow himself to be left behind so he could carry his information to the other Senserte.

· · · ·

"And that's it, really," Lastor concluded. "The rest you know."

Michael and Arrina nodded.

It isn't nearly as bad as we feared, but is Sora at the top of the food chain, or is she working for someone else?

She knew they wouldn't be certain until someone tried to activate one of the paintings.

Just then, Mathalla returned. "Clear skies over Tremora tonight."

Arrina and Michael let out sighs of relief.

Hopefully it's the same over Aaronsglade. The sooner Jonathan gets our message, the better I will feel about this.

Chapter 23

Their two days in Tremora dragged out into nearly three because a storm had settled over the lighthouse like an angry elemental. More than once, Lastor wondered out loud if it was the same elemental they had crossed in the mountains.

Arrina retained hope that word would come from Jonathan, but she was not entirely surprised when no arrow arrived from Aaronsglade. The group of three Wefals and two Farlanders would have to find a Wen to send an arrow, which would be hard enough, but finding one willing to break the Aaronsglade ordinance and risk crossing the Nosamae would be next to impossible.

She worried about them, but she also trusted the soundness of Jonathan's judgment to keep them out of trouble.

As long as they don't run into the arms of Sora's allies, whoever they might be.

They received four letters from Zori on the second night, though. That seemed to hint at quick reversals of circumstances, but at least it meant they had not been captured or killed. She unrolled the first and read it to the Senserte.

> *Arrina,*
>
> *Larus's Gift has already reached the Onra River, and we will be in the Palace of Morning Mist at dawn. We should be able to find transport from there to Zerlerin. I really don't want to go there again, but Rokia isn't going to hand over the Diadem of Elvenkind to us just because I ask her for it, and if someone already stole it she has every reason to lie.*
>
> *The one bright spot is that if Davur and Ravud can just keep their mouths shut for a few more hours*

Vudar's reaction should be hilarious. Almost makes the
prospect of a trip to Zerlerin worth it. Almost.
More news when I have some.
Until then, I am yours truly,
Zori ad'Korona

"Palace of Morning Mist?" Lastor asked. "I thought they were going to Meorin."

"They're two names for the same place," Mathalla explained.

"And Zerlerin?"

Mathalla shrugged. "The Romin have their secrets just as we do. It's an old word for 'Palace of Tears,' but I couldn't say where or what it is."

"Probably another Romin city," Torminth suggested.

Tajek recited something softly in his native language, and heads turned his way.

He smiled sheepishly. "My apologies. This is a story from Aelkindom I have heard before. I will try to translate." He recited in Wenri. "The children of the First Empress wished for thirteen floating palaces, and magic granted their request. The first was the Palace of Morning Mist — Meorin in Elven. The second was Berin, the Palace of Fog. The third and fourth were Toverin and Dammerin, the Palaces of Lightning and Thunder. The fifth was Zerlerin, the Palace of Tears." He paused. "I can't remember the names of the rest, but they were all cities or fortresses hidden in clouds."

Michael looked thoughtful. "Do the stories say anything more about Zerlerin?"

Tajek shook his head. "Only that many called it by another name — Gaherin."

"The Palace of Ghosts," Mathalla translated.

"Cheerful," Michael said drily.

Lastor crossed his arms in a pout. "I can't believe I missed out on a palace full of ghosts."

Arrina shook her head in disbelief and unrolled the second letter.

• • • •

The four Senserte climbed to the canopy with the nimble sureness of Wen who had lived in the trees their whole lives. It didn't hurt that the vines and branches bent and twisted their way into Zori's hands and under her feet, so the Marusak brothers needed only to follow her. Even the fading light posed little impediment to their ascent, as Ravud saw in darkness as easily as in daylight.

Nevertheless, there were a few muttered curses now that no Farlanders or Wefals were around to hear them. Most of them came from Vudar.

"Haven't you Romin discovered how to make ladders yet?" he growled. "I mean I know you just invented the wheel like thirty years ago, so that's probably asking a lot, but a ladder's really a simple contraption."

"What's the matter, baby brother?" Davur asked from several yards above.

"He just misses his elemental," Ravud, in between the two, said.

"You know, you're going to need to get used to this idea that hard work may occasionally be required of you," Davur called back, fingers probing for the next handhold as Zori's foot left it. "Besides, what kind of Sutol is afraid of heights? What would father say?"

Vudar winced as the rough bark of the tree scraped the skin off one knuckle. "I'm not afraid of heights, and climbing trees isn't hard work," he objected. "I'm just saying there are more efficient ways of getting from floor to canopy than this."

"Ropes, pulleys, and platforms?" Ravud asked with a snort of laughter. "You've clearly spent too much time around Jonathan and the Farlanders."

"All I'm asking for is a ladder. Easy for you to poke fun. You're not the one groping around in the dark unable to tell vines from snakes."

"The snakes are the slithery ones," Ravud explained.

"So I gathered. Thank you."

"Davur can't see in the dark, either, and you don't hear him complaining about the climb, do you?"

"I'm complaining in silence," Davur called down. "How much farther to the canopy?"

Ravud paused. "Maybe ten feet. Zori's climbing into it now."

"Glad to hear that," Vudar said. "I've heard there's a tree in Romina that you can climb forever and never reach the top. I was beginning to wonder."

"It doesn't go on forever," Zori called back cheerfully. "It just goes up to one of the Thirteen Floating Palaces — not even one of the ones that's high in the air, either."

"How high up is it?" Vudar asked.

"Viserin?" Leaves rustled as Zori ascended into the ceiling of over-lapping branches. "Maybe five thousand feet. From the top you can see into King Larus's own bedroom."

"And you don't use ladders to climb it?"

Zori snorted. "Of course not."

"Please tell me that's not where we're going," Vudar said. He could hear more rustling as Davur reached the canopy, and a twig landed on his upturned face.

"Rest easy. It's just a small outpost. We'd only need to go there if Rokia happened to be there." Which, Zori was certain, she would not be.

"I don't believe for a moment that the commander general of Romina has the time to climb 5,000-foot trees."

Davur laughed. "She's teasing you, Vudar. No one climbs to the floating palaces."

"How do they get there, then?"

"You'll see," Zori called down. "Don't you dare spoil the surprise, Davur."

"Is that wise?" Davur asked. "I don't want him to faint when he sees the great Romin catapult."

"The what?!?" Vudar exclaimed. His hand found the first branches of the canopy.

"I'm with Vudar," Ravud said. "When did you grow a sense of humor, Davur? You've been spending too much time around Stipator and Arrina."

"Bah," Davur called back.

"Ah. That's more like the eldest brother we grew up with," Ravud said with mock relief.

Once he was safely nestled in the branches of the canopy, Vudar stopped climbing.

"You've only got ten feet left, and the rest of the climb is easy," Ravud called down.

"Great. Then I won't slow you down much if I take a break and wait for my shoulders to stop throbbing."

"Climbing is good for you. Builds the strong arm muscles you need for archery."

"Yes. I remember when Davur said the same thing to you several years back. I doubt you much cared for it, either."

"Oh, he didn't," Davur threw in. "And he was even climbing a ladder at the time."

Zori and Vudar laughed. Ravud muttered something under his breath.

"You can spend the night there if you're comfortable, Vudar," Zori said. "We can't get inside Meorna until morning even if we wanted to. This is as good a place to sleep as any."

"Could you toss me a couple pieces of fruit when you have a chance?" Vudar asked. "I can't tell a coconut from a skullberry in the dark."

The four ate a meal of fruit brought forth by Zori's magic and went to sleep in the branches of the canopy. She woke them in the predawn, and the brothers climbed slowly up to the top of the canopy, balancing on a path of living branches that had been woven together for just this purpose. A heavy mist cloaked everything around them.

Zori and the Marusak brothers reached Meorna at dawn, but then no one ever reached the Palace of Morning Mist anytime else. It appeared each morning when the sun lit the mist above the rainforest canopy — a city of curling wisps of shadow just barely visible in the early light. As the sun warmed the air, the mist would fade away, and the city would vanish until the next morning's mist.

"Where does it go the rest of the day?" Vudar asked.

Zori shrugged. "Nowhere. Elsewhere. No one really knows. Those who leave the city during the day vanish into the mist and are never heard from again."

Other figures appeared — some walking toward the city, others away from it. They were all little more than shadows in the mist. The branches of the canopy were not so much a path or road as a broad mat spreading out all around Meorna.

Vudar adjusted the bandolier of small glass bottles filled with colored liquids as he walked. "And those who leave at night?"

The other two brothers had similar bandoliers. All four Senserte had a bow and quiver of arrows, as well as a rapier and dagger. Davur and Vudar had extra quivers, while Ravud carried a collapsible spyglass and machete.

Zori frowned. "The less said about their fates the better."

They could make out buildings now. Meorna's walls and roofs bent and curled in graceful patterns rather than practical ones. No architect, no city planner had designed its rolling streets or the houses that hung impossibly like lanterns from half-arches of shifting mist. Like the Palace of Doors, Meorna was a powerful mirakla, which meant it didn't follow most of the rules other places did. It was a dream, a wish made real. All the floating palaces were.

The Palace of Fog could be in any place shrouded in thick fog. Ancient Elves had used it to transport armies, although no one had seen it in millennia. Any thundercloud could hide Toverin or Dammerin — weapons of the Empire that could strike enemies with lightning, whirlwinds, and massive hail. Both served the commander general. Zori wondered if the Palace of Tears was under her cousin's command as well.

"Isn't Rokia's house that way?" Ravud asked, brushing a lock of bright purple hair off his face.

"Yes, but we won't be going there today," Zori said.

She didn't elaborate on that, but they all knew why. First, she knew Romina better than all the Senserte put together. Second, the commander general no doubt had plenty of spies with Wen hearing — both adults and children.

The four of them reached a small square surrounded by tall white spires ascending into the grey mist above. A thick rope of braided white and grey mist hung down from the sky at the center of the square. Zori removed a handful of silver coins from a trouser pocket and pressed one into the hands of each of the brothers.

"What's this for?" Vudar asked.

Ravud chuckled and winked at his younger brother.

Davur nodded his understanding as he took the coins. "You don't trust her either, do you?"

Zori's face betrayed none of her usual good humor. "Just stay close to me."

She pulled the cord hard. Several seconds later, a massive bell sounded from high in the sky. Zori held up her coin and motioned for the brothers to do the same. Then she pulled the cord three more times.

Davur and Ravud carefully adjusted their equipment as though preparing for a battle.

Vudar mimicked them awkwardly. "What's going on?" he whispered.

"Four for Zerlerin!" Zori shouted at the sky.

The huge reptilian jaws of an air elemental descended from the mist. A long neck, wings the size of ships, and a pair of massive clawed arms followed. The air elemental leveled off a dozen feet above the square but did not slow down.

Davur and Zori held their ground. Ravud's body tensed as though expecting pain. Vudar shrieked like a little Farlander girl and dove onto his belly, arms covering his head.

The elemental's front claws snatched Zori and Davur. A back claw grabbed Ravud, who let out a short gasp as it lifted him off his feet. For a moment it looked like Vudar had evaded it entirely, but then the snaking grey tail lashed out and grabbed the youngest brother by both ankles.

The elemental's wings tilted, and they lifted up sharply, leaving a trail of Vudar's obscenities in their wake. Meorna vanished into the mist below.

Zori couldn't hold back a long scream of exhilaration and wouldn't have tried to even if she could. Life with the Senserte was exciting, but how she missed these little pleasures of home.

Tiny beads of water spattered against her face and clothes as the elemental flew upward. The elemental abruptly burst above the mist and into the early morning sunlight, and for a moment the light blinded her. When her vision cleared, she saw only the morning mist stretched out far below them, already beginning to thin in the warming air.

• • • •

"It never let me have any fun, but sometimes I miss my elemental," Lastor said wistfully.

"How do the Wen survive their children?" Michael asked with a shake of his head.

"First-cyclers are usually harmless just as long as you stay away from their crèche," Torminth said.

"Far, far away from it," Mathalla amended.

"Floating palaces," Arrina mused. "Are they actually fortresses in the sky?"

"So the old legends say," Tajek said. "They're cities hidden in clouds."

"What of Meorna and, um, the Palace of Fog?" Michael asked.

Tajek shrugged.

"I've been in plenty of clouds," Lastor said. "They're just fog, really, unless you get really high up. So maybe fog is just a cloud close to the ground."

"Have you ever seen one of these floating palaces?" Michael asked.

Lastor shook his head. "I just learned about them today. There are a lot of clouds in the sky."

"I have, I think," Arrina told them. "Back when we were in the balloon."

Lastor's jaw dropped. "Really? Why didn't you tell me about it?"

"I had other things on my mind at the time — like not falling to my death," Arrina said. She held out the letter. "Are you going to let me finish reading?"

Lastor crossed his arms in an exaggerated pout. Michael waved her on. Arrina frowned as she read.

> ... *Vudar did have an extra pair of pants, and we gave him some time to recover after we landed at Zerlerin. We had to wait to enter anyway. The Warden is capricious, and tiresome, and talks too much.*
>
> *The less said about our time in Zerlerin, however, the better. It was soon evident that the diadem was not in the Mausoleum of the Last King. From what we could gather, it never reached it. I have my suspicions, which I will bring to my cousin tomorrow. The night's rest will give Ravud and Vudar time to recover — do not worry, none of their injuries were life-threatening and my talent will have mostly healed them before we meet again. Though sleep will be hard to come by, I suppose.*
>
> *Hopefully, I will have better news tomorrow.*
>
> *Until then, I am yours truly,*
> *Zori ad'Korona*

"That's it?" Lastor demanded. "She's not even going to tell us about the ghosts?"

Mathalla looked thoughtful. "Some places in the Valley are best left to the imagination. I suspect the Palace of Tears might be one of them."

Arrina unrolled the next letter.

Chapter 24

Zori stopped the ad'Marusak brothers in the square before the Diadeza, the former residence of Romina's kings and queens. No stone walls swirled with such shades of gray and white as these, and no towers anywhere bent quite the way these did. As they watched, a child flew out of one wall with a poof, spinning head over heels out over the city. Two seconds later, half the wall exploded with a wet bang as an elemental burst out to catch its charge.

She grinned, remembering her own childhood.

"They turned it into a crèche." Vudar shook his head. "Look what those kids have done to it!"

He was pointing to a rainbow-colored tower, craggy and solid, clearly transformed by some child's magic. Zori thought it must be a mirakla of its own — a mirakla of a mirakla, and a reminder that not all of them made any kind of sense.

"So she doesn't live here," Ravud said. "Why not?"

Zori spoke over the muffled, rolling thunder of the crèche. "Rokia wants the people to know she is one of them, so she lives like the people do."

Except she has larger estates in other parts of the country, Zori thought. *Her modest Meorna home is like the free election she's promised us for a decade — an ultimately empty gesture.* She stopped that caravan of thought before her rage was reignited.

"Come on," she said, a bit more tartly than she intended. *I must be calm with her. We are cousins, after all.* It was still bitter to know that her own family, the Koronas, who had been one of the king's most powerful allies, had thrown their weight behind the commander general under a hundred promises of which not one had been delivered.

Not to mention Valni. Surreptitiously, she wiped her eyes, and prayed to Mira that she could hold herself together in front of Rokia.

Zori led her troupe two streets down from the Diadeza to a circular building formed from a dozen towers of varying heights, some of which started bending around each other a few stories up. Several official Romin walked briskly out of a tower as they arrived, and Zori smiled at the two guards as she asked to see Rokia. They were sent inside, up three flights of stairs with few complaints, and put in a waiting room.

Ravud and Davur flopped down on a red couch, and Zori adjusted her dress and sat on the edge of a wooden chair. Vudar wandered over to the window, looked out and then leapt back, falling on the floor and clawing at the green and white rug.

"The city's falling!" he cried, panicking.

Ravud and Davur exchanged a satisfied grin and went to save their flailing brother. Zori's tension lowered ever so slightly. She glanced out the window, which was in one of the bent towers. The road and city were tilted nearly on their side, but people and carts moved normally.

A secretary in blue and black livery approached.

"The commander general will see her cousin and her escorts now," the man said.

"Thank you," Zori replied. She smoothed her dress as she stood, and Vudar, properly sedated, offered her his arm. Flanked by Ravud and Davur, she entered her cousin's study.

Commander General Rokia ad'Puisia rose as they entered. She was tall and broad-shouldered, with a hawk nose and a complexion just starting to show her 22 cycles — almost middle age. Her close-cropped, orange hair showed gray at the roots, evidence it was dyed. She wore the same blue and black uniform, but gold frocking, gold buttons and a rack of medals adorned hers, and the jacket looked like it had been worn only twice.

She bared her teeth in what might have been a smile, and stiffly embraced Zori.

"Welcome to Meorna. Allow me to provide you a bed for the night," she said in ritual greeting. "A meal and beds will be prepared for you. There are facilities for freshening up, which you do seem to need. I must warn you about trying to leave the city unless it is, indeed, morning."

"Praise to the Mother of the Trees," Zori said quietly.

Rokia stiffened a little bit more. "Yes, praise to Mira." She walked around her desk and sat down.

"Thank you, commander general." Zori looked over her shoulder as Vudar pulled up a plush blue stool. She sat on the edge of it, and the brothers stood two steps behind her. She watched Rokia's green eyes, pupils tiny little black holes of wariness, dart from brother to brother. One hand, wearing three gold rings, self-consciously pushed papers around on the desk. Finally, Rokia seemed to come to some decision, and visibly relaxed.

"Zori ad'Korona. It's so nice to see you again. What brings you back to Meorna?" The commander general picked up an ornate chalice and sipped from it, then gestured with the chalice to the secretary.

"Commander general, we are here on Senserte business," Zori said, hands clasped in front of her. She hoped the brothers had all listened to her about keeping their hands visible.

The secretary offered her a crystal goblet of water with lime. Zori gratefully took it, and tried not to gulp it down.

Her cousin waved the title aside. "Please, Zori. I am not my position, and we are cousins. Call me Rokia."

You look exactly like your position, Zori thought. *Anyone would be confused.* But she knew Rokia like to play these little games, in an attempt to be a politician. Those who spoke to her deferentially using her official title were graced with the opportunity to use her name, and those who did not often found themselves thrown from the waiting room window.

"As you say." Zori gestured at the three brothers behind her. "My companions are the ad'Marusak brothers. I believe you have met Davur and Ravud. Vudar is their younger brother."

"Commander general." They did not bow, but that was the Sutol custom. Zori had not been able to talk them around.

"Sutola's children are always welcome in Meorna. Please, I am not so formal. Call me Rokia." She gestured to a bench along the wall. "And take a seat. You look like a regiment standing there."

Ravud and Davur didn't need to be asked twice, but they moved the bench away from the wall, so they could be involved in the conversation. After they had settled, Zori took a deep breath.

"Rokia, the Senserte have learned of a plot to steal the Diadem of Elvenkind from Romina. The ad'Marusak brothers and I ask you to let us help you foil this audacious burglary." Despite the familiarity of her tone Zori kept her eyes lowered. She made a supplicating gesture.

"The Diadem was buried with the last king in the Zerlerin," Rokia replied briskly. "Those few who dare to plunder grave goods from the Palace of Tears never return. The residents make certain of that. Your thieves will forever guard the very treasure they hoped to steal."

The thief who stole it sits before me. "I have already spoken to the residents of Zerlerin. They assured me the Diadem of Elvenkind was never interred in the Mausoleum of the Last King. It would appear it was intercepted in transit. We would find it and return it to the Romin."

Rokia shifted slightly, her hands adjusting the papers on her desk. When she spoke, it was without the feigned joviality. "I find it difficult to believe you would return to the Palace of Tears. No. I find it impossible. I know you better than that."

At one time, I thought you would make the world perfect, Zori thought, lifting her head and meeting her cousin's hard eyes. She slowly reached to her collar to take off the necklace she wore, and felt anger and sadness rise up in her. *At one time, I would have followed you anywhere.*

The golden medallion on the end of the chain flashed in the morning light as Zori placed it on the desk.

"A token from your brother, Kivit, freely given me to prove I speak the truth."

Rokia said nothing, but Zori could practically feel the heat of her gaze on the medallion. The commander general took it silently, turning it over in her hands, inspecting it. Zori breathed deeply and sat up straighter.

"I know the state coffers were empty after the coup d'etat, and you needed to raise money to consolidate your power. No one knows how many miraklas the last king kept in the Diadeza, but such things have value."

Rokia's head lifted a little from the medallion. Her pupils had swallowed her irises, and redness rimmed her eyes. It was starting to spread to her face, but Zori pressed on.

"Some could be traded for gold, others given as gifts to secure loyalty. You did what you had to hold our nation together, which is laudable." Zori had gotten very good at pronouncing that lie over the past ten years. "By itself the Diadem of Elvenkind has useful properties but none that cannot be replicated by other miraklas. Alone, it is a painful reminder of Romina's monarchy." *Something everyone wants to erase from our history.*

"No one wants to remember our king. Not anymore," Rokia said harshly.

"If you wore it for the protection it conferred, the Romin would wonder whether they merely traded a king for a queen."

"That's why I sent it to Zerlerin ..."

"But why bury it in the Palace of Tears when you can get a good price for it?" Zori stood up and slammed her hand on the desk. She froze as something sharp bit her neck. Rokia was a mixture of surprise and fear — but no rage.

Zori tried to look out of the corner of her eye. A guard had materialized out of nowhere, the point of her sword pressed into her neck. She felt a bead of blood roll down her throat. Zori slowly removed her hand from the desk, wondering what had happened to the brothers. She had told them not to act unless she said, but they were impetuous at best. She pressed on.

"You are above wasting the people's resources, commander general. Why else would you offer amnesty to the monarchists?"

The sword dug a little deeper, and the bead became a trickle.

Rokia stared at her, shaking slightly. She pulled the amulet's chain hard in her hand. *Hardness doesn't bend,* Zori thought. *Hardness shatters. This is why someone else makes the plans with the Senserte. I have no control.* She prepared herself for the worst.

After a long moment, the chain loosened, leaving a faint line across the commander general's hand. The amulet in her palm had bent.

"At ease."

The sword left her neck. Zori risked a glance over her shoulder at the brothers. Four more guards had pinned them with blades before they had even risen. She gestured low to them — *I'm fine. Everything is under control.* She hoped it was true. *This can still be salvaged, but I must wait for another opening.*

Rokia cleared her throat. "It would have been wasteful to execute them." She studied the bent medallion a second before looking up at Zori again. A tear had fallen down her cheek. "Zerlerin's ... residents ... refused to let us bury the diadem there. It no doubt reminded them of all the abuses they suffered at the hands of centuries of tyrannical monarchs."

More lies, Zori thought, but stilled her tongue. The guards had appeared from nowhere, and had not yet vanished. The commander general continued, "I believe it was sold to some collector of antiquities, but it hardly seems worth Senserte attention. A thief would be hard-pressed to find a buyer for it, and it is no great treasure on its own."

228

"It is harmless without the Orb of Elvenkind," Zori conceded. "However..."

With a slight flourish, Davur handed her the letter from Arrina, which Zori gave to Rokia, taking on the supplicant's pose again as the commander general opened it and read.

"This must be a lie. The Palace of Doors is so unassailable it has become proverbial. Not even the Floating Palaces are so famously inviolable."

"You are welcome to confirm the tale with the Tremor, commander general," Zori said demurely.

Rokia harrumphed. "If this is true, someone went to a lot of effort ..."

"If the diadem is with a collector, it would be much more easily retrieved." Zori cursed herself for interrupting again. "My apologies, commander general, but the thought of the orb and the diadem in the same person's hands scares me." The brothers murmured assent behind her.

"Those miraklas must not be allowed to serve the same master again," Rokia said hoarsely.

"I agree with you, and so do the Senserte. Please don't make us waste what little time we may have."

"I want it back."

Wouldn't it be nice to sell it again? "We'll return it to you."

Rokia rubbed the bent medallion. "I'm not as cold as I used to be, Zori. I'm afraid, despite my best efforts, that this life is making me soft." She smoothed the wrinkled paper, then spoke quietly. "The collector's name is Heilur ad'Mastios. My secretary can tell you how to find him."

• • • •

"Zori lost control like that?" Michael sounded surprised. "She doesn't lose control like that."

"Ah, but she often thinks she does. It was probably a much more civil conversation than she gives herself credit for," Arrina said. She looked back down at the letter. "Let's see. 'Luckily, we did not have to go the Bizarreum. I would have found it hard to explain to the brothers why I had to drug them insensible to get there, although I do have a stash of their sleep peach wine just for such a case. But Heilur has long since closed up shop, and lived in an attic in Meorin."

• • • •

The attic was small, and the short Wen who lived there was not happy to have all four of them inside. He never stopped fussing over one thing or the other, dodging around them to move something or dust it. When he did stop, he twitched, reminding Zori of nothing less than a squirrel. And the attic was his hoard, filled floor to ceiling with piles of junk.

"He could give Jonathan a run for his life," Davur joked.

"Who? What?" Heilur asked. "Don't touch anything." It was the fourth time he'd said it.

"Our friend," Zori asked. "He has a room like this, but I don't think it's for the same purpose. You were once a merchant in the Bizarreum, were you not?"

"I was, I was. I sold mirakla to other people, sometimes for mirakla, and sometimes for," he coughed into his hand and wiped it on his stained shirt, "talents." He licked his hand.

"Talents?" Vudar asked. "You mean, someone would do something for you?"

"No," Zori said as Heilur started to giggle. "Coin doesn't usually work in the Bizarreum. Vendors sometimes want other things. There's a mirakla that allows you to pay with your magical talent. You give it as your price."

Vudar looked disgusted.

"Don't wager on anything," Ravud added, nodding with the merchant. "Don't drink anything. You might make a choice you will regret."

"You have quite a collection," Davur said. "What's your most valuable item?"

"Replicas!" The man tripped over Vudar's foot and smiled gratefully as he was caught. His hands found a box, and he opened it before them "The Star Ring. The Moon Ring. Gorgeous, aren't they? Go ahead, you can touch these, they're not real."

Zori picked up a Star Ring. The dozens of star diamonds in it caught the light as she turned it, and for a second the world went white.

"Good, huh? Wide silver band decorated with over two hundred tiny star diamonds. I'm sure you can see them sparkle with inner light, so you know I'm not selling you bits of glass. It's a perfect replica of the original. I also have a fair number of Moon Rings — heavy gold decorated with four moon pearls that change colors with the cycle of each moon."

"You make ... copies of miraklas?" Vudar asked, voice a mixture of disbelief and horror.

Heilur blinked at him. After a moment he shook his head, his expression just as horrified. "Not the way you seem to think! I am but a simple jeweler." He shivered. "I was but a simple jeweler."

"Do you ... Did you make replicas of any other miraklan jewelry?" Zori asked.

Heilur gave them a sly smile. "I would never attempt to make a replica of any piece of jewelry I haven't personally seen."

When that silenced the four Senserte, the jeweler's smile broadened to a grin. He pushed the box into Vudar's face again.

Did he trade the Diadem for the Moon Ring and Star Ring?

Zori dismissed the thought, twirling the Star Ring around her finger.

That's ridiculous. Both rings were lost two hundred years ago — thrown into the ocean, or so Stormhaven and Kukuia both claim. No mirakla stays lost forever, and even the keys to Nosamae Ascending were bound to re-emerge eventually, but the Kuku and Havens destroyed every detailed sketch of the rings they could find to keep anyone from recognizing them.

Of the brothers, Davur caught on first. "You've seen the Moon and Star Rings?" he demanded.

Heilur held up the box. "A jeweler does not give away his wares for free. I think we should talk price before I say anything more."

"I thought you were no longer a jeweler."

"I'm feeling invigorated. I might try to open shop up again."

"What did you have in mind?" Zori asked.

"Forty dai for one ring. Seventy-five for the matched set," he said without hesitation.

"Done," Zori said. Heilur held out a hand, and she counted the money into it from her purse.

The jeweler pocketed the coins and seemed to become even more animated. "I made my fortune in the Bizarreum by taking materials produced by miraklas and working them into my jewelry. I had several contacts in Turuna who provide gems that glow, hum, or change color, as well as seaside merchants dealing in miraklan shellfish with remarkable decorative properties — such as the four species of lunar oysters that produce moon pearls. After the commander general took control of Romina, her new government needed money, which I had in abundance. In exchange, she gave me the Diadem of Elvenkind." He winked at them. "I thought maybe I could earn some money creating replicas of it to sell ..."

"I can't see that working," Ravud interrupted.

"To say they sold poorly would be a vast understatement. So I stopped." Heilur closed the box and put it away. "The diadem was worthless to me, so I buried it in my strongbox for most a cycle, doing other things. Several months ago, a letter arrived from a museum curator interested in purchasing it for a collection in Kukuia."

"You sold it to her?" Vudar asked.

"Only because she knew how to trade. If she had offered me money, then, I'd have laughed in her face."

"Only miraklas should purchase other miraklas," Zori said. "You traded the diadem for the rings."

"I was suspicious, at first. Everyone knows they were thrown into the ocean after the Nosamae War. The Wen woman brought them to me in the Bizarreum, and they behaved exactly as they did in the stories." His hand dipped into his pocket and jingled the money there, his eyes moist with excitement. "But. But. But."

"But what?"

"I don't know what happened after I opened the strongbox to get the diadem. When I came to my senses, the woman, the diadem and the rings were gone. And someone had looted my tent. I lost everything."

Zori looked around and stifled a laugh.

"Did she drug you?" Davur asked.

He shook his head. "I'm not that much of a fool. I take precautions, especially when exchanging the most valuable mirakla in my possession. It's more likely that my prospective buyer wasn't a Wen at all."

"What was she?"

"I can't prove it, mind you, but I suspect I was robbed by an enchantress."

"In Romina? In the Bizarreum itself?"

Heilur shrugged. "The precautions we take with outsiders to prevent them from remembering how to reach the Bizarreum would be less effective against an enchantress, right?"

"This happened just a few months ago?" Davur asked.

"Half a year now."

• • • •

"If our targets have the diadem, and both rings, they could be quite formidable," Arrina read. "If they retrieve the orb, they would be nearly invulnerable to most of our tricks. Be careful, Arrina, and please don't let them get the orb." She put the letter down and stared at the rest. Mathalla and Torminth looked uncomfortable. She raised an eyebrow at them.

"It might be worth sparing a thought for the key miraklas," Mathalla conceded in a hesitant voice. "They have their own properties."

"So we are learning," Michael muttered.

"Stipator told me Theo's Sword makes the wielder a master swordsman," Arrina said. "And I suspect Jacob's Bow works similarly for archery."

"It's more than mastery. They make the impossible commonplace," Mathalla corrected. "Whoever heard of a Farlander winning an archery contest against Wen archers? Only Jacob Premier."

"What do the other four miraklas do?" Arrina asked.

Silence answered her.

"Stormhaven and Kukuia didn't rid themselves of the wedding rings just to keep anyone from activating one of the paintings, did they?" she prompted.

Mathalla sighed. "Not entirely, no. You grew up among Wen, Arrina. You know how miraklas come to be. Wen children imagine things, and sometimes they become real. A Wen who wears the Star Ring becomes a heroic figure, able to change his magical talent to fit every situation. A Farlander wearing the Moon Ring embodies the stories Wen children heard about Nosamae from the adults — possessing powerful magic but prone to terrible villainy."

"Are you saying the rings are sentient?" Michael asked. "That they can control the ones who wear them?"

Mathalla shook his head and looked uncomfortable, almost embarrassed. "They respond to the wearer's voice. Certain phrases activate them. For the Star Ring, the Wen has to shout the name of the Wen talent he wants to use in, um, sort of a bold, heroic voice. It won't respond to just anyone. It likes baritones most. Tenors and basses can sometimes learn to talk to it right."

Arrina raised an eyebrow. "So, shout 'Lightfoot Magic' to gain your ability to walk on water or air?"

"Yes. Aside from being a bit showy, it can be a bit illogical to shout to gain Tasticon's talent for Unseen Presence."

"How long does it last?" Michael asked, always curious about the workings of magic.

Mathalla shrugged. "Until it stops being exciting, I guess. Both rings work better when lots of people are watching the wearer use them." He spread his hands helplessly. "They're the invention of a child's imagination, and so they have a child's sense of how such things should work."

Despite the vagueness of the answer, Michael absorbed this eagerly. "What about the Moon Ring? Are its principles similar?"

"Yes. The Moon Ring favors contralto voices, instead. However, the Wen child obviously didn't know what enchantresses call their spells, so the commands work a little, er, differently."

"It uses descriptive names, instead?" Michael ventured.

Another heavy sigh and a brief look at Torminth. "It is activated by saying villainous things."

Michael gave him a blank look. "Like?"

"Well, understand that while the Kuku knew most of the commands for the Star Ring, the people of Stormhaven only ever learned a few of the Moon Ring's commands. You know how sometimes you make it so magic can't affect you?"

Michael nodded. "The counterspell cloak. What the Marrishlanders call skin of the demon."

"Yes. The command phrase for that one is 'Pitiful fools! Your puny magic is no match for the power of a Nosama.' It must be shouted with absolute confidence. Laughing maniacally appears to increase the duration of its protection..."

Michael regarded him intently. "You're serious, aren't you?"

Mathalla nodded. "The rings have one other property when two different people wear them. If a Farlander wears the Moon Ring and a Wen the Star Ring, the Wen cannot be touched by Farlander magic, and the Farlander cannot be affected by Wen magic."

Michael looked at all of them hard. "I wish someone would have mentioned this to me before now."

"I never dreamed the rings would ever find their way back to the Valley," Mathalla said. "This was supposed to be a rescue mission with punishment for the kidnapper, remember?"

"You haven't told us where Aaronma keeps Nosamae Ascending or how the two paintings came to be, either, Michael," Torminth reminded him.

"It isn't really relevant. We know how to activate them and what they do."

"Do we?" Torminth asked. "There are two stories. The first is they weaken the magic of the enemy. The second is they strengthen the magic of the victor. Some say enchantment was more powerful then, that the Wen activated Nosamae Descending to restore balance between Wen and Farlander magic."

Michael shook his head. "No one knows for certain. Most of the records and Nosamae were destroyed, and Farlanders don't live as long as Wen. As to why a Wen child would happen to create a mirakla that granted Farlander enchantresses more power, we've heard the same legends you have." His expression hardened. "I'm not naïve enough to believe no enchantress has tried to force a Wen child to create a mirakla. However, I can assure you none has ever succeeded. Those who claim otherwise have always proven to be frauds."

"Enough," Arrina said to Wen and Farlander alike.

Kukuia and Aaronsglade were not friends. Their peoples had spilled each others' blood many times. The last border war was only five years ago. Only Pithdai's intervention had prevented it from dragging on longer. Michael and Mathalla seldom talked about it.

"I'm sorry, Arrina," Michael told her sincerely, his gaze falling deferentially.

Mathalla and Torminth crossed their arms over their chests and bowed to Michael in apology.

"I also wish I had known the properties of the key miraklas," Arrina said. She felt lied to, but what were they supposed to have done? "An enchantress invulnerable to Wen magic complicates matters."

"She is only invulnerable so long as a Wen wears the Star Ring," Mathalla corrected.

Arrina considered this for a moment. "What would happen if a Wefal wore the Star Ring?"

"Wefals do not have Wen talents, so I doubt the Star Ring could grant them to you."

"Would the immunity still work both ways?"

Mathalla hestitated. He was clearly more uncertain than evasive, now. "Possibly. It may not work at all. The Kuku rid themselves of the Star Ring before Wefals were...recognized."

She glanced at Michael, found his expression thoughtful.

"What of the diadem and the orb?" Michael asked.

Everyone looked to Lastor, who was sitting crosslegged under the table, watching a pair of squawkers wrestling.

"Lastor?" Arrina prompted.

He didn't even look up at them, clearly reciting some memorized lesson. "Many millennia ago, the Wen and Turu were part of Aelkindom, the Elven empire in the fabled city of Satuana in the mountains between desert and rainforest. As symbols of her authority, the empress wore the Diadem of Elvenkind and carried the Orb of Elvenkind. When the Turu betrayed Aelkindom, the empress brought them into Flekar — what we call the Flecterran Valley — and built a new capital near what would become Pithdai."

The adults in the room waited for Lastor to continue, but he didn't.

"What do they do?" Michael asked.

Lastor shrugged. "I don't remember. That teacher was boring."

"We could ask his grandfather," Arrina suggested.

"No need," Tajek said suddenly. "The Turu remember Aelkindom, though of course our version says the Wen betrayed the empress and stole the Aelkindom Crown and Sphere." His expression was grave as he explained. "By itself, the crown protected the wearer from poisons and disease, as well as any magic fruit or potions, including what you call saat. The sphere protected from weapons — much like my skin is proof against metal, except it works on wood, stone, flesh, and anything else that is not magic. The one who carries both can issue commands to Wen and Turu that cannot be disobeyed."

"Will they work in the hands of a Farlander?" Michael asked even as Arrina asked, "Can they control Farlanders and Wefals?"

Tajek held up his hands as though to ward them off. "Our Blood Priests' histories do not mention the crown or sphere after the fall of Aelkindom. The Farlanders did not come to Elven lands until centuries after that."

Michael looked profoundly unhappy. Mathalla seemed ashamed as Torminth patted his arm and whispered words of comfort. Arrina felt slightly sick to her stomach but also exhilarated.

Mira's leafy skirt, I'm turning into Stipator!

Only Lastor seemed entirely unperturbed. He crawled out from under the table and dusted off his bare knees. "We're Senserte. The surer our enemies are of victory, the more inevitable and absolute their defeat, right?"

"Who told you that?" Michael asked.

"Sounds like Stipator," Arrina said with an amazed shake of her head.

Lastor shook his head as he sat crosslegged in a chair. "Jonathan."

"Oh," Arrina managed. That bit of context had stripped away much of the heroic air Lastor had given it. Jonathan worked so hard to keep them out of danger, and that sometimes meant convincing targets that the Senserte were no threat to them.

There is a time for bravado and a time to feign weakness.

"We'll have to work this information into the plan, but it doesn't change the bones of it," Arrina told them. "Lastor, I'm going to write a few letters I'll need you to send by arrow even if you have to travel far from Tremora to reach clear skies."

Lastor nodded by grabbing his feet and rocking forward and back on the seat of the chair.

"Arrina, wait," Michael said. He looked as guilty as Mathalla, now. "There's something you need to know."

"Nosamae Ascending is in Aaronsglade, isn't it?" Tajak guessed.

"Yes," Michael said slowly.

"I knew it!" Torminth cried as if he had just won a bet.

Michael continued as if the Wen hadn't spoken. "Specifically, it's in the Nosamae War Memorial Museum."

"Sora's museum," Arrina said.

He nodded slowly.

"That means she already has access to all but one of the miraklas she needs to activate either painting."

"And she's already on her way to collect the final piece while the Senserte are scattered across the Valley!" Mathalla amended.

Michael shrugged. "It just means we need to be ready to move into the climax faster than any of us expected."

Much faster. Suddenly there didn't seem to be any time.

ACT IV

Chapter 25

The abandoned lighthouse on the rocky island in Phantom Lake marked the current boundary between Sutola and Pithdai. After the last war between the two Wen nations, Pithdai had built it so the Sutol could warn away boats that came too close to the border. Larus had hoped it would keep any of his subjects from violating the truce.

From the look of it, the lighthouse had never been occupied by anyone other than Pith and Petersine fishermen, hunters, and foragers. Those seemed to regard it as a haven in the event of foul weather or a campsite for their expeditions. Net fragments. Broken arrows. Rotten husks of fruit. Remnants of cookfires.

Not an especially safe place to keep a mirakla as powerful as Gates of Tremora, Arrina thought.

Bringing it within the borders of Sutola was out of the question though. The Sutol knew enough of the painting's legend to see the potential threat it presented. What faster way to bring an enemy army into the heart of their country than through a painting? It would not be the first time Pith and Sutol armies had used the painting to transport troops between the kingdoms without passing through territory they did not control.

Phantom Lake's lighthouse served as a reminder of the stark cultural differences between Pith and Sutol. Both were Wen nations. Whereas Pithdai deliberately positioned itself as the diplomatic capital of the Flecterran Union, Sutola had joined the federation simply to ensure the other member states didn't take action against it. The lay of the two lands told a story of a deeper philosophical split.

Most of the kingdom of Pithdai was carefully cultivated rainforest or jungle, with occasional open spaces for crops. It was hard to tell where civilization ended and wilderness began. The capital might have extended halfway to the border with Stormhaven or ended two miles south of the Kaeruli Lake for all the layperson might know.

In truth, though, all of it was carefully planned. The Pith left some parts of the land truly wild, but even those served a purpose as places for Wen to hunt and camp for sport. They served as training grounds for Pith soldiers, homeguard, and the nation's future leaders, as well as venues for the execution hunts of criminals who had committed murder or treason. Stipator had taken Arrina and Jonathan to just such a preserve to train them in the use of their magic.

Sutola lacked the centralized government of Pithdai and maintained the old ways. Their Council of Leaves was made up of elders who made decisions for the entire nation by consensus. It met only rarely except in times of war. Sometimes years would pass between council gatherings. They maintained no ground roads, lived in tree homes, and did almost nothing to shape the rainforest around them. Their forest was as untouched as they could make it, and each Wen would defend it to her death.

Though perhaps well-intentioned, the border lighthouse had been doomed to disuse from the beginning. Most Sutol politely scoffed at anyone who slept on the ground. This included Farlanders and Wefals, but they maintained a special disdain for Wen who had strayed far enough from the old way to build palaces of stone for themselves. Certainly no Sutol would willingly spend the night in a structure as artificial as a lighthouse. Even the ad'Marusak brothers, who were anomalies among their people for traveling with a mixed group like the Senserte, slept in the canopy as often as they could. Their wagon didn't have a bed or hammock, as they wouldn't dare risk another Sutol accusing them of ground sleeping.

Heavy rain drenched them every night of the first five days of their journey to Seleine, and the unbroken darkness of the forest floor wore at their tempers. Mathalla and Lastor served as scouts, frequently breaking through the canopy to navigate. Without these constant peeks, they would have gotten thoroughly lost. All the landmarks were visible only from the canopy and emergent layers. The rainforest floor was a labyrinth of tree trunks that were largely indistinguishable from one another.

The rain poured from the sky with a vengeance on the afternoon of the sixth day, but it fortunately let up that night, allowing them to sleep and send messages to their fellow Senserte. An arrow pinioned Arrina's sleeve while she slept. She found it surprising that it hadn't woken her, but the past several days had been exhausting and she was far from her full strength.

As she opened her eyes in the dim twilight of the forest floor and pulled the arrow out of the ground, the other Senserte looked up from their breakfast.

"Word from Jonathan, I hope?" Michael asked.

Arrina unrolled the letter. Its date preceded their departure from Romina. The writing was neither her twin's nor Zori's. She frowned and peeked at the signature at the end.

"It's from Etha."

The Farlander's eyes widened and he stood. "Etha?"

Arrina nodded. Her frown deepened. "And it's dated four days before our confrontation in Tremora."

Michael looked to Lastor.

The young Wen shook his head. "Sora ordered Corina to keep me below decks while we were in Aaronsglade."

Michael nodded. "She probably didn't want your magic attracting any unwanted attention."

Arrina unrolled the letter and read:

> Arrina,
>
> Nothing has gone as planned. Poresa and Jonathan have been arrested, and the Bronze Leviathan and its crew seized by the Nosamae. Stipator is missing. Kara went to the Nosamae with Michael's letter of introduction, but that was two days ago and I've received no word.
>
> I spotted watchers near our rendezvous point, so I didn't dare return and wait for the others. I thought it best to explain our situation to you, so I'm no longer in Aaronsglade. I don't know how much longer I can stay ahead of anyone hunting me.
>
> Here's how it happened.

• • • •

Etha had not grown up in Aaronsglade, nor had she spent much time in it. In fact, this was her first time visiting it without Michael leading the way. She reminded herself that this meant she was far more familiar with the city than any of the Senserte with her, and felt her stomach flip over again.

"All of that is Aaronsglade?" Poresa asked as Stipator and Jonathan rowed toward the dock. The harbor could accommodate the Bronze Leviathan, but that would require a sail master, and too much of the Senserte equipment would raise eyebrows with customs even if it never left the ship.

"More or less," Etha answered.

The city was on Maiden Island, but all that most people had heard about was the new Exult Spire — most often referred to as the Spire. The three-tiered, limestone-walled behemoth had been leveled in the Nosamae War, and this version had been finished about sixty years ago. It was famous in legend and lore, but it was not half of the island, and all the residents of Maiden Island considered themselves living in Aaronsglade.

From the harbor stretched the wide, flat expanse of Ma'Lara's Field. Already in her young apprenticeship, Michael had tested Etha on the history of the Nosamae War. Several battles had been fought around Aaronsglade, and each field was still remembered, if only locally. The field, though, had been turned into sprawling housing, from little better than huts to two-storey stone buildings. South of the city, near the other harbor, was Ma'Patricia's Field. A great road ran north and south across the island, bisecting the Fields, and connecting the massive bridges with the mainland to the Exult Spire.

"More or less?" Poresa asked with a playful laugh mimicked by the two squawkers, Jabber and Garble. "Sometimes I remember whose apprentice you are."

Etha flushed. "It depends on who you ask is all. Some say no. The same goes for the Ma'Patricia's Field."

"More like Pithdai than the Palace of Doors, in other words," Jonathan said, coming to her rescue.

"Yes."

"What's the security like?" Stipator asked between straining strokes of the oars. He hadn't fully regained the strength he lost on Gulinora Island. "We've all heard the stories."

I don't know, she wanted to say. *With Michael, we weren't trying to do anything that required me to know.* But she had to answer, so she thought about what she had seen.

Nosamae enforcers seldom came to the Field except to quell large riots or to escort visiting dignitaries along the least offensive roads to the capital. Neighborhood police varied in competence and corruption depending on what part of Ma'Lara's Field one visited, but Etha could not begin to tell the Senserte which ones were dangerous and which were safe.

"It depends on what part of the city you're in," she admitted at the end. "The Nosamae can't be everywhere at once."

"Are there any especially seedy parts of town?" Stipator asked with a smirk. "You know the kind." He winked at her.

Etha felt her cheeks redden. *After spending half a year with him, you'd think he wouldn't be able to embarrass me anymore.*

"Stipator, enough," Kara said coldly from her spot at the front of the boat. "Enchantresses don't have to be anywhere near the spot they're surveilling, but enforcement is apt to be lighter at the edges, so Etha's sentiment is accurate."

Etha remembered something Michael had said in a lecture. "Only enchantresses can police enchantresses," she said. "The Nosamae must watch for unlicensed magic."

Kara turned around and looked at Etha, her expression thoughtful. After a moment she nodded and turned back to the city. "They use a lot of magic here. I'm not used to being able to see a difference in the flow from so far away."

"You're not using magic, are you?" Jonathan radiated tension. "You remember what Michael told us."

"Nothing detectable at this range, no."

"That's not what I asked," Jonathan said, frown deepening.

"You worry too much."

"Just because you know the risks..."

"Stuff it, Jonathan. This is what I do best."

They joined a few other rowboats making a line for the harbor pier under the direction of a sail master in a tiny sailboat, which she seemed to be able to whip around them as if they were standing still. The stink of the harbor filled Etha's nose as they got closer to the pier, reminding her of home, and a few minutes later, Jonathan was helping her onto dry land.

"How did they rebuild the Spire?" Poresa was asking. The massive, three-tiered structure was in much better view from here.

Etha shrugged.

"One of Michael's mysterious looks?" Kara guessed.

She nodded.

"And that's where we're headed?" Poresa asked.

"Once we get through visitor registration. Michael thinks we should start by finding out whether this museum is real," Etha said and immediately cringed inwardly. *That's it. Make it sound like you can't do anything unless someone tells you what to do.* "It will probably be on the First Tier, the lowest level of the city where mostly non-enchantresses live and Nosamae patrols are light."

"What if the museum isn't real?" Poresa asked. "Or what if it's not on the First Tier?"

"Michael's letter will get us to his mother, and she should be able to help us," Jonathan said.

"Assuming she's not behind these thefts," Kara said coolly.

"Which is why it's our back-up plan," Jonathan reminded her between clenched teeth. "Otherwise, we'd go to the Nosamae first."

Etha knew from Michael's lectures that it was more complicated than that. The Nosamae had factions, some of them bitterly opposed to each other. M'Elizabeth ad'Alice was the leader of one such group, and while Michael trusted his mother completely he also hinted that her direct involvement in a Senserte mission might induce some rival factions to interfere with it.

But if I say anything, Kara will question Michael's judgment, and I'll have to defend him and I'm not sure who is listening.

"Please don't make the customs people angry at us," Jonathan told Stipator as they approached the Harbor Gate to the First Tier of the Spire.

"Me? What would I do?" Stipator feigned shock.

Etha glanced back at the harbor as Kara efficiently found their documents and presented them to the agent. The apprentice loved the docks. The sounds of the mooring lines stretching and scraping against the planks, the bustling of the workers, traders and masters, and the general transientness of the place — it was never the same, yet all harbors were similar. She squeezed her pack to her chest, imagining she could feel her knives in there.

My cousin taught me to throw on the docks, she thought. *He could fly almost like a Wen child across the masts of Stormhaven. He was ...* Even starting to think of him conjured up her mother's face and made her cringe.

"Etha!"

She ran to catch up with the Senserte, pushing her past back down.

• • • •

She led them to Michael's First Tier safehouse — a narrow, three-storey stone house that backed up against the base of the Second Tier, and only six houses down from the stairs up there. She had not known about it until Michael told them. When she had come with him, they had stayed on the Second Tier, which was limited to Nosamae and their apprentices — with permission. The Third Tier was even more restrictive, allowing only the Council and its designated aides access. Even Michael had not yet been there, or so he said.

As Kara unlocked the door, Jonathan gave her the look she saw him direct at the balloon before it took off, a sort of, will-it-work expression.

"I think we passed the house twice on the way here," Stipator said, walking past them and following Kara inside. "No judgment, you know, I'm just healing here and could use a drink. Is this place stocked with cheese?"

Etha flushed.

"But she did help us find the museum," Jonathan added casually, turning her by the elbow and directing her inside.

Embarrassed, she went straight for the stairs, looking for a bedroom. *Michael told us all the directions, I didn't have to be leading! And I didn't even see the museum, what was Jonathan talking about?* Kara was already on the landing.

"Men." Kara sighed. "If it's not right the first time, they complain until their beards grow full."

"That might take a while for Jonathan," Etha heard herself say, then cursed inwardly. *We are all friends here!*

Kara snorted and placed a hand over her smile. She opened a door, then turned and opened another. "I'll take this one."

Etha went into the other one, which was smaller, and put her bag on the bed. She quickly unpacked. Her clothes were hung or placed in the small dresser and her costume jewelry and toiletries laid out before the small mirror. She pulled out her knives and a coiled whip — *Your reach isn't long enough for a sword, so we have to make you longer* — and found the false baseboard she had asked Michael about.

I'm glad Kara didn't take this room, she thought, hiding the knives and whip, just as Garble trotted in. "Eta! Eta!"

"It's Etha." She pushed the baseboard into place.

"Pie!"

"We're still being surveilled," Kara noted, sticking her head into the room.

"It's just routine," Etha assured her as she shooed the stray squawker out. "You could start a fire in the kitchen stove to make us tea, and I promise no one will arrest us." *I did tell you Michael had permits to use magic in this house — it's supposed to be for his apprentices.*

"What if I ward the house against surveillance?" Kara asked.

Etha shrugged. "It should be fine."

"I'll make them false input wards just in case."

Etha had nothing to add to that, because she had no idea what Kara was talking about. Being Michael's apprentice had gifted her with a lot of history and a lot of warning, but very little knowledge of enchanting. She followed a cheerfully refreshed Poresa down the stairs to the dining room, where Garble and Stipator each had a fist full of pie, and Jonathan was playing in the fireplace.

"Have you heard of a fork, Garble?" Poresa said. "I know Stipator could use some training."

Jabber jumped up on the table with a fork and stabbed the pie. Stipator swallowed what he was chewing and winked at Poresa, cheeks stained with purple berries. Etha couldn't help but smile despite the grossness. She took a seat and shooed Garble away as he tried to offer her pie.

Kara came down a few seconds later, warily scanning every corner, and sat two seats away from Etha.

Jonathan cleared his throat. "Since Etha has helped us to establish that the Nosamae War Memorial Museum is real, and that it's also close to our current location, we can now decide what to do next."

Etha put one of her hands on the table. "I'm sorry, but I'm not sure what you're talking about."

Her face grew hot as she blushed. *An enchantress would just accept the credit. She wouldn't let on that she knew less than people thought she did.*

The other Senserte stared at her.

Stipator abruptly burst into laughter, which only made Etha blush more. "Poresa owes me ten dai! I told you she was lost."

"I wasn't lost," Etha said softly, even though she knew it was a lie. "I simply wasn't sure exactly how to get here."

"Stipator, enough," Poresa said sharply, throwing a concerned look in Etha's direction.

"You're just upset that I won." Stipator smirked.

Etha wanted to stand up, go to her bedroom, and lock herself inside for the rest of the night. It wasn't as if the Senserte needed her now that they were inside the First Tier. But she respected Jonathan too much to do that. And she didn't want to worry Poresa, either, or make Michael look bad in the eyes of Kara.

I am his apprentice, after all, and my actions reflect on him.

And so she clasped her hands under the table and tried not to feel too small.

• • • •

Hours later, when the plans were settled without much input from Etha, Jonathan suggested they all get some sleep. Etha didn't move after everyone had left. Sleep was still some distance away, and she felt she had to consider ways to make a larger contribution to the plan. She took one of the lamps and went to the house's small library. There were books in here intended only for the eyes of an enchantress, she knew, books she sometimes wondered if she would ever be permitted to read.

Most apprenticeships take three or four years, she reminded herself. *You've only been at it for six months.*

But it still frustrated her that she was the only Senserte without magic. Even the Wen had their gifts, each of them useful in several circumstances.

Etha fought the temptation to break the rules, to pick up some text on advanced theory or a book of specialized enchantments. Michael wasn't here to stop her, and all the other Senserte were asleep or soon would be. Here was one subtitled "Warding Against Input Wards" that would have been useful earlier.

They're probably enchanted to keep anyone from reading them without permission, she told herself. *They probably won't make sense until I've learned the basic principles. Even if I learn something helpful, I'll be in trouble if Michael finds out I knew about it before he taught me about it.*

In the end, her fingers found a perfectly ordinary history of the Nosamae War. She tucked the thick tome under her arm and picked up the lamp.

At the least this is likely to help me fall asleep.

As she walked into the darkened living room, a woman spoke.

"Ah. That's where you went."

Etha nearly jumped out of her skin. Kara sat on one of the couches, her face a mask of shadow in the dim light.

"I didn't see you there," Etha said before she realized how obvious that was.

"Late night reading?"

Etha held up the book so the title was clearly visible, relieved that she hadn't taken something illicit. "If I'm going to play the excited niece, auntie, I should know a little bit about what I'm so excited about."

"You don't have to play as a child if you don't want to, Etha."

"I know you're not going to need my help," she admitted with a heavy sigh as she slumped into the couch on the other side. When Etha had suggested she and Kara go as aunt and niece, Stipator had voiced an opinion that he would make a better companion for Kara, because he could do more. She put the lamp on the low table between them, which cast more light on the enchantress's face.

"Don't take Stipator's little tantrum seriously. He and Jonathan have always had differences of opinion, and he can be careless with that tongue of his. You're an enchantress's apprentice, which means one day you'll be just as valuable and just as feared as we are."

But what about right now? Etha wanted to ask. *Without magic I'm just an apprentice among the Senserte. They treat me kindly, but there is nothing I can do that someone else can't do better.*

She didn't want to make the conversation more awkward than it had already become, though, so she said nothing.

After a long moment Kara said, "If you want to be a guide or cousin or friend tomorrow that will be just as good. More than anything I need an extra set of eyes to help me get a handle on the layout and warn me if it looks like we're being followed or watched."

So you're bringing along the only person who walked past the museum twice and never even noticed, Etha thought glumly.

She shook her head. "Arrina is right. The part chooses the player. If I'm a child, I can wander into places I shouldn't go or create a distraction when you need one. And none of that keeps me from watching your back. It's just the best part I can play in all this."

"I wanted you to know that just because you often disguise yourself as a child doesn't mean I think of you as one. You're as much a woman as I am and a lot cleverer than you let on."

Etha wasn't sure how to respond to this. Kara meant well, certainly, but telling a woman of twenty-five that she wasn't a child still fell short of complimentary. She hefted the history book meaningfully. "I should probably get reading if I don't want to be up too late."

Kara seemed to accept this, for she stood up and went to the stairs. Etha followed her up, carrying the flickering lantern. It needed more oil, but the lamp in her bedroom would still have a full reservoir.

How did I not see the museum when we walked past? she berated herself silently. *I was probably distracted looking for something familiar while wondering whether the others knew I had gotten them lost, but they must think I'm so stupid.*

She tried to push it out of her mind and focus on the next day.

"Good night, Etha," Kara said.

Etha mumbled a like response and closed the door behind her. She lit the lamp on the nightstand and blew out the nearly empty one. She sat on the bed with the pillows behind her back and opened the history book to read.

The dry writing soon made her drowsy, and it didn't help that most of the history she knew from Michael's lectures on the subject. It seemed very important to him that enchantresses never again make the mistake of those old Nosamae. Her eyelids drooped briefly, but she recovered herself.

With a sigh she began to skim, looking for small facts that a child might find interesting. She settled on a passage about famous wands used in the Nosamae War to fight the Wen children with their equally potent magic. Once she finished that, she moved on to a passage about the purges that followed the war — the names and great deeds of powerful enchantresses who were snuffed out by their own people for their magical abilities.

This proved too much for Etha after a day spent sailing, walking, and planning, and she fell asleep curled around the book like a talisman.

• • • •

"When is she going to get to the good parts?" Lastor complained loudly.

"It can't be long, now," Torminth assured him. Then he barked a laugh. "Unless she spends several pages describing who woke her up and what everyone talked about at breakfast."

Arrina scanned the next page quickly and quietly moved it to the back of the stack of folded paper.

"We're going to be listening to you read this letter all day!" Lastor protested.

"I'm sure she has a very good reason for telling us about these things," Arrina told him. "They could be important later."

"You should probably continue reading," Michael said.

Arrina did so.

Chapter 26

"That was a little pricier to get into than I thought it would be, but for my favorite niece, I think it is worth it!"

"Well, we don't want just any Fielder coming in here," the old man said as he handed over two bronze tokens. "You keep those on you, and return them when you leave."

"Thank you!"

As they passed through the red brick wall and onto the grounds of the museum, Etha bit her tongue from telling Kara there was a good reason she hadn't noticed the museum. *That low brick wall is taller than me!*

"I wonder who the patrons are who help keep this place running," Kara asked delightfully. "There certainly aren't that many history viewers!"

Kara's feigned cheerfulness reminded Etha that she had to be exuberant as well, so she stopped at the first display in the front room, and read the inscription out loud.

"Ma'Pearl's fountain was one of the first designed for modern indoor plumbing, and veterans from the Second Battle of Ma'Lara's Field once drank from it." The water trickled down the two tiers of the fountain, pushing feathers to the edge of the water. She glanced up to the half-open skylight, four stories above her. *Indoor plumbing means there's sewage, and feathers means birds get in here, and probably squawkers.*

She did not look at Kara to confirm it, but took the woman's hand and pulled her into the first gallery, where sealed glass cases built into the walls displayed lengths of wood, bone, metal, and gemstones ranging from barely a hand in length to large enough to double as a cudgel.

Etha practically ran from one to another, loudly telling her imaginary aunt everything she knew about each one. Most of the time, this meant reading the small card in each glass case, although the previous night's reading had not been entirely wasted.

Kara, meanwhile, played the part of the delightfully indifferent adult in the company of an overstimulated child. Etha knew the enchantress was actually examining the enchantments protecting the museum from intrusion.

Etha quickly discovered that most of the wands were replicas — mere physical copies of originals lost or destroyed during the purge of enchantresses after the Nosamae War. The only supposedly real one she recognized was the infamous Archon-Killer, which was one of the few wands capable of killing Wen first-cyclers.

During the war, the Nosamae created it in response to the Rain of Fire that destroyed Aaronsglade. In a single day, one Nosamae used the Archon-Killer to wipe out the creches of most of the southern cities of Romina. They called it the Archon-Killer not because it killed the Wen leaders of those communities but because, so the legend went, the Archons committed suicide out of grief when they learned what the wand had done.

Though she knew that the Rain of Fire had killed tens of thousands of innocent people in Aaronsglade, the mere thought sent a shudder through Etha. Wars in the Flecterran Valley had never been affairs of honor or restraint, and sometimes it seemed that only the fear that the other nations would intervene prevented border skirmishes from exploding into conflicts with catastrophic death tolls.

Even if this is the real Archon-Killer, its magic has long since faded away. Who would keep such a terrible weapon charged and ready for the next war?

"We should probably look at some of the other exhibits, sweetie," Kara said.

Her voice was louder, less matronly than usual for this role. Etha realized this probably hadn't been the first time Kara had tried to get her attention.

"Sorry, Auntie," Etha said with a child's apologetic meekness. "I was just looking at the Archon-Killer."

Kara's eyes widened ever so slightly, but they soon returned to their tour of the museum.

They passed from gallery to gallery, feigning interest even though they were both beginning to feel the pressure of time. However intense a child's enthusiasm, her capacity to remain focused for long periods of time was limited, so the longer Etha played her part, the less believable it would become.

They found the Nosamae Ascending gallery on the third floor. The six key miraklas hung on wall hooks or sat in simple glass cases on pedestals not even secured to the ground, which made it clear at once that they were mere copies and not even ones made of materials worth stealing. Nosamae Ascending hung in a display case the size of a small room walled off from the gallery by a thick sheet of glass. To one side of the painting was a heavy metal door. All these trappings had the combined effect of making a painting of not impressive size look even smaller. Etha could have fit it into a backpack without removing it from its frame.

Kara stared at the painting, carefully examining the security protecting it. Etha flitted from one of the keys to another, although she was too short to look at any of them closely. They hadn't seen many other museum patrons, but letting Kara be seen looking at Nosamae Ascending the way a student of history might was a lesser evil than being caught doing so furtively. When she had exhausted the other options in the gallery, Etha pressed her face against the glass of the oversized Nosamae Ascending display case.

It showed a wedding scene with a Farlander bride and a Wen groom standing in front of a crowd, leaning forward into their first kiss as husband and wife. The bride wore the Diadem of Elvenkind and held the Orb of Elvenkind in her right hand. The groom wore Jacob's Bow across his shoulder and carried Theo's Sword at his hip. Their hands were clasped. From this distance Etha couldn't make out the Star Ring on the groom's hand or the Moon Ring on the bride's. Two thrones stood on the dais behind the pair, and above the thrones hung a painting only two inches wide. Nosamae knelt in chains before a Wen king.

Etha froze. *That's not right. It should be Wen lords kneeling before a councilor of Aaronsglade.*

She wordlessly tugged Kara's sleeve. After a moment, the enchantress crouched as if to speak to her niece.

"Who are the people in the painting behind the couple?" Etha asked.

Kara looked and the painting, face going slightly pale. After a moment's hesitation she carefully described the painting within Nosamae Ascending. Both of them focused on remaining in character for the last several minutes of their tour of the museum.

Once they left and Kara confirmed they were not being tailed, the two Farlanders returned to the safehouse. Poresa slept on one of the couches. Etha knew the Wefal's mind was at the museum, riding her squawkers' senses and directing their movements. There was no sign of the other Senserte.

Kara frowned. "Stipator?" she called loudly enough to be heard anywhere in the house.

She received no reply. Kara eyes got a faraway look.

"He's not here, but nor is anyone else," Kara announced. "I'm not surprised. He can't ever stick to the plan."

Etha relaxed. Kara had already sat down on the couch opposite Poresa. Etha took up her usual position on her chair, although the girl's skirt she wore meant she didn't cross her legs this time.

"He probably got bored and went looking for trouble," Kara said, blowing a lock of black hair that had fallen out of its braid back over her head. "Which means they'll probably have another argument we'll have to sit through."

"If they do, we should offer to go to the market for supplies," Etha suggested.

Kara laughed. "Just don't leave me alone with them."

"Kara! Eta! Kara! Eta!" cried two small voices from the back door. Moments later, Garble and Jabber ran into the living room and chased each other around the room.

Kara and Etha exchanged a look, but at that moment Poresa sat up, grey eyes bloodshot, strawberry blond hair disarrayed.

"Is everything alright?" Kara asked.

"Yes." Poresa's voice was hoarse. "Could you bring me something to drink?"

Etha hopped off her chair and retrieved a decanter of spring-chilled paleberry wine from the cellar. She handed a glass to Poresa.

"Where is Stipator?" Poresa asked, looking around the room.

"We don't know. Obviously not guarding you like he should," Kara answered.

Poresa shrugged. "I was fine anyway."

"Did you find a way in?" Etha asked, sitting down again.

Poresa nodded as she sipped her paleberry wine. "The squawkers passed Jonathan on the way here, so let's give him a moment. It will save us repeating the same stories twice."

They didn't wait more than a minute before Jonathan strode into the room, a sheaf of papers tucked under one arm.

"Where's Stipator?" he asked.

Poresa shrugged.

Jonathan visibly struggled to control his irritation, but he did not comment further on Stipator's absence. "Matters are worse than I thought. Sora is the museum's de facto curator. This is a bit strange because traditionally only Nosamae are appointed to the post, but Sora isn't a Nosama. She has made several trips beyond Aaronma in the last year."

"The other key miraklas?" Poresa murmured, chewing her lip.

Jonathan nodded, face grim. "The museum is, for all intents and purposes, hers. She has access to every mirakla, wand, and talisman in it, including Nosamae Ascending."

"If the Nosamae appointed her to the post, they might be behind all this." Poresa shifted in her seat. "If that's the case, we can't possibly stop them from restarting the Nosamae War."

"I don't think they are," Kara said. "Or at least if they were, they probably aren't anymore."

The enchantress's words commanded their attention. Etha started to hug her knees to her chest unconsciously before realizing she was still wearing a skirt. She planted her feet firmly a few inches above the floor and let Kara do the talking.

The enchantress blew the stray lock of hair back over her head. "Someone switched the paintings. Nosamae Descending is in the gallery in the place where Nosamae Ascending once hung."

"How?" Jonathan asked, brow furrowed.

"The museum's security is excellent but not impenetrable," Kara said. "Someone familiar with all the precautions could defeat them."

"And if Sora is involved, she would have easy access," Poresa noted.

"Even if it wasn't her, it wouldn't need to be a Nosama." Kara smiled sourly. "Any competent diviner could manage it if she had skilled accomplices to carry out the burglary."

"But why replace it at all?" Poresa objected. "Kara can't be the only one who will notice that the painting within the painting is wrong."

Etha considered correcting this. After all, she had been the one who spotted the swap, not Kara. But claiming credit was just a distraction from the mission and the discussion at hand, so she remained silent.

"It was probably a recent change," Jonathan said. "Perhaps the thieves took Nosamae Ascending somewhere else. They may not want to keep it in such plain sight as in a museum."

"What now?" Poresa asked, looking at Jonathan intently.

Jonathan ran a hand through his short blue-blond hair. "Someone in Aaronsglade will notice the swap, and I'm not sure they'll simply hand it over to Pithdai, especially if Nosamae Ascending is missing. We need to retrieve it, and we need to do it tomorrow night." He shook his head. "I wish we could do it tonight. There's no telling how soon someone will notice the switch or what the Nosamae will do once they do — step up security at the very least."

"Then we should do it tonight," Poresa said.

"We have no idea what the museum's security is like overnight. I'm not willing to risk the whole mission by going in blind."

The front door opened, and Stipator walked into the room. He was missing one boot, and his clothes and copper-colored hair were drenched as if he had fallen into a lake.

"Stipator!" Poresa cried with only the tiniest note of reproach. "Where have you been?"

"Speaking of risking the whole mission," Jonathan muttered under his breath. Etha felt the same.

Stipator waved one arm vaguely. Several drops of water spattered onto the floor. "It occurred to me that an aqueduct runs into the museum's basement, and I discovered that the intake was both large enough to squeeze into and entirely unguarded."

Jonathan glanced at Poresa.

"It's a dead end. Getting into the basement is easy, but the reinforced door at the top of the stairs..." She shook her head. "Better to go through one of the windows. Faster, too. The gallery is on the third floor."

Stipator twirled his mustache. "You might be right about that, Poresa. I didn't spend a lot of time trying doorknobs. I found a room piled high with Pithdai's paintings, though. It seems Sora unloaded her haul here."

Etha held her breath. *Of course! If the painting was here, then Sora has been here. Is she still here?*

"We suspected as much," Jonathan said. "They replaced Nosamae Ascending with Nosamae Descending in the third-floor gallery. We don't yet know exactly why."

Stipator twirled his mustache. "Actually, I think I can help you with that. I'll admit I didn't have time for a full inventory. I saw Sun's First Rising and several mundane paintings I recognize from Pithdai, but then Sora and Herald came down the stairs, so I fled."

"I don't believe that for a minute," Kara said drily.

Stipator shrugged. "I eavesdropped for a few minutes, yes, but mostly because I had to cover up all the paintings I had uncovered."

"And?" Poresa prompted.

"Herald seemed annoyed that they hadn't stolen Jacob's Bow from Seleine yet. He said the original plan was to activate Nosamae Ascending in Aaronsglade, and taking it out of Aaronma was too risky. He seemed concerned that the Senserte would interfere and demanded to know why Sora hadn't killed Arrina and Stipator when she had them in her power. Sora then reminded him that she regarded him as an advisor only, and that she had several good reasons not to meet us with deadly force."

She must be in charge, Etha thought. She crossed her arms on her chest tightly, consciously keeping her legs down when she wanted to hug them.

"I did a bit of snooping around the docks and found out Sora and her allies are setting sail tonight on a racing yacht," Stipator added.

"Any idea where they're bound?"

"No, but I think we can narrow it down to three destinations."

"Seleine, Romina, or the Palace of Doors," Poresa supplied.

Stipator grinned. "We could hire our own fast boat. Tail them to find out."

"No," Jonathan said with a note of finality. "That wasn't a part of the plan."

"Plans can change," Stipator persisted.

"Not this one. Listen, we've got Senserte waiting for Sora's gang in both Romina and Tremora. We could sail hard for Seleine, but with three Wefals, two Farlanders, and no Wen, we're not likely to be greeted with open arms by the Sutol. It doesn't matter who our parents are."

That's true enough, Etha thought. *No more than Zori and the ad'Marusak brothers would have been welcome in Aaronsglade.*

"If Sora plans to activate Nosamae Ascending, of course we'll do everything we can to stop her," Jonathan continued. "But even the Senserte can make mistakes, and if we fail we need a way to restore the balance of power."

"You intend to steal Nosamae Descending." Kara's face was as expressionless as her voice.

"Nosamae Descending belongs to Pithdai," Jonathan corrected. "We're simply taking it back."

"Why not just go to the Nosamae and demand they return the stolen art?" Kara asked. "We still have that letter of introduction to Michael's mother."

Stipator smirked. "Because he knows you won't need me for a diplomatic mission to the Nosamae, and he thinks I'll feel free to chase Sora."

"Michael said the letter was to be an absolute last resort," Jonathan reminded them.

"More of a last resort than stealing miraklas from an art museum in Aaronsglade, though?" Kara demanded.

"Kara," Etha said softly. "It's more complicated than it sounds. The Nosamae are not ... monolithic."

Kara pursed her lips for a moment before responding. "Very well. Stipator will get his museum heist. What's the plan, Jonathan?"

Within an hour they had sketched out the night's events. Stipator would enter the museum alone with one of the convincing replicas of Nosamae Ascending available in a marketplace near the museum.

· · · ·

"Oh, what did they do? I'll bet she has all the details," Lastor asked, and Arrina looked up at to see even Mathalla and Torminth leaning forward in anticipation.

"Etha's a good writer," Torminth said, and Mathalla had an approving nod. Michael sighed.

So did Arrina. She skimmed the page. "It looks like there was some kind of talisman to prevent wards from going off, which of course needed to be triggered by Jonathan, but Stipator went ... Oh dear."

"What?"

"She writes that Jonathan, Stipator, and Poresa formed a complete meld."

Michael whistled lowly.

"What's that?" Lastor asked.

"An internal, external, and mental mystic combining their powers — but each has to give some control up, especially the internal." The idea scared Arrina, but she imagined Stipator would have protested more than even Etha wrote. She stared at the letter in horror. *What was Jonathan thinking?*

But it made sense, a little. If Nosamae Ascending was activated, then it would be imperative to have Nosamae Descending. And here, it appeared, was a window.

"Even though Etha's opening suggests it did not work ..." Arrina felt dread rise in her.

"Read on," Michael said. "Let's get this over with."

• • • •

Some hours later, after the Senserte had eaten dinner, Kara and Etha sat on the couches opposite each other, drinking tea. Two clean, square dinner plates a foot on a side sat on the low table between them.

The two of them said nothing, although they could both feel the tension as they waited for the others to activate the relay. It had been nearly an hour since the others had left, and that spoke of at least a small complication.

Ghostly images of a metal rod against the shadow of some shrubbery abruptly appeared in the air a few inches above each plate.

Poresa's whisper hissed out of the image. "Is the relay working now?"

Kara let out a relieved breath and set down her teacup. She touched the edge of one of the plates and spoke. "Yes, Poresa."

"Sorry for the delay," Jonathan said quietly. "We had a little trouble getting one of the other relay rods in place."

"We're glad you're all safe, Jonathan," Etha said as she touched a plate.

"Etha says she's glad we're safe," Poresa repeated. "Stipator is getting ready to start his climb. We'll create the meld in two minutes."

"Sounds good, Poresa," Kara replied. "We're ready here."

The enchantress removed her hand from the dinner plate and took up her tea. She smiled at Etha. "I'd say we got the easy part of the job: drinking tea with maybe a glass of wine later. We could spend most of the heist talking about boys, if we wanted."

Etha wrinkled her nose. "Anything but that."

The image above the plates changed to a brick wall. A gloved left hand and a bare right hand stretched out in the view.

Kara touched a plate. "We have your eyes, Stipator. Can you hear us?"

"Yes." The hands fell out of sight. "Give me just a moment to put on this eye patch."

"Remember, glove in bag. Bare hand to set the token down. If nothing else, stick to that plan."

Stipator did not answer.

A few seconds later, a dark space filled the image above the plate that represented Stipator's right eye. The darkness was almost immediately replaced by a sort of colorful fog moving like a slow river. Etha could still make out the bricks, but the motes of green, red, yellow, blue, and several duller, almost faded colors partially obscured the view.

"Is that the flow?" Etha asked softly.

Kara looked into her eyes. "I can't answer any of your questions about what you see through the eye patch. Michael will explain it all to you when you're ready for that knowledge." Kara turned back to the images, touching the plate. "The patch is working. We also have your ears. Jonathan, do you want to test your meld?"

The Senserte spent several minutes testing to make sure Jonathan, Poresa, and the Farlanders could all access Stipator's senses and that everyone could communicate easily. Between the eye patch, the tokens, and the meld, it was as if all five of them were in one body.

At last, Stipator lost patience. "I'm going to get started," he said, and the bricks seemed to flow down like a waterfall.

Kara poured herself some more tea, refilled Etha's nearly empty cup, and sat back. "Now, where were we?"

"I have a question. I hope you don't think it presumptive of me to ask," Etha said.

Kara motioned for her to continue, watching the jerky movements on the plate.

"Earlier you suggested that Michael's mother might be behind all this. Before that, you seemed quick to cast suspicion on Pithdai. It sounds like you don't think Sora is working on her own. Why?"

"This whole thing has felt wrong to me from the moment the letter arrived, at nearly the last moment it could have." She tapped one finger on the table. "What would have happened if Jonathan hadn't come up with some plan to get a least a couple Senserte there in time?"

We voted to go, Etha thought. *Larus might have wanted the Senserte, but he couldn't have known he'd get them. Wait, is that what she's saying?*

"I think Sora would have made good on her threats," Etha said, not believing herself.

Kara's lip curled. "I don't think she would, but let's assume you're right. Kaspar is dead. How does Larus react? What happens in Pithdai, when Larus's line ends and his relatives squabble over the throne? As like as not, Larus is assassinated long before he can punish anyone."

Etha started in horror. "Do you believe this is a succession dispute?"

"I am not ruling it out."

They focused on Stipator again, as he inched carefully through a hallway, pausing at every breath. Kara pulled out a pocket watch and tapped it a few times, eyes darting back and forth between the flow and face. Etha jumped again as Kara spoke.

"Let's say Kaspar is dead. Larus sends his homeguard to deal with Sora — but he's certain she's a Nosama and wants to restart the Nosamae War. You don't have to be the King of Tremora to see where that goes."

Etha nodded, rubbing her arms. *The Union gets rallied against Aaronma, and the war happens anyway.*

"Here's another one. The Nosamae decide they want to activate the painting, but they want plausible deniability if it fails. So they need a cat's paw — Sora. They even give her assistants with useful talents."

"The last thing the Nosamae want is another Nosamae War."

Stipator peeked three times around a corner before darting to another doorway.

"They have good reason to fear *losing* another Nosamae War."

"I still can't believe that of them."

Kara breathed deeply. "I am just not ruling out any possibilities, no matter how small. You said yourself they aren't monolithic."

And some factions might be tempted, Etha thought.

"Maybe Kaspar's just a boy in love. Maybe he sees an opportunity to increase his power over the Farlanders."

"And the same for Canolos and Sutola's Wen?"

"Now you're catching on. And what do we know about Herald? Aflighan would just love for civil war to come to the Union. And we know even less about the other, younger enchantress. Is she an Aaron, a Jacob, or a Haven? All of them could gain or lose if one of the paintings is activated."

"She could also be working alone."

Kara shrugged, studying the image showed the flow for several minutes. At last she touched the plate and spoke, "Corridor security isn't as bad as I feared, Stipator."

"Does that mean I don't have to lay down a trail of these coins?" Stipator whispered.

"Leave the trail, but consider yourself safe to improvise if you must."

Kara removed her hand from the plate.

"Do you still think it wiser to let Sora's group work without our interference?" Etha asked.

Kara shook her head. "As much as I hate to admit it, this struggle would have happened with or without us. Whoever decided to get us involved knew exactly how to attract our attention, and now that we're here we have no good way to extricate ourselves."

"Kara, I'm at the door behind the Nosamae Ascending display," Stipator whispered.

The heavy lock looked like it had been torn off.

Did Jonathan's part of the meld not work? Etha wondered.

Kara touched the plate. "Open the door a crack and look through it with the eye patch."

As Stipator complied, there was a tinkling noise as of a window being broken far away. The image shifted abruptly as the Wefal turned his head at the sound and then again as he turned back and threw the door open. A Farlander woman lay on the floor of the gallery in a pool of her own blood.

Stipator swore under his breath and swept into the room. He swung his head around to look at the painting or, as it turned out, where the painting had been only a few hours ago.

"Someone just beat us to it," Stipator whispered. He had enough time to take a single step toward the exit before the image of the flow became as a solid wall of color in an elaborate pattern.

When the color faded a split second later, both images winked out.

Kara swore under her breath and touched the plate. "Jonathan? Poresa?"

The images flickered back to life, but now both showed Jonathan through Poresa's eyes. He looked grave. "Any chance you can extract Stipator?"

Kara shook her head, seeming to forget that he couldn't see her. "The museum is in lockdown."

"You can counter enchantments," Jonathan objected. "Whoever stole the painting also hurt or killed the guard. It'll look bad for Stipator if..."

"I don't have that kind of time," Kara cut him off. "Get as far away from the museum as possible. We have to use the letter."

Jonathan seemed to weigh this for a moment. At last he nodded. "We'll meet you at the safehouse soon."

"Make it the Bronze Leviathan," Kara said. "And be sure to pull up the relay rod before you go or it will lead them right here. Good luck."

The double images of Jonathan flickered and vanished.

Kara looked up at Etha. "We need to leave. Now."

Etha hopped off the couch and ran to her room. She opened the hidden panel and removed her knives and the whip. She put it on and returned to the living room. Kara was unarmed, but she had her satchel slung over one shoulder and was in the process of slipping several rings onto her fingers.

"Are we going to the ship?"

"Not yet. They'll be hunting for his accomplices. We need to go to ground for the night somewhere they won't expect. Do you know of any abandoned buildings nearby?"

Etha flushed. "No."

"Inns in seedy parts of town?"

"The First Tier doesn't really have seedy parts."

Kara pulled open the back door of the safehouse. "Then I hope your sandals are comfortable, because we're going to be walking until dawn."

"We could go to a tea house," Etha suggested. "Many near the University are open all night."

"Because apprentices stay up late studying?"

"Or need a place to sober up before returning to their dormatories. And apprentices don't go to the University. These are the enchantresses."

Kara closed the door behind them. "That should work. Lead on."

The tea shop Etha chose was among the largest and busiest. Neither of them seemed likely to fall asleep, but they kept the tea coming anyway so as not raise any eyebrows. No one seemed to take any notice of Kara, but then her jewelry marked her as one of them. Etha drew stares, though, as she always did when she spent any time in a place that catered only to adults.

I'm probably the only woman alive who is looking forward to gray hair, she thought glumly.

A few hours before dawn, rumor of the burglary at the Nosamae War Memorial Museum passed through the shop. Etha hoped she was hiding her own nervousness as well as Kara, who seemed entirely engrossed in her conversation with Etha about Flecterran Union politics. But the enchantresses spoke of the crime as a matter of curiosity, and no one looked at Kara or Etha twice.

When the sky turned gray, the two left behind a pile of small coins and stepped into the morning mist. By the time they reached the docks, the sun had burned away most of the fog, but a few wisps hung in the air along the water. They came up short when they saw the Bronze Leviathan tied up at one of the piers. Aaronma customs officials walked up the gang-plank, flanked by Nosamae enforcers.

"That was quick," Kara murmured.

Etha didn't bother responding. The Nosamae enforcers routinely tracked down renegade enchantresses. Surely they could identify the ship that had brought a mirakla thief into the city.

"I'm running out of ideas," Kara announced as they walked through the busy streets. "Will our documents still let me into the First Tier?"

"Yes, but they surely have your name by now. We were lucky they didn't ask for our papers when we left."

"It won't have my name on it or yours," Kara confided with a small smile.

Etha didn't question that. The enchantress had probably been in Aaronsglade long enough to analyze the patterns of its scans for magic and might be able to avoid notice.

"And what will I do?" Etha asked.

"I assume the ban on magic doesn't hold outside of the city. Get a message back to the others. Let them know what happened. We might need to explore … political extraction."

Etha sighed heavily. Arrina wasn't going to like that.

Chapter 27

"That was two days ago," Arrina read. "I'm staying at an inn a few miles outside of Aaronsglade, but I'm not sure what to do next. Most or all the Pith art Sora stole is in Aaronsglade, and it isn't clear into whose hands Nosamae Ascending and Nosamae Descending have fallen. Be careful. If Kara is right, this might be more complicated than finding one villain and punishing him. Humbly at your service I am Etha ad'Lisa."

"That is … discouraging," Mathalla said. "If Sutola is involved in this little power struggle, our welcome in Seleine could be rather cold."

"It doesn't even have to be all of Sutola," Arrina reminded him grimly. "Canolos is the son of the archon of Seleine, and he clearly has his own plans in this. If his mother is involved …"

"Whatever happens, we can't let them activate either painting," Michael said. "This time we can't let them get away."

"Then we should get moving," Lastor said with an unmistakable note of complaint in his voice.

None of them could argue with that.

The arrow that landed at Arrina's feet that afternoon gave them little cause for hope. She looked up toward the canopy, staring up at the scattered array of bows angled down at them. It was generally safe to assume that any Wen pointing a bow at ground travelers had a talent to make it nearly impossible to miss her target, and even the ones without magic abilities like Davur's or Canolos's were doubtless better archers than most Farlanders and Wefals.

"They look angry," Tajek said softly at her back.

Arrina motioned him to silence. Many Wen had her father's talent for hearing, and it would not do to provoke them.

I think it's safe to say Sora got here before we did.

She raised her hands above her head with palms upraised.

"Who goes there?" someone shouted from the row of bows. It was a child's voice, one maybe Lastor's age but probably younger.

Arrina glanced in Michael's direction without moving her head. The Farlander stood frozen in midstep.

"Travelers from Pithdai," Arrina said. She didn't insult the Sutol by shouting, knowing at least some of them could hear her even from the canopy. She touched her magic, heightened her own hearing until she could make out the calls of every bird and monkey in the trees above her. "Mira's followers who keep her code. Praise to the Mother of the Trees. We seek shelter and story for the night. Will Seleine offer hospitality?"

"What are you names?" The same voice, a girl's voice, but she did not shout this time.

"We would speak with your archon," Arrina replied. "In good time, we may trade our names with yours."

"Well said." A woman's voice, older, seemingly from directly behind the Senserte.

Arrina smiled slightly as she saw Tajek out of the corner of her eye, head weaving as he looked for the source. She was hidden with unseen presence or capable of speaking through the trees, Arrina guessed. The latter talent was most common among Tremor but Sutol frequently possessed it.

"Partor, allow our guests up," the woman's voice commanded, and this time it came from somewhere in the canopy.

The Wen tree town was larger than it looked from the ground. They may have been walking under it in the jungle for some time. The Senserte climbed the ladder dropped for them and joined a woman who looked old enough to be any of their mothers on one of the platforms between the trees. Another level could be made out above them, as well, near the tops of the ancient trees, three of which formed the heart of the town.

The archon, who introduced herself as Berilla without being asked, greeted Mathalla, Torminth, and Lastor with a kiss on each cheek that each of them returned in kind. She then kissed Arrina, Michael, and, with a raised eyebrow, Tajek on the right cheek. Arrina and Michael were familiar with this Sutol greeting, which they used even with enemies, and returned it with two kisses.

Tajek reciprocated the single kiss awkwardly, seemingly unaware that Wen always received a double-kiss. "Greetings of peace from the Nankek, archon."

Berilla seemed not to take offense at this. "You are far from home. Do you miss it?"

The Turu brushed his hand across his chest. "At times, archon, but it is a small price to pay to keep such exalted company."

"You come from the east, by way of Phantom Lake." She didn't phrase it as a question. Sutol hospitality said stories must be traded, but no questions could be asked regarding who and where guests came from.

Arrina glanced at everyone, and kept her mouth shut.

The silence stretched for a heartbeat longer than comfortable, and then Berilla beckoned them to follow her. Lastor led, following the archon along a rope bridge away from the center of the tree town. Mathalla and Torminth followed. Arrina hung back with Michael and Tajek. She noted absently that while no one pointed arrows their way, many Wen archers maintained watchful stances toward the visitors, particularly interested in the Farlander among them.

"Anything?" she asked Michael softly.

He shrugged and shook his head, which was the signal that meant he had not detected anything but that he had his doubts. Arrina had a basic understanding that enchantresses had a more difficult time scanning long distances in rainforests and jungles than in open or mountainous terrain. The explanation was apparently a secret — one of many Michael said enchantresses were expected to keep.

He climbed off the bridge and smiled wanly at Berilla, who stood next to the room they would stay in. "I thank you, mother. May Mira's breath bless you with many more years."

Berilla's stern face didn't change, nor did she speak.

They were on a platform fifty feet above the ground, made from shaped wood notched into the tree and tightly bound with vines. The platform was a circle around the tree, with two rope bridges leading off at right angles, allowing some privacy on the far side. There was more than enough room for the six of them.

"Welcome to Seleine," Berilla said formally. "Allow me to take you into my home for the night. I will prepare a meal and beds for you. We have scheduled rains here if you would like to shower."

"Thank you, mother," Arrina responded just as formally. "We will accept your hospitality."

Berilla gestured to the platform. "The five of you will sleep here. Your enchantress will receive special quarters." She grabbed Michael by the arm.

Tajek stepped between her and Michael.

"We'd prefer our friend to stay with us," he said firmly.

The air filled with the creaks of bows being drawn and the hiss of swords and knives sliding from sheaths. The archon reached up — she didn't have to reach too far, Arrina realized, she was almost as tall as Tajek, though slimmer — and put her hand on the Turu's shoulder.

"No harm will come to him as long as you do not behave in a way unbecoming of guests." She released Tajek, and he stepped to one side, looking at Arrina helplessly.

Arrina deliberately avoided looking at all those hidden bows waiting for them to take aggressive action. She took Michael's free hand. The Farlander looked at her with a strained expression on his face.

"Mother, please forgive us, but we have not shared fruit with you," she said.

Now the older Wen's stern face cracked. The sign was tiny, barely noticeable, but the wrinkles that appeared at the eyes were of a restrained smile. At that moment, Arrina felt she could trust the archon of Seleine under any other circumstances but this one. Something more was at work here.

Sora may still be here and in command of the orb and diadem.

The code said that once a community peeled fruit with its guests, neither side could betray each other. Some claimed a mirakla or Mira herself enforced these brief treaties, but history showed only tradition bound either party to the arrangement.

Berilla called for fruit and wine.

The archon held up a basket of oranges, purple bananas, and a single spikefruit. "Mira, Lady of the Forest, your hands give us generously of the fruits of the land. May it nourish us and give us no cause for conflict."

She took the spikefruit and peeled off its green skin to reveal the pale gold flesh beneath before dividing it into slices.

The language of the bounty, Arrina realized. *Sharing an orange means friendship, so it's the most common. Bananas are for family — yellow for guests of equal age, purple for younger, blue for elder. And spikefruit?*

She wracked her brain in search of childhood lessons on the subject. She hadn't had much use for this information, though Jonathan sometimes used the tradition in the troupe's plays. Mathalla seemed to notice it, as well, for he frowned fractionally as he watched Berilla finish peeling the spikefruit.

"We share the fruit under Mira's auspices," the six travelers answered. Each of them took a slice, and hostess and guests ate them together.

Berilla took the pitcher of wine and poured it into each of seven wooden cups on a tray. "Mira, mother of the trees, you taught us to give up our power in our search for peace and understanding."

That's the prayer before taking saat, Arrina knew. She had heard it countless times when diplomats came to Pithdai Palace.

"Glory to the Mother of the Trees." They each took a cup, dribbled a small amount on the platform, and drank the rest.

Arrina expected to taste the strong sweetness of saat in her wine, but she tasted only the refreshing coolness of lemon, lime, and mango.

As a boy collected the cups, Berilla beckoned Michael again. "If you are satisfied you are indeed our guests, we will take your friend. I will leave my grandson, Nijel, to assist you as needed. Please join us for dinner when the sun touches the horizon." She bowed slightly to them, then ushered the Farlander off.

Arrina nodded, feeling slightly guilty she had forced the ceremony. *Like a daughter trying on her mother's clothes after being told not to.* They watched as Michael was led away until they could no longer see him for the trees.

At least the Wen of the town had stopped pointing arrows their way. She touched her magic experimentally and found it still ready to answer her call.

She pretended to give us saat but didn't, Arrina noted. She still couldn't remember the meaning of spikefruit.

Nijel was younger even than Lastor — perhaps ten years old and in full command of Wen magic. He was watching her carefully. Several minutes after Berilla left, he came to a conclusion. "You're Larus's girl, aren't you?" he blurted.

"If by that you mean his daughter, then yes," she told him. "My name is Arrina ad'Anna. I can introduce the others if you'd like."

"Grandma didn't recognize you," Nijel said as if it was Arrina's fault. "I should go tell her."

Oh I'm fairly certain she did.

"She asked you to watch us," Arrina reminded him. She watched his face contort — surely he didn't really want to do this, but his grandmother was a formidable woman. After a few seconds of discomfort, Arrina placed a hand on his shoulder. "You may tell her later. We are not going anywhere. Come, Nijel, tell me about your town. The festival of Dark Moon's Passing was a few days ago, right?"

"Four days," he said, and then stopped again, mouth opening. "But I'm not supposed to talk to strangers about that."

All right, Arrina thought, *that's why everyone's on edge.* She looked right, then back at him. "How about we play a game of cards?"

Lastor took up the cue and appeared with a pack in his hand. The boy was eager to play.

When she was certain Nijel was distracted, she plucked Mathalla's sleeve. "What was that fruit we shared?" she asked innocently.

The big Wen caught the intense look in her eye and recognized the falseness of the question. "Spikefruit. It's mentioned in the third act of Beware the Blue Eclipse."

Arrina knew the troupe's plays well, and she recognized the reference at once. The play concerned the betrayal and murder of King Luxias. Someone who knew about the conspiracy to assassinate him sent him a spikefruit as a warning, but his brother, who was in league with the conspirators, convinced him it had been sent to frighten him into refusing to meet with a Sutol envoy.

Spikefruit. The enemy is among us.

Arrina nodded in simple acknowledgment.

Chapter 28

An hour or so passed, and then a young Wen girl came flying over the rope bridge, feet lightly patting on the railing as she danced across like a tightrope walker.

"Those were the days," Mathalla said softly, smiling as the girl landed lightly right behind Nijel.

"You should drop those cards," the girl said, poking twice at his hand.

"Shut up, Cleo," Nijel said. "I know how to play."

"Grandma sent me to invite the guests to dinner."

Nijel scowled, the universal symbol for "hello, annoying little sister." He put his cards down carefully and stood up. Arrina and the other Senserte also stood.

"Friends of Mira," the boy said formally, "would you please join us at our evening meal this ..." He stopped, eyes rolling nervously.

"Join us for dinner this evening," the girl corrected.

Nijel blew out a big sigh. "Yes, would you please join us for dinner this evening?"

"We would be honored," Arrina said, smiling.

They followed the two children — Nijel took the main route, but Cleorame, who he said was his cousin, not sister, danced around ahead of them, feet and hands touching everything. Lastor contented himself with walking under the bridge, his feet touching directly under Mathalla's. Arrina could tell Nijel wanted to chase her, but his sullen stubbornness kept his feet marching like a Farlander's.

When they reached the low-ceilinged dining room, five Wen hovered behind Berilla at the entrance. Arrina recognized one of them with bright pink hair at once.

She gasped softly and heard an echoing grunt from Mathalla.

"Canolos," Arrina said with a stiff nod. "Where is Kaspar?"

"Unharmed and much safer now that the Nosamae's agent has been neutralized."

"Nosamae's agent?" Arrina repeated, resisting the urge to name names.

Canolos only gave her a mysterious smile. "Please join us for dinner, and we'll be happy to explain the depths of this Aaronsglade conspiracy. Mother?"

"Welcome to Seleine." Berilla sounded strained. "I apologize for the tension of our initial greeting, but you'll better understand it once my son explains it. " She then introduced the Wen with her: Canolos, Partor, and three others who were a sister, an aunt, and her own daughter.

Everyone adhered strictly to the protocols of welcoming guests. The tension there was palpable. Only Nijel and Cleorame seemed unaware of it. Arrina frowned but followed the Wen into the chamber, which consisted of two large wooden platforms that acted as floor and ceiling, stretched between two trees instead of wrapping around one like most of the platforms. They sat on tiny pallets at the long, low table, which was little more than a beam.

Arrina sat across from Canolos, with the other Senserte on her side of the table, facing the Wen on the other side. Berilla directed Nijel and Cleorame as she served the food with a rigorously formal demeanor. Canolos kept his hands carefully folded in his lap, concealed under the lip of the table.

"I must ask after my friend," Arrina said to Canolos as Cleorame filled their tall wooden cups with water and Nijel filled the smaller cups with a deep red wine.

"He will join us after dinner," Canolos said. "We will talk more of it after we eat."

Arrina's stomach knotted. She didn't believe for an instant that Michael was an agent of the Nosamae — at least not one involved in the kind of conspiracy Canolos hinted at. *That doesn't mean the people of Seleine will not believe he is.*

"Arrina?" Tajek asked. The Turu looked on the point of leaping into action.

"It would be rude to refuse our hosts' hospitality," Arrina told them all.

The children brought in trays of peeled fruit and sliced meat — all of it arranged in neat rows so it could be eaten with fingers with a minimum of mess. The Senserte ate the simply seasoned food mechanically. Arrina made a conscious effort to eat as much as she could stomach. She would need its strength soon enough. The meal passed in silence, and as Nijel refilled their wine cups, Arrina felt some of the tension leave the room. She finished her second cup and turned it upside down, but Mathalla gestured for a third.

Finally Cleorame and Nijel brought out the dessert, small bowls of canopy honey and big bowls of nuts: pecan, walnut, blacknut, and almond, cracked and ready for dipping.

"Now," Berilla said, causing silence to drift down the table. "You refused to give your names to our sentries. Please, do us the courtesy of introducing yourselves to me."

Arrina glanced at Canolos, who smiled slightly and made no move to explain anything. She looked down at her plate, carefully wiping honey and salt off her hands. She sipped water before introducing each of them in turn. Berilla gave no indication of surprise at any of their identities. Arrina turned her attention to Canolos. "You promised us an explanation."

"According to tradition, we would now exchange the stories of our homes," Berilla noted.

"Under the circumstances, I think that can wait, mother," Canolos said. "I believe we owe her an explanation sooner rather than later."

Berilla nodded solemnly. "As you say, Canolos."

"You hinted at a conspiracy," Arrina prompted.

Canolos smiled. "Oh yes. Aaronsglade has had designs on the Pith throne for decades, carefully infiltrating the palace and subverting Wen at the highest levels of your government. They would like nothing so much as for ancient King Larus's sole heir to mysteriously vanish, assuring a bloody succession war whose outcome they can sway to their favor."

"I find that a bit incredible," Arrina told him. "Who is this agent you claim to have neutralized?"

For an answer, Canolos gestured to Nijel, who stood at the entrance. A moment later, Michael walked into the dining chamber. He looked no different from when she had last seen him, although he wore a defeated expression.

The Wen around the table made motions to rise, but Canolos stayed them with a hand. "No need, cousins. He has tasted saat and is unarmed."

"Michael is Aaronsglade's agent?" Arrina demanded, not bothering to conceal her incredulity.

"Yes, and now that he knows the game is up, he will confess his betrayal to you," Canolos told them all.

"Arrina, my fellow Senserte, and people of Seleine, my name is Michael ad'Aaron, and I am a traitor."

The Wen of Seleine murmured, but Arrina spoke over them. "Wait!" She stood up and looked Michael in the eyes. "Uncle, are your bruises and tears from sorrows or fears?"

Michael frowned. "I know this must be difficult for you to hear, Arrina."

Arrina lowered her eyelids at Michael's incorrect response. *Either he has been enchanted, or this isn't Michael at all.*

"Difficult?" she asked as she strolled forward with one hand in her pocket, clutching the cool wooden disc hidden there. "What do you intend to do with him?"

Berilla spoke delicately. "He is our guest under the code of hospitality, but once he leaves Seleine, he no longer has that protection."

"You intend to dose him with saat and send a hunting party to execute him before it wears off," Mathalla said, shaking with outrage. Arrina knew every Senserte knew Uncle Father by heart — the play was as popular as it was timeless.

"King Larus would do no less," Canolos insisted. "It is too dangerous to let a rogue enchantress live."

Indeed it may be at that, Arrina thought.

Without giving a sign of her intentions, she slid the disc out of her pocket and in one motion pressed it to the back of Michael's hand. The disc went cold, and Michael immediately turned into Corina. She squirmed slightly, but Arrina's grip was firm.

Arrina dragged the young enchantress toward the table as she rounded on Canolos. "This is an imposter! Archon, you are being played for a fool."

None of the Wen in the room made any move toward Canolos or Corina.

"I'm sure my son can explain this little misunderstanding," Berilla said.

"What misunderstanding?" Lastor demanded, and several nearby leaves began to smolder and smoke. "Where have you taken our friend?"

Canolos managed a tight smile. "In the name of the Empress, remember that Michael ad'Aaron confessed to conspiring against the Pith, which means the Nosamae's designs on Sutola cannot be far behind. He was just escorted out of the room."

"Outrageous!" Partor cried. "We must stop them now!"

Canolos regarded Arrina coolly. "As long as you adhere to the code of hospitality, you will not be harmed. Release Corina, and tell your Senserte to keep their hands away from their weapons."

"In the name of the Empress, explain yourself," Mathalla snarled.

None of the Seleine Wen made any motion to obey, although Arrina had to admit it had been worth a try. *It would appear the diadem can allow others to speak on the wearer's behalf.*

"Arrina?" Canolos prompted.

Arrina released Corina and stuck the wooden disc back in her pocket.

"Ah no," Canolos said with a cluck of his tongue. He held out his hand. "We're not using talismans this time. Turn out all your pockets and place the contents on the table."

"Arrina?" Tajek asked.

"Do as he says," she said.

The Senserte removed the talismans they had hidden on their person. Lastor tried to keep one in reserve, but Corina detected it somehow, and it ended up on the pile.

The young enchantress made no motion, but after a moment she spoke. "They're neutralized."

"Good. Tell Sora our guests are safe," Canolos ordered.

Corrina nodded once and left.

Canolos's expression changed from arrogant calm to furtiveness. "In the name of the Empress, never think about anything that happens between now and the time the Empress arrives. In the name of the Empress, it is time to exchange stories."

"Let us tell you some stories of our town," Berilla said, beaming. "And you can share your stories with us in turn."

"Your pardon, mother." Canolos smiled. "Arrina brings me an important message from her father, and we should discuss it at once. We will be nearby, so pay us no notice."

"Of course, son," Berilla said, patting his hand.

Canolos's eyes met Arrina's, and he gestured with his right hand, his left bent behind his back again. Arrina rose and joined him in a corner beneath a shroud of hanging leaves.

"Let us be frank with one another," Canolos said.

Arrina immediately slapped him hard across his left cheek. His head turned from the blow, and his pale cheek turned bright red.

He doesn't have it, which means Sora does.

Canolos looked on the point of laughing, but he fought down his amusement.

"That wasn't quite what I had in mind." He touched his red cheek. "If I weren't promised to another, I might respond to your little flirtation the way Stipator would."

If you even try it, you'll spend the rest of your life pissing from a squat! Arrina thought fiercely, but she instead forced herself to remain calm.

"How does it feel to let an enchantress subjugate your family?" Arrina asked.

That worked.

Canolos frowned. "They aren't enchanted. Legends about miraklas mingle freely with the truth. Some experimentation is required to sort out the two."

"Learn anything of interest?" Arrina almost snarled.

"Yes. " Canolos made no move to elaborate.

Arrina prodded him further. "So you've given her the orb and diadem. How is that any different from handing over the Valley to a new Nosama tyrant?"

"You are in no position to judge me. If not for the Senserte she would never have gotten the orb or Theo's Sword," Canolos whispered. "Your brother came with Sora of his own volition. Pithdai's homeguard is too vigilant to allow an enchantress to practice her arts so close to Larus's heir. Of course the instant he was out of their reach, she had no such limits. He won't leave her willingly. You will need to rescue him, but I'm sure you already knew that."

"And Michael?"

Canolos shrugged. "We need a scapegoat to convince Seleine to give us Jacob's Bow. His confession was convenient."

"You mean to murder him?"

"Of course not. He has no doubt escaped by now, and hopefully he will flee Sutola. Not everyone in Seleine has been ... mellowed by Sora. They won't deliver him to her as planned. She is tired of running from you, you know. You're in for a fight you can't win. Your enchanter can't change that, but I'll see to it that you have your opportunity to escape. Do not fail to bring Kaspar out of Seleine with you."

"You intend to stay behind with Sora?"

"Yes. Someone needs to stop her from using Nosamae Ascending."

"How do you intend to do that?"

Canolos gave her a mysterious smile, and Arrina knew he was planning to swap Nosamae Ascending for Nosamae Descending at the last moment.

Kara is right. Everyone has a stake in this.

"Is she acting on her own?" Arrina asked for the sake of appearances.

Canolos shook his head. "There is no time to explain. She will be here soon."

Arrina had expected a lie, not an evasion, but perhaps Canolos guessed she knew him well enough to tell when he was lying. She returned to her place at the table. The post-dinner storytelling had just concluded.

A few minutes later, four figures walked into the dining area. Sora led the little group. Kaspar followed at her heels. Corina brought up the rear. Michael was on her arm, his eyes glassy and lifeless. Arrina risked a glare at Canolos, but he seemed momentarily just as surprised as she was.

Where is Herald? she wondered silently.

Sora wore an elegant diadem that looked to have been woven of golden saat leaves and silver vines. She carried the Orb of Elvenkind in her right hand and wore a silver ring on her left with four rounded stones — one each of green, blue, yellow, and black. The stones glowed faintly in the shape of the current phases of the moons.

The Moon Ring.

"Arrina and her Senserte. What an unexpected surprise," Sora purred as she surveyed the room. "But where is your brave Wefal friend?"

"That is none of your concern," Arrina snapped. Michael had told her stories about what enchantresses could do. As light a touch as he used on their jobs, she had seen him subdue several people at once with his magic without apparent effort. "Release us, and return Kaspar to me at once."

Sora tilted her head back and laughed long and loud. "You are hardly in a position to make demands, Arrina." Sora looked at the Moon Ring and stretched her hand toward the table as she spoke. "Look upon the power of the Nosamae and humble yourself!" she shouted, and the stones of the ring flared bright with light.

A wave of nausea swept over Arrina.

She wanted to laugh, and cry, and fight, and weep, and ... the emotions coalesced into devotion, pounding, head-searing devotion for the woman with the ring, for the dark mistress who ruled all. She wanted to kiss her, to obey her every command. She felt this sink into her, like it was searching for that small ball that could still scream "this isn't right." The power consumed her.

Arrina gritted her teeth, fighting it. "Release us," she croaked, "or Stipator sends Nosamae Ascending to the bottom of Kaeruli."

And then, the ball popped, and Arrina lost herself in the worship of her enemy.

Chapter 29

When Arrina regained her awareness, she was kneeling on a wooden platform overlooking all of Seleine. Just before the horizon she could see the line of red-leaved trees that marked the southern border of the Blood Preserve. The morning sun shone down on her, and there was the unmistakably sweet taste of saat in her mouth.

Sora and Michael stood in front of her. Canolos stood slightly to one side, his arms folded. The other Senserte lay unconscious all around, as if they had fallen asleep in mid-grovel. Berilla and the other Wen of the town were nowhere to be seen.

Sora frowned at Arrina. "Do you really expect me to believe that you broke into the Nosamae War Memorial Museum and stole one of Aaronma's most precious national treasures without being apprehended by the Nosamae?"

If I'm not dead or enchanted already, she must not have called my bluff.

Arrina shrugged. "It wasn't even the hardest heist we've ever pulled. Canolos and Kaspar both know about some of the jobs we've done in the line of duty."

"An interesting lie but not a very convincing one, Ma'Sora," Canolos said. "We have Nosamae Ascending. Herald is bringing it from our yacht even now."

Arrina took a chance. "Herald is bringing Nosamae Descending. He means to trick you into activating the wrong painting."

Canolos's eyes went wide.

Sora turned to Michael, whose eyes were still glassy. "Is she telling the truth?"

Arrina froze and silently cursed herself. *It was a beautiful lie. Too bad it didn't last.*

"Yes, Ma'Sora," Michael droned. "Herald switched the paintings again just before you left Aaronsglade. I was there when she gave Stipator the order."

Arrina fell over to hide her surprise. Hope filled her as Canolos roughly returned her to a kneeling position, but by then, she had regained her composure.

Sora returned her attention to Arrina. "You must cancel your order."

"I can't. I can delay it by arrow, but I can only cancel it in person."

Sora sneered. "That is easily arranged. Wefals aren't the only ones who can change faces."

Arrina laughed. "Stipator would spot an imposter as easily as I spotted yours."

"I can force you to give me your password."

"Password? The Senserte rely on nothing so easily discovered. We have the scripts of scores of Jonathan's plays memorized for our shows. We practice them constantly for our performances, but they serve a second purpose. If Stipator recites one line and I fail to respond with the next, he'll know you're a phony."

That, at least, wasn't a lie. Well, not entirely. They all had their favorite challenges and responses. She had a pretty good idea which lines Stipator would quote.

"An enchantress can convince him that he has heard the response," Sora snarled.

"The way two enchantresses had no trouble subduing the Senserte at Tremora?" Arrina countered. "It's not as though he will be alone. Canolos knows the company we keep. Enchantresses aren't the only ones who can force an enemy to act against his interests."

Poresa would have been furious at having her magic used as a threat like that. She employed her powers as a mental mystic against the unwilling even less readily than Michael did.

Sora's forced smile showed all of her teeth. "How long before ad'Bryan's heir does his worst?"

"Pray for clear skies, Sora." Arrina snorted. "Not long enough for you to break us the way you did Tasticon. Or Kaspar."

Sora looked genuinely surprised. "You think I've enchanted your half-brother?"

Arrina nodded gravely.

"You wound me!" Sora cried, but her tone was mocking.

Arrina wanted to snarl or shout or hurl Sora off the platform and into the canopy below.

She still has orb and diadem though. I can't hurt her, and she knows it. Even if I could, it would not stop someone else from trying to do the same thing she is. Arrina clenched her fists.

"Sora, we have what we came for," Canolos said suddenly, and for the first time Arrina noticed the familiar, elaborately decorated rapier at his hip and the ivory white bow that crossed his chest.

Theo's Sword and Jacob's Bow. The only key I haven't seen yet is the Star Ring.

"It is all for nothing without Nosamae Ascending!" Sora snarled at him.

"She's lying," Canolos said slowly. "We've been a step ahead of her from the beginning. I don't think her Senserte have suddenly gained the upper hand."

"And if she isn't?"

"You have confirmation from Michael that I'm not," Arrina reminded her.

"Sora, my love," called a new voice. Kaspar stood on the platform. Behind him, Corina stepped off the ladder, brushing her skirt. "This is unnecessary."

Sora's expression softened at once, and she turned to the prince. "Kaspar, my sweet, I thought you were resting for the journey ahead."

Arrina expected Kaspar to make accusations, threats, or demands. Instead, he simply smiled warmly at the enchantress.

"Helping you is more important than my rest. Please release Arrina and her Senserte."

"Sora, no!" Canolos almost shouted, his hand gripping the hilt of the rapier.

"They are no threat to you. In fact, they can help you."

"That's ridiculous," Canolos snapped. "They are dangerous enough alive. If free, they will continue to hound us or worse."

Anger lit Kaspar's face. Arrina saw her father's rage in his eyes. He didn't raise his voice. "If you lay a finger on my sister, Canolos, I will make you regret it."

"The panther cub tests his roar," Canolos said with a sneer. "You don't have nearly your father's bite, though, nor do you have any say on what we do or don't do."

Kaspar still looked angry, but he seemed to be struggling. "We've been friends since we were children. Please don't force me to forget that."

"We were friends once, yes. That was before you tried to replace me in Sora's affections. She has promised herself to me. Me!"

Kaspar sighed heavily. "If you love her, Canolos, why have you plotted to betray her?"

Sora mouthed the word "betray" but did not move.

"It's true, Sora. Canolos didn't give the Senserte saat as you instructed. He hoped they would take me away from you when they escaped." Kaspar held up his right hand. The ring on the first finger there sparkled as if with a thousand tiny stars. "The trees have ears. I am continually amazed by what they overhear."

That must be the Star Ring, Arrina thought.

"You are as glib as your mule of a sister!" Canolos snarled. "Sora, you can't possibly believe him!"

Sora said nothing.

"Herald is bringing Nosamae Descending because Canolos told him to. They will use you to activate it or find some other Farlander woman to press into the deed."

Sora shook her head in silent denial.

Kaspar spread his hands apologetically. "You have the diadem. Order him to give you an account of his conversation with Arrina."

Canolos readied and drew Jacob's Bow in one smooth action, and Kaspar froze in its aim. The arrow left the bow so quickly that Arrina had no time to move before it streaked toward her half-brother.

"No!" shrieked Sora, and Arrina thought she heard Corina echo it.

A gust of wind flicked the arrow aside, and it buried itself in the wood of the platform at Kaspar's feet.

His Wen talent saved him. He knew it would.

Arrina scrambled to her feet and tackled Canolos before he could draw back the bow a second time. She need not have bothered, though. The pink-haired Wen lay rigid beneath her, his muscles arrested.

Sora was breathing heavily, her face a flushed mask of rage staring down at Canolos.

Kaspar was at her side in an instant. "My love, are you alright? I didn't mean to alarm you like that."

Sora threw her arms around his neck and pressed her lips to his. He ran a hand through her hair absently and made soothing noises.

Arrina picked herself up. "It would be best if you gave yourself up, Sora," she said gently. "If you are under another's orders, the Senserte can offer you sanctuary from them if you give us their names."

Sora released Kaspar and shook her head. All her cool arrogance was back. "I don't think you understand, Arrina. Your Senserte have not defeated me, nor will they."

"However much Canolos comes to regret betraying you, it will be as nothing if you persist in this folly," Arrina said. "Yours will be a story used to teach children what happens to those who seek power through injustice."

Sora drew herself up, all weakness cast aside. Arrina's legs buckled under her, and she prostrated herself in front of the enchantress' glory. "Give me three days, and you will serve me as Tasticon did."

"Sora, please don't," Kaspar pleaded, taking her arm.

"She isn't giving me a choice."

"You don't need to break them to retrieve Nosamae Ascending," Kaspar said softly. "They will deliver it to me as a wedding present."

Arrina wanted to ask him what he was talking about, but her mouth would not move.

"Are you saying what I think you are?" Sora asked, laying a hand against Kaspar's cheek.

"Yes, Sora." He sounded earnest. "Canolos hoped to use you to activate Nosamae Descending. He never loved you the way I do. Rule at my side as you would have had him rule at yours."

"But your father ..."

"... is a Wen and subject to the diadem as surely as the people of Seleine. He cannot stand in the way of our love."

"Kaspar," said Corina from her place by the ladder. Her face was three large Os of surprise.

"Will you marry me, Sora?"

"Yes, Kaspar!" Sora breathed, pressing her lips to his.

Corina made a choking gasp, but if anyone but Arrina noticed her, they didn't react.

The pair kissed and touched each others' faces for several minutes, hands and tongues wandering over each other. Everyone else remained stretched out on the platform except Michael, whose vacant expression twitched ever so slightly as if he wanted to clear his throat.

Eventually, the young Wen and the middle-aged Farlander pulled back slightly, still staring into one anothers' eyes longingly.

Sora nodded, and Arrina felt the pressure of the enchantment ease. She still could not have acted against either her half-brother or his lover.

"I do not want for us to be enemies, Arrina," Sora said with a tiny, smug smile. "We will soon be family, after all. Contact your Wefal friend and have him bring Nosamae Ascending to Pithdai's palace with all haste. You do not want to keep a bride waiting for her wedding night."

"And if I refuse?" Arrina asked.

"If you refuse, I will in no way feel responsible for what happens to the Flecterran Union. With diadem and orb, I am already the Empress of the Elves. There will be war until I am wed, and you will be responsible for that bloodshed. When I am crowned by the power of the miraklan painting, I will rule the Valley wisely and justly."

"I offer you my assurances she will keep her word, Arrina," Kaspar said, face and voice solemn. "And as you are still Pith, you are bound to obey me."

If Sora is letting us off her leash, we may yet surprise her.

"As Crown Prince Kaspar commands me, I will obey," Arrina responded.

Kaspar grinned like a love-sick fool.

Sora turned her attention to Canolos's inert body. "What to do with our traitor?" she mused. "Bow and sword are yours, of course, but what to do with Canolos?"

"He was my friend once."

"Perhaps, but he tried to murder you, darling. Do you think he would canopy dive if I asked it of him?"

"Without hesitation," Kaspar said at once. "Who could resist your charms, my sweet?" Kaspar caught the hand that held the orb and kissed the back of it. "I would do it even if you had neither diadem nor enchantress's art."

Sora suddenly smiled. "Ah, but my love, you could survive it. Your talent."

Another kiss of the hand. "Even if you drugged me first with saat, I would gladly dive for you."

Sora blushed like a woman in her teens.

When did Kaspar learn to speak like that? Arrina wondered silently, caught between amusement and disgust. *Did father woo my mother like this?*

"But I do not think it necessary," Kaspar told her, pressing his lips to her neck. "Command him to stay in Seleine. When we are well away from here, you can take off that heavy crown to release the people here from its power. They will remember what happened. They will know his role in it. Let him face their justice. Wen can be ever so much more patient in dispensing punishment than we can afford to be right now."

Sora turned her attention to Arrina. "We will leave Seleine immediately. Do not attempt to follow us. I will see you and Nosamae Ascending in Pithdai at the next turning of the green moon, or else the Pith will kneel before me."

Kaspar turned to Sora, taking her hand in his. "Come, my love. You will be the first Farlander to canopy dive as safely as a Wen child."

Sora's eyes lit up. "That sounds exhilarating."

The pair stepped off the platform and vanished through the leaves of the canopy below.

Mathalla, Torminth, and Lastor scrambled to their feet with outraged cries. Michael rubbed his eyes as if he had just woken up.

"Nobody move," Arrina urged all of them. "Michael, give us a line."

"When breaks the hull against these rocks, you'll have your choice of men to wed," Michael said before anyone could act.

Arrina responded just as quickly. "And what of those I do not choose?"

"That is up to you, my daughter," Mathalla said, reciting the next line. "I will spare them, send them away, or drown them in the foam."

"I will choose one for now, and if he displease me, Father, make an end to him so I may choose another," Torminth continued.

Lastor continued with a grin. "All the seamen on that ship will be yours to do with as you wish." He giggled at the innuendo.

Tajek looked at them a bit blankly for a moment. "The Isle of Enchantment," he said slowly.

The Turu hadn't been with the Senserte long enough to memorize all their plays, but he already recognized them.

"And the synopsis?" Michael prompted.

"A comedy about an evil enchanter who lives alone on an island with his daughter. She wants to leave the island to find a husband, but her father fears she won't return, so he causes a ship to crash into their island. He forces all the sailors who survive to engage in strange contests for her hand in marriage, each one more ridiculous than the last, and then kills each one in a fit of paternal overprotectiveness on the morning after the wedding night. The cleverest sailor deliberately loses all the contests until he is the only one left, and then he sneaks her away from the island on their wedding night, and they live happily far from her father."

All the Senserte nodded in unison, and Tajek looked relieved.

The Senserte held their breaths for a full minute before anyone dared speak.

"It's safe," Michael announced. "Even the trees can't hear us right now."

His magic prevents magical spying, and there is no one close enough to overhear us without magic, Arrina knew. It was a common enough tactic for an enchantress.

"How is it that all of us were dosed with saat, but you were not?" Tajek asked.

Michael gestured to Canolos where he lay on the edge of the platform as if he was sleeping. "He had the saat wine for the fruit peeling ceremony replaced with ordinary wine."

"We already know that," Torminth reminded him. "We weren't dosed either until after Sora arrived, while we were charmed."

"Ah yes. I took that first cup in good faith, as befits a guest. The second cup was thrust upon me by force, though, so I'm not ashamed to admit I didn't let it touch my lips." He brushed the edge of his ear, touching each of his four earrings.

"Why switch out the saat only to give us saat later, though?" Lastor asked.

"Canolos probably thought Michael would escape from Sora and then come rescue us," Arrina mused.

Michael snorted. "With all those Wen archers chewing tasa petals and watching me? That would have been suicide. I've learned some tricks from you and Stipator. A moment of feigned weakness wins the day more often than an hour of heroic glory."

"It would have played into Sora's hands even more than her clumsy imposter routine, at least in the eyes of the archon," Arrina said.

She addressed Lastor. "Once the saat wears off, I need you to bring us paper, ink, and bows. We need to let the others know what happened here."

Lastor nodded.

"I hate to bring this up," Mathalla said with a frown, "but how does

Prince Kaspar fit into all of this?"

Arrina shook her head. "I can't tell if he is still in love with Sora or is so afraid of her that he doesn't dare give her any other impression."

"I think it's complicated," Michael said. "She appears to be the driving force, but he has some control over her, too. "

"Canolos claimed Sora enchanted Kaspar," Arrina noted.

When Michael spoke again, he did so with careful deliberation. "Many charmers choose that path because they have always been lonely. They know charmers can make anyone respect and obey them, but they don't realize what a two-edged sword that power can be. If you'll forgive me for this parallel, they become like young women who get their way solely by using their beauty. It can actually make them feel more isolated, especially because charmers are so often reviled for the magic they wield. To fight that, most set boundaries about who they will and will not enchant. Quite often, friends and lovers are taboo, as they're the only ones who appreciate the charmer for who she is and not because of the power she wields against them."

"But nothing says they can't change their minds." Arrina nodded. "If one of them betrays the charmer or tells her something she doesn't want to hear, she might violate that taboo."

Michael shrugged. "Unfortunately, yes."

"So you think Sora trusts Kaspar, but he knows that if she stops trusting him, she will simply abandon him the way she did Canolos and Herald," Arrina said.

Mathalla raised an eyebrow. "How is it that you saw this whole exchange while the rest of us slept?"

"She chose to talk to me," Arrina said.

"She thought I was safely enchanted," Michael explained.

"Thought you were?" Mathalla persisted. "Don't tell me an enchantress couldn't tell the difference. "

The enchanter gave him a mysterious smile. "I was enchanted the way Lastor was enchanted. I looked enchanted and knew how best to pretend to remain so, but I was not compelled by Sora's magic."

Arrina made the connection first. "Corina's false enchantment. You figured out how she did it?"

"Not exactly."

Arrina jumped and turned. She had completely forgotten about Corina.

"Ah, Corina," Michael said. "I guess Kaspar's enchantment on Sora is effective."

"It helps when I am camouflaged." The braided, brown-eyed Far-lander stepped gingerly forward. "I'll need to rejoin Sora soon, but I had to talk with you."

"Understood," Arrina said.

"Your brother doesn't share Sora's ambitions. He wasn't even con-vinced that she wanted to use Nosamae Ascending until after we left Tremora."

"How long have you known?" Torminth asked.

She gave him a pained smile. "Much longer, but I didn't want to abandon Kaspar before I convinced him of it."

"How did you fall in with her?" Torminth asked.

Corina shrugged. "I'm a thief. A burglar. A swindler. Whatever you want to call me. Sora hired me to help her steal some things, and I agreed for a reasonable price. It doesn't matter, because I have no interest in re-starting the Nosamae War, and I'm not fool enough to make enemies of the Senserte." She hugged herself. "Kaspar told us about what you do."

"We only punish the leaders, not the accomplices," Lastor assured her cheerfully.

"Yeah, well I'd rather not take that chance."

"Tajek here might accidentally catch you by surprise over a railing," Mathalla said with a small laugh.

Corina frowned in confusion.

"Never mind him," Arrina told her. "Do you know where we can find Nosamae Ascending?"

She shook her head. "It was on the yacht when we put ashore at Red Lake, but Canolos might have told Herald to get rid of it."

Arrina looked at Mathalla.

He nodded. "I know how to get to Red Lake."

"We need to intercept Herald first," Michael said. "Both paintings are equally dangerous."

"I should go before I'm missed," Corina said. "Kaspar will need me."

"We understand," Arrina assured her. "Thank you again for helping us."

Corina nodded once and left the platform.

Chapter 30

"I want answers, and you are going to provide them," Arrina said.

Canolos did not fight the ropes that bound him to a wooden chair. They were still on the emergent layer platform, sweating in the sweltering afternoon heat. Arrina sat on a chair facing him. There was no sign of any of the other Senserte, but he could just make out the voices of Wen in the canopy below.

"I can understand if you wish to test me the way you did Tasticon, Ma'Sora. I know you're angry with me, but I can explain."

Arrina snorted a laugh. "Don't play the charmer's victim with me, Canolos. Sora has orb and diadem. There would be no reason for her to waste time with a loyalty test, and you know it."

Canolos gave her a blank look.

"Let me explain your situation," Arrina said airily. "You've betrayed your family and country by handing over the keys to Nosamae Ascending to an enchantress who clearly has every intention of activating it. In a few hours, Sora will remove the Diadem of Elvenkind, and everyone will remember your role in her theft of Jacob's Bow. Justice will no doubt fall on you very hard, your mother's position notwithstanding."

Canolos pursed his lips a moment before speaking. "You assume that they will simply accept your accusations as truth. This is not Pithdai." He sneered. "There will be a trial. I will have an opportunity to defend myself."

"Michael can force you to answer my questions long before then."

Canolos shook his head. "Even Sora couldn't do that in the matter of hours you have. Do you think the Sutol will let a Pith subject one of their own to the enchantments of a Nosama's scion?"

"We could convince them of the necessity."

"You're wasting precious time, Arrina. I know you. As long as I'm not the one you want to punish, I'm safe from both you and your pet enchantresses." He smiled. "You may think you can force me to whatever you want simply because you've taken me prisoner, but you can't."

"I can and I will," Arrina said coldly.

Canolos chuckled. "And I say you won't. I'm not guilty of the crime you assume I've committed. You recall that Ma'Sora is a Nosama, right?"

"She is not a Nosama," Arrina retorted hotly.

He shrugged. "Perhaps she lied about that, but your friend Tasticon can tell you with certainty that she is an enchantress of some skill. Do you think I had any choice but to do as she wished?"

"Then why did you try to murder Kaspar?"

Canolos flushed, rage lighting his eyes. "He provokes a mad enchantress with the intention that I would suffer a worse fate than Tasticon, and you accuse *me* of attempting murder? It's not always the one with the dagger who delivers death."

Arrina frowned slightly. "If you wish death on Kaspar and don't want Sora to use Nosamae Ascending, why refuse to help us stop her?"

Canolos hesitated.

Arrina smiled slightly, as if she had just won a bet. "Let me give you some friendly advice. Keep your lies simple, or you are more likely to get caught in them."

"You'd know about lying, wouldn't you, Arrina?" Canolos snarled.

She let the bait slide. "Give me the truth, and we can go our separate ways. I won't even speak against you when you face your people."

Canolos stared at her in stony silence.

She spoke with the voice of reason, almost kindly. "Whoever is trying to activate either of these paintings will be brought to justice, with your cooperation or without it. You are running out of time to tell me what I need to know."

"What do you want me to tell you?" Canolos snapped. "Do you want to know who is behind all of this?"

Arrina shook her head.

"Your half-brother, of course," Canolos continued before she could respond further. "Isn't it obvious?"

If the hasty revelation shocked her, Arrina didn't show it. She continued as if they were on a stroll by a lake. "I have only two questions, but that isn't one of them."

"Of course this was never about justice. You Senserte destroy lives to punish crimes, but as soon as the heir to the Pith throne is guilty, you refuse to take it to its logical conclusion!"

"You as much as confessed that you intended to activate Nosamae Descending," Arrina reminded him.

Canolos opened his mouth, but Arrina clamped a hand over it.

"No more lies, no more games, or I really will hand you over to Michael," she said harshly into his ear. "We are not pursuing a petty crime tyrant. These miraklan paintings could tear the Flecterran Union apart. Weighing that against a single city's laws or even the wrath of a nation of the Union, we will do what we must to protect the Union as a whole." She leaned back so he could see her tight smile. "I'm sure even your mother would understand that."

He turned his head slightly to uncover his mouth, and Arrina let him go. "What do you want to know?"

"Where is Nosamae Ascending? What will your friend Herald do with it?"

He hesitated.

"My patience is running out."

"Get your face out of mine, and maybe I'll tell you," he growled.

Arrina leaned back in her chair. "Well?"

"In the Empress's name, kill the Senserte!" Canolos shrieked suddenly.

His Wefal interrogator looked unsurprised, and no Wen archers appeared from the canopy to pepper her with arrows.

"There's your confession, Arrina," Arrina said to someone who was not standing next to her on the platform.

"That is not a confession," noted a familiar voice — his mother's voice — from the empty space next to his interrogator.

Canolos tried to open his mouth to speak to her, but it refused to move. The area around him abruptly shifted, and instead of the emergent layer platform in the afternoon, he sat tied to a chair in his mother's personal study shortly after nightfall, although the muggy night air felt as hot as afternoon had. The Senserte were there, as was his mother, looking deeply unhappy with the situation. His interrogator was no longer Arrina, but Michael.

The enchanter's face was a thunderhead, but he spoke like a tranquil day. "We had the sense to wait until the saat and diadem wore off, obviously."

"Mother, tell them they can't do this to me," Canolos pleaded.

Berilla's frown deepened, and she spoke to Arrina instead of her son. "I can promise you he wasn't acting on the orders of the Council of Leaves. The Sutol don't wish to restart the Nosamae War any more than the Pith do."

"If the fate of the entire Valley didn't rest on his testimony, archon, we would never have suggested this," Arrina told Berilla. "I can't tell you how much I regret that it has come to this, but if we don't retrieve both paintings, who knows who will use them?"

"I'm your son!" Canolos cried.

His mother merely shrugged without even acknowledging him, though her eyes were wet. "He is my son."

"I know," Arrina said gently, squeezing Berilla's arm.

"You say your mental mystic can make him forget the pain your enchanter will inflict. Is there any danger to him?" the archon asked, clearly looking for reassurance.

"Michael's illusions will do no physical damage, and Poresa will erase all memory of those few hours of pain it takes to extract the truth," Arrina said. "Michael's magic will even prevent him from crying out. I know you don't want this to be public knowledge in Seleine."

Berilla took a deep breath, as though considering this.

"Mother, no!" Canolos wailed. "She's a Pith spy! Arrest her. Arrest them all!"

Berilla seemed not to hear him, though, and at a motion of Michael's hand, the pink-haired Wen's voice failed him.

The archon nodded once. "For the good of the Union." She looked at Canolos for the first time since he had regained consciousness. She looked angry. "You have disgraced me and with me all of Seleine. Even if Sora was in charge, you should have found a way to neutralize her yourself or, at the least, warned us of the danger before she put on the diadem. You did not, and for that alone you will be tried for treason under our nation's laws. I cannot prevent that."

Canolos's mouth opened and closed like that of a fish out of water, his voice stolen. Michael's frown deepened, and Canolos felt a tingling itch in his hands, like the pain of a mild burn that was slowly spreading to the rest of his body.

"We could," Mathalla said suddenly, and Berilla looked at him in search of some explanation. "Rather, the ad'Marusak brothers' father could offer him a lighter sentence if he cooperated with us. It is his prerogative to extend pardons to criminals."

"He maintains he is innocent," Berilla noted.

"He won't for much longer," Michael said absently, and Canolos felt the pain creeping up his arms.

Berilla flew to her knees in front of her son. "Canolos, please! You have to tell them what you know." She started weeping but still didn't lay a hand on him, as if he carried some contagious disease incurable by Wen magic. "I just know Sora had you enchanted the whole time and was using you to get Jacob's Bow, but there is no reason to lie to them about it and every reason to tell them what you can."

Canolos felt the burning itch reach his shoulders. "Herald has orders to leave Nosamae Ascending on the yacht." His face flooded with relief at the sound of his own voice. "He was to bring it here after ... later. He's bringing Nosamae Descending here." He frowned. "I'm surprised he hasn't arrived yet."

"Perhaps he got lost," Mathalla suggested.

The itching sensation stopped advancing. "No," Canolos persisted. "His sense of direction is unerring. He should have arrived before sunset. He ..." Canolos's eyes suddenly widened.

The pain was gone. His mother was gone. The chair and ropes were gone, and he lay on a wooden platform. Canolos could feel the sun shining on him, which meant he had to be above the emergent layer, but he couldn't so much as open his eyes.

• • • •

Arrina watched the silent interrogation. To all appearances, Michael simply sat next to Canolos's sleeping body with an intent expression for nearly an hour.

"What is he doing?" Tajek asked her, clearly unnerved.

Arrina bit her lower lip. *I'm not sure I can answer that question.*

"Oh, you know enchantresses," Lastor said with a manic grin from where he sat crosslegged. "He's making Canolos dream all sorts of terrible pain so he'll tell Michael what we need to know."

Tajek seemed taken aback by this. He opened his mouth, but at that moment Michael stirred from his concentration.

"Well?" Arrina prompted.

Michael frowned slightly. "You understand that complex illusions are not my area of expertise. I knew there would be a lot of inconsistencies that could tip him off. I tried to mitigate it by creating a dream within a dream."

"Is that a yes or a no?"

"A yes with regrets, maybe?" Michael said with an almost pained smile. "I'm afraid … I'm afraid I had to inflict some pain as part of the illusion."

Lastor mouthed "I told you so" at Tajek, who looked horrified.

Arrina knew Michael's interest in this mission was at least equal to her own, and possibly even greater.

Will I need to ask Poresa to do the one thing with her magic she has told me never to ask of her?

"How much pain?" Arrina asked slowly.

Michael looked instantly shocked, almost wounded. "No, no, no!" He waved both hands at her in denial. "It's nothing like that. Certainly nothing that will do permanent damage. To his mind, I mean. Just enough to give the impression that it would get much worse. I thought for sure he'd spot the flaws if I let the illusion run too long."

The other Senserte waited.

Michael blew out a breath and pointed at his face. "Being up here in the sun all day, well, I have a sunburn. So I made him feel like he did, too."

"Wen don't get sunburns," Mathalla observed.

"Yes, exactly! So he naturally assumed it was some kind of fire illusion."

"We believe you," Arrina assured him. "And Nosamae Ascending?"

Michael brightened. "Ah yes. The plan was for Herald to leave it on the yacht. I suspect Canolos didn't want to risk it making its way into enemy hands once he had activated Nosamae Descending."

"How soon is Herald expected?" Arrina asked.

"Before sunset today."

"How can he be sure?" Mathalla asked. "The rainforest is difficult to navigate. Even the Sutol don't promise arrival times."

Michael shrugged. "Canolos claims Herald has some infallible sense of direction. I'm afraid I know next to nothing about Aflangi magic."

Arrina absently noted that the saat had finally worn off. "I know even less."

"Is there any chance Herald is behind this?" Torminth asked. "Activation of either painting may well weaken Wen or Farlander magic. At the least, it will probably start a civil war. Aflighan is always eyeing our northern border, and either situation would give them a chance to strike the Union while we're weak."

"I don't know," Arrina admitted. "Hopefully we can find that out tonight."

"What should we do to Canolos?" Lastor asked with a malicious gleam in his eyes. "It's been too long since we covered someone in honey and flowers and set the bees after them. I was talking to Nijel a little during dinner, and I'm sure he'd love to help."

"It's been a long time since *you've* done that," Torminth corrected. "Even Stipator thought that was a bit much, remember?"

Mathalla shook his head. "He has confessed to nothing that will stand in a Sutol trial. If Berilla respects her nation's laws at all, she'll at least have Canolos arrested until she can investigate further."

Arrina remembered the moment the arrow had left Jacob's Bow, aimed at her half-brother by this pink-haired Wen at Michael's feet. She recalled the arrows Canolos had shot into Stipator's legs to cripple him. She thought of the man's lies and his betrayal.

He deserves punishment for the crimes he committed.

She forced it aside.

Coming from me, punishment would not be justice. I might enjoy the chance to have revenge, but I am Senserte. Until I have proof that he is the one behind this conspiracy, he is not mine to sentence.

"He is Seleine's concern now," she told them. "Once we're sure Sora has removed the diadem, we'll dose him with saat and turn him over to the archon's custody."

The other Senserte nodded at this, and only Lastor seemed a little disappointed.

Lastor and I, Arrina corrected silently, but she said, "Let's discuss what to do about Herald."

Chapter 31

As afternoon waned into evening, thunder boomed to the west of Seleine, promising the day's ration of torrential downpour. An hour's walk to the east of the Wen city, a lone traveler made his way along the forest floor with none of the usual hesitation that marked rainforest travel.

"Again we meet," Tajek said as he stepped out from behind a tree and into Herald's path.

Juxtaposed this way the two made for an interesting set. Both were huge, and even more hugely muscled, figures. Herald had long blond hair, a shaggy mane of a beard, pale blue eyes, and skin as white as the flesh of a cassava tuber. Tajek's skin was a deep brown, almost black, and he had dark brown eyes and black hair shaved down to stubble on his head and face. The Turu carried no weapons, while the Aflangi wore a pair of heavy battle axes in loops at his belt.

The axes were in Herald's hands before the Turu could act, but the Aflangi didn't attack.

Tajek grinned, showing off white teeth. "Did you forget our last match?"

Herald seemed to notice the axes in his hands as if they had moved there of their own accord. He maintained a defensive posture. "I haven't, but we both know you're not alone."

"True enough," Mathalla said, stepping into position a few paces behind Herald, sword at the ready.

Torminth and Arrina completed the circle, swords out. The blades of all three swords burst into flames as Torminth ignited the blood he had rubbed on them earlier.

"We don't want to hurt you, Herald," Arrina assured him. "Canolos and Sora have failed. Drop your weapons and hand over Nosamae Descending."

Herald's bushy eyebrows rose slightly. "To dislike causing harm is a weakness, and the Godhead chooses the heralds of his coming from among his strongest servants."

"You cannot stand against us all," Tajek pointed out. "If you stand and fight, you might be killed."

"The fear of death is also a weakness the Godhead does not tolerate," Herald said, gripping his axes more tightly.

"Your death wouldn't achieve your Godhead's aims in the Flecterran Valley," Arrina said.

"You do not know the Godhead's aims, or you would not say such a thing." He smiled grimly. "I cannot betray his intentions if I am slain, for only the Godhead can raise the dead to serve."

Michael stepped into Herald's view — filling a gap between Arrina and Tajek. Like Tajek, he held no weapon, but like the Turu he was dangerous in spite of that. "Do not be so certain you can keep your secrets from us. We are the Senserte." The enchanter fingered one of his earrings.

Herald stiffened slightly, but he showed no sign of prostrating himself. "I serve only one master, charlatan, and you are not he!"

Michael had just enough time to look surprised before Herald sprang at him, burying one of the axes in the enchanter's chest.

Arrina touched her body's magic, and the chaos unfolded around her in slow motion. Torminth, Mathalla, and Tajek sprang toward Herald with snarls even as the back of Michael's head hit the rainforest floor. Tajek ripped the other axe out of Herald's hand and raised it for a killing blow. Swords passed through the Aflangi's torso in two places, their flames extinguished in his flesh.

Arrina wanted to join them, but she saw blood pouring out of Michael's wound, his eyes already glazing.

"Lastor! Healing now!" she shouted.

The young Wen dropped from a branch far above and seemed to float lazily toward Michael's still form. Arrina tore her attention away from the Farlander, her heart in her stomach with fear for him.

She expected to see Herald satisfyingly headless on the rainforest floor, but the Aflangi continued to surprise her. A foot kicked Tajek backward with impossible force, sending the Turu flying past one enormous tree trunk and into a second with an unpleasant crunch. Bright blood flecked Herald's beard, though Arrina couldn't tell whether it was his or Michael's.

The pair of sword thrusts seemed to have had all the effect of stabbing a slab of meat. The fire had cauterized both wounds, so there was no blood, but the Aflangi didn't seem concerned or impeded. If anything, he looked even stronger than he had been a moment before.

Lastor alighted at Michael's side and pressed a hand to the wound. The gout of blood immediately stopped, but Arrina wasn't sure if it was magic or something terrible. Herald swung his axe at Torminth's midsection, but the Wen backed up just quickly enough to turn a mortal blow into a ruined shirt and a scratch along his belly.

The two of them can't stand against Herald.

They had been so confident that Michael could bring the Aflangi to heel as easily as he had Canolos and countless other pawns of their various marks. With one blow, Herald had felled that hope.

Arrina drew her sword. This was no time for regrets.

Herald smiled at her as she approached. "Your big friend was right. I can't defeat all of you at once."

Mathalla attempted to blindside him, but the Aflangi ducked the sword thrust and grabbed the blade. Blood dripped from his hand, but with a twist, Mathalla's rapier blade snapped off three inches from the hilt. Herald flipped the Wen over his shoulder and onto the ground in front of him, leaving Mathalla wheezing for breath.

Torminth sank a shoulder under Herald's guard, throwing the Aflangi back before he could bring an axe down on Mathalla. Herald tucked into a roll and came back to his feet with his back against a tree.

"The painting is in my pack," Herald said with a gesture over his shoulder. "Come and take it from me if you can."

Arrina sprang forward even as Herald leapt straight up, and only her heightened reflexes kept her from embedding her rapier in the tree. She glanced up, expecting to see the Aflangi diving at her with his axe in both hands, but her opponent had caught hold of a branch twenty feet above the forest floor and was ascending the tree with incredible speed.

"This Aflangi sorcerer may even be harder to catch than a Wen child," Arrina muttered.

She leapt up the tree, using her magic to nearly match his pace. Below her, Torminth tossed his sword to Mathalla, who had caught his breath enough to join the chase, running up the trunk of the tree as if gravity was a problem other people had.

Lastor looked at Arrina longingly, no doubt anxious to join the action. She paused only long enough to shake her head, and he followed her gaze first to Michael and then to Tajek, who still lay crumpled and unmoving against the tree where he had landed.

"We'll catch him, Arrina," Mathalla called to her as he ran past. "A fifth moon will wax full in the sky before someone bests me in the canopy!"

A moment later, the Wen vanished into the ceiling of leaves above them.

Still so confident, Arrina thought as she ascended. *So was Michael. So was I. But perhaps this is beyond even the Senserte.*

She glanced down once more. Michael and Tajek hadn't moved, but Lastor was holding the Turu's head in his hands now.

Stabilized in time or dead? Arrina wondered. *And how bad is Tajek's injury?*

She noticed Torminth's eyes on her.

Will I deliver your lover back to you, or will I fail him as I failed Tajek and Michael?

Torminth suddenly grinned and gave her an enthusiastic thumbs-up.

We are Senserte. We must trust each other.

Her doubts vanished as surely as the ground below disappeared beneath the layers of canopy. If they were still there, she at least had no further awareness of them.

The chase was on.

Traveling across the canopy of the rainforest approached walking on water for sheer impossibility and easily surpassed it in terms of peril. A plunge into a river or lake was hardly dangerous at all so long as no lake monsters or murderfish lurked beneath the surface. Trying to walk on water and failing meant getting wet and having to swim. A single misstep while leaping from branch to leaf-covered branch meant a swift and quite often fatal drop a hundred feet or more to the forest floor. It was only slightly less dangerous than canopy diving — and at least that only required the diver to get lucky once, while a canopy runner had to make hundreds of safe steps across a hundred branches that might or might not be strong enough to support a person's weight.

Wen children did it all the time, of course, but their magic kept them from falling. Mathalla's Wen talent worked the same way, though it wouldn't help if he ran afoul of a canopy cat or poisonous snake up here.

An internal mystic could do it, but Arrina knew she would pay a price for this chase.

The forest ceiling spread out around her — an endless plain of leaves of a thousand shades of green. A million flowers of tens of thousands of shapes and bright colors. Birds and insects and monkeys and reptiles of every color imaginable crawled and clambored and flitted on top of it. The hot Valley sun caught on floating seeds with fuzzy threads in every color of the rainbow, the spinning motes whirling and turning in the wind like beads and pieces of glass in a kaleidoscope.

To the west, not nearly as far way as Arrina would have liked, storm clouds approached. Even from this distance she could see the torrential rain the black cloud was unleashing and the bolts of lightning dancing from cloud to trees and from cloud to cloud. It had already blasted a black scar into one emergent tree's enormous branches. The wind it brought with it was like the inside of an oven filled with pots of boiling water, but even that felt cool compared to the air in the sun-drenched upper canopy.

Once the rain starts, the footing up here will become even more treacherous.

Arrina scanned the canopy, looking for signs of Herald or Mathalla. She spotted two figures running north, quickly closing the gap between themselves and the line of red leaves that marked the southern border of the Blood Preserve. Herald seemed to be slowly losing ground to the Wen, but it wasn't impossible that the Aflangi would reach the Blood Preserve before Mathalla caught up to him.

Is he running that way because he doesn't know the danger or because he does?

Magic tingling in every vein in her body, Arrina set out across the carpet of leaves at a run. Three steps later, she made her first misstep and only barely avoided a drop to the rainforest floor by catching another branch only a few feet down.

She gritted her teeth against the futility of it all as she regained the canopy.

It hardly seems fair. Incredible strength. Toughness to match Tajek's. Speed and grace to match an internal mystic's. And he canopy runs like a Wen child. Doesn't his magic have any limits at all?

At that moment Arrina saw the tiny shape that was Herald dip below the trees.

Perhaps not entirely without limits, then, Arrina thought, loping from branch to branch and dodging the snapping jaws of lazy snakes. *Aflangi sorcerers must be like Nosamae who hide their power until they must bring it to bear.*

Almost a minute later Herald reappeared and continued his run, but she and Mathalla had both gained a hundred yards or more from the misstep. Arrina dared to hope they might have more such turns of good fortune.

The air darkened, and Arrina felt the first few drops of rain.

A dozen steps later, the cloud poured on her like an upended bucket that could never be emptied.

Her foot slipped on a wet leaf, and though she caught herself before dropping through the canopy floor, one sandal slipped off and spiraled as it fell into the twilight below. She could see Mathalla, but Herald was lost somewhere beyond the curtain of rain in front of her.

A canopy cat loomed up at her, its many-colored coat of iridescent fur less impressive in the rain. Its huge paws and jaws lost none of their effect, however, and neither did its roar. Arrina vaulted over it and for once landed solidly on a sturdy branch.

With luck it's more surprised than hungry.

Arrina pushed it out of her mind for the moment. Canopy cats were stalkers, not chasers.

Not even creatures born to the canopy are foolish enough to chase across it.

The next several yards of branches swayed in the wind and dipped under her weight. The other sandal was only making the footing more treacherous, so she kicked it off.

It landed in an enormous flower that filled and overflowed like a pale purple fountain in the rain. Tiny waterfowl swam in it. Their beaks dipped down to snap at Mira only knew what.

Sky minnows, maybe?

Arrina lost track of Mathalla. His magic was much better suited to this than hers. She kept running in the same direction, or at least as near as she could make out in the rain.

At least I'm not paying a high a price for it — not like under the lake.

The price of doing ordinary things to an extraordinary degree was always cheaper than doing something no Wefal body could do or be on its own. Changing faces carried a far smaller cost than breathing water or healing a major injury overnight, and even that was a high price to pay compared to running and balancing quickly as she was now.

If I grew wings to fly, that would cost me dearly.

Not that it would do her any good in this weather. The rain would be a physical weight pressing down on everything, even if the wind hadn't been so wild. Certainly no birds or insects were flitting around up here right now.

Besides, she had never tried that before. Jonathan seemed to think human flight was more complicated than growing huge bird wings. This was no time to try and fail.

The rain diminished for a fraction of a second between outpourings, and in that moment Arrina caught motion out of the corner of her right eye. One shadow, maybe two. Possibly human. Possibly a large archon monkey. Then the curtain of water fell again, blotting it from sight. Arrina changed directions.

It has to be better than running blind.

She slipped again, caught hold of a slippery branch. It broke, and she plunged into the canopy. Branches whipped her face and arms and completely tore off the right sleeve of her shirt. A pair of buttons popped off as well, falling like copper drops of rain through canopy and understory. Arrina clutched a vine, which almost tore free, but it broke her downward momentum.

A tree with sturdy-looking branches looked close enough. She pumped her legs once, twice, three times. The vine tore loose above her, but Arrina was already flying through the open air. Her hand found a branch and slipped a little but held. She pulled herself up and scrambled back onto the carpet of leaves.

She quickly realized she had lost her bearings. Her head whipped back and forth in the rain, eyes straining for a sign of Mathalla or Herald. The rain pressed down on her, and she noted absently that the buttons she had lost were the top two, baring cleavage down which water streamed like tiny rivers. The ugly slash on her shoulder from one of the branches dripped blood that mingled with the rain and stained the remnants of her pale blue shirt.

Not enough blood to slow me down, though. I'd best save my strength for Herald.

In all she had already sacrificed a pound — a modest price that would rise precipitously if she suffered any serious injuries.

"Where are you?" she murmured.

The rain ebbed.

There.

The pair of shadows certainly weren't archon monkeys. Arrina caught the outline of an axe and the the stance of a Wen fencer impossibly balanced on the tip of an outstretched branch. Arrina put a hand to the sword at her side and ran to join the battle.

Even in the driving rain she could see their shadows. Herald's axe severed the branch. Mathalla's sword plunged at something Herald was using as a shield, but it glanced off without penetrating.

A hole abruptly opened up in front of her, and Arrina only barely skidded to a halt in front of it. Hole was actually the wrong word, as it was an opening in the canopy like a wide clearing too large to jump. She could see all the way down to the rainforest floor.

Mathalla took a kick to the knee and only barely ducked under the wide swing of the axe that followed.

Arrina gritted her teeth and started skirting around the edge of the opening. She had barely taken ten steps before she saw the sea of red leaves directly in front of her, blocking her path.

The Blood Preserve. That would explain why they turned aside instead of continuing north.

An enormous blood red flower opened its bud in Arrina's direction. Its mouth full of thorny teeth dripped black venom and saliva.

Not going that way, she decided, circling around the hole.

Herald jumped into the air and spun into a kick that connected with the side of Mathalla's face, knocking the Wen back several yards closer to the Blood Preserve. The Aflangi landed on a weak spot in the canopy, though, and he plunged up to his armpits before hooking his arm around a branch. His axe disappeared into the sea of leaves, but his backpack landed on the canopy a foot away.

That was his shield. A sword wouldn't pierce a miraklan painting.

Arrina drew her sword and ran toward them. She felt the ribbon holding up her hair finally give way, and the long blue-blond braid fell across her back, bouncing as she jumped and ran across the branches of the canopy. Mathalla stood up from where he lay in midair — a remarkable sight even for someone raised among Wen — rubbing his jaw. The Wen moved slowly, unsteady on his feet and seemingly still stunned by the blow, but he showed no sign of giving up the fight.

Herald looked at the two of them converging on him and sneered. "I could still defeat you both, but this chase is testing the limits of the Godhead's patience with me."

A hand snaked out and grabbed one strap of the backpack.

"You wanted me to give you Nosamae Descending? Here. It's yours."

Arrina slowed to a trot. Herald abruptly swung the backpack over his head and released it so it sailed through the rain.

"Fetch, dogs!" the Aflangi shouted, and then he was gone, laughing as he let himself slide through the canopy.

The backpack landed on the bed of red leaves, bounced once, and fell into the Blood Preserve.

Chapter 32

Arrina ran toward the line of red leaves, sliding her sword in its sheath as she danced from branch to branch. The Blood Preserve seemed to sense her coming, for all its deadly flora and wicked fauna twisted and sang and chittered at her loudly enough that even the thunder couldn't drown it out.

"Arrina, no!" Mathalla shouted, and she stopped short.

"Herald will turn up again, and we'll deal with him then."

"That's the Blood Preserve."

"I know that, Mathalla. The painting can't be more than fifty feet from the edge. Whatever monsters lurk there, I think I can handle them for two minutes."

Mathalla regarded her gravely, putting up his own sword. "The Blood Preserve isn't the place where monsters live, Arrina. It's the place where *nightmares* go, the kinds of nightmares that terrify Wen children."

Arrina was already climbing down one of the trees into the canopy just outside the Blood Preserve.

"Fifty feet in and fifty feet back."

Mathalla walked down the trunk next to her. "A hundred feet or a hundred miles, it's too dangerous."

"I can't just leave it in the Blood Preserve. Sora had us in her power on Gulinora Island. She took us prisoner with ease in Seleine. She would have bested us at Tremora if she had stayed. If she beats us again, Nosamae Descending is our only hope of reversing the damage she does."

The damage we *did by all but giving her both Theo's Sword and the Orb of Elvenkind.*

"We can beat her this time. Most of her allies have turned against us."

"But we've lost Jonathan, Stipator, Poresa, Kara, and Etha. We don't have time to convince the Nosamae to release them to us."

Assuming they still remember who we are when we see them again.

"The Wen say a mirakla never stays lost. It only falls out of use for a time. Someday someone will recover it."

Arrina's braid caught on a tangle of branches. She pulled it free, alighted on a wide branch, and took a moment to knot it around her head before continuing downward. "Someday could be after a century of Farlander rule, assuming Aflighan's Godhead doesn't conquer the Flecterran Union before then. And someone could be a Wen as ambitious as Canolos and just as willing to hunt down the key miraklas as Sora was."

"More likely it will be a Wen child when our need is great," Mathalla noted. "Or else one looking for a grand adventure."

Arrina grabbed a long vine and descended it hand-over-hand into the understory. "You can't know when it will happen, though. A Wen might recover Nosamae Descending in a month or in a millennium. We know where it is right now, and we're right here."

She reached the end of the vine and dropped the last ten feet to the rainforest floor. Mathalla strolled casually down the rest of the tree trunk.

"If you won't trust the mirakla, Arrina, at least trust your fellow Senserte." He almost had to jog to keep pace with her now.

"The Aaronsglade heist was a failure. I'm not sure how or when we'll free Jonathan, Stipator and the others from the Nosamae or whether our friends will still recognize us if we do. We can't possibly stop Sora without them. We can't just let her win!"

The black bark of the Blood Preserve's trees loomed in front of them. Mathalla laid a hand on the back of her shoulder.

"Arrina, you are going into the one place in the Flecterran Valley where I will not follow you." He sounded sad. "Nor will I let any of the other Senserte go in after you. If you go forward, you come back on your own or not at all. Do you understand me?"

Arrina shook him off. "Yes. The Senserte are only involved in this because I got you involved. It probably cost Michael his life, and others may die, as well. I never expected you to follow me."

Mathalla took a step back from the Blood Preserve. "If you intend to go, go, but don't forget what you're looking for. Get the painting and get out as quickly as you can."

"Of course."

"Good luck, Arrina, and good hunting."

Arrina took the final step out of Sutola and into the Blood Preserve.

• • • •

The rain, though noticeable, did not fall nearly as heavily on the rainforest floor as it did on the canopy. The clouds turned the usual twilight beneath the canopy into a darkness verging on a moonless night's. A trickle of magic allowed Arrina to see clearly, although she soon wasn't sure she wanted to. What fell as rain elsewhere looked like drops of dark blood. Rivulets ran down every tree as if from terrible wounds higher up. In a matter of moments, the rest of her shirt matched the spots where she had bled on it, the pale blue turned dark and sticky.

A rain of blood is no more dangerous than a rain of water. Stay focused.

Arrina picked her way carefully across the floor of the Blood Preserve on bare feet. She kicked a stone a few yards in, and it rolled into her view. The empty eye sockets of a human skull stared back at her, and it was then she noticed that bones littered the rainforest floor like branches and fruit.

Bones are no more dangerous than branches, she reminded herself, but her heart's rhythm intensified.

The first tree she came to was covered in severed hands that had been nailed to the trunk — Wen, Wefal, Farlander. She even saw one that could have belonged to a Turu.

She fought back a laugh.

These aren't nightmares. These are tales told to children meant to give them nightmares!

A peal of distant thunder rolled through the air.

I'm also too old to be afraid of thunder! she thought fiercely, skirting around the hand tree and deeper into the Blood Preserve. *Twenty feet, so far, maybe thirty. I should be able to see it soon.*

The thunder came again, closer now. And again. And again in the same slow, steady rhythm — like the tread of enormous feet.

Arrina remembered the fins of the shark giants they had seen from the balloon. Her search for Herald's backpack became a bit more frantic.

Monsters are flesh and blood. They can probably be killed. If they can't be killed, they can be outwitted. If they can't be outwitted, I can still outrun them. I won't be more than fifty feet from the border of the Blood Preserve.

Arrina found human bones in endless variety on the rainforest floor, some of them large enough to rival Tajek's, others small enough to belong to children or even infants.

A black snake darted out of a skull and sank its fangs into her calf. Arrina's sword moved from its sheath and through the serpent's neck in the space of a breath, but she could already feel the poison working, turning her blood to fire in the veins of her leg. She set her magic to work on it, and the pain began to subside.

Arrina grinned. *Glad to see this place of nightmares has some teeth, at least.*

The footsteps were getting closer. She thought she caught a brief hint of movement farther into the Blood Preserve, but the trunks of trees wider than houses blocked more than that.

Arrina frowned, scanning the rainforest floor one more time without success.

Perhaps it didn't fall all the way down.

She looked up and caught sight of a tree in the understory covered with fruit shaped like human heads severed by an executioner's axe. Another had a dozen corpses hanging from ropes around their necks, their hands bound behind their backs. A lone Wen hung from a third by ropes at his hands and feet, body writhing in agony as needle-beaked black birds pecked at his eyes, but he made no sound. Arrina noticed absently that the third tree was covered in severed tongues the way the hand tree had been covered in hands.

Then she saw it, hanging from the branch of an understory tree covered in vines. *No, not vines — human intestines.* Arrina frowned. *There are not enough people in the entire Union to leave this many bones and body parts.*

She grabbed one of the — *better to think of them as vines anyway* — that dangled just within reach. It was wet, slick, and oozing and dripping something foul-smelling.

It's only about twenty feet up. Get the painting and get out of the Blood Preserve.

Arrina climbed the intestine vine. Her braid bounced against her back, drops of what couldn't possibly be blood oozing out of it and down past her belt, soaking into her pants.

Harmless storyteller's horror or no, she was looking forward to a bath and a change of clothes.

One of the black birds with needle beaks took an interest in her as she climbed, stabbing into her rump where she couldn't reach. Arrina cursed at it but kept climbing.

No poison, and it can't drain enough of my blood even to make me lightheaded.

The thunder was closer. A prolonged cracking could only be the tower of a tree breaking under a huge foot; the cacophony of snapping branches and squealing of small animals must be the tree falling. The vine she climbed shuddered in her fingers.

Arrina pushed it aside. The backpack hung only a few feet away now. She pulled herself up and brushed it once with the tips of her fingers before getting a grip on it. The vine shuddered again, but a hard tug brought the backpack free.

She let out a sigh of relief and slid one-handed down the intestine vine.

"Is that the best you can do?" she asked as she dropped from the bottom and onto the rainforest floor. "This didn't even give me a rope burn."

As if in answer, the vine Arrina had been climbing let loose a stream of foulness onto her head. She took three steps away from it, wiping the filth off her face where it had run into her right eye. She took a moment to crush the mosquito bird on her leg, as well. It died with a tiny hiss.

"Arrina!"

Her sword was out in an instant. The half-seen figure in the stinking undergrowth sounded a lot like Lastor.

"Whoa! I'm glad to see you, too." The figure laughed cheerfully. One of its ears was dangling by its skin.

After a moment her vision cleared enough to see that the figure looked like Lastor, too.

"Isn't this place neat?" it asked, casually ripping of a piece off severed tongue bark. "Very convincing, don't you think?"

"Where are the others?" Arrina asked, still not letting down her guard.

It looked suddenly very serious. "There was nothing I could do. Tajek's neck was broken. And Michael ..."

Arrina's heart pounded in her chest. *This is just an illusion. Whatever this Lastor creature is just wants to frighten me.* Suddenly his ear was normal.

"If I find you spoke falsely to me of my son's betrayal, your blood will water my orchard, and I will take great delight in feeding on the flesh of those fruits!" Arrina shouted over the pounding of the rain on the canopy high above.

"Arrina, it's me!" it protested.

"Answer me or die," Arrina growled.

It has to be a lie. Has to be!

"As if you even could," the Wen-shaped illusion mumbled, scratching an elbow. "But fine. The truth I swear I saw myself and heard with these two ears. Heris is as false as your wife is true." He said it flatly. "Really and truly it's me."

She blinked at him and put up her sword. *It's really Lastor. But that means ...*

Arrina collapsed to the forest floor, barely noticing the bones snapping under her knees. "Tell me everything."

Thunder so close the ground trembled beneath her.

"If you have the painting, we should be going. You saw most of it anyway. Michael had an axe in his chest. He was dead before he hit the ground. Tajek I might have saved if I'd gone to him first, but it was too late for him, too. Torminth was too slow to follow you. Have you seen Mathalla?"

"He wouldn't follow me." Arrina thought on that for just a moment. "He didn't warn you away from following me?"

Lastor shook his head. "I didn't see him, but I found this."

The young Wen held out a sword. She immediately recognized it as Torminth's.

"Where?" she demanded.

"On the rainforest floor just outside the Blood Preserve."

"Exactly where he left it."

A round object rolled out from behind a tree and stopped directly between them. She found herself staring into Mathalla's sightless eyes. Herald stepped into view, his axe dripping with blood or rain or some combination of both.

"And once I've finished my business with you, I'll return it to its owner point-first." Herald smiled wickedly.

Arrina sprang to her feet, sword in one hand, backpack with the painting in the other. Herald lunged at her, but she was already on the move. The blade shattered an empty skull where she had been a moment before.

Tears stung her eyes — half grief, half the grime that still dripped down her forehead from the intestine vines. "You had no reason to hurt him! He was no threat to you."

Herald jumped high over her, axe poised for an overhand strike with both hands. Arrina rolled clear, drawing a line of blood across the Aflangi's cheek with her sword.

"Reason? What reason must there be to hurt someone weaker than I am? I am the Godhead's herald. I am the strong who lays low the weak. Soon all the Flecterran Union will kneel before me!"

Each sentence was punctuated by a swing of the battle axe. Arrina ducked and dodged the first four. On the fifth, she blocked the attack with the backpack. The blade touched the canvas hidden inside and stopped dead, not even pushing her back.

"Is Sora taking orders from the Godhead?" Arrina demanded, advancing with shield up and sword flicking out at the Aflangi. "Do we need to humble him as we have humbled so many like him?"

Her braid swung around and tangled in the guard of her sword. Herald circled around and let fly a backhanded swing.

"You are welcome to try such absurd acts of defiance, but you will serve him a hundred times as long in death as you defied him in life."

Arrina ducked the axe and rolled away from the downward follow-up.

"But to your question, no. Sora doesn't serve the Godhead yet."

Arrina stood up with her back against the hand tree. An axe blade whistled at her neck. She rolled around, presenting the backpack arm, and the blade bit into the wood. The fingers of the damaged hand bark twitched as if in pain.

"So she is working for herself."

Arrina's sword slashed open Herald's arm, but he didn't even wince. The Aflangi pulled his axe free of the tree and advanced upon her, slowly now.

"Don't be a fool," he snarled. "The answer has been right in front of your eyes the whole time. Canolos, Sora, Kaspar — all of them tools in the hands of another whose interests happen to be the Godhead's, as well. The Senserte too are nothing but dupes."

The axe swung in a wide arc, which Arrina blocked with the backpack. Her sword pierced his shoulder, but the wound didn't even bleed as she slid the blade out again.

"Who then?"

Herald took several steps back, and the two circled each other.

"I'm almost tempted to let you live, Arrina. The truth will destroy you more completely than my axe ever could. I'd ask the Godhead to raise you so you could carry it until the end of the world, but your corpse would rot long before it reached Aflighan. More's the pity."

Arrina and Herald met in a whirl of steel. Her sword got tangled in her braid again, and this time it plucked the sword from her fingers. Herald grinned and advanced with incredible speed.

Not helpless yet, Arrina thought with a dark smile of her own.

She sidestepped Herald's advance and slipped behind him. The end of her braid sat in her hand, so she swung it over Herald's neck and pulled it under his chin, almost toppling him onto her.

"Who?!?" she shouted in the Aflangi's ear.

Herald made a strangling noise, clutching his throat. Abruptly he leaned forward, flipping her over his head and onto the ground below.

Conveniently within reach of my sword, Arrina thought, grabbing its hilt and rolling clear of the next attack.

Herald was breathing heavily. "Very well, I'll tell you. The villain behind Sora — the one you believe you will bring to Senserte justice — is King Larus of Pithdai."

It's a trick.

But the Aflangi didn't suddenly renew his attack and attempt to finish her with a rain of blows. He simply stood there at the ready and soaked in her reaction.

It's a lie.

But she saw how it could fit the facts. Her father had executed the only witnesses to Kaspar's kidnapping. He had agreed to hand over Pithdai's miraklan paintings as ransom. He had sent the Senserte to make the exchange, and he certainly must have guessed they would not let it end at that, might even have recognized the possibility that they would help Sora steal all the keys simply to bring her to perfect justice for her crimes.

"Father is a man of peace," Arrina all but shouted. "He would never ..."

"He is a man at the end of his life who wishes to leave behind a legacy," Herald countered. "Diplomacy is a tool for holding power as war is a tool for seizing it. He never hesitated to use either."

"I don't believe you."

"You believe me, Arrina. You know I'm right. You know there is no other explanation." Herald took a single step with each sentence, and Arrina took a matching step backward. "As promised, this is the kind of knowledge that kills. It has extinguished your trust in Larus, and now my axe will extinguish your life."

Arrina backed into the trunk of a tree. A hundred squirming tongues licked and probed her neck and legs and back. Her sword didn't waver, though, and she held up the backpack.

Wherever it leads, she thought, tears flowing down her cheeks and mingling with the blood rain. *I am Senserte, and I swore to follow this wherever it leads.*

Chapter 33

A wall of fire suddenly sprang up in front of Herald.

"You'll do no such thing," Lastor said, moving next to Arrina and grasping her left hand as best he could around the backpack. "Arrina isn't alone. The Senserte are with her."

"What's left of them," Herald returned with a laugh.

Lastor only stood up straighter. "I am Senserte, and *I* am with her. You murdered our friends, and we will hunt you wherever you go. When you die, you will die praying your Godhead never finds a way to bring you back to life or whatever it is he does to dead people!"

Herald laughed wildly, and the wall of flame flickered out. "A child? A single child against the might of one of the heralds of ..."

His beard and hair vanished in a flash of fire, leaving face and pate blackened and blistering. Lastor let go of Arrina's hand and stepped in front of her.

"I would stand with Arrina against your Godhead and all his twisted, murdering servants."

Herald raised his axe, but it turned into a bouquet of writhing snakes in his hands, each of their heads a different color. The Aflangi tossed the serpents aside and seemed on the point of advancing another step, but his body froze.

"So long as Wen have magic to wield, Aflighan will never gain a foothold in the Flecterran Valley." Lastor took a small step forward. "Never!"

The shout echoed, and the rain of blood suddenly stopped. The thundering footsteps were running away now. Fear flickered across Herald's face, and he took a small step backward even as Lastor took another forward step.

Feline shapes as high as the Wen's shoulder came out from behind trees, huge, twisted shadows of the canopy cats Larus's executioners trained to track criminals. They stalked slowly toward the Aflangi, growling low in their throats or hissing through teeth like daggers. The bones of the Blood Preserve crunched beneath their heavy paws.

"Run, Herald," Lastor said in a near-whisper. "Run and hope some monster of the Blood Preserve catches up with you before we do. "No nightmare here or in any other land will show as much patience in killing you as we will."

Arrina had taken a step forward, but she froze at those last words.

Sixteen hours my kidnapper ran from my father's men. Thirty-six hours more before they let him die.

Herald, however, wasted no time. He turned and fled deeper into the Blood Preserve, the shadowy canopy cats snapping and snarling at his heels, driving him without ever quite catching up.

Lastor looked over his shoulder at her with a bloodthirsty grin that bordered on madness. "Kill him with me, Arrina."

Herald killed Michael, Tajek, and Mathalla, and he shows no remorse for those crimes or any others he has committed in his Godhead's service.

Arrina took a few steps in the direction Herald had fled.

"In the Godhead's service," she murmured, and something woke in her. Rage and the pain of her grief tried to strangle the words, but they had already left her lips.

"Arrina?" Lastor prompted.

She abruptly slammed her sword into its sheath and turned her back. "We are Senserte. We strike the master, never the servant."

"We are Senserte?" Lastor demanded. "That's what you have to say? He killed three of our friends. He would have killed you if I hadn't stopped him, and if we let him escape he'll keep trying to kill us and the rest of our friends. And all you have to say is that we are Senserte?!?"

Arrina turned back to him. "The Blood Preserve is a place of nightmares. Even a creature such as Herald should fear it. Let it render the judgment that we cannot."

"No!" Lastor shouted, red rain streaming down his face like tears of blood. He started walking backward in the direction Herald and the shadowy canopy cats had run. "He doesn't deserve to get away. He needs to die before he kills again!"

A part of her — a sizable part of her, in fact — wanted to do it. Aflighan had raided the Union before. The Godhead's soldiers had burned homes, killed innocent people, and taken prisoners for purposes no one dared guess. And Herald was a part of that. He was complicit, at best, and more than likely glad to do it.

"Lastor," she said softly, and then choked.

Mathalla, how will Torminth ever forgive me? Tajek, will your uncle still wish to build a tunnel between Wen and Turu when he learns what I let happen to you? And Michael, sweet Michael ...

She swallowed the tears. "Lastor, if you go, I cannot follow."

She spoke the words as though they had been written for someone else. She had put no passion in them, could not. Michael would have been disappointed with her delivery of the line.

If you could be here, I would be glad even for your disappointment.

"Someone else may have written the words for you, but you must make them your own," he had told her once long ago.

They're not my words. I'm just echoing Mathalla, and there is nothing left of him but his echoes.

Lastor looked disappointed as he turned his back on her. "I never expected you to follow me."

He ran deeper into the Blood Preserve.

"Lastor, no!" she shouted, but he didn't respond.

This is the Blood Preserve. The monsters that live here come from the nightmares of Wen children so young they are almost impossible to hurt. These are the things that frighten those who fear nothing.

Arrina took a step toward where Lastor had gone.

His magic is powerful but not powerful enough. If I don't convince him to leave the Blood Preserve, it will kill him, and it will be my fault.

Another step. First Michael and Tajek. Then Mathalla. She couldn't bear to lose another Senserte. She suddenly stopped, Lastor's final words echoing in her memory.

"I never expected you to follow me." Those were my words to Mathalla.

She took a step back.

And the words I said to Lastor were the same as the ones Mathalla said to me.

Mathalla knew the legends about the Blood Preserve. "If you go forward, you come back on your own or not at all," he had said.

Another of Mathalla's warnings leapt into her mind.

Get the painting and get out as quickly as you can.

Arrina turned on her heel, bare foot grinding against a bone fragment on the rainforest floor, and ran. She fled from Herald. She abandoned Lastor.

Frustrated howls filled the air behind her as she ran. Arrina didn't look back. She passed the intestine vines. She ran past the tongue and head trees. She vaulted over a shadowy canopy cat and a sharp piece of bone sank into the bottom of her foot as she landed.

Only Wefal magic prevented her from falling, from limping, from slowing down enough for the creatures behind her to run her down and add her bones to the Blood Preserve's grisly collection.

Fifty feet in and fifty feet back, but how much farther did I wander in my fight with Herald?

The carpet of bones abruptly gave way to the leafy compost of the rainforest. She ran past trees that weren't covered in tongues or heads or hands. She wanted to run away forever, even though the howls of her pursuers had faded away, and it was only by chance that she collided with Lastor.

Not collided, she realized at once. *He stepped into my path. But I left him back in...*

"Arrina, what's wrong?" Lastor asked, looking more concerned than she had ever seen him.

"Never ask that question of someone who survived the Blood Preserve," said another voice, familiar and yet...

Arrina tilted her head as she stood. Mathalla leaned against a massive tree.

"Mathalla, you're alive!" she cried and hurled herself against him.

He hugged her awkwardly. "Y-yes."

"Where's Torminth?"

"He's back with the others," Mathalla told her.

"Others?"

Please let it all be a nightmare.

The Wen pushed himself free of her embrace gently, and she saw the splotches of brown slime and blood rain that had dripped off of her, staining his dark green shirt. "I won't ask but I can guess. Michael is badly hurt, but he'll live. Tajek just had a bump on the head. They'll both be fine. And you? Did you find what you were looking for?"

Arrina held up the backpack. Her hands were trembling, and she was surprised by how thin her arms had gotten. She froze, calling her magic to check her health. Mathalla accepted the pack.

I burned eight pounds, she noted. *More than I expected, but not as much as I can afford.*

Now that the danger had passed, she dismissed her magic.

Mathalla opened the bag and withdrew a painting only a foot long and tall. It showed a wedding scene with a Farlander bride and a Wen groom standing in front of a crowd, leaning forward into their first kiss as husband and wife. The bride wore the Diadem of Elvenkind and held the Orb of Elvenkind in her right hand. The groom wore Jacob's Bow across his shoulder and carried Theo's Sword at his hip. Their hands were clasped, and Arrina could just barely make out the Star Ring on the groom's hand and the Moon Ring on the bride's. Two thrones stood on the dais behind the pair, and above the thrones hung a painting only two inches wide.

Lastor squinted at it and Mathalla frowned.

From her vantage point Arrina couldn't make out the details of the painting within the painting. From what she knew about Nosamae Descending, it showed Nosamae in chains kneeling in front of a Wen king. Nosamae Ascending was identical except reversed — Wen lords kneeling before a councillor of Aaronsglade.

"Hard to imagine, isn't it, that something so small could end a war and break the power of the Nosamae?" Mathalla said softly.

"And it might happen again," Lastor noted cheerfully. "Do you think Canolos was right about it giving Wen adults back their magic?"

"The only way to find out is to use it, which we would never do, but I doubt it," Mathalla said, sliding the painting back into the pack.

"Of course not. We're Senserte," Lastor declared proudly. His eyes grew curious. "But you can see why maybe someone not Senserte would consider it, can't you?"

Mathalla simply nodded.

The encounter with Lastor. The fight with Herald. It was all just a nightmare made by that place, Arrina reminded herself. *Kaspar isn't behind all of this, and Father definitely isn't.*

She could almost hear the Blood Preserve laughing at her.

The only nightmare ever to escape the Blood Preserve, she thought with a shiver. *We must be absolutely sure.*

"We can't afford to make any more mistakes," Arrina said. "If we fail at Pithdai, it could destroy the Flecterran Union."

Lastor and Mathalla looked at her with serious expressions but said nothing.

"We should return to the others to let them know we're safe," Arrina said.

They returned to Seleine. Berilla had placed her son under arrest in a small tree house they occasionally used as a prison, although she seemed less convinced of Canolos's guilt than did Arrina. When the Senserte returned to the quarters the archon of Seleine had given them, Nijel and Cleorame had already claimed them for one of their card games. Arrina had the sense that the children were not there by accident.

Let them spy. We have nothing to hide.

Arrina explained the situation to the others.

"I hate to suggest such a thing," Tajek said slowly, "but there are other ways to put a stop Sora. She is friendless and surrounded by enemies. Let her set down the orb for even a moment, and a knife can open her throat the same as anyone else's."

"That isn't the Senserte way!" Lastor said fiercely.

Tajek shrugged. "If this becomes a choice between your code and your nation, which do you choose?"

Lastor fumed.

"I do not like that solution, but Tajek isn't wrong," Mathalla admitted after a long moment's consideration. "We've never played for such stakes as these. If we fail, the best we can hope for is civil war. And when there is civil war in the Valley, there are raiders from the mountains."

"But it's still murder!" Lastor cried. "That's not how we work."

Arrina felt a small surge of pride at the young Wen's vehemence.

We've taught him well, Stipator and me. How could I have believed that Lastor in the Blood Preserve was the same as this one?

Because he had known the response to the test line, of course — a response no doubt somehow stolen from her memory just as the rest of the nightmarish situation had been. The fake Lastor was a reflection of her fear and anger. If she had been paying attention to his attitude instead of his lines, she would have seen it sooner.

Sometimes the players make the play, not the script.

"We can't do this without the other Senserte," Mathalla persisted. "We lost most of our information gatherers in the Aaronsglade debacle, and we've never pulled off a heist without Stipator and Jonathan. We may have to put the Valley ahead of our principles just this once."

Lastor opened his mouth to counter, but another voice interrupted him.

"It has been a challenging day," Michael said from where he sat with his back against a tree. His face was still pale. "I propose we rest tonight. Send word to Zori and the brothers to meet us at Phantom Lake. Who knows? We might yet receive news of Jonathan and the others. At the least their captors will send their demands."

Chapter 34

Arrina ran through the Blood Preserve, pursued by Herald, her father's homeguard, and the black canopy cats. Arrows whispered all around her. One passed so close she could feel the feathers against her cheek. Her heart hammered, but her limbs felt heavy and sluggish.

A lance of bone from the forest floor stabbed one foot, but still she ran. Limping, she tried to call on her magic, but it did not come. She licked dry lips and found the sweetness of saat there.

"Run!" Herald bellowed. "You will march a thousand miles in the service of the Godhead for every mile you run from me tonight!"

Arrina ran. Another volley of arrows flitted past her. One hit a tree trunk within her reach as she ran. Another tangled itself in her hair, letting loose her long braid. A third creased her cheek, leaving a line of blood that tickled her jaw.

Arrina jerked awake, her hand flying to her face. Her fingers found an arrow in the turf there, a thick roll of paper tied around the shaft. Her stomach knotted in dread. Only Etha wrote such lengthy epistles. *What more could have gone wrong?* It was too dark to read.

"Lastor," she called.

The young Wen didn't answer.

He's probably as tired as any of us.

Arrina went to the embers of their cook fire, added some wood, and stirred it to flickering life. It wasn't a candle, but it would do. She unrolled the letter and read:

"So much has happened in the last few days that it's probably best if I just start at the beginning."

• • • •

It's been a week and they haven't responded.

Etha sipped her tea and pretended to be interested in the book in her hands. Its cover was tattered not because it was old but because it was so cheaply made. The content was of no higher quality — a tale of an unlikely romance set in a wildly inaccurate Aaronsglade, translated badly from Kafthean.

There are not this many trees here, she thought, picking up a fallen page and inserting it back into the book. *It could be the weather. You haven't seen the stars for the last two nights.*

The hero of the story bested the Pirate King of Aaronsglade in some elaborate strategy board game called Push Power. Then he claimed the Pirate King's crown and set free his beloved Princess of Jacobston. There were so many things wrong with this book Etha didn't even know where to start.

Maybe they ran into trouble of their own in Tremora. Maybe the thieves set a trap for the Senserte in the Palace of Doors.

Etha flipped quickly through the next several pages where the author described how the heroine expressed her gratitude to the hero for rescuing her. Long paragraphs described acts for which Etha did not have the Kafthean vocabulary, although she learned several words in that language she had never wanted to know.

Why do they always wait to be rescued? Can't they do anything for themselves? Etha abruptly threw the book down on the table, scattering half its pages. *And just what am I doing? Nothing. Hoping either the Senserte here in Aaronsglade find a way to escape, or the Senserte who aren't in Aaronsglade will show up and rescue our lost friends. Either way, I'm the one really being rescued.*

"What's a little girl doing here all alone?" asked a man to her right. He reeked of cheap spirits and smoke.

Etha slid her chair back from the table several inches. "Find another table," she told him as forcefully as her high-pitched voice would allow.

The man looked down at her and spotted the two knives at her belt. His eyes went wide for a moment.

One dagger in a belt is a tool, Etha's cousin had taught her. *Two daggers is a warning. Three is a threat that invites challenge.*

The drunken lout placed a hand on her table. "Your mother sent me to bring you home." His face was comically grave. "She says something has happened to your father."

Etha's eyes met his, and she gave him a tight smile. With a sharp tchunk the tip of one of her knives buried itself in the table between his outstretched fingers. Her eyes hadn't even flicked in that direction. A heartbeat later, her other knife was out of its sheath, the tip of the blade an inch from his inner thigh.

Wear two, but always carry at least three, Etha's cousin used to say, before they sent him away, before they told her she couldn't see him again.

The man stumbled backward, leaving a drip of sweat on the table near the knife. Etha watched him until he found another table, and only then noticed the few other teashop patrons watching her. She felt a flush rise to her cheeks.

But I did something, she thought, checking the tip of her knife. She sheathed it, and stood up. *I've told the Senserte that both Nosamae Ascending and Nosamae Descending had been stolen, and whatever they decided, I have nothing more to add. I certainly cannot recover them.*

She literally had no value to the Senserte just now, in this teashop across Maiden Lake from Aaronsglade. Patrons could walk right off their skiffs into the ship; it was a two-hour sail back to Ma'Lara's Field. All her value was tied up in Kara, Stipator, Poresa, and Jonathan.

Michael would have found a way to retrieve them, she thought, tossing a couple of lei on the table. She left the tattered book behind, found passage on a skiff heading across the lake, and settled in, fingers sliding up and down the smooth handle of one of her knives.

She realized she had not drawn her knives since she had become Michael's apprentice. She had not needed them while she was under the Senserte protection. Her mother and uncle could not reach her, and she had thought magic would protect her. But she had not learned any magic.

I have nothing to lose. This isn't Romina. The worst that can happen is that I'll be arrested with the others.

She had her knives. Where Michael constantly preached about the why of magic, her cousin had only pointed out the sharp end and the handle, and straightened her grip and wrist, and directed her to the target on the straw mattress against the wall. Later, he demonstrated the smooth flowing motion of a throw, one hand on her wrist, the other on her elbow, urging her to relax.

Your decision should be done without thought. The motion should be instinctive.

The thought was strangely liberating. She had been assigned to the extraction team, so she might as well act like it.

"Hey little girl, we're here."

Etha looked up at the old sailor, who was reaching out a veined hand to help her off the boat.

"Oh, I'm sorry," he said as she took his hand. "My wife would love to have your youthful looks."

"That's fine."

Etha walked into Ma'Lara's Field, thoughtfully rubbing the knife at her belt.

• • • •

"Ma'am, please stop for a moment."

Etha briskly turned into a side street, then ran until she found an alley. She whipped the blue and white cotton dress over her head and stuffed it into a crate of carrots. Underneath, she wore knee-high shorts and a smudged muslin shirt. She pulled a child's cap out of the shorts and stuffed her ribboned pigtails into it, then ran out into the street, acting for all the world like a boy who was up to something innocently mischievous.

The gate guards for the First Tier had allowed the woman with three kids to move on already, the kids much louder now than they were when Etha had snuck in like an older sister. The mother was too tired to scold the kids into silence. Two guards were leaving the house to search for a girl in a blue and white dress who had snuck into the city, and their eyes passed right over Etha. She did her best impression of Stipator's smirk, and turned up into the city.

If you've taught me one thing, Michael, it's how to do costume changes in a heartbeat. Her papers to get into Aaronsglade should still be good, but she was uncertain if her name would still be circulated. So she had had to find another way to get inside.

And for my next scene, I will have to borrow from our Senserte tricks. Since she could not make her hand into a razor, she carefully palmed an iron coin with a razor-sharp edge and made for the gate to the Second Tier.

As she wound her way through the city, Etha listened for any rumors of the museum heist. She heard a few, but everyone seemed to agree that the thieves had been caught and that nothing had been stolen. The museum had already reopened to the public.

That's why the price is just high enough to be uncomfortable. The Nosamae want to make it look accessible to the public but want to discourage people from visiting it.

That made some sense. The museum held reminders of the Nosamae's greatest defeat and greatest shame. It existed because they wanted to look like they had learned this lesson of history and did not intend to repeat what all Aarons regarded as a tragic mistake, an overreach by enchantresses not as enlightened and humble as the current Nosamae.

Nosamae Ascending was real. How many of its other relics of the Nosamae War are, as well?

Etha watched the crowd flow out of the Second Tier. Most of the bureaucrats and merchants who worked there lived on the First Tier. They would return home for lunch and the three hours' rest of setat, and then they would return in the late afternoon to finish their daily tasks.

A boy of about twelve led a mule into the First Tier. His belt had two pouches — a heavier one that probably held coins and a smaller one that was of greater interest to her. A man who was probably the lad's father walked several feet ahead of him. Etha tailed the boy.

She had done this a score of times for the Senserte, had practiced doing it a thousand times. Etha tried not to think about how that had been in remote villages like Mattock, not in Aaronsglade with its seemingly all-seeing Nosamae enforcers.

A quick motion and it was done. Coin and pouch were in Etha's pocket before she had taken two steps.

She remained tense as she walked away, half-expecting a cry of "stop thief." People surrounded them on all sides. Someone surely saw the theft and would raise an alarm.

Fifty feet.

Or maybe some officer of the watch tailed her, hoping to track her to a local thief master. He would apprehend her as soon as she tried to pass through the gate onto the Second Tier. Etha forced herself not to look over her shoulder, not to appear hurried, and certainly not to run.

The gate to the Second Tier came into sight — not the one the boy and his father had come out of. Too much risk that the entry guard would recognize the name and realize it did not match the face.

Etha took refuge briefly in an alley, took the boy's identification papers out of the pouch and stuffed the pouch with its cut leather cords back in her pocket.

It will be bad enough to be going the wrong way at the midday break.

Traffic onto the Second Tier at this time of day was light. Etha joined the trickle. Most of those around her wore the rings and earrings common among enchantresses. More were women than men. Etha saw no other boys going this way.

"I forgot something, and my father sent me back to get it," Etha rehearsed silently. *What did I forget?*

Her mind went blank. She suddenly couldn't think of anything a merchant's son would need to retrieve that couldn't wait until setat.

And why would I bring my backpack in with me?

"Your papers, please," said a voice in front of her.

Etha bit back panic and mutely held out the folded identification. The gatekeeper frowned as she unfolded it, and Etha thought for sure the woman had seen through her ruse. The agent made a note in a nearby ledger and handed the papers back to Etha.

She took them numbly and continued on her way, still expecting an outcry any moment. It would be like the First Tier gate, except this time they would send enchantresses to catch her. She wouldn't slip a noose like that just by changing clothes, and certainly not by running away.

She knew the Second Tier a little better than she knew the first, although she was in an unfamiliar neighborhood.

I need to find a place to change costumes.

She couldn't go where she needed to go dressed like a merchant's boy. Etha eventually found a commerce street, one of the few places on the Second Tier where enchantresses and non-enchantresses mingled freely. She found a public house that sold kebabs to a mixed clientele and made her way to its lavatory.

The boy's clothes fell to the polished mosaic floor. She unwound the wrapping around her chest, rubbed briefly at the indentations it had made under her armpits. She had passed for a boy before without the wrapping, but she hadn't wanted to risk it here in Aaronsglade.

She swept off the hat and untied the pink ribbons from her black hair, finger-combed it out so it hung to her shoulders in only slightly bedraggled curls.

Out of the backpack came a simple long white skirt. She cinched it tight with her belt, hung her coiled whip from it, peacebound the two daggers. Then Etha took out a dark blue blouse studded with hundreds of clear crystals in patterns that matched several dry season constellations. Simple sandals went into the backpack, and fine sandals with more crystals went on her feet.

It was the outfit of an enchantress's apprentice. The constellations on her blouse marked her as an apprentice of an ad'Aaron — the family line that had given the city its name so many centuries ago. The ad'Aarons had ruled the city long before the formation of the Nosamae, when Farlander women weren't allowed to learn magic.

Etha stuffed the clothes back in the bag, adjusted the strap to make it a shoulder bag again, and left the lavatory. She briefly worried someone would notice the wrinkles in her clothes, but that fear passed quickly. Everyone in Aaronsglade was focused on getting something to eat before the hottest part of the day.

Etha made her way to the gate through which the boy and his father had come. She turned over the pouch with the boy's papers to a member of the watch standing nearby. She spun a brief story about finding it on the ground. It must have gotten caught and snapped the leather cords. The watchman assured her they knew the boy well and would make sure he got it back before setat.

"Thank you, sir," she said and turned, clasping her bag in both hands before herself, and disappeared into the crowd.

• • • •

In the small front lawn of Michael's house was a pump that drew fresh water from the Second Tier's underground plumbing. Etha drankly deeply from the well, and rinsed the sweat off her face and arms. Walking around in the sun had left her thirsty and tired — hungry, too, but she dared not leave the house now.

How much time will it take to deliver my letter to M'Elizabeth ad'Alice? she wondered. Handing letters to the messengers at the gate to the Third Tier was the primary way for people to communicate with the city's leaders, but even though the short missive she had written for M'Elizabeth had been labeled as coming from Sa'Michael ad'Aaron, her own son, Etha could not know how much priority the Nosama would put on her words.

She sat down on the wicker bench on the front porch as clouds rolled over the city with a crack of thunder. The afternoon rain began with big, fat drops, then got stronger, until it felt as though a cool mist was blowing through the porch. Etha hugged her knees to her chest, trying to keep her eyes open, but the steady thrumming of the rain on the roof lulled her to sleep.

When she woke, the rain had stopped, and the shadows were long on the street. The watch would be clearing the streets soon. She sat up, panic rising.

"Where is your master, apprentice?" asked a woman's voice from the wicker chair on the other side of the porch.

Etha pushed the black curls out of her eyes. A Farlander woman in her late fifties sat in the chair, her graying hair pulled back into a long ponytail. She had half a dozen earrings in each ear and her face was a mask of cool control.

Etha scrambled to her feet and dropped into a hasty curtsy. "Nosama."

The enchantress said nothing, and Etha remembered she had been asked a question.

"Sa'Michael is in Tremora, Nosama."

The enchantress raised an eyebrow. "Remarkable to find you on the Second Tier without him."

Etha felt the blush heat her face, and her stomach knotted. Was this M'Elizabeth or a Nosama enforcer here to arrest her? Her eyes flicked to where she had left her shoulder bag, but it was missing. Only then did she notice it sitting at the Nosama's feet.

"This is perhaps not the best place for this conversation," the older woman said. She didn't smile mysteriously, didn't frown threateningly, didn't show any sign whatsoever of her mood or intentions. "Not all my peers share my appreciation for the sort of audacity you've displayed today."

Appreciation is good, Etha thought. Then again, Michael sometimes expressed his appreciation of the clever schemes of the sort of villains the Senserte routinely and ruthlessly destroyed.

"You're a quiet one," the enchantress commented.

"Yes, Nosama," Etha said dumbly. This whole plan had been doomed from the start, and now she would be arrested the same as the other Senserte.

"Shall we go inside?"

"I don't have my key, Nosama."

The woman reached into the small purse on the seat next to her as she stood. "Don't worry. I brought mine."

"You're M'Elizabeth ad'Alice."

"And you're Etha ad'Lisa," the Nosama countered as she unlocked the door and pushed it open.

The lamps in the living room lit themselves immediately, one of Michael's little flourishes. An enchantress of Michael's pedigree and rank was expected to have countless such spells to impress visitors and ensure their comfort.

"Let's have a closer look at you," the Nosama said once Etha was sitting comfortably on the sofa near the heatless flames of the living room fireplace. "My eyes aren't as good in the dark as they used to be."

Etha sat with her hands in her lap as the enchantress studied her. She wasn't sure what to do or say next. Simply getting access to Michael's mother had seemed an impossible enough plan for one day. Convincing M'Elizabeth to intervene was not even on the table. Either the Nosama would act or she wouldn't, and Etha wasn't sure she could sway the Nosama one way or another.

"You're not sleeping with my son, are you?"

Etha blushed furiously. "N-no, Nosama," she stammered.

M'Elizabeth's eyes bored into hers. "Don't lie to me, apprentice. If you are, it would be best for you if I find out about it now instead of when your belly is round and I have to deal with the scandal of a grandchild born of my son's apprentice."

"It's the truth, Nosama. I would never..." Etha paused, tried to regain her composure. That arrow had reminded her too much of home, of her mother. "Do you really think so little of me that you assume he's teaching me for sex?"

That hadn't been what she meant to say. It was irrelevant to the very serious situation that had brought her here.

I come here to ask for her help and then I insult her?

M'Elizabeth's eyes widened fractionally at the heat in Etha's voice, but there was none of Michael's thunderhead in the Nosama's face.

"I think you misunderstand me," the enchantress said soothingly. "If he were, he would be the one in the wrong, not you. Enchantresses are forbidden from taking apprentices as lovers or lovers as apprentices. Yet it sometimes happens secretly." She looked almost embarrassed, the first sign of emotion Etha had seen in her so far. "An enchanter can keep an apprentice silent, can ensure her cooperation with threats and magic. The Nosamae established the universities of Aaronma in part to prevent opportunities for such abuse, and any lone enchantress who takes on an apprentice becomes the subject of rumors. This is doubly true of enchanters with young, quiet, female apprentices."

"Oh," Etha managed. Her studies had not yet progressed into the finer points of enchantress ethics, although it made sense.

Far more sense than ostracizing your teenage daughter for one foolish mistake.

Etha's life had been filled with the uncomfortable social consequences of a decision she was taught to despise but without which she would never have been born. Her reputable Stormhaven relatives acknowledged no contradiction in this. As far as they were concerned, it would have been more acceptable if Etha had not come into the world. Her mother, Tudi, never openly admitted to sharing their assessment, but Etha knew what her mother had given up on her account and often wondered whether she truly thought it worth the bother.

Tudi's family could have taken an unauthorized marriage to a poor young sea captain in stride. Such things happened even among the children of the Princes of Stormhaven — as inevitable, if unpleasant, as storms at sea. But for the shy youngest daughter of one of the most powerful sea merchants in the world to get swept up in a whirlwind romance with a pirate captain was more than even Tudi's father could shrug off with a jolly laugh. And to let that brief tryst bear fruit?

Etha's grandfather was not a cruel man. He would not let his daughter or grandchild starve, but the living he furnished them with could hardly be called generous, and every iron florr of it came with a reminder that Tudi would not have needed his support if she had married into a good family.

"You took risks to talk to me face-to-face," M'Elizabeth said into the long silence. "What do you need to say?"

Utterly unprepared for this question, Etha told the Nosama the truth. *If she's as disturbed by these thefts as the Senserte are, she is more likely to help. And if she's behind them, she already knows what we are doing, and my disappearance will not create any great inconvenience for the other Senserte.*

"Sora ad'Serra," M'Elizabeth murmured when Etha's tale was done. "You say she's falsely claiming to be a Nosama?"

Etha nodded gravely.

The enchantress pursed her lips, which brought out the lines in her face. "That is truly unfortunate for her."

"You've heard of her?"

"Yes. We went to the university together, although we moved in different circles. She became quite a skilled charmer and hoped to become a Nosama enforcer. Many of her friends became Nosamae."

"What happened?"

M'Elizabeth made an almost dismissive motion with one hand. "Oh, the usual trap that gets young charmers — she fell in love, he jilted her, and she tried to win him back with magic."

"She broke the law."

The enchantress nodded. "She was expelled from the enforcer training program, forbidden ever from being a Nosama. Expelled charmers have trouble finding work in Aaronma. People don't trust them, and rightly so."

"How did she end up as curator of a museum?"

M'Elizabeth sighed. "One of her professors, Ma'Molly ad'Mary, took pity on her. She believed Sora's was a crime of youthful jealousy. She was the curator of the Nosamae War Memorial Museum at the time, and she offered Sora a job as assistant curator. It wasn't what Sora wanted, but she had no other offers.

"Twenty-five, thirty years she served as Ma'Molly's assistant, traveling the world acquiring Nosamae War artifacts that had made their way overseas. Every few years she would make a formal appeal to the Council of Aaronsglade asking them to forgive her youthful indiscretion and let her become a Nosama enforcer."

"The council denied her requests."

M'Elizabeth gave a small shrug. "It's our law. No one who enslaves another for personal gain is permitted to learn our secrets. The Nosamae cannot afford another Nosamae War."

"With Nosamae Ascending stolen, that seems a real danger. She'd need the key miraklas, though."

M'Elizabeth pursed her lips a moment, as though considering whether she should share what she knew. "Ma'Molly and her assistant visited Kafthey about five years ago on museum business. She notified the council that she had found the Moon Ring by accident and had opted not to acquire it. It was safer there than in Aaronma — less of a temptation to thieves, less likely to attract the scrutiny of the other nations of the Union. She didn't even tell us exactly where she had encountered it.

She worried someone on the council might be tempted by it."

"But Sora was there."

Etha's stomach knotted. Kukuia and Stormhaven had sent a ship to cast the rings into the ocean, but it had never returned from its mission. Everyone assumed it had been lost at sea, sunk by a hurricane or broken on reefs in unexplored waters. The Princes of Stormhaven later learned from a survivor that the ship and rings had been captured by Kafthean pirates. They saw no reason to investigate further or make the incident public. Kaftheans wouldn't recognize the rings as miraklas, after all, and so they would probably find their way to the fingers of some Kafthean prince or in a bank's vault.

"Precisely. She knew exactly where to find it, which is why the next twist in the tale still doesn't sit right with me. A little more than a year ago, Ma'Molly died in the museum. The death looked natural — the sudden collapse of a very old woman, not a mysterious accident or shattered glass of poisoned wine. Sora found the body and reported it, but we had no reason to suspect foul play. One of my colleagues on the council thought otherwise, though, and she had Sora put to the question."

"Old enemy from university?"

"I don't know. Regardless, Sora had no memory of committing such a crime. A charmer could have altered her own memories, of course, but what possible motive could she have had to murder the only Nosama who cared about her? The council ultimately issued an apology, and Sora returned to work at the museum as its temporary curator."

"Temporary?"

"The position is a political appointment. Traditionally, only a Nosama can hold the post."

"But an exception could be made."

"Yes, but even so a charmer wouldn't be the best candidate. A diviner or artificer would be a better fit. The council granted Sora the curatorship temporarily, until such time as our Arts and Culture Committee found a more suitable candidate."

"That was a year ago?"

"Yes. Appointments usually don't take that long, but as I'm not on that committee, it was of little interest to me. Our temporary curator made some strange friends in the last year, and she has been doing more acquisitions work than curating. I think someone was delaying the appointment deliberately to use as a lever against Sora."

"So she's working for someone else."

M'Elizabeth shook her head. "She was, but she isn't anymore. The councillor who insisted on putting Sora to the question? The committee appointed her niece to the curator position about a week ago."

"Before or after Nosamae Ascending was stolen from the museum?"

"Before. Sora has ample motivation to lash out against the one who has been using her."

Against all the Nosamae, in fact, Etha mused. *Sora set herself on a road to ruin the moment she abused her power, when she was no older than I am now.*

"She has gone rogue."

"Yes. What she is doing could destroy the Union. She must be stopped."

"What of the councillor who was using her?" Etha demanded. "She orchestrated this, and she needs to be punished for it."

"She will be, I assure you, but not by the Senserte. Only enchantresses can police enchantresses, and only the Nosamae can police the Nosamae."

Etha considered this. From what Michael had told her about the Nosamae, M'Elizabeth had a point. "Does that mean you already know who it is, or are you telling the Senserte to stay out of Aaronma politics?"

The Nosama frowned, and Etha saw a bit of the thunderhead Michael sometimes wore. "The Senserte came into our capital under false pretenses and broke our laws," M'Elizabeth said frostily. "I will arrange for their release, but they will not be allowed in Aaronsglade again."

Etha knew she should back down. She wasn't Arrina. She didn't have the Wefal's dogged obsession with achieving poetic justice. The Nosama could easily make all the Senserte in Aaronsglade forget everything they had learned if she pushed the Nosama too hard.

"Was the letter Kara carried intercepted, or were you the one who had her arrested?"

"Are you accusing *me* of being Sora's secret patron?" M'Elizabeth demanded. Outrage crept into her voice.

"No, but others among the Senserte might, especially if the friends they sent to Aaronsglade disappear or forget. Your whole tale of Sora's history could be a fabrication. I can't prove otherwise." Etha made a helpless gesture and spoke more soothingly. "I know you don't want any outsiders to find out that you have a rogue among the Nosamae. I'm not asking you to unmask her in front of the entire Union. Keep your shameful secret if you must, so long as justice is done, but if you want the Nosamae to look blameless in this, help us bring down Sora in her moment of triumph."

There. Arrina would like that bit.

M'Elizabeth considered this. Etha could see the calculation in her eyes. Was she weighing the risks of involving herself with the Senserte? Was she considering the possibility that Etha was bluffing? Was she thinking about the best way to have all the Senerte assassinated without the murders being traced back to her?

The Nosama abruptly smiled — a tight, forced smile, but still a smile. "Michael would be so proud." It was a mark of her distraction that she forgot to include the honorific Sa. "The Nosamae will take part in your elaborate morality play, but in a role of our choosing."

"Thank you, Nosama," Etha said, awkwardly attempting to stand up and curtsy at the same time.

The frown returned, imperious this time. "Do not thank the ones you blackmail. I will send your Senserte here. Tell them to enjoy the marvels of Aaronsglade while they can. It is the last opportunity to do so any of them will get. I'll be in contact with you until this unfortunate situation has been resolved."

With that M'Elizabeth threw the house key on a low table and swept out of the room.

Chapter 35

"Kara complains about her confiscated jewelry, Stipator has some gaps in his memory concerning the location of the safehouse, and Poresa has been particularly quiet these last few days, but we're all unharmed. Even the squawkers have recovered," Arrina read to the Senserte gathered around the remnants of their campfire. "Please send us news soon. Humbly at your service I am Etha ad'Lisa. P.S. Jonathan sends his love. He asked me to write this letter because I saw the events and he didn't. He'll take over the letter-writing duties after this."

"At least the letters will be a lot shorter," Torminth said with a bark of a laugh. "I would have loved to have seen the look on the moon shooter's face when she handed him that roll of paper."

Lastor abruptly woke up from where he was dozing in a hammock of vines. "What did I miss? Did she get inside Aaronsglade?"

"They're safe," Tajek summarized.

"She should have said that at the beginning," Lastor grumbled.

"What's so funny, Michael?" Mathalla asked.

The enchanter had been shaking his head and laughing for most of Etha's description of her conversation with his mother.

"She manipulated a Nosama perfectly and she has no idea why it worked," Michael said as though that explained everything. When he saw their blank looks, he elaborated. "Mother has been trying to bury the Nosamae War for decades. She'd make the whole Union forget the entire thing if she could. A rumor that she was actually behind a plot to use Nosamae Ascending is so utterly, ludicrously out of character for her that it would spread like pollen on the wind."

"She'd rather not get involved at all?" Arrina guessed.

"It'll take months for her to regain her standing in the Council of Aaronsglade. M'Elizabeth doesn't spend her influence frivolously like that."

"She has an angle," Mathalla said.

"You could put it that way." The enchanter smiled slightly. "She's using the situation to further Aaronma's interests. Fortunately for all of us, what my mother considers in Aaronma's interests are also in the Union's interests."

Mathalla snorted a laugh but didn't dispute the statement.

"What do we do next?" Tajek asked.

"I'd suggest letting the Nosamae deal with Sora," Michael said.

"That doesn't sound like much fun," Lastor said. A line of large spiders crawled up and down one of his arms.

"The Nosamae are powerful but proud," Mathalla said. "They will come to Pithdai like a rain of sledgehammers, and I fear for those Sora holds hostage with orb and diadem. There will be blood."

Michael quickly objected, and the two of them were off.

Arrina had grown tired of their arguments. "Peace, both of you."

They had the decency to look ashamed.

"What do you suggest we do?" Michael asked.

Arrina reached a decision. "Stick to the plan."

"What? How?" Mathalla demanded.

"Don't you see? We're now in the perfect position to stop Sora exactly the way we originally intended."

Mathalla raised an eyebrow, and Tajek tilted his head in confusion. Only Lastor seemed not to question this.

"Sora has defeated us at every turn," Arrina explained. "That was our plan from the start, remember?"

"Our plan was to let her thwart us," Mathalla admitted, "but she's actually done it multiple times — Gulinora Island, Romina, Aaronsglade, and now Seleine. The only one we actually planned was Tremora."

"We did fine in Seleine," Lastor objected. "Canolos betrayed her, Herald ran away, and we found out Corina and Kaspar are secretly trying to stop her."

"All of that was because Canolos made so many mistakes," Mathalla reminded them.

"It was very clumsy for a betrayal," Tajek agreed.

"Yes. Take Corina and Kaspar out of that, and we're all groveling at Sora's feet begging for her to command us," Mathalla said.

"Right, so Sora has beaten us every time," Arrina admitted, "but she can't be certain we didn't mean for her to beat us."

"I'm not following you," Mathalla told her.

"No matter how much Canolos and the others warned her about us, she must be feeling pretty confident that she'll see through any trick we try to play on her."

"Well yes, but she's justified in thinking that," Mathalla pointed out.

"She's the one with the elaborate plan to seize control of the Flecterran Union, but she's all alone with this single goal she'll stop at nothing to achieve."

"A goal she's very close to achieving."

"So much the better. Here's the thing. We don't have to defeat her with every swindle we throw her way. In order to stop her, in order to make her and everyone else think the Senserte had the whole thing planned from the start, we only have to trick her once."

Lastor was grinning but didn't seem to catch the implications. Tajek looked confused. Mathalla looked thoughtful.

"She's not Reck. No matter how paranoid we make her, she's never going to fall for the Nidela routine. She isn't looking for allies. She doesn't think she'll need them."

"Ah, but she does. She needs one person — a Wen man she can trust."

"It would appear that position has already been filled," Tajek noted drily.

"If he shows any signs of betraying her, she'll just use the diadem or her charms to force him to finish what he started." Realization spread across Mathalla's face. "You cut these things very fine, Arrina, very fine indeed."

"What?" Lastor demanded. "What's the new plan?"

Arrina put a hand on the young Wen's shoulder. "Tell the others to meet in the director's tent. It's almost time for the blow-off."

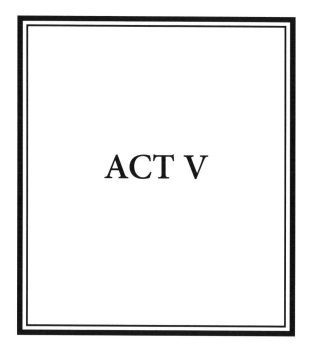

ACT V

Chapter 36

The director's tent had been set up miles from Pithdai proper, in a clearing in the rainforest home to cultured flora and fauna, but far from any Wen, Farlander, or Wefal home. Arrina walked across the damp earth toward it, balance perfect, motion graceful, thoughts focused.

It was twilight, and the animal sounds of day had begun to give away to the cries of the night's creatures. The tee-dee of the spry cockerel faded into the too-hoo of the slant-faced owl, and the howls of the swinger monkeys into the laughter of the moon chimps. Closer to the tent, the voices of the Senserte added to the rainforest's hum.

All of us creatures have a place in Mira's theater, Arrina thought as she walked into the shadow of the tent, pausing by the entrance as thunder rolled above and a wet breeze tried to open her cloak.

"White?" Poresa's question cut above the noise.

"White is the easiest to stain." Arrina should have known Poresa was talking to Lastor. Only he or Stipator would be so flamboyant. "Any drop of blood I spill, forevermore will stain me; every cut I suffer, hence will sing my ruin to all."

But his reason is new. That line is from The Envoy of Romina. I wonder if he will stick to the plan this time. Arrina strode quietly to the other side of the entrance. Lightning flashed across the sky.

"What did you dose me with, you Romin witch?" Vudar sounded more annoyed than angry. "It tastes as bad as Davur's experimental brews."

"If it doesn't taste bad, it will not heal you. And Davur makes some wonderful brews." Zori's laugh was tinged with something Arrina couldn't quite grasp, and again, the Wefal wondered about Zori's past, and what had happened to bring her to the Senserte.

Whatever secrets she keeps, she never lets them come between us.

"Did you get attacked by ghosts?" Lastor asked loudly, and the whole room quieted.

"They're not ghosts," Zori said tiredly. "They're nothing so simple as that."

"Nor would I. It would be like speaking of the nightmares of the Blood Preserve," Davur added, but the comfortable mood seemed damped.

Something tugged on Arrina's boot top, and she looked down to see Jabber. *So Poresa knows I'm here,* she thought, placing a finger to her lips. The squawker mimicked the motion.

"Tajek, tell us a story about the desert!" Poresa said into the silence in the room. "Tell us a joke from Turuna."

"A joke? What is a joke in Turuna?" Arrina could feel the big man standing up and pacing. "Why did the duck cross the Riphil?"

"Why?"

"It wanted to see if the crocodiles were smaller."

Arrina put a hand over her smile. That was Tajek, full of strange stories and a humor no one else understood. *But he was undeniably our best defense against Herald.*

But it had worked, and now a round of jokes started, lightening everyone's mood. Arrina took a deep breath as the sky opened and rain started to fall. The smells of earth and leaves and water filled her lungs.

Mathalla and Torminth walked up to the entrance, fingers laced together, but did not seem to see her. She held back as the flap opened, spilling laughter and light into the clearing, then shut again.

They reminded Arrina that not all became Senserte for the same reasons. The Kuku endured dangers and poor weather and worse roads because of the people they travelled with. They often said they regarded the Senserte as family — as more than family, for in Kukuia, Mathalla and Torminth had to pretend to be something they were not.

"Waiting to make an entrance, sis?"

Arrina smiled and turned to pull Jonathan into a crushing embrace.

"Whoa, it's not as if you haven't seen me since we got back," he said, smiling and squeezing her hard.

"I don't know if I'll get much of a chance in the coming days," she said.

Jonathan grinned.

"They know I'm here, anyway," she added.

"Then let's go in. It's starting to get wet, and I don't have materials to make an umbrella."

"A few more minutes."

He shrugged, then crouched into the shadows better, holding a finger up to urge her to be quiet. Arrina glanced up before ducking down. Stipator was sauntering to the tent flap, arm in arm with Kara. Etha followed, almost invisible in their shadow.

She did her part, and more. But she needs to understand that directors stay behind the scenes. Someday, Arrina knew better now, Etha could be the Director. She felt a tear in her eye. *But no time soon.*

Jonathan leapt at Stipator with a loud cry just as the battlemaster let Kara go and opened the flap with a flourish. The two tumbled into the side of the tent, laughing, and Kara's face was a picture of fury. Arrina just caught a knife disappearing back up Etha's sleeve, and let her own breath out. Etha gave her a small wave, then entered the tent.

"That wasn't in the plan!" Stipator said, jumping to his feet and brushing himself off. "I was going to usher our beautiful Kara in with great respect and dignity!"

Everyone else was laughing, and Jonathan's voice was full of smile. "I'm just getting you back for all the times you didn't stick to the plan!"

The flap fell, and Arrina was left to the rain again, but there was Michael, hobbling up the path on a crutch because he had refused a magical device of Jonathan's. He wore a wide-brimmed hat to try to keep some of the rain off him, but it did not seem to be working. Arrina ran over to help him.

"Ah, the chair appears," Michael said affectionately. "But it appears I need a leg, not a chair."

"Then I can be a leg," Arrina offered, taking the crutch and putting her shoulder in its place. She wrapped an arm around his waist, and he draped his over her shoulder.

"I was thinking," they both said at the same time, and then laughed.

"You first," Michael said.

"I was thinking how well Etha did, and that she could be a great director one day, but I don't want to lose you." She let it out in a rush.

"We don't want to lose you," he corrected.

"No," she said, kissing his hand.

"Ah."

"What were you thinking?" she asked.

"I don't know anymore."

"Come on, you guys!" Lastor called from the tent flap. "I can't take another Turu joke!"

"We're coming!" Arrina called.

"I think there must be a better plan," Michael said as they reached the shadow of the tent. "Something simpler, something that doesn't rely on so many small things going right."

"We planned for when those go wrong," Arrina said.

Michael lifted his arm off her shoulder and took the crutch back. He smiled down at her. "Maybe we could find a way to limit those small things."

"I'd rather be prepared for everything than run into a surprise."

Michael smiled and touched her cheek. "I think we can have a few wild cards up our sleeves, just in case."

"What do you want to do to the plan?" Arrina was surprised. The Senserte had hammered out the details of the plan the night before, with much tea and manioca involved. It had been hard enough to battle the expected tweaks without having any unexpected ones.

"You'll see." Michael scrunched up his face.

"That's not a smirk," she chuckled. "You don't look a thing like Stipator."

"I'll have to work on that." And he lifted the tent flap with a flourish to make Stipator proud, and escorted Arrina into the director's tent for their green room. Everyone gave a cheer.

"Let us begin," Arrina said, assuming her role.

Everyone found a chair in the sixteen arranged in a circle, a torch between each one. Arrina sat with seven Senserte to her left and right, across from the empty chair. She surveyed her troupe with affection.

Sora has not faced all fifteen Senserte at once. Our history is littered with the ruined villains who tried that feat and failed.

"Director, call the roll," Arrina ordered.

Michael leaned forward. "Pardon me if I don't stand. I was waylaid on the road here by something large and made of metal."

"Hear, hear," Vudar grunted.

"Facechanger, Chairwoman. Are you here?"

"I am," Arrina answered.

"Are you Senserte?"

"I am the poisoned wine, the executor of unexpected justice. I am she who throws open the final curtain. My name is Arrina ad'Anna, and

I am Senserte."

"That always gives me chills," Kara stage-whispered to Etha, who nodded. Arrina grinned at them.

"Extractor, Playwright," Michael intoned. "Are you here?"

"I am," Jonathan answered from Arrina's left.

"Are you Senserte?"

"I am the springworker, the engine-builder, the breaker of locks. My name is Jonathan ad'Pithius, and I am Senserte."

"Two for two," Stipator mumbled.

"Shh," Tajek said, gently smacking him on the side of the head.

"Ouch."

Michael kept calling names, and one by one they answered. Arrina watched their faces as they declared themselves Senserte — Poresa's soothing demeanor, Kara's open confidence, the three brothers' wary closeness. Mathalla and Tasticon stood together, as much one person as any of them. Zori's confidence was steely compared to Kara's, and giant Tajek's enthusiasm was potent.

"I guess that's everyone," Michael said, leaning back with a smile.

"Now wait," Stipator and Etha had leapt up at the same time, and their words were echoed by Lastor, who harrumphed theatrically and flopped back into his chair.

Stipator and Etha glared at each other for a few seconds, and Arrina thought it would actually come to blows. Stipator backed down, though, with a twirl of his moustache and a glint in his eye.

"You did not call us," Etha said, her high-pitched voice hardly squeaking. "You did not call for ... Trickster, Battlemaster."

Stipator rose again, smiling. "They also call me some much less flattering things, but that never bothered me. I'm reckless. I'm incorrigible. I'm constantly going off-script. I trust my improvisation over anyone's carefully laid plan. I am Stipator ad'Bryan, and I am Senserte."

"And, um, Protégé and Wild Card," Etha continued.

Lastor walked across the circle and shook Etha's hand. He was taller than her, and glowed in his white outfit.

"I am the righter of wrongs, the punisher of the unjust, the one whose appearance is either a welcome relief or the end of the world. I am Lastor ad'Remos, and I am Senserte." He bowed to her.

"Of course, yourself, Director. Um. Thunderhead." She jumped as a sharp crack of thunder happened after she said the word.

Arrina stifled a laugh. Most of the people had jumped, but the thunder could not have been coincidence. Michael's smile was proof of that.

"I am the talisman-maker, the show-stopper, and the dramatic ... pause," Michael said. "I am Sa'Michael ad'Aaron, and I am Senserte." He gestured to Etha. "Shadow, Dagger Thief, are you here?"

"I am," Etha said, sitting down.

"Are you Senserte?"

"I am the swarm of bees, the audacious rescuer, the one who cannot be caught. My name is Etha ad'Lisa, and I am Senserte."

"Good, good," Jonathan murmured to Arrina's left.

"We are Senserte," Michael started the words, but everyone joined in. "The secret eyes of justice. It is our duty to punish those who let wealth and power corrupt them.

"We rise above the politics of our homelands and our peoples. We band together in a common cause."

Arrina put an arm around Jonathan's shoulders, and took Michael's hand with the other. Davur and Ravud held up Vudar between them, with Stipator and Zori flanking them. They joined in a circle, a little lopsided until Tajek lifted Michael to them.

"We see the corruption of the rich and powerful. We hear the cries of the weak and the poor." They almost shouted the words, Lastor and Stipator loudest of all.

"We are the hands of justice who humble the arrogant, ruin the miser, and destroy those who threaten peaceful folk with violence!"

Arrina stepped into the circle's center and urged them to hush, turning on her heels to meet everyone's eyes.

"It is our sacred duty to seek the source of the corruption and eradicate it," she whispered, barely louder than the pounding rain. "No one comes to the Senserte with a pure heart. No one is infallible or invulnerable. It is only by serving justice that the Senserte are pure. And only our perfect loyalty to and trust in each other ensures that we will never fail. Do you have as much faith in your fellow Senserte as you that the sun will rise in the morning?"

"We do," came the hushed response.

"Will you be a worthy vessel of their trust?"

"We will."

"Many powers may be arrayed against us, and yet not all those whom we fear are villains may prove to be beyond redemption. We will exercise restraint. We will show mercy if we can."

"And those who refuse it?" Stipator growled.

This was part of the script, so Jonathan didn't hesitate in his reply. "We will shatter their plans like pottery."

"We will break them like ill-tempered horses," Poresa said.

"We will catch them and bind them fast," Kara said.

"We will steal that which they most desire in the moment they acquire it," Etha said.

"We will drive away everyone they ever loved," the ad'Marusak brothers said. "They will live out their lives cursed by strangers, surrounded by enemies, and mocked by everyone who has heard tales of their crime."

"And we will lay bare their crime for all to see," Zori said. "Theirs will be a story used to instruct children, to warn them of what can happen to those who abuse their power."

"Their names will burn in their infamy," Torminth said.

"The wind will carry news of their destruction to every ear in the Valley," Mathalla said.

"Everyone they meet will be as sympathetic to their plight as are the snows and stones of the avalanche," Tajek said.

"They will want to forget," Michael said.

"They will long for death," Stipator declared.

"And we will deny them even that," Lastor said.

"We are Senserte," Arrina repeated. "We will not ignore the terrible crimes committed by these enemies of the Union and its peoples. There will be justice — as swift and terrible as a poisonous snake. By Mira do we swear it."

"By Mira do we swear it," responded the other Senserte in a unanimous hiss.

Despite the fire, the tent felt suddenly very cold. Fifteen Senserte took their seats and began their final preparations.

Chapter 37

Arrina sat in the director's tent with Michael after all the other Senserte had left. No one was sure of the time-table, but everyone had to be ready when the moment arrived.

"Didn't Lastor's aunt tell us Gates of Tremora was the only way into the Palace of Doors from outside Tremora?" Michael asked.

"No," Arrina corrected. "She said it was the only way into the Palace of Doors that bypassed its defenses."

Michael's small changes had been universally accepted, and she was glad for it. For once, even Jonathan had agreed. *The final hand at the table is what you've been saving your wild cards for,* Michael had said.

The Senserte would hold nothing back, and Arrina was proud, because this was personal to her and Jonathan as much as it was a job for the troupe.

"Do you have any idea how many such gates exist?"

Arrina shook her head. "I doubt Mariah would approve of Lastor revealing the existence of just this one. It implies that the Tremor have many more such doors, which could lead to some awkward questions from other nations in the Union."

"At least it helps us position our resources more quickly than would otherwise be possible." Michael tugged at his earrings. "I'm worried about our entrance. Our role in this seems overly complicated. Is there really nothing you and Stipator can do to make yourself immune to saat?"

Arrina laughed lightly. "If only we could. Internal mystics have been trying to figure that out for centuries. It doesn't have anything to do with swallowing it or tasting it. A drop on the lips is enough. One Wefal sealed his mouth completely with magic, but a drop of saat where his mouth should have been neutralized his magic. We'll have to rely on your talismans."

"I was afraid that might be the answer."

"I thought you said someone chewing tasa petals couldn't see the enchantment hidden in them?"

He waved dismissively. "Of course, but if an enchantress scrutinizes them she'll figure it out pretty quickly."

"Kind of like Kara's fake mirakla spell."

"Exactly."

Arrina rubbed his other earrings until he took her hand. She grinned at him.

"I'm more worried that Herald will show up for the finale," she said. "The Nosamae are at least a known quantity. We have no idea what an Aflangi sorcerer is capable of. We only know he shows none of Sora's hesitation to kill."

Michael pressed his hands to his temples. "There are so many ways this can go wrong. Even with your hometown advantage I feel like there's something we're forgetting."

Arrina shrugged. "Probably, but you know how it is. Plan the mission to death and improvise around anything you couldn't plan for."

• • • •

Kaspar paced furiously in his suite. Corina sat on the chair at his desk.

Sora was somewhere in the palace eliminating the last of the pockets of resistance to her rule. The guards at the palace gate had suspected nothing until it was too late. Most of the homeguard had been taken just as unawares. The rest discovered that simply placing wax in their ears protected them from the commands of the diadem and orb. It had no effect on the soldiers already in the enchantress's thrall, however, and in spite of her earlier assurances, people had died in the fight to defend their king and queen.

Larus had ordered the surrender, and it wasn't until he and Aora were prisoners that anyone realized his elven hearing had probably made him vulnerable to Sora's commands even though his ears were plugged with wax. Those who remained free of the imperial commands fought a losing battle in the palace. She insisted Kaspar stay in his suite so he wouldn't accidentally fall under the power of diadem and orb.

"Kaspar, you're pacing again."

He paused for a few seconds. "Sorry, sorry. I just feel so helpless. What was I thinking?"

"You weren't," she said gently, placing her hand on his arm. "You were in love, and it blinded you to who she was and what she was trying to achieve until it was too late."

"She'll be back soon. She'll want to celebrate her victory." He shuddered. "I dare not refuse her, but after the things she has done in Pithdai..." He eyed Theo's Sword where it hung on the wall over his bed. "I wish I had the courage."

Corina's grip on his arm tightened. She guessed his thoughts. "That might delay her ascent but would not stop it."

"I've been such a naïve fool, and now I will be forced to marry the woman who enslaved my parents."

"She was not the woman you thought she was. You are not the first person to suffer love blindness, and you won't be the last."

"I should have listened to you sooner."

"Who were you more likely to listen to — a woman you only just met who told you from the start that she was a thief, or the friend you've known since you were a boy?"

"I just ... I just don't see any way out of this."

"Every trap has an exit. The only things she believes in are her right to rule and your love for her. Maintain that illusion." Corina looked into his eyes hard. "You will get one and only one opportunity to betray her. She is vulnerable to no one else.

"Are you telling me to murder her?"

"Is it murder to prevent a tyrant from throwing the Valley into civil war? To prevent Herald's Godhead from taking our people captive while we refight the Nosamae War?"

Kaspar's shoulders slumped. "I'm not sure I have that in me."

"Then you are right. There is no way out of this for you."

There was a knock on the door to the suite. Sora had returned.

• • • •

"Could you quit glowing for a minute?"

Lastor wasn't sure he liked this more confident Etha, but since she was already showing signs of wearing off, he let it be. He polished a button and looked at his cards.

"No. Your turn."

Etha drew a card and discarded it. "Saat," she said, showing all her cards.

"Again?"

"You should have checked my sleeves."

An arrow tchunked into the deck, a thin script tied to its shaft. Lastor pulled it off and unrolled it. He scanned it quickly, and then smiled broadly. It was from Nijel in Seleine.

"Oh no," Etha said, voice rising an octave. "Stick to the plan."

"Read this and tell me what the plan is," he said, handing it to her and rising. "I'll be right back."

He darted out of the room in the Palace of Doors before she could respond, just noticing as she picked it up and rose to her feet.

• • • •

"In the name of the Empress, release me," Canolos commanded.

Promin didn't respond as he set the plate of fruit on the floor of the small house that had become the prison cell of the mayor's son. The young member of Seleine's small police force had found the pink-haired man's demands insulting at first and then amusing, but now he regarded the constant stream of commands as merely annoying. They were the pathetic rantings of a madman who had betrayed his family and nation for the sake of a Farlander woman who had turned against him.

An hour later, Canolos tried again. He had nothing better to do. He had experimented with the diadem and orb. Sora had left Seleine three days ago. Eventually she would have to put on the diadem again, and when she did all the Wen she had enthralled with it before would be her subjects again. She had ordered the people of Seleine to obey Canolos and had failed to rescind that order before leaving.

Not all of them had heard the order, though. She had enough sense to stay away from the crèche, and a couple foraging parties missed all the excitement. But having most of the town in his power was better than having none of it under his control.

Night fell. Canolos heard footsteps on the platform outside his prison.

"In the name of the Empress, release me at once!"

Silence answered him. He hadn't really expected Sora to be wearing the diadem at this hour anyway. Canolos laid down on the sleeping mat. An instant after he closed his eyes, he heard a key turn in the lock.

Had it finally worked, or had someone gotten tired of listening to him? Perhaps they had guessed his intentions and were coming to gag him.

A huge shadow filled the doorway. A half-moon axe hung at its hip.

"Where have you been?" Canolos asked.

Herald only grunted. He took the chain of the Wen's manacles in both hands and snapped the links between them like fine threads. He did the same for the leg irons.

"Where is Nosamae Descending?"

"Do you hope I will kill everyone in your village, Wen?" Herald hissed.

Canolos shook his head.

"Then hold your tongue until we are quit of it."

"I need to go to my house first." When the Aflangi didn't object, he added, "It is on our way."

Herald grunted again. Once they got there Canolos wasted no time. He took his bow, a quiver of arrows, and a bandolier of glass vials. Everything else they would be able to find along the way.

They fled across the rainforest floor. The canopy offered more direct routes, but they were more likely to be spotted and pursued by first-cyclers and their elementals there. Canolos suspected Herald could outrun those, but he knew he couldn't.

At last the pitch darkness of night became the twilight of forest floor day. Canolos called a halt. His feet and legs were aching, and he was breathing heavily.

"Tell me. Did you kill everyone before you rescued me?"

Herald did not seem winded, although sweat streamed down his face and soaked his shirt. "No. It would not have furthered the Godhead's aims enough."

Canolos had long since learned not to ask Herald about the Godhead's mysterious goals.

After the moment had passed, the huge Aflangi continued, "I expected we would be pursued. It appears we are not."

A rustle in the canopy drew their eyes upward, but it was only a monkey.

"Where have you been?" Canolos demanded. "You were supposed to bring Nosamae Descending to Seleine days ago."

"Had I done so, it would have implicated you."

"So where have you hidden it?"

"I cast it into the Blood Preserve to keep it from falling into the hands of the Senserte."

"And do you plan to retrieve it, oh fearless Herald of the Godhead?"

Herald did not lick his lips. His eyes did not shift nervously. He didn't betray the smallest regret as he spoke. "No. It would not further the Godhead's aims enough to justify the price."

Canolos barked a laugh. "You're afraid! What nightmares terrify an Aflangi sorcerer, I wonder?"

"Your Blood Preserve does not frighten me. The Godhead can visit nightmares upon those who displease him that are beyond the imagination of any Wen child!"

"And you're afraid that if you spend his power frivolously he will be angry with you."

Herald said nothing.

"At least you came back for me, but I'm sure it is because you think I can still be useful to your Godhead."

He didn't bother to deny it. "We will go to Pithdai."

"Why?"

"It is not the place of the lesser to question the greater."

Canolos waved that aside. "You don't intend to stop Sora. You wouldn't undo all the work you've done to make her empress. That would waste the Godhead's strength. You *want* the civil war she will set off."

"She cannot be allowed to remain empress. Even with Wen magic diminished, an empress could be a rallying point."

"Ha! I knew it! Your Godhead wants maximum chaos. You mean to steal diadem, orb, or both."

"I am no sneak thief."

"Ah, but it will require tremendous resources to march into Pithdai and attempt to slaughter your way to the new empress. You know I can help reduce that price."

Again, Herald offered no denial, which was as good as an assent. "You know ways into the palace I do not. You know where to find Empire of Brass. While the palace guards are distracted by the army within, Sora will be more vulnerable."

"That won't work. The inner vault was built with such breaches in mind. A few first-cyclers could turn back the invasion. I have a better idea, one that will cost you even less than storming the throne room."

"I will tell the Godhead of your cooperation. Perhaps he will give you an honored place among the dead enemies who serve him."

Canolos didn't respond to that. Instead, he took one of the small bottles of clear liquid from his bandolier. "Miraklan liquors are a Sutol specialty," Canolos said. "We'll drink this before we enter the palace, and it will render us undetectable by eye and ear for at least an hour. That should be long enough to reach Sora and pluck the diadem off her head if you choose."

"This will not work on me." A hint of suspicion. "The Godhead protects me from all toxins, be they mundane or magical."

"Don't tell me you can't relinquish that protection long enough for it to take effect. I have business in Pithdai, too, and I need you as a distraction so I can carry out my plans. I have nothing to gain by poisoning you."

"I will consider your suggestion," Herald said.

"Consider it while you flee the canopy cats. We are not beyond my mother's reach yet." He unstoppered the bottle and drank it down in a single gulp, his face screwing up from the strength of the vintage.

Herald held out a hand. "Give it to me now."

Canolos shook his head as he began to melt away like a soap bubble deteriorating in mid-air. "I trust you, Herald, but not that much. Meet me in The Emerald Orchid in Pithdai on the morning of Sora's wedding day, and I will show you the secret way into the palace."

"Canolos, get back here!" Herald growled, but he received no reply. He snarled and ran with supernatural speed away from Seleine.

· · · ·

"Cleo wanted to tell the archon what we saw, but I knew the best people to tell would be the Senserte. And no matter where you were, you, Lastor, would be the one who would do something. Go get him!" It was signed Nijel, and there was a note at the bottom. "Please be careful. Cleo."

Etha took a deep breath.

This was what Michael had planned for in his change in our plans. Lastor, the wild card. Now I have who knows how long to have a new plan.

Flabbergasted panic threatened to overwhelm her. Etha forced it down. *You bluffed your way into the Second Tier of Aaronsglade. You can handle this.*

After all, if you don't, Jonathan won't be alive to kill you.

Chapter 38

Stipator and Arrina walked down the broad cobblestone road that led to the wall-less palace of Pithdai. Each wore a lithe rapier at the waist, and Arrina carried the canvas pack that contained Nosamae Ascending. The lighter morning rain had finally stopped, leaving puddles of water in their path that Arrina carefully walked around as if she feared her feet would get wet through her low leather shoes.

"Give us a kiss for luck, dear," Stipator said suddenly.

Arrina hesitated, glancing around at the busy streets. "Is that wise?"

Stipator chuckled. "Afraid we'll start rumors? Honey, there are already stranger rumors about you out there. Quickly now, while no one is staring at us."

Arrina smiled slightly and planted a brief kiss on Stipator's lips.

"The mustache tickles," Arrina told him. "Maybe you should try growing one."

"I like all your earrings, too. You should wear them more often," Stipator said, touching the side of Arrina's face gently. "Good luck, Arrina."

"Good luck, Stipator," Arrina said, catching her companion's hand briefly in hers. "Now let's deliver this mirakla."

"And this painting, too," Stipator laughed.

The pair continued toward the palace.

• • • •

Michael sat on the couch in his wagon, putting the finishing touches on a pair of fine silver chains. A small garnet hung from one, a tiny sapphire from the other. A trio of the troupe's disguise masks lay on the table next to an empty tumbler that had held honey wine not long ago.

There was a knock on the door.

"Almost ready," Michael called absently. "Come in."

The door opened, and Arrina stepped through it, closing it behind her. She looked the part of a royal sister going to a wedding on a hot afternoon in Pithdai — a bright skirt in a pattern with flowers and palm trees and a short-sleeved white shirt trimmed with lace and embroidered with patterns of crystals like constellations of stars. Her outfit was not all frills, though. The sword at her side was all business, as were the travel sandals on her feet and the ring of blue-blond hair pinned up instead of worn down.

Arrina leaned her back heavily against the door, breathing heavily, her breasts rising up and down. "Michael, I'm so glad I found you. We have so little time!" she gasped.

"What's wrong, Arrina?"

He half-stood, but she was at the foot of his couch in an instant, pushing him back into it.

Her eyes flicked to a simple cane leaning in a corner of the wagon and then back into his, drowning him in a blue as wide as a clear sky, as bottomless as Kaeruli Lake. "Tell me, Michael. Are you fully recovered from your injury?" she asked, still breathing heavily on him.

He tilted his head slightly at the question. "You know I have. Zori said so herself days ago."

"Good. Then let's not waste any more time!" Arrina threw herself on him, kissing his cheeks, probing his mouth with her tongue. Her knees straddled his thighs, pinning him down.

"Urmf?" Michael managed, but if any surprise still lingered, the reality of the beautiful woman in his arms quickly swept it aside.

Her hands found his belt — his, the buttons on her shirt.

"What is going on in here?" another Arrina in an identical outfit demanded from the door.

Michael hadn't even heard it open. He froze, but the first Arrina remained insistent.

"Let her watch, my love," she breathed in Michael's ear.

"Stipator!" the new Arrina shouted. "What are you doing?"

The Arrina on the couch broke off the madly passionate kisses and leaned back on her heels. "Just getting into character." Finger and thumb pinched the air to one side of her lip.

Michael pushed the Arrina in his lap away with an irritated growl. "Stipator, you are such an *asshole* sometimes!"

The not-Arrina was laughing in gales as she picked herself up off the floor. "He's a decent kisser once you get him going," she confided to her twin.

Michael picked himself up off the couch with extreme awkwardness. "Enough of this nonsense, Stipator. You're not even in costume, yet." He picked up the masks on the table, glanced at them, and flicked one to the laughing woman. "I'm sorry, Arrina," he said to the mustached man at the door, handing over another mask.

The real Arrina burst into laughter. "*You're* sorry? I feel like I'm the one who owes you an apology. After all, my body and clothes just tried to seduce you." She glanced at the not-Arrina. "Even though he's been warned not to do this sort of thing before."

The not-Arrina deliberately avoided her twin's gaze, focusing all her efforts on tying the mask around her face. In a flicker, not-Arrina became Ravud and gave Arrina a shy smile. "What's a little prank between brothers such as we?"

Arrina sighed heavily and slipped on a mask, becoming Davur. "Let me put it the way Jonathan would. Stick to the plan."

"I always do!" Ravud said cheerfully.

"Yes, your own plan," Michael muttered, his mask turning him into Vudar.

Ravud grinned. "We should have a toast. The brothers Marusak always have a drink before a job."

Davur started to object, but it was too late. Ravud had already set out three tumblers and was examining Michael's fruit liquor collection.

Vudar sighed and retrieved the corkscrew. In a moment they all had a glass of banana liqueur in hand.

Ravud raised his in their direction. "We brothers three will always be side-by-side to victory!"

Davur and Vudar raised their glasses as well. "Side-by-side to victory!"

The three clinked glasses, drained them in one go, and set them down on the table.

"Let's get going, boys," Davur said. "Be dears and carry the painting."

"You don't think Kara will have any trouble convincing your mom to let her inside, do you?" Vudar asked Davur. "This whole plan rather hinges on it."

"Oh, I'm sure she'll manage," Davur said. "If not, Jonathan will have to assemble that monstrous contraption of his very, very quickly."

· · · ·

"I don't know what you're after, young woman, but I'm not about to let five strangers into my house just because they claim to be friends of my children," Peggy ad'Anna shouted from the second story window, the crank crossbow pointed at the redheaded Farlander standing at the gate outside.

Davur, Ravud, and Vudar gave Kara uncertain looks. Poresa merely stood carefully behind the ad'Marusak brothers and tried to keep Jabber, one of her pet squawkers, from climbing down from her shoulder.

"Jonathan will be here in a couple hours to assemble the machine he told you about," Kara explained.

"Jonathan!" cried Jabber, and Poresa shushed him.

"He sent you a letter, remember?" Kara called.

"If you think I've gone senile in my old age, you're badly mistaken. Jonathan hasn't sent me a letter in weeks."

Kara blinked. "He sent it by moon shot three days ago."

"Sure he did, girl. Convenient what with all the cloudy nights we've had. I'm not letting you in, and that's final!"

"We could force our way in," Ravud suggested softly.

A crossbow quarrel tchunked into the side of the cart behind them. Kara and the ad'Marusak brothers scrambled for cover, even Ravud on his crutch. A moment later, Poresa gave a squeak and did the same.

"Haven't gone deaf in my old age, either," Peggy shouted from behind the cover of the arrow slit as she reloaded her crossbow. "First one tries it gets worse than a warning shot!"

"What now?" Poresa asked.

All of them were looking at Kara.

"It's for her own good," Ravud said, rubbing his sore calf through the bandages.

"And ours, too," Vudar added, peeking over the canvas covering the cart's contents for just a moment before ducking down again. "Hurry. I think she's almost done reloading."

Kara sighed heavily. "If Jonathan cancels our dinner plans because I charmed his mother, I'll be very unhappy with all of you."

"Dinner plans?" Poresa grinned. "Something casual or something intimate and romantic?"

Vudar cleared his throat. "Ladies, can we gossip some time when no one is trying to shoot us?"

• • • •

Zori looked at the blueprint dubiously for the hundredth time. Tajek and Jonathan sat on a space on the floor of Jonathan's wagon that he had cleared soon after dawn.

"Can't we just build another balloon?" she asked. "At least we have it on good authority that it could fly."

"Tajek, wrap that rope around where the sticks overlap between where I'm holding them. A little to the left. No. My left, your right."

"There?"

"Close enough. It's not an exact science. Well, actually it is, but I'll make it work." Jonathan didn't turn away from the project at hand. "Zori, it would be too obvious. The homeguard would shoot it down before it reached the palace." To Tajek, "Don't use maidknots like that one. It'll just come undone. Use roundknots with a monkeyhead."

Tajek gave him a blank look.

"You've no idea what a monkeyhead knot is, do you?" Jonathan asked.

Tajek shook his head.

"It's like a ... nevermind. You hold the sticks here, and I'll show you," Jonathan said. Then to Zori, "Besides, the wind is wrong, and the garden isn't really big enough for a balloon that would carry all three of us."

"Oh, I see," Tajek said. "The knot is an elbaryud. I know it, just by a different name."

Jonathan looked relieved. "Oh good, because we're on a schedule and we're running behind already. " He looked at the frame of the device with consternation. "Ah, you've got them all done in maidknots. We'll have to retie them all."

"I've got them," Zori said. "The last thing any of us needs is for this whole thing to come apart."

Garble, one of Poresa's squawkers, lifted his head up from the chair where he had been sleeping. "Jonathan?"

"What is it, Poresa?" Jonathan said without looking up. One of the sticks of the frame snapped in his hands, and he cursed.

"We seem to have run into a bit of a snag," Poresa said.

"I'll get another piece," Tajek offered.

Jonathan shook his head. "We've used up every scrap we have, and we don't have time to look for more. We'll just have to tie it together and hopes it holds long enough."

"Jonathan?" Poresa prompted through Garble.

"Sorry, Poresa, but we're a bit busy at the moment. Zori, Tajek, if you two have these knots, I'll get started on the flaps."

"It's your mother," Poresa said.

"Has she been killed?" Jonathan asked, adjusting a tie.

"No."

"Kidnapped?" He reached over and retied a knot.

"No."

"Then what's the problem?"

"She's just being, um, noncooperative."

"Poresa, I've got six hours of work to do in three. Figure something out."

"She has a crossbow."

"And she's a lousy shot."

"She's your mother."

"And Arrina is my sister, but you know how she can be. Stick to the plan."

Garble's mouth hung open for a long moment, and then the squawker curled up and went back to sleep.

"Tajek, somewhere in that pile of papers over there is a bear trap. Could you find it and bring it over here? I need to cannibalize the springs for this next bit."

Chapter 39

Pithdai's square throne room, like most of the palace grounds, was open to the sky, protected from the daily rains by Wen children or, in rare cases, a large canopy of waxed silk that rested on the almost invisible latticework that covered the room.

It was a large garden square surrounded by a wide aisle supported on columns of white marble carved to look like tree trunks and buttresses covered in flowering vines. Above the aisle were marble walls speckled with scores of windows and half a dozen small balconies — pale blue marble created by Turun children thousands of years ago, in the days of the Elven Empire. Each opening in the wall was surrounded by a tile mosaic that symbolized a star, one of the four moons, or, directly over the throne, the sun.

At the back of the throne room stood a double door made of olka and decorated with hundreds of tiny purple flowers arranged into the purple tree that was Pithdai's crest — planted in the wood and kept alive with the magic of Wen children. A wide walkway of dark red marble flagstones, flanked on either side by expertly shaped trees covered in fragrant purple flowers, led from the main door to the Postulant's Terrace — a raised column of vine-covered red marble eight feet high and twenty feet across reached by a winding stair on either side.

Beyond that rose a single tree twenty feet across that stretched out purple-flowered branches. Carved into the trunk six feet higher than the Postulant's Terrace was a large grotto with two thrones of living wood, upon which sat King Larus and Queen Aora. A short flight of stairs led from the grotto to the Postulant's Terrace, and at least a dozen bows were ready to be pointed in that direction from the windows at any moment.

The smaller thrones to either side of them were intended for the future king and queen until their coronation. Sora sat in the Consort Throne, but the Heir Throne was empty when the homeguard escorted Arrina and Stipator into the chamber.

Arrina and Stipator had been disarmed, and the contents of the backpack examined.

"Have you brought the wedding present?" Sora asked sweetly.

The acoustic qualities of the throne grotto made her voice boom and echo throughout the palace. Dozens of brightly plumaged birds that had perched on the overhead lattice squawked in unison and took flight at the sound. The scores of domesticated squawkers that lived in the garden took up the question with a flawless imitation of Sora's voice, so the echo of it only faded after several minutes of pandemonium.

"We have," Arrina said, holding out the backpack with the square object in it.

"We have! We have!" cried the squawkers.

Sora gestured with the hand that held the Orb, and the two caught a glimpse of the Diadem on her head. "Bring it to me."

"To me! To me!" echoed the squawkers.

Arrina and Stipator climbed the stair to the Postulant's Terrace.

"Is there any way to stop them from doing that?" Sora demanded of Larus and Aora. Her words echoed off the balconies.

Larus shook his head and spoke softly. "Squawkers mimic voices, Empress. They don't understand the words they speak. When you are sitting, your voice is among the softest. Standing, though, it is easily the loudest."

"Why do you even let them in here?"

"In here? In here?" cried the squawkers.

Larus spoke quietly. "It is an old tradition, Empress. They discourage courtiers from spreading whispers unheard by the king ad queen. They add weight to royal decrees. They remind us also that only animals speak simply by repeating what they have heard, while wise advisors must bring new ideas."

"If I may be so bold, Empress," Aora added hesitantly, "they are also small, clever, and fond of people and gardens, so there is no good way to keep them out of the throne room."

"You could have them all killed," Sora suggested.

"You could have them all killed!" the squawkers cried.

"If my empress commands, I will obey," Larus said.

Sora dismissed it with a gesture of the orb. "Perhaps after the wedding. I have more pressing matters."

"After! Killed! Pressing matters!"

Sora ground her teeth. Arrina and Stipator waited on the terrace for her pleasure. They bowed with arms crossed across their chests.

"Your majesties. Ma'Sora," Arrina said, and Stipator echoed it. The squawkers took up the chant at once.

Sora walked down to the Postulant's Terrace and held out her empty hand. Arrrina held out the canvas pack.

"Take it out. Let me look at it."

"Look! Look!"

Arrina obeyed, holding Nosamae Ascending out to Sora. The enchantress stared at it for a long moment, her frown deepening to a scowl.

"This is a forgery."

"A forgery! You could have them all killed!" the squawkers cried enthusiastically, and that actually brought a small smile to Sora's lips.

• • • •

Garble stopped chasing a wad of discarded paper and trotted over to Jonathan, who was still bent over his contraption of wood and rope and paper thin leather. He glanced up at the awkward-looking creature of fur and feathers.

"Vudar and I are in position, as is Kara. I can only assume the other two are, as well."

"Glad to hear it," Jonathan said. "What's going on?"

"Mathalla and Torminth are bringing the first fake to the terrace now."

"Right on schedule."

"At least someone is," Zori muttered behind him from where she sat struggling to pull the leather cover into position over a piece of the wooden frame.

"Is everything going well there?" Poresa asked through Garble.

"It will be fine," Jonathan said. "I had to make a few last-minute changes to the flaps."

"Because he forgot we still have to get it out of the wagon!" Zori threw in.

Jonathan turned his head to shout back. "I told you I could blow the roof off with pyrotechnic chemicals, but you seemed to think that might be dangerous." He returned his attention to Poresa's squawker. "You got the business with my mother sorted out then?"

There was a long pause. "About that ..."

"What?"

"It took some convincing, but once she believed our story, well, she wanted to come with us."

"You told her no, of course — tied her up and hid her in a closet or whatever it took to keep her from doing that?"

"Um."

"Where is she now?"

"Oh, she's with me. She promised not to do anything but watch. She said something about seeing how you and Arrina spend your time away from home."

He exhaled loudly. "See that she keeps that promise. Pith are notoriously bad at that."

"I will."

"Anything else?"

"Out of curiosity, does that secret passage lead anywhere else? We saw a few other tunnels leading off."

Jonathan allowed a small chuckle. "I'm guessing some rulers have had one secret lover, while others have had several."

"Where do they lead?"

"Other nice houses, I imagine. Our parents forbade us from going down there."

"Oh. Hold on. Sora just noticed the forgery, and I think she's about to order them killed," Garble said in a rush. "Gotta go."

The squawker stalked over to the trigger mechanism and sniffed at it. Garble lifted a paw to grab it. Jonathan shooed it in a near panic.

"No, no, no! Get away from that. Bad squawker!"

Garble looked up at him. "Bad squawker!" it shouted, and then it scampered off to look for the lost ball of paper.

• • • •

To Canolos' surprise, Herald was waiting for him when he reached the Emerald Orchid.

"Two of the Senserte half-breeds just went into the palace with Nosamae Ascending," the Aflangi whispered. He looked less than pleased. "You will lead me inside now."

Canolos looked around the room. He saw no familiar face in the crowd, but he knew the Senserte too well for that. No one had pursued him out of Seleine, and he didn't have time for further complications.

"Of course," he said to Herald, removing two bottles from his bandolier. He hoped that in the dim light the Aflangi wouldn't notice the liquid in the one Canolos gave him was slightly pink.

"How will I follow you if we're both invisible?" Herald asked as he opened the bottle.

"Two invisible people can see each other," Canolos lied.

The Aflangi seemed to accept this, and both of them drank their vials of liquor in quick gulps. Canolos' face twisted as the alcohol went immediately to his head.

"You call that liquor?" Herald asked with a booming laugh. "I've had harsher wines than this."

"Sweet as peaches?" Canolos asked.

The Aflangi's giant's mouth opened to reply, but then his eyelids slammed shut and his head struck the table.

"He's yours to do with as you like," Canolos said to the air as his hands became transparent. "I'll trouble you no more."

A child's laughter wafted out of the Emerald Orchid as he left it behind.

• • • •

Davur and Vudar, dressed fairly convincingly as two members of the homeguard, patrolled corridors of Pithdai's palace. At each intersection, Vudar reached a silk-gloved hand into a pouch and handed Davur a small but thick copper coin. Davur, who wore no gloves, dropped each coin on the floor as they walked.

"Think we've dropped enough?" Vudar whispered.

Davur shrugged. "Poresa said she'd send a squawker as soon as she got word from Kara."

"We haven't seen any since we entered this wing."

Two of the homeguard turned a corner ahead of them, heading their way. Davur and Vudar turned stepped into a side passage, sweating profusely.

"Why couldn't we have been servants?" Vudar asked once they were certain they had not been noted. "Cold-infiltrating an elite royal guard where everyone knows everyone else is next to impossible."

"Not as impossible as two armed servants making their way to the roof of the throne room," Davur said. "Now give me another of Kara's coppers."

Vudar harrumphed and handed him another coin from the pouch.

• • • •

Sora seemed on the point of giving a harsh order but hesitated, perhaps deciding exactly what kind of terrible sentence to pass on the Senserte.

"A proxy, not a forgery, um, Empress," Arrina said hastily. "The real one is at the Palace of Doors."

"You were told to bring it here."

"Bring it here!" cried the squawkers.

"And we are, Nosama. We thought it too dangerous to transport overland all the way from Tremora, so we've arranged for our associates to bring Gates of Tremora here today. Now."

A long silence followed. Arrina looked uncomfortable.

"I wonder why it's taking them so long?" Arrina wondered, looking to Stipator for help.

"It's a big painting," Stipator explained. "Or maybe they were stopped by the guards?"

Sora's frown deepened.

"Guards! Guards!" repeated the squawkers.

• • • •

"Anything yet, Kara?" Poresa asked through Jabber, who sat curled up contentedly in Kara's lap.

Kara glanced at the silver mirror she had hung on the wall and frowned. "Not yet. They're probably having a hard time navigating in the royal wing without being stopped by the homeguard."

"She's running out of patience, and if I nudge her much more, she's going to notice. We need a plan now."

Kara chewed her lip. "Have her arrest Peggy."

Jabber let out a squawk. "Jonathan will kill us both if we ..."

"No, I mean have her send someone here. That should buy the boys some time to lay down more eyes. Sora probably would have done it already if she had thought of it first."

"How are you going to keep them from sweetening your lips?"

"Sora isn't the only enchantress in Pithdai. " Kara smiled slightly. "Please, do it quickly before those muscle heads dig themselves any deeper."

Jabber curled up in Kara's lap and promptly fell asleep.

• • • •

Sora's smile carried venom. "Do you know who I forgot entirely to invite to the wedding, Arrina? Your mother. Perhaps if I bring her here she can help you remember where you hid Nosamae Ascending."

"Oh, it's not hidden, and it will be here very soon," Arrina assured her, but sweat was running down her forehead. "Besides, Mom and Kaspar were never very close, so there's really no need to ..."

"Oh, but I insist," Sora said. "Sergeant, send eight men to arrest Peggy ad'Anna."

"At once, Empress," said one of the homeguardsmen near the entrance. "Where can we find her?"

"Your majesty?"

"Spicetown," Larus said at once. "Stucco house two stories tall with a wrought iron gate at the front. It's a bit of a fortress, so be careful."

"Yes, your majesty." The guards bowed deeply toward him, turned, and left.

"Eh ..." was all Arrina could manage, the look of panic on her face mirroring Stipator's.

"And sergeant?" Sora called before he had gone too far. "Spread the word. I want everyone entering the palace dosed with saat — no exceptions. Am I understood?"

"As you command, Empress."

• • • •

"How many do we have left?" Davur asked quietly.

Vudar glanced inside the pouch. "Three or four."

"Are we really that lost, or has Poresa forgotten about us?" Davur muttered.

A squawk from a side passage halted their steps. The two brothers followed it and found a three-legged squawker watching them.

"Poresa?" Vudar whispered.

"Poresa!" cried the squawker, and both of them shushed it.

Davur glanced into the main corridor furtively to make sure they hadn't been noticed but found it empty.

"Sorry," the squawker said softly. "Things are a bit hectic here. Good work. Go to phase three."

Both of them heaved a sigh of relief, and the squawker waddled away.

"Let's find a staircase," Davur said.

• • • •

"Peggy ad'Anna, open up in the name of the king."

An old Farlander woman stepped out of the garden and into the passage leading to the front gate, leaning heavily on a cane. "At once, sir. Could you please tell me what this is about?"

"You're being invited to a wedding."

Peggy's eyebrows rose, but she didn't raise any issue with this as she unlocked the gate. The sergeant held out a small glass bottle filled with a golden liquid.

"What's this?"

"Saat, madam."

"I'm not an enchantress."

"We're sorry, but this is the Empress's orders."

"Of course, dearie," Peggy said agreeably, taking the bottle.

As she lifted it, her cane clattered to the ground. All eight pairs of eyes followed it. Peggy leaned over stiffly and picked it up again, and only then did they look at her again. She handed the empty saat bottle back to the sergeant with a smile.

"There you are, dearie. Lips nice and sweetened like the nice Empress ordered. Lead on."

As soon as they were gone, Jabber slipped through the bars of the front gate and scampered to an alley a few blocks away from the palace where Davur, Ravud, and Vudar passed the time next to a large painting covered by canvas.

"Kaspar's suite!" the squawker cried. "Now! Now!"

Davur and Vudar looked at each other.

"Aren't you supposed to be with Kara, Jabber?" Vudar asked.

"She'll meet you there. Quickly!" Jabber squawked, and then he ran off.

"What part of 'stick to the plan' is so hard?" Vudar grumbled.

"Things don't always go the way you plan them," Ravud said, twirling his non-existent mustache for the hundredth time."

"Stop that. You'll give yourself away," Vudar complained.

"I thought giving ourselves away was the plan."

Vudar scowled.

"Careful. You'll give yourself away," Ravud said in imitation.

"Heave ho, gentlemen," Davur said, gesturing to the painting. "We've got a long day's work ahead of us."

• • • •

"Of course I suspected from the start that you were bluffing." Sora tapped Stipator on the shoulder with the Orb and turned away with an evil grin.

"Bluffing!" cried the squawkers.

Both the Wefals stood stock still, sweat trickling down their faces.

"I know my museum's defenses, and even with an enchantress or two you'd have a difficult time breaking into it. Add to that Aaronsglade has the strictest magic laws in the Valley, and it is clear you were lying from the start. It is no matter, though. That simply means I have to bring the painting here myself. However shall we spend the time you force me to wait?"

"However you wish, Empress," Arrina and Stipator said in unison.

Sora laughed, and the squawkers laughed with her. "Stipator's famed bravado has fled, and the Pith princess who offered me her protection when *she* was in *my* power and not the other way around appears to know fear after all!"

The eight homeguardsmen returned, escorting an ancient-looking Farlander woman between them.

"Peggy ad'Anna, I presume?" Sora asked.

"I was told there would be a wedding," Peggy said. "There are no decorations, dearie."

"A wedding! A wedding!" the squawkers shouted.

Arrina and Stipator turned, their faces draining of color.

Sora laughed at their discomfort. She addressed Peggy. "There has been a small delay, but I insist you remain my guest until that happy day." She delivered an unpleasant smile. "I'm sure we'll become very close friends in just a few short days. Bring her to me."

The homeguardsmen escorted Peggy to the Postulant's Terrace firmly but not roughly. The old woman seemed unperturbed by this.

When she reached the Postulant's Terrace, however, Sora frowned.

"Wait. You're not …" she began, and then she and Peggy locked gazes.

More than a minute passed as the two stared at each other. At the end, Peggy flickered once and became Kara, who fell to her knees in front of Sora, head bowed.

"Dose her with saat," Sora ordered. She was breathing heavily as if she had just won some epic battle against an equal opponent.

"As you command, Empress," Arrina and Stipator said at once, but the homeguard and squawkers drowned them out as they said the same.

The doors to the throne room opened, and the ad'Marusak brothers entered carrying a huge painting between them. They spared a moment's attention for the black-haired Farlander kneeling on the Postulant's Terrace, and Vudar mouthed "Kara," but Davur stepped forward fearlessly.

"Empress Ma'Sora," he said, unbowed as was Sutol custom. "We're sorry it took so long, but your host's guards took many more precautions than we anticipated."

"Six doses of saat?" Ravud complained. "I know we're carrying a famous miraklan painting through which armies have marched and that we once vowed to destroy you utterly for the crime you're committing here — Senserte and all — but that strikes me as a bit much."

Sora pointed at Ravud. "Silence!"

"Silence! Silence!" cried the squawkers.

"Yes, Empress," Ravud droned.

Davur glanced at his brother, looking concerned. "I apologize humbly for my brother's insolence, Empress. I believe Arrina and Stipator have explained our purpose here?"

"Yes."

"And I can certainly see why you might be afraid it is some trap. We Senserte are famed for them, after all."

"Trap! Trap!"

Sora gave the three a sour look that shifted into a clever smile. "You bear a family resemblance. You are the Marasuk brothers, aren't you?"

"Yes, Empress Ma'Sora. I am Davur. The silent one is Ravud. And the youngest here is Vudar."

"Tell me if this is a trap, Davur."

"Of course not, Empress," Davur said. "It simply seemed the safest way to transport Nosamae Ascending. We can have it sent overland, if you'd prefer."

"Very well. Sergeant, remove the canvas, but see that it is not pointed in my direction."

"Yes, Empress."

The homeguardsman obeyed wordlessly. When nothing happened, Sora spoke again.

"What do you see on the other side, sergeant?"

"The main gallery in Tremora, Empress."

"Besides that," Sora grated.

"A pile of paintings and statues. There's a young Wen boy sitting right in front of the door."

"No army?"

"No one else at all. The Wen is standing up. I think he might walk through."

Sora suddenly relaxed. "Let him. The diadem will contain him if needed. Turn the painting around so I can see into it."

The homeguardsmen obeyed. Davur, Ravud, and Vudar stepped back into the aisle near the throne room door to give them more room. Lastor stepped through Gates of Tremora a moment later. He bowed outrageously to Sora.

"Empress, my name is Lastor, crown prince of Tremora and youngest of the Senserte. I ask your permission to present to you Nosamae Ascending."

"Of course. That was the agreement."

"And the other paintings stolen from Pithdai."

Sora said nothing.

"As well as, incidentally, all the other works of art in your care at the Nosamae War Memorial Museum." Lastor grinned as he pulled a golden wand out from behind his back.

Two dozen bows creaked from windows and balconies and Lastor froze.

"Put that down," Sora ordered. "Slowly!"

Lastor obeyed, carefully setting the wand down on the flagstones. "What is it? The plaque said it was something called Archon Slayer, but I didn't have time to read the rest of it. Museum burglary and all."

"Sergeant, give him saat. Lastor, don't resist him."

Lastor stiffened slightly and took the bottle without argument.

"Sergeant, take your squad in and bring out all the art in that pile, but most especially Nosamae Ascending."

"Yes, Empress."

The eight homeguardsmen stepped through Gates of Tremora and into the gallery beyond.

"There is a lot of art, Empress," Lastor noted. "You might want to send more people."

"Anything amiss, sergeant?" Sora asked.

"No, Empress."

"Any sign of Nosamae Ascending?"

"Not yet, Empress."

"We put it on the bottom," Lastor said cheerfully.

Sora snarled, and the squawkers mocked her like a bunch of Wen children.

"Very well. Send more. I want that art unloaded as quickly as possible. Lastor, stay exactly where you are."

"Yes, Empress."

Thirty minutes passed. Then an hour. At last, the homeguard brought out Nosamae Ascending.

Sora examined it from afar before waving the man forward. "Bring it to me."

The sergeant obeyed.

"Your dagger, sir."

"You disarmed us, Empress," Arrina and Stipator said at once, even as the homeguardsman handed her his dagger.

Sora eyed them. "Mock me now if you wish, but I will make you suffer when this day is through."

"Thank you, Empress," Arrina said.

"Silence," Sora hissed.

She stabbed the dagger at the painting, right at the Wen groom, but the blade didn't even scratch the paint, much less cut through it. She nodded, satisfied.

"Hang it over the thrones and let Prince Kaspar know his bride is waiting for him."

Arrina and Stipator moved forward.

"Halt," Sora said, and the two obeyed instantly. She frowned. "You two are acting very strangely."

The two said nothing.

"Stipator, slap Arrina."

Neither moved.

"You, slap him."

Arrina struck Stipator a blow across his cheek. Sora stared at each of them intently.

"You, explain why you didn't slap her when I told you to slap Arrina."

"She isn't Arrina."

"Who is she?"

"Mathalla ad'Stontal, eldest son of the vice primary of the Coastal Republic of Kukuia," Stipator said.

"Pitiful fools!" Sora shouted, pointing the Moon Ring in their direction. "Your puny magic is no match for the power of a Nosama." She laughed maniacally, and suddenly Arrina and Stipator were Mathalla and Torminth, glassy-eyed and in the thrall of the Diadem of Elvenkind. Each wore a simple cloth mask that covered just the top half of the face, held on by a piece of string.

"What is this?" she demanded, ripping it off Mathalla.

"One of Michael's disguise masks," Mathalla said.

"If neither of you are Arrina, where is she?"

"Rescuing Kaspar."

"And for our next trick," Lastor announced from the floor in front of Gates of Tremora, "a disappearing act!"

The young Wen jumped through Gates of Tremora, and the gates closed behind him. Sora reached up and touched her head as if to confirm the diadem was still there. Sora appeared to notice for the first time that the large painting had been blocking her view of the throne room entrance.

"Did the other three go through, too?" she demanded.

"No, Empress," the sergeant said. "They left while we were moving the art."

"And you just let them go?"

The sergeant looked confused, as if he hadn't thought about it before now.

"Go to Kaspar's chambers and ... never mind. I'll go myself. Attend me!"

Sora stormed down the stairs and out of the throne room.

Chapter 40

"How many?" Davur asked the three-legged squawker in a whisper.

"Twelve," it said.

"That leaves six for us," Davur noted as he pulled the vial out of his pocket and poured its contents onto a cloth.

He handed it to Vudar and prepared a second for himself.

"Three to one odds. How wonderful."

"Better than eight to one. I'll take the lower galleries. You take the upper."

Vudar nodded.

• • • •

"It isn't too late, you know," Corina reminded him. "I can manage the homeguard in your suite. We could escape and be on a ship before she even realizes we're gone."

Kaspar threw a bit of wax from the wicker table off his balcony. "I can't. My cooperation is the only thing keeping her from hurting my parents or others."

Corina leaned forward. "How many died when she captured the palace?" she hissed.

"What could I have done? They wouldn't listen because they thought she had me enchanted."

"You're just going to stand at her side and hope for the best?"

"If it comes to that, yes." Kaspar sighed. "I'm Wen and she's Farlander. She'll be empress for five or six cycles at most, assuming someone doesn't overthrow her. I won't even be middle-aged by then."

"Thirty years is a long time to sit and do nothing."

"Whatever you might say, Corina, this is my own fault. I must endure the consequences in the name of peace. It's my duty."

"If you had the stomach you could prevent it from being necessary."

Kaspar picked at the remnants of the previous night's tapers where they had melted onto the table. "I might find it in me to be as ruthless and merciless as my parents one day, but that's not who I am." He sighed heavily. "Besides, Arrina and Jonathan, the Senserte, are still out there."

"You have a great deal of faith in your Wefal kin."

"So does my father. He doesn't often misplace his trust."

"I hope you're right." Corina stood up. "Let's get you into your wedding things. You'll want to look your best for your bride."

Kaspar followed in silence

There was a knock on the front door of the suite. Kaspar looked at Corina and shook his head.

"Yes?" she called.

"The Empress wishes to tell Kaspar that his bride is waiting for him," came the muffled reply.

"He says he's almost ready. He just wants this day to be perfect."

"You know, some girls get jealous if you spend a lot of time letting another woman dress you."

Corina and Kaspar looked at each other wide-eyed.

"Just a little while longer," Corina called back.

"I'll let her know. Oh, did you need us to replace these homeguardsmen outside your door?"

"What?" Kaspar asked.

Corina put a hand over his mouth inelegantly.

"I think I recognize that voice," he whispered around her fingers.

"Why would he need replacements?"

"The ones out here seem to have come down with a case of being knocked unconscious, and I'm a bit worried we might get blamed for it."

Kaspar pushed Corina's hand out of the way and flew to the door. He opened all the locks while the homeguardsmen inside the suite remained completely oblivious. Three familiar Wen faces greeted him.

"Davur?" Kaspar gasped. "Ravud, Vudar! Come in."

The three came inside and dragged two unconscious homeguardsmen in with them. Kaspar closed and bolted the door.

"Is everything else under control here?" Ravud said, hooking a thumb in the direction of the motionless homeguardsmen.

Corina nodded.

"We're obviously here to rescue you," Ravud said, twitching a nonexistent mustache. "You want to be rescued this time, right?"

"Yes," Kaspar said, looking greatly relieved.

"Do you know whether Sora is working for anyone else?" Vudar asked.

"Not that I've seen," Corina said. "She has been making the plans and giving the orders from the start. Herald worked with her because he thought a civil war in the Flecterran Valley would be good for Aflighan's Godhead."

"He explained that to us at length," Davur said morosely.

"Did you catch him, too?" Kaspar asked.

Davur sighed. "Unfortunately not. He gave us a choice between him and our mission and correctly guessed which we'd choose. Any chance he'll show up for the finale?"

Kaspar shrugged. "It's hard to say. Canolos knew him better than I did, and I knew Canolos less well than I thought."

"He helped for his own reasons, as well," Corina explained. "But I'm sure you've taken care of him."

"We left him to Seleine's justice as Kaspar suggested," Vudar explained.

"I hope they are not too cruel in punishing him," Kaspar said softly. "I believe he loved Sora as I did. Herald used jealousy of me to tempt him. I think he hoped it meant Sora would have no choice but to have him. I'm not sure which of them is the bigger fool." He sighed.

"Do you want to stop her?" Ravud's question cracked through the air like a whip.

"Of course," Kaspar said.

"Go through with the wedding. We have given her Nosamae Descending instead of Nosamae Ascending, and she's fallen for the trick."

"How?" Corina asked.

Ravud grinned. "One of the Senserte is very, very good at forgery. When she was younger, she was quite the rogue. Sleight of hand, burglary, you name it. Learning magic only made her better at it."

"A bit like you, Corina," Kaspar said.

"In any case, if you go through with this wedding, it will either break the power of Farlander magic or increase the power of Wen magic. Either way, she'll be vulnerable, and the Senserte will take care of the rest."

"But won't that still disrupt the balance between Wen and Farlanders?" Kaspar asked.

"Yes, but you'll be in control of it instead of the crazy enchantress who is currently barking orders at your parents."

Kaspar touched his fingers to his chin as he considered this. "Unless you have Nosamae Ascending handy to immediately reverse the effect, I can't do that. I'd be jeopardizing the peace of the entire Union. It would be a tremendous violation of the trust Pithdai has earned from the other nations. We'd lose a century of relative peace." He shook his head violently. "Please tell me you have some back-up plan."

Ravud grinned and tousled Kaspar's bright blue hair. "Congratulations, you've passed the test."

"Test?" Corina repeated.

"You were worried that *I* might be behind all this?!?" Kaspar sputtered, pale face flushed.

Davur sighed. "We've never taken on a job like this."

"Our list of suspects included you, King Larus, and the Nosamae," Ravud said with a smirk.

"No, it didn't," Vudar said tiredly.

"Sorry, but Kara was the only one assuming otherwise," Davur said.

"And the story isn't over yet," Ravud noted. "So don't dismiss the possibility just yet."

Vudar fumed silently.

Kaspar grinned. "You three are really breaking character. I wouldn't take you for the ad'Marusak brothers for an instant."

Ravud grinned and took off his mask, revealing Arrina.

"Sis!" Kaspar cried, hugging her warmly.

Davur cleared his throat and removed his mask. "Actually, I'm Arrina, not this lout."

"I missed you too, kid," not-Arrina said enthusiastically.

"And Michael?" Kaspar guessed.

Vudar nodded and removed his mask.

A familiar squawker scrambled in from the balcony. It was Jabber.

"Poresa. What's our status?" Michael asked it.

"We've had a complication here and an improvisation there, but the plan isn't on fire yet."

"That's a relief," Arrina said.

"I hate to break up the family reunion, but Sora just found out the brothers skipped out while she and the guards were distracted by Lastor." The squawker rubbed a paw across its nose. "Actually, I'm almost certain that wasn't Lastor. The orb and diadem didn't work on him."

"She's sending more guards?" Michael asked.

"She's coming here personally."

"Can you stop her, Michael?" Corina asked. "I think you could have beaten us both back in Tremora if you'd wanted to."

The enchanter shook his head. "Sora isn't that kind of fool, and neither are Pithdai's guards."

"Six doses of saat between the front door and the throne room!" not-Arrina exclaimed. "That's even more than usual."

"Tasa-chewers in just about every window, too," Michael noted. "I don't have the right talismans for a showdown with a charmer."

"Speaking of which," Arrina said, reaching down her shirt and removing the piece of cloth where the silver chains were hidden.

"We don't have much time, Kaspar, but we absolutely need your help," Arrina told them. "Yours too, Corina."

• • • •

"You expect us to ride in that?" Tajek asked incredulously.

"That" was a small wooden cart with its wheels removed. Jonathan had bolted a long bench and leather restraining harnesses to the floor. Small, mysterious paper packages had been glued to each bolt.

"That's your remarkable conveyance?" Zori asked with equal skepticism at the wooden contraption nearby, occupying much of the open space in the garden. "You're going to fling us at Pithdai with a catapult?"

"It's not a catapult," Jonathan said a little defensively. "Catapults are driven by torsion — ropes all wound up. In order to launch our intended payload into the air as high as we need to go, we'd need a catapult the size of a barn with more rope than you'll find on all the ships of an entire naval fleet." He patted the device next to him. "This is a trebuchet."

"Trebuchet," Tajek repeated, testing out the new word. "Spending time with you, I learn new words every day. Is 'trebuchet' an obscure Flecterran synonym for 'suicide'?"

"It is a kind of siege engine."

"I know what a trebuchet is!" Tajek snapped. "This is ludicrous!"

"This is one of Jonathan's contraptions," Zori reminded him with a smile. "I'm sure it's perfectly safe. " She tapped one of the mysterious packages lightly. "Assuming it works at all. The worst case scenario is that maybe we'll put a hole in the side of the throne room large enough for the other Senserte to escape through." She made it sound no worse than all of the Senserte performing a swindle naked.

"Not just any trebuchet, either." He gestured at the machine. "Most of them require long arms because the counterweight drops around the axle, which robs it of a lot of force. On this one, the arm is on a wheeled track so the counterweight drops straight down. It's still a big piece of machinery, but it'll get us aloft, after which we drop the extra weight and deploy our apparatus."

Zori shook her head in excited wonder, clapping Jonathan on the shoulder, but Tajek still looked genuinely terrified by this prospect.

Jonathan gave him an encouraging smile. "Look, it's not all just math. It doesn't just look good on paper. It will work. I promise."

Tajek looked to Zori for some confirmation of this.

She shrugged. "When Poresa tells me a mark is lying, I believe her. When Michael tells me the talisman he is giving me will render me invisible, I trust him. I have equal faith in Jonathan in matters of wheels and springs."

Tajek nodded once. "Then I will trust your trust. Is there anything else you need, Jonathan?"

"Just the helmets. Don't look at me like that. They're for in case we fall while climbing down."

Tajek sighed and walked away.

"You are sure this is safe, right?" Zori asked as soon as the Turu was out of earshot.

"The trebuchet and cart will function exactly as I described." Jonathan's smile approached a rictus. "We shouldn't have any problems until after the wings deploy. After that, there are just too many variables to be certain, but I should be able to hold it together."

"Oh. That's comforting, then," Zori said, but she certainly didn't look comforted.

Garble climbed down from the orange tree where it had been snacking on butterflies and padded over to them.

"Sora just went to Kaspar's suite," Poresa said through the squawker. "I hope you're almost ready."

"Nearly," Jonathan said. "What do you plan to do with Mom when Sora orders a search?"

"It's not like they'll find us before we're ready. It's all part of the plan, remember?"

"It wouldn't be the first surprise of the day. Kara?"

Garble's silence stretched out for nearly a minute. "She'll be fine, even if I have to make her forget the confrontation with Sora, she'll be fine."

"She knows what she's doing, but Mom knows just enough about this to give us away."

"Oh, is that it?" Poresa sounded somewhere between amused and annoyed. "I've convinced her to stay hidden in the balcony until the finale."

"Convinced or *convinced*?"

"Please don't think what I did in Aaronsglade means you're now allowed to ask me that question," Poresa said crisply.

"I know. Sorry. I was just curious. Mom can be unreasonable at times."

"I assure you your mother is a perfectly sane and rational woman, Jonathan."

"Of course she is." A beat. "You did the right thing in Aaronsglade, you know. There was no time to get permission, and we couldn't have confirmed M'Elizabeth's suspicions with that hole in in our memories."

"Speaking of Aaronsglade, she came with the Aaronma contingent, so I wouldn't count her out yet."

"Did she take the bait?"

"Stuck it up the sleeve of her uniform while Sora wasn't looking."

Tajek returned with the pot-like helmets, and the three of them put them on, pulling the leather chin straps tight.

"Good. Let's see if she tries to change the script," Jonathan said. "We're ready and waiting for your signal, Poresa."

"Try not to die," Garble said with a bark of a laugh.

• • • •

The door to Kaspar's suite burst open and eight homeguardsmen poured in followed by Sora. Corina let out a shriek of surprise, but Kaspar stood his ground.

"My love, we have everything under control," he said, pointing to the trio of Wen lying trussed on the ground and overseen by four of his homeguardsmen.

Sora stared at Corina and Kaspar intently, rage blazing, but said nothing right away.

"Sora, dear, it's just me. Those three over there snuck in and tried to convince me to betray you, but they've been dealt with."

"Betray how?" Sora snapped, still staring at Kaspar like he might turn into a giant lizard at any moment. "They finally gave me Nosamae Ascending. They tried to trick me with a fake and even sent an enchantress to kill me, but I beat them. I beat them all!"

Kaspar kissed her forehead gently. She showed her age, but this woman was not the withered husk Lastor had described. Her hair was black with some strands of gray, but she wasn't unattractive for all that. Nor did she look like she had once been some famous beauty — simply an ordinary Farlander woman who had endured decades of frustrated hopes.

"Not yet, my love. That is the betrayal I warned you about. The Senserte mean to trick you into activating Nosamae Descending, instead. They disguised it as Nosamae Ascending."

Sora's eyes widened, and her face hardened. "How?"

"They must have had access to both, and one of their enchantresses is also a skilled painter."

Sora turned her attention to the trio on the floor. "You stole every painting in my museum just to trick me? Even though you know what I can do with this?" She pointed at the diadem.

Ravud shrugged.

She turned back to the prince, raging. "I've kept my promise to you, Kaspar! I haven't harmed a hair on any of their heads out of love for you. And still they defy me!"

"They are Senserte. That's what they do. I warned you about that, didn't I?"

"We're giving you one last chance, Sora," Ravud said. "Surrender the miraklas you stole, and we will show you mercy. Commit this terrible crime, and yours will be a story used to warn children of the dangers of pride."

Sora whirled on him. "I know those words, though the voice is unfamiliar." Her hands probed Ravud's head and pulled away a previously hidden mask, revealing Arrina beneath. "You!"

Arrina regarded her with a mellow expression, and lifted one hand to her cheek, where Sora's fingernail had scratched it.

Sora stepped away quickly. "How did you get free?"

Arrina smiled mysteriously, and her thumb and forefinger touched her upper lip for just a moment. "You cannot fetter the Eyes of Justice."

"That remains to be seen," Sora snapped.

Kaspar cleared his throat, and Sora tensed for just a moment before pulling masks off the other two ad'Marusak brothers.

"Michael and Stipator. Well, well. I'm gathering quite the collection of Senserte today. Perhaps I should put you on display in a museum, perhaps one specializing in fools who wrongly thought being born to a powerful family makes them better than those who are of … lesser station."

"Technically, that would be a menagerie," Arrina said. "Museums are for dead things."

Sora gave her a thin smile. "It depends on how quickly you can deliver the real Nosamae Ascending to me. Guards, dose the three of them with saat and bring them to the throne room."

"Yes, Empress," the homeguardsmen said in unison.

"And tie Arrina's hands again. Better still, find some manacles."

The guards entered the room.

"Corina, go with them."

The younger enchantress dropped a small curtsy. "Yes, Ma'Sora."

When they were alone, Sora kissed Kaspar, a long, lingering kiss that left them both breathless.

"I'm tempted to keep you here for a little while longer." Sora planted sucking kisses on his neck. "They made us wait, so let's make them wait, too."

Kaspar pulled away slightly, kissing her forehead.

"What's wrong, my love?"

"The Senserte aren't the only ones who might try to stop us today, and if they fail, how long can we hold out against the combined might of the Union?"

"A duel between enchantresses looks like nothing more than a staring contest to an observer. It is a silent battle of wills, a contest of subtle power. At the end, one enchantress kneels, and the other commands her. It is never otherwise, not even if one does not resist the other." Steel crept into her voice. "Politics is the same. I will not kneel unless I am defeated, and I will not be defeated so long as I wield Nosamae Ascending and its key miraklas. If the Wen defy me, you and I will wed again, and their magic will wither. If the Farlanders rebel, we will wed under Nosamae Descending until orb and diadem allow me to wield a nation of invincible Wen who obey me without question."

"And the Wefals?"

"Both sides hate them. Most likely the winners will conquer Ulangoshi and Petersine. If they don't kill off the Wefals, they'll leave them broken and without a homeland."

The prince kissed Sora tenderly on the cheek. "If that is your decision, my love, I will support it." He took her hand in his and pressed the Star Ring into it. "We'll convince the Senserte to give you Nosamae Ascending, and we'll get married today even if we have to do it by moonlight."

Sora removed the Moon Ring and handed it to Kaspar, who slipped it into his pocket.

"A moonlight wedding would be a bit romantic, but let's hope it doesn't take that long," she told him. "Are you ready?"

Kaspar belted on Theo's Sword and slipped Jacob's Bow and a quiver of arrows across his shoulder. He nodded and held out an arm.

She took it. "Then let's go, my prince."

Chapter 41

"Down with the Empress!" the squawkers in the throne room shouted as Sora and Kaspar returned.

The grin on Arrina's face told a pretty clear story. Manacles bound her hands, but she twisted in them as though a motion of her wrists might free her.

"You," Sora snapped at Arrina. "Deliver Nosamae Ascending to me, or I will order such slaughter in the streets of Pithdai that they will spit your name as a curse."

Arrina's wrists never stopped moving, but the manacles showed no sign of giving way. She smirked. "Are we beginning to lose patience, Nosama? You must have put years of your life into this already. What are a few hours or even a few days more? Or are you afraid word of your intentions will reach someone — someone you fear? The Nosamae, perhaps?"

"I grow tired of your insolence!" Sora shrieked.

Arrina's knees buckled, and she prostrated herself before the enchantress. Kaspar, Stipator, and Michael looked on with horror. Standing near the homeguard, Corina's eyes flickered with an anger like a coming storm.

Sora leaned over and touched the side of Arrina's face. "Tell me where to find Nosamae Ascending, and no more tricks!"

Arrina sat back on her heels, whatever spell the enchantress had called either broken or easing. Only a fraction of her defiance remained. "The door will open again at the end of the sixth hour."

"Do it now," Sora commanded.

Arrina shook her head, panting for breath. "This was pre-arranged. We have no way of communicating with Tremora before then. Even if you torture us or order the homeguard to murder Pith, it will not get you what you want any sooner. You will have to wait."

"Wait! Wait!" the squawkers repeated.

Sora ground her teeth. "Then we will wait. In the meantime, halt all traffic into or out of the palace, and I want it searched from top to bottom for any other Senserte. All of them will be dosed with saat every hour." She flung both her arms in the air. "Now!"

"Now! Now!" cried the squawkers.

The throne room exploded into action.

"Not you," she snapped at Mathalla and Torminth, who had started descending the stairs from the Postulant's Terrace.

• • • •

The squawkers in the throne room maintained a steady chorus of insults while the homeguard searched futilely for the remaining Senserte. Mathalla and Torminth supplied the names of Poresa and the ad'Marusak brothers but seemed not to know where they had hidden themselves.

"You're responsible for patrolling every inch of this palace against intruders," Sora raged at the sergeant after the third report of nothing. "How is it that you can't even find one of these intruders?"

"I'm sorry, Empress. We will keep looking."

Sora collapsed into the Consort Throne, and Kaspar took his seat next to his father. Corina sat at the top of the stairs leading to the thrones from the Postulant's Terrace.

• • • •

Somewhere beyond the throne room, a homeguardsman called the hour. As the last of the Senserte in the palace took up their positions, Poresa came awake in their hiding place in the balcony directly across from the thrones. Ravud sat next to her, silently watching Sora. Balls of wax plugged his ears. Peggy sat at the rear of the balcony, a step away from the tapestry they had chosen for her hiding place in case someone unexpected found them.

Poresa touched his hand. "Five forty-five," she told him in his mind. "Fifteen minutes to go."

Ravud simply nodded. "How are you holding up?" he thought back to her along the link she had created.

"I'm spread thin, but I can manage."

"Jonathan is ready?"

"It's Jonathan, what do you think?"

"Any idea how he intends to get into the palace now that Sora has locked the doors?"

"None I can share without endangering the plan. Your brothers are in place, though. I know you worried about them."

"They can take care of themselves," Ravud insisted. "How is the palace's supply of saat?"

"The first barrel is empty, and the new one they brought out of the basement isn't saat."

"Everything according to plan, then."

"Yes."

"Makes you nervous, doesn't it?"

Poresa startled as the door to the balcony opened. She glanced at Peggy, reached out a tendril of her mind, "Hide."

The middle aged Farlander woman slipped behind the curtain.

"Tell whoever just came onto the balcony that she's early," Poresa thought.

Ravud nodded and slipped away.

"We need to buy them at least another quarter hour," Ravud whispered to the newcomer in the shadows. "Come back at six."

The door clicked shut. There was a muffled cry, and then the sound of someone falling to the floor.

Poresa's head whipped around, her mind seeking the person in the shadows. Whoever it was had already moved to the other side, out of her sight and out of her power. She tried to turn her head back, but it refused to move. She had just enough time to dip into a trance and send a final message before something heavy struck the back of her head.

• • • •

"Now, Vudar! Now!" a squawker shrieked.

Vudar frowned. "It's only five forty-five."

The squawker did not reply as it scrambled down into the throne room guarden in search of more insects.

The youngest ad'Marusak brother removed an arrow from his quiver and fitted it onto the bowstring.

"Had to go wrong eventually," he muttered. "It always does."

• • • •

"I found two of them!" someone cried from one of the balconies.

The throne room fell silent except for the calls of birds from the mesh high above.

"Don't just stand there!" Sora shouted. "Bring them to me!"

"Yes, Empress," said the entire room at once, including Mathalla and Torminth.

"Not you two," Sora said to them. "And would someone please keep Stipator from escaping?"

Stipator had climbed to his feet and was trying to leave the room in spite of the manacles on his ankles. A pair of homeguardsmen pushed him back to the floor.

On the throne, Sora rubbed her eyes and had to catch the diadem to keep it from falling off her head.

A short while later the homeguard carried the limp forms of Poresa and Ravud into the throne room. Ravud bled from a shallow cut to the head, and Poresa had a large lump at the base of her skull.

"Well, are they alive?" Sora asked.

One of the homeguardsmen checked each of them. "Yes, Empress. Unconcious, though."

"Dose them with saat and put them with the others."

"Yes, Empress."

"They would have been of much better use to me conscious, though," she muttered.

"Poresa is a mental mystic," Kaspar explained. "Conscious, she could have subdued her attackers easily. She was probably behind the squawkers earlier."

"Really? How did she avoid the saat?"

Kaspar shrugged. "The Senserte are clever."

"What they are is annoying." Sora leaned on the arm of the throne. "I am so tired of this farce."

High overhead, an arrow flew through the mesh and exploded into a purple flower of fire above the palace.

"Show time!" Arrina shouted. She tilted her head back and laughed.

• • • •

"Was that sound the signal?" Tajek asked.

"Yes," Jonathan said as he fussed with the contraption they had assembled that morning. "They're early, which means something has gone wrong. Someday, everyone will learn to stick with the plan. That means it's our job to get this swindle back on schedule. Hopefully they clear the palace crèche before we get there, or this will be a messy landing. Climb aboard."

Zori and Tajek took their places on the bench and strapped themselves in. Jonathan examined their restraints carefully, corrected one strap Tajek had not quite placed in the right place, and hung the folded device over their shoulders. He pulled out a handful of bolts, which flew out of his hands and burrowed into the pre-drilled holes in the bench back to secure the contraption to it, transforming a short bench into a trio of high-backed chairs.

"The device behind us will support our heads during launch," he explained as he took his place on the bench. "Don't lean forward until we're near the apex of our trajectory."

"How will we know?" Tajek asked. Sweat ran down his shaved head and down his cheeks.

Jonathan adjusted his straps, and the device at his back moved of its own accord to cushion his neck and head. "Oh, you'll know."

At a gesture of his hand, the trebuchet's release lever moved, and then the whole world lurched around them.

The ground fell away. A hundred feet. Two hundred feet. Three hundred feet. Nearly all their momentum was upward. Birds whipped past them with surprised squawks. One hit Tajek in the leg, drawing a line of blood there before spiraling to its death.

"Stage two," Jonathan shouted over the screaming wind.

The paper-wrapped packages exploded, detaching their restraints and the wing apparatus from the bench and cart, which fell away below them. The cart tumbled as it plummeted toward a small pond far below. A few terrified heartbeats was all it took for the three passengers to tilt forward with a lurch, seeming on the verge of joining it.

"Apex," Jonathan announced. "Deploying wings."

Nothing happened.

Tajek and Zori started swearing in unison, united in vehemence if not in language. Jonathan craned his neck as they entered the first tumble. He looked more annoyed than concerned, as if this was nothing but a test run that might send him back to his jungle of a wagon, rather than a fatal miscalculation that could turn all of them into bloody smears on the roof of one of the buildings below.

A parrot had flown into the contraption and gotten stuck in its moving parts, keeping the whole apparatus from opening. Jonathan gestured at the bird, but it still writhed in its death throes, rendering it immune to his magic.

"Jonathan! Do something!" Zori shouted.

He glanced at the ground. It was coming closer now instead of moving farther away. The three completed their first full somersault and started into their second, blue turning to green and then to blue again. He drew a knife from his belt and waited.

"I don't feel well," Tajek moaned.

"Now, Jonathan! Now!" Zori screamed.

Jonathan ignored her, picking his moment with a precision only an external mystic could achieve. The dagger flew, knocking the dying bird loose before falling hilt first. The wings opened a fraction of a second later, perfectly angled to catch the wind and give them a few seconds of lift.

Their altitude stabilized with a lurch, and Tajek vomited above a busy marketplace. The winged contraption was moving forward quickly now, so none of them saw whether the Turu's nausea or Jonathan's knife caused any collateral damage.

The palace of Pithdai lay in front of them, still well below their altitude and holding steady. Flaps at the back of the contraption moved in response to Jonathan's silent acts of will, making minor corrections in their approach.

Zori shrieked again, this time in exhilaration. Tajek did not share her enthusiasm, but nor did he decorate any other unsuspecting shopkeepers with the contents of his stomach.

"Wax in your ears, now," Jonathan said.

"There are still children on the roof," Tajek said, pointing. "And those would be the elementals, right?"

"If the sun will rise tomorrow, trust the Senserte," Zori said with conviction. "Wax."

Jonathan's gritted teeth told the real story. Something else had gone wrong.

• • • •

Vudar was gasping for breath as he reached the bend in the corridor. He rounded it but found only a window overlooking the throne room. He cursed silently but vigorously.

How many windows does this pile of rocks need?

He turned back, picked another corridor, found another dead end.

I should have studied Jonathan's map more carefully.

Yet another dead end.

Seriously? How many places can a bell tower hide?

Kara and Poresa had worked up some silent communication and navigation system involving Kara's coins and the squawkers that ran wild throughout the palace. With Kara and Poresa captured, though, Vudar was on his own, and he had to admit that he was completely lost.

Davur will have to think of something. There isn't enough time.

Vudar wound his way along the corridors until he found another window. He drew back an arrow, focused his will, and loosed. The shaft flickered with white light so bright it made everyone below cover their eyes for a moment. It landed, quivering, at the foot of the Postulant's Terrace and burst into short-lived flames.

• • • •

What are you doing, Vudar? Davur raged silently as his feet pounded down the stairs leading from the gallery. *Jonathan must be on his way by now, and we still haven't cleared the roof!*

Something else had gone wrong, and he was nowhere near the bell tower to sound the alarm.

Time to make a new plan, as Stipator would say.

He emerged from a service entrance near the Postulant Terrace, his homeguardsman uniform soaked in sweat.

"Empress! Someone has opened Empire of Brass. The inner vault is overrun. We need the crèche to drive them back before they reach the throne room!"

Sora said something, but Davur couldn't hear it through the wax plugs in his ears.

He spun on his heel and shouted over his shoulder. "There's no time to waste!"

He ran out of the throne room before anyone could respond.

That'll have to do. Arrina saw the arrow, too. She'll play along.

His heart pounded as he ran up the stairs. He needed to get back into position before the next phase. They had planned more distractions than they were likely to need, but they didn't have fifteen minutes of them to spare.

• • • •

"Come back here, I said!" Sora shouted at the homeguardsman's back.

"Back! Back!" screamed the squawkers.

She turned to the thrones next to her, saw the fear written on Larus's and Aora's faces. "Another Senserte game?"

Kaspar shook his head violently. "I can't believe that of them. Too many innocent people will die if Empire of Brass breaches the inner vault. We need to sound the alarm."

"What did he mean by needing the crèche?"

King Larus pushed himself to his feet, leaning heavily on the arms of the throne. "Please sound the alarm, Empress. We'll explain later."

"Ten thousand Wen died in the last Brass Empire incursion," Kaspar told her by way of summary. "Only the first-cyclers of the palace crèche can drive them back."

"Very well," Sora said. "Sound your alarm."

A moment later, a great bell rang high above the throne room. Dozens of small shadows danced across the mesh overhead. Childish laughter echoed down. The throne room became almost as dark as night as the cloudy bodies of many air elementals followed their young charges.

When the last of the shadows had passed, King Larus slumped into his throne with a relieved sight. "Thank you, Empress."

"Yes, thank you," Arrina called. She held her manacles in one hand and the leg irons in the other. She twirled a non-existent mustache and tossed the shackles aside. "Farewell!" she shouted over her shoulder as she ran through the throne room doors.

"Stop her!" Sora shouted. "Bring her back!"

A veritable mob of homeguardsmen took up the chase. Mathalla and Torminth vanished into the crowd before Sora could stop them, but she kept Larus and Aora from joining the search party.

The enchantress rubbed the bridge of her nose in irritation. Kaspar patted her hand comfortingly.

A chorus of surprised squawks and the movement of many wings filtered down to Sora from the mesh above the throne room. A split second later, there was a whoosh as something much larger than a bird hit the mesh. Two other whooshes as more bodies hit the mesh. Then a crash as a harness and set of wood-and-leather wings slammed into the roof on the far side, skidded, and fell off the side of the palace. Two breaths before the crunch that told her the contraption had landed on another roof two stories lower.

She couldn't see the source of the commotion clearly from the throne, so she stood up and looked. Three figures scrambled from the center of the mesh, which they had apparently used as a safety net. Two others helped them to the roof.

"How many acts does this Senserte comedy have?" Sora demanded of no one in particular.

No one answered. She was alone except for Kaspar, Corina, Larus, and Aora.

The mesh fell as if every line securing it to the roof had been cut at the same time. It folded like a falling cloth over the purple tree, draping the tree, the throne, and the Postulant's Terrace in a net of fine cords. Figures scrambled down the mesh in front of her.

"Come back! Come back!" Sora shrieked. "Stop the Senserte!"

"Senserte! Senserte!" shouted the squawkers.

• • • •

The fleeing Arrina stopped running a few strides outside the doors and leaned against a wall. The pursuing homeguardsmen halted nearby. Mathalla and Torminth had only enough time to draw their swords before collapsing to the floor. Arrina smirked at them.

"Has it worn off yet?" one of the homeguardsment demanded.

"Alas no, but we didn't really expect that it would. Michael and Arrina are the ones that matter. We just need to keep Sora from getting married for a little while longer."

"Wait. Aren't you…?"

Arrina twirled her absent mustache. "Disguises within disguises, Nosama."

Sora's voice echoed from the throne room. "Stop the Senserte!"

"How long do you want us to wait?" the not-homeguardsman asked.

"A minute, maybe two. Enough time for her to sweat but not long enough for her to get desperate," not-Arrina said.

"What about you?"

"Stuff wax in the ears of Mathalla and Torminth and let them take me prisoner in about five minutes. That should put us back on schedule, and Sora will enjoy the irony."

• • • •

Zori, Davur, and Vudar cut openings in the mesh and scrambled along the branches of the great tree. Jonathan and Tajek climbed to the ground. Jonathan went to the captured Senserte, and the manacles dropped from their wrists and ankles. Tajek lifted the bottom of the mesh and advanced on the Postulant's Terrace.

"Homeguard, stop the Senserte!" Sora shrieked as the Turu climbed the stairs leading to the terrace.

Corina drew a copper rod and pointed it at him, but nothing happened. Tajek did not hasten his steps but nor did he hesitate. When he reached the terrace, he punched Corina hard in the gut and flung her off the side. She lay on the ground, wheezing.

Tajek smiled at Sora and placed his foot on the first step. An arrow hit the mesh, bounced off. Several others had the same effect. Then one slipped through and hit the Turu in the back. Its metal head tchinked off him.

"Turu, halt!" Sora ordered, but Tajek did not obey. "Look upon the power of the Nosamae and humble yourself!" she shouted.

But the Moon Ring was in Kaspar's pocket, so Tajek kept coming. Overhead, Zori and the two ad'Marusak brothers climbed closer.

Sora took a step backward and wielded her own magic. The Turu and the three Wen froze in place and then collapsed onto the stairs leading from the thrones to the Postulant's Terrace.

"Kara, Arrina. Now!" Jonathan shouted from the other side of the mesh.

Sora simply watched the events unfold with a satisfied smile.

Mathalla and Torminth escorted Arrina back into the throne room. The manacles bound her hands and feet again. Kara remained kneeling on the Postulant's Terrace, and whatever spell she was meant to activate never came into play.

Sora stood up from her throne and applauded with a grin, holding the Orb in the crook of her elbow. "Oh, very entertaining. I can see why the poor and downtrodden love your plays so much. This has really been quite an exceptional wedding present." Her gaze hardened, and she took the Orb in hand again. "However, it is not the one you promised me in Seleine. Homeguard, seize the Senserte and dose them with saat again. And cut this net down!"

Alone against dozens of homeguardsmen, Jonathan threw down his knives and let them take him prisoner.

"Since we're waiting for a Pith to deliver on her promise, we might as well redecorate. Hang the paintings back where they belong while we wait."

"Yes, Empress."

At that moment, the sixth hour arrived, and Gates of Tremora swung slowly open. A surprised-looking Lastor looked back at them through the gate.

"Lastor, close the gate!" Arrina screamed at him, but of course he couldn't hear her.

He stepped through the gate.

"No!" Arrina shrieked, tearing at her blue-blond hair.

"Stay where you are, Lastor," Sora commanded.

The young Wen stiffened. "Yes, Empress."

Sora smiled slightly. "Do you know where Nosamae Ascending is, Lastor?"

"Yes, Empress."

"Lastor, bring me Nosamae Ascending — the real Nosamae Ascending. Now."

"Yes, Empress."

Chapter 42

Once Lastor was dosed with saat, Sora spent a full hour scrutinizing Nosamae Ascending. At last, she stood up.

"Homeguard, hang this on the wall behind the thrones. King Larus, Queen Aora, please stand over there by the throne room gates until I have need of you."

"Yes, Empress," they answered.

Sora descended the stairs to the Postulant's Terrace and then a second set of stairs until she stood in front of the manacled and heavily guarded Senserte. Poresa and Ravud had regained consciousness but could not remember the face of the Wen who had attacked them. "No doubt one of the homeguard," Sora mused. Kara had joined her fellows, still acting humbly toward Sora.

"Let's count the Senserte." Sora clasped her hands together amicably. "Are we missing anyone?"

"Etha," the Wen among them replied immediately.

Sora looked to Kaspar for explanation. "Michael's apprentice. She has no magic of her own, however, so she is no threat to you ... us."

"Good," Sora purred. "Homeguard, cover up Gates of Tremora. Also, dose the Senserte with more saat just for good measure. I want no further surprise visitors or any other interruptions." She held out a hand to Kaspar. "Let's get married, my prince."

He took it, and they walked up the stairs to the thrones.

"Corina, where are you?"

"Here, Ma'Sora," the enchantress answered from behind the great tree where she had been hiding.

"Please begin the ceremony," Sora said.

The young enchantress ascended the steps and smiled as she took each of their hands. "Mira, bless this happy couple and bring them joy in this new life they are beginning together."

Sora gazed into Kaspar's eyes, looking not like the middle-aged woman who had set herself up as empress of a people she did not claim as her own but a young woman entering into a long-awaited marriage.

"Ma'Sora ad'Serra, do you come here of your own free will with the intention of mingling yourself in marriage with this man?"

"I do."

"Prince Kaspar ad'Pithius, do you come here of your own free will with the intention of mingling yourself in marriage with this woman?"

"I do."

"Marriage marks the place where two souls touch, where two hearts and bodies overlap. A wedding is simply the public acknowledgment of that contact. It is an awareness of the place where roads cross, where two rivers flow into each other, or where two trees weave their branches together. These two people are here because they have felt each other's touch and wish to recognize it publically. In Mira's name, do those gathered recognize that place where these souls touch?"

In the small crowd of Senserte, Stipator turned away, face in his hands.

"We do," answered the rest of those gathered.

"One relationship does not dissolve all those that came before it or prevent any others from coming to be. The tree that touches the branches of one touches the branches of others — must touch them. Two trees that stand alone will be swept away by the rain. Only a forest of trees can endure the hardships of wind and rain. Will you share sun and rain with each other as two trees in a rainforest?"

"We will," Sora and Kaspar said together.

"Then exchange any tokens of your affection and seal your marriage with a kiss," Corina said.

Sora took the Star Ring from a tiny pocket and slid it onto Kaspar's finger. Kaspar then placed the Moon Ring on Sora's finger. Sora leaned forward to kiss her new husband, her eyes closed, but the lips that met hers were not Kaspar's but Arrina's.

The entire throne room burst into raucous laughter. Someone had pulled down the sheet that was covering Gates of Tremora, and an audience of a hundred Wen sat in chairs on the floor of the Alliance Gallery in the Palace of Doors. Most pointed and laughed at Sora, but some of the especially well-dressed among them whispered warnings into the ears of children sitting next to them.

Arrina smiled weakly at the enchantress. "You can't say we didn't warn you."

Corina suddenly shifted to reveal Michael beneath the disguise, his face hardened into a thunderhead. Sora's magic withered against it.

She opened her mouth to shout some command, but Arrina's arm moved more quickly. The Diadem of Elvenkind bounced down the stairs and fell onto the flagstone floor beyond.

Michael stared intently at Sora, who stared back with growing horror. Arrina pulled off the Star Ring and stuck it into her pocket.

"Pitiful fools!" Sora shouted, pointing the Moon Ring at Michael. "Your puny magic is ... mmph." She cut off as Arrina's hand covered her mouth and twisted the Orb of Elvenkind out of her fingers.

Arrina tossed the Orb behind the thrones.

Bows creaked from every balcony and window and took aim at Sora. The homeguard had not a single Wen among them, now — only Wefals and Farlanders. Some of the Wefals bore a familial resemblance to Stipator. Many of the Farlanders wore the abundance of earrings favored by the wealthy families of Aaronsglade.

Michael turned to Larus and Aora, who still stood near the entrance to the throne room, rage growing in their eyes as the Diadem's power faded away.

"With your permission, your majesties, the council of Aaronsglade wishes to conduct the trial here and now as a warning to any who might consider this course of action in the future."

Larus regarded Sora without pity, eyes full of rage. He waved for Michael to continue. Aora's mouth was a thin, hard line, the corners slightly upturned as if looking forward to whatever came next.

"Sora ad'Serra, kneel and prepare to stand trial for your crimes," Michael ordered thunderously.

Sora fell to her knees with her back to the thrones, her arms limp at her sides, her mouth working silently. Arrina crept in and removed the Moon Ring from the enchantress's finger and pocketed it.

Michael looked to one of the Farlander women standing among the Senserte who had been disguised as a homeguardsman. "M'Elizabeth, the accused awaits your judgment as an archon of Aaronsglade."

The homeguardsman flickered, becoming a Farlander woman in her late fifties, her face a mask of cool control with no pity in evidence.

M'Elizabeth ad'Alice ascended the stairs first to the Postulant's Terrace and then to the throne grotto. Arrina made way for her, slipping behind her father's throne. She quietly removed Nosamae Ascending from its place on the wall as Michael's Nosama mother spoke.

"You have been caught in the act of impersonating a Nosama, criminal abuse of magical knowledge, and conspiring to a crime so unthinkable that even high treason does not adequately describe it," M'Elizabeth paused a moment and then continued with a sneer. "Let all who would bear witness to these crimes say guilty."

"Guilty!" shouted the crowd.

"Guilty! Guilty!" repeated the squawkers.

Tears leaked out of Sora's eyes, but she still could not respond.

"You have further been accused of crimes against the interests of every nation in the Flecterran Union. Many of those nations' laws would sentence you to death for your crimes against them."

"Death! Death!" chanted the squawkers enthusiastically.

"You are, however, a citizen of Aaronsglade, and our laws do not allow for a death sentence. Instead, you will be returned to Aaronsglade where you will be stripped of your knowledge and experience as an enchantress. Until the end of your days you will bear a mark that forbids any enchantress from teaching you to wield magic again. We will then give you back your freedom to make of the remainder of your life what you can."

Sora shook her head in mute denial, shaking with silent sobs.

M'Elizabeth turned on her heel in dismissal and descended the stairs. She gestured idly over her shoulder. "Dose her with saat and prepare her for transport."

"Yes, Nosama," chorused several Farlanders.

"Bring Nosamae Ascending and any other art from Aaronsglade back, as well."

One of the Farlander women quietly let the Archon's Wand drop to the ground from where she had hidden it up her sleeve. She had blond hair streaked with grey and wore white clothes decorated with patches of blue like a mostly cloudy sky.

That's our rogue Nosama, Arrina thought, silently memorizing her appearance so she could share the information with M'Elizabeth later. *No fool, though. She saw that she could do nothing to salvage her plan, so she abandoned it. One to watch.*

"Rise, Sora," Michael commanded.

The woman remained on her knees as if frozen, her eyes wide in fear. Arrina frowned and glanced at the balconies. Canolos stood on the balcony where Poresa and Ravud had been hiding, his bow pointed at Sora. He had already released the string, and the arrow was in motion.

Arrina clutched Nosamae Ascending in both hands and leapt in front of Sora. The arrow struck the painting solidly without penetrating, and Arrina's motion carried her off the stairs and into the gap between the Postulant's Terrace and the purple tree of Pithdai. She landed feet-first, and the tip of Theo's Sword touched the ground, reminding her that she still carried two miraklas.

Not enough time to intercept the next arrow, she thought, fitting an arrow to Jacob's Bow.

Arrina heard her mother's wordless scream and then a meaty slap. Arrina feared the worst as she came out from behind the Postulant's Terrace, bow raised to the balcony just in time to see Canolos tumble over it, shrieking, his bow flying from his hand. Arrows scattered from his quiver and clattered to the ground. He landed on one of the purple-flowered trees to either side of the walkway.

Up in the balcony, Peggy shook out her hand. The other Senserte looked at her with wide eyes and then to Arrina.

"You didn't think she got it from my side of the family, did you?" King Larus asked drily.

On the other side of the throne room, the Farlanders M'Elizabeth had brought from Aaronsglade by way of the Palace of Doors escorted Sora down the stairs from the Postulant's Terrace and toward where Gates of Tremora hung on the wall. The missing homeguardsmen were coming through the painting from the Palace of Doors, taking the swords and bows from the imposters who had stolen them.

Arrina put up Jacob's Bow as she joined the gathering of Senserte. Mathalla and the ad'Marusak brothers dragged Canolos out of the tree. Out of the corner of her eye she noticed her father and M'Elizabeth engaged in some serious conversation. She moved to eavesdrop.

"Pithdai would welcome a permanent envoy from Aaronma," Larus was saying. "We owe the Nosamae a debt."

"We could not have done it without your Senserte," M'Elizabeth countered gracefully.

His Senserte? Arrina thought, forcing down the impulse to snort a laugh.

"Then let our two nations leave behind our bloody history and come closer together in friendship," the king said with his broadest smile.

Did they plan all this, or are they merely taking advantage of the opportunity? Arrina wondered.

She decided it didn't really matter so long as neither was trying to start a civil war. She walked back to the other Senserte.

"How did you replace the homeguard without Sora noticing?" Canolos asked.

Tajek looked to Michael, who shrugged.

"My mother, M'Elizabeth, placed a layer of illusion on the surface of the painting to show Sora and any others what she expected to see. The miraklan nature of the painting made it almost impossible to detect it. As the homeguardsmen stepped through the painting, the Aarons enchanted them and created disguises for our allies."

"It prevented any bloodshed in case Sora broke her promise to Kaspar not to harm the Senserte," Arrina explained.

"It was the only promise she kept," Canolos muttered.

The false Michael and Stipator removed their disguises, becoming Corina and Kaspar.

"This is hardly fair," not-Arrina complained. "Everyone else looks like themselves again except me.

"That's why you kept delaying, isn't it?" Kaspar asked. "So the saat the homeguard gave Arrina and Michael had enough time to wear off?"

Arrina nodded. "We also wanted to catch her in her moment of triumph, when she thought she had beaten us and once we had witnesses from every nation watching. The Wen stayed in the Palace of Doors, since magic from one side of Gates of Tremora can't affect the other side. The story will spread, and everyone will know what Sora attempted and that the Senserte let her write her own confession before breaking her. Which brings me to another order of business." She turned to Canolos.

The Sutol Wen flinched slightly.

"After your role in Sora's crime, why would you come here to murder her?"

"Don't you think she deserved to die?" Canolos asked hotly.

"Don't feed us that," Arrina said. "You're no vigilante."

"Sora wasn't your target," Kaspar said softly. "I was, wasn't I, Canolos?"

Canolos said nothing.

"You wanted to take my place at her side. You thought she would respect you again if I was dead. The moment I kissed her, if Wen magic stopped, it would no longer protect me from your arrow. You didn't expect me to turn into Arrina. You didn't expect Sora to fail."

Arrina picked up the thread. "You couldn't find Kaspar anywhere else in the throne room, but you still had that arrow nocked and nowhere to fire it. No one had seen you, and you had one chance to shoot before someone noticed you. You chose Sora. Why?"

"Jealousy?" Stipator guessed.

"Revenge?" Michael suggested.

"To keep her from testifying against you in Sutola?" Arrina asked.

"Love!" Canolos hissed, and his shoulders slumped. "You heard the sentence M'Elizabeth passed. If I had been in Sora's position, I would rather be dead. Wouldn't you?"

No one spoke, but Corina and Kaspar looked guilty.

"Yes, I tried to convince her to activate Nosamae Descending, instead, and she refused. Yes, I lied to her in Seleine, but that was just to get Kaspar out of the way. I could tell that she was more in love with him than with me, and I also knew he would betray her. I saw the way he and Corina talked, and I knew he would discard Sora as soon as he no longer feared her. I, at least, was faithful to her, Kaspar, which is more than I can say for you or Corina!"

Kaspar dropped his gaze, and Corina took his hand.

"I betrayed everything I was just to be with her — my family, my nation, my whole race! She took it all with her when she left Seleine, and she gave me nothing but her scorn in return."

"She left you your life," Corina reminded him. "Actually, Kaspar left you your life, and the Senserte left you an opportunity to defend your innocence to the people of Seleine. You squandered both."

"What will you do with me? Will you make me forget her the way you will make her forget me?"

Davur shook his head. "You will come with us to stand trial in Sutola's capital. The High Archon will decide what further punishment your crimes merit."

"Dose him with saat and put him in the dungeons until the ad'Marusak brothers can arrange his transport," Queen Aora ordered.

The homeguard obeyed. Canolos didn't even bother to resist them.

"I'm guessing we're returning the key miraklas to their home countries, yes?" Stipator asked. "Because I'd really like my sword back."

Michael shrugged, and none of the other Senserte objected.

"That's probably best," Arrina agreed.

Stipator took Theo's Sword. Zori took the diadem. Kaspar handed over the Star Ring to Mathalla. Davur took Jacob's Bow with only a slight scowl from Kara. Not-Lastor removed the mask to reveal Etha, who accepted the Moon Ring.

"Have any of you seen Lastor?" Etha asked.

Jonathan twitched.

"No," Michael said. "We thought he was with you."

Etha shook her head. "He left the Palace of Doors late this morning, but I thought he'd be back by now."

"Any idea where he went?" Michael asked.

"He went to Pithdai to take care of something important," she said.

"A renegade enchantress tried to activate Nosamae Ascending!" Jonathan raged. "What could possibly be more important?"

• • • •

Herald woke with a snort and immediately coughed as a feather went up his nose. The sack over his head blocked his sight, but he was standing upright, ankles in manacles chained to bolts near his feet, arms stretched out on an upright crosspiece, wrists chained. The creak of wheels and the lurch of the ground beneath him indicated he was on a cart of some kind.

He ripped the chains free with the strength granted him by the Godhead!

Rather, he tried to, but they were too strong for him. More correctly, he was not strong enough for the chains. Something had happened to him. An intense sweetness filled his mouth.

"Ah, you're awake," said a voice. A boy's voice. A slightly familiar voice.

The cart or wagon tilted forward slightly, and a wind scourged Herald's skin. He was naked, he realized. Not bare, though. A sticky substance covered his body, like dried honey. Something more, as well.

Feathers. Hundreds or even thousands of feathers covered his body from toe to head.

Speaking of his head, someone had shaved it, but it wasn't a clean shave. He could feel a few tufts of hair poking the inside of the sack.

They had also mangled his beard, trimming it like a topiary bush into some shape Herald couldn't see.

His mustache stank of death. It took him a moment to realize it wasn't his mustache. It was some dead rodent that had been affixed to his upper lip with the same sticky goo that kept the feathers from blowing away. It was rotting. Herald could feel maggots wriggling there, some of them crawling their way into his mouth. He spat them out.

"Who are you?" Herald asked. "Whatever you are being paid, the Godhead will pay more."

The young voice at the front of the cart burst into laughter. "The Senserte don't care about money. I'm doing this because you tried to start a civil war in the Flecterran Union, and you need to be punished for that."

Herald snorted. "Punished? You mean killed? I am not afraid of death."

"No," said the voice. "You almost killed Michael, which makes me really mad, but I am Senserte, and we aren't murderers."

"If you won't kill me, I will kill you. You cannot keep me prisoner forever."

"Better do it soon, then. We're almost there."

"Are you going to leave me in the wilderness to be devoured by your jungle cats? That is a cowardly way to kill a man."

"I'm not doing that either. What part of 'I am Senserte' don't you understand?"

"I'm not afraid of death."

"Yes, you've already said that a few times." Herald could almost hear the boy rolling his eyes. "The Senserte aren't executioners. We believe in the rule of law and let the courts decide what punishment to administer."

The cart lurched to a halt.

"Only we don't have jurisdiction over people who aren't citizens of the Flecterran Union, so there's no one in the Valley we can hand you over to for judgment."

"If you kill me, the Godhead will kill you."

"You're not much good at conversation, are you?" asked the boy. He was closer, now. "You're not a citizen of the Union, so we can't punish you. Instead, we send you back to your country with an explanation of your crime and just let your courts decide what punishment you've earned."

"There is no judge in Aflighan except the Godhead!" Herald said righteously.

"Great. Then I've brought you to the right place."

The boy whipped the bag off Herald's head, and he blinked in the bright Aflangi sunlight. Less than a mile away stood Baummorder Keep, the Godhead's southernmost garrison.

Lastor stood in front of him, grinning. "We'll let your Godhead pass sentence on you. I'm sure he'll be every bit as merciful as we Senserte have been."

Herald's eyes widened, and his face paled further. Then he saw the mirrors around him, showing him every side of his body.

The dead rodent was the least of it. The colored feathers had been arranged into vaguely suggestive patterns, but he might have expected that. His beard had been cut into the shape of a horse's legs, tail, and ass, which was creative but not damning. Last, Herald caught sight of the words carved into the hair of his head, which simply said "I failed" in Aflangi.

He blinked at that simple sentence. Lastor had fled in Herald's moment of inattention, and riders approached from Baummorder Keep.

Herald looked at the mirror again, strained to see those letters. "I failed."

Herald strained at his chains uselessly and howled in terror of the punishment that awaited him.

The End

ABOUT THE AUTHORS

Eric Zawadzki

Eric spent his Midwestern childhood reading fantasy, so it probably isn't surprising that he came to idealize stories of going to a far-off land. When no wizard showed up to tell him he was the heir to some otherworldly throne or the only one who could defeat the nefarious designs of a dark god, Eric took this whole questing hero thing into his own hands.

While backpacking alone in Poland without so much as a phrasebook, he met many strangers who gave him advice and directions. One family even took him in for the night, feeding him and asking him about his travels. No bandits or wolves, but that's probably for the best. He still has nightmares about that wolfman from The Neverending Story.

He lived for a time among the majestic mountains of Colorado before seeking his one true love, Beth, on the frozen wastelands of Minnesota. They married on a beautiful spring day and are in the process of living happily ever after with their son.

Matthew Schick

Indiana had a slogan in Matt's childhood: "There's more than corn in Indiana." Driving around the state, he agreed — there were also soybeans and vast, flat skies. He found inspiration because there was so much room for it, inspiration to explore, to fill himself with variety, and to write with them in mind.

He now lives in Charlottesville, Va., with his lady, whom he met while working as a journalist in Hawaii. He ended up in Hawaii after doing similar work in Colorado and Virginia, and going to college in Wisconsin. In his explorations, he has found people, food and experiences that made each place an inspiration for the worlds in which he writes.

· · ·

The words of a prophecy brought Matthew and Eric together for the first time when they were 14. Not ones to fight destiny, they quickly began a collaboration that has flourished even after they discovered girls, went to different colleges, and lived half an ocean apart. Fate briefly brought them both to Minneapolis, only to fling Matt away again, but they concocted a scheme to finally publish their works and throw off the prophecy altogether.

Made in the USA
Middletown, DE
12 January 2015